THE BLACK AND TAN SUMMER

Ireland's turbulent year of 1920

C.A. POWELL

ISBN: 1484000463
ISBN 13: 9781484000465

ACKNOWLEDGEMENTS

Front Cover Art by Gisela Pizzatto. http://www.gpizzatto.com.br/

The song sung by the Tans in Chapter 1 is from *Goodbye-ee* by R. P. Weston and Bert Lee (1915).

To Carole Rashbrook – "uber oo"

ONE

Oblivious to the Din of his Fellows

Ireland: July 24th 1920

Shouts of high-spirited banter issued from the merry group of policemen, sitting in the back of the open-topped truck as it sped along the country lane. Most were thrilled at the arrival of the Auxiliary Officer, Captain Bashford. He had presented himself at the barracks an hour before, wanting to see some familiar faces from Flanders – men from his old regiment, his boys and adoring disciples.

The vehicle hit a bump, which caused the Reserve Policemen to bounce from the bench, while the standing Auxiliary clung to the wooden frame behind the driving cabin. All the men cheered as they landed with a thud, engulfed in reckless fun.

"Don't go losing your beret, Sir," yelled a thick-set man called Baker, as the rest of the policemen chuckled at the noble-looking Auxiliary. "We keep peaked constabulary cap and beret tucked between our feet. It was the first thing we learnt travelling along bumpy lanes in the back of a lorry."

"Not my beret, that wouldn't do at all," replied the Auxiliary with feigned pride – gleefully patronising the men before him.

"Yeah," shouted Turpin. "It'll give old Callaghan something to gloat about. He's pretty sore at you, Sir. The old mick wanted you travel up front in his car."

Jones leaned over the side of the truck to roar at the Inspector's car ahead of them. "The Captain's one of us, Pongo!"

"Calm down Jones, he'll hear you," cursed Sergeant Bradley of the Regular Royal Irish Constabulary. Like the rest of his Regular Police colleagues, he was not happy about the new Auxiliary Officer turning up at the barracks. Bashford had overexcited the Black and Tan Reserves and, to Bradley's surprise, had merely chuckled at Jones's antics.

The Auxiliary leaned back against the wooden frame, lightly scratching the bridge of his Roman nose and regarding the Reserve Policemen before him. He was inquisitive about those not from his old unit, therefore unfamiliar. His interest was captured by a lean, young man of about twenty-five years, who appeared strangely detached from the happy banter. The man was daydreaming – lost in the tranquil, green splendour of the Irish countryside bathed in morning summer.

"Hayward's in dreamland again," shouted Turpin in his usual brash manner. He was following the Auxiliary's line of vision.

Henry Hayward ignored the comment, allowing the summer breeze to sweep his thin, brown hair over his wind-whipped face. His spirit was free, like those of the men around him, though his joy was of a more private and tranquil nature. A feeling of solitude wrapped him in a peaceful blanket – comforting him from the harsh years that had gone by. Ireland had seduced him in spiritual ways, bringing a welcome freshness to his life.

"He's taken his ball in," teased Higgins. "He's dreaming about all those Irish lasses, aren't you, Hayward?"

"Are you, Hayward?" asked Jones in a clear, well-spoken voice. He was very imaginative where women were concerned. "Is she one of those untamed women with a fiery temper and wild, auburn hair?"

"Yeah, one of those hot-blooded, Celtic girls would give thee a right old sorting out," giggled Wright, growing excited as he took off his spectacles to wipe the sweat glistening on his nose.

A roar of coarse laughter arose from the policemen picturing quiet Hayward being seduced by a gamely Irish lady. He looked up and grinned – raising an eyebrow, allowing them to know he was not a shy boy. They were trying to lure him in with frolics – he could indulge if the mood took him, but on this occasion he was not to be enticed, and would not respond beyond a cheeky smile.

"Leave the lad alone now, fellas," laughed Sergeant Bradley, knowing that Hayward was in one of his whims. He found him to be the most agreeable of his Black and Tan Reserves.

"Dreamer, is he?" enquired Bashford.

"Sometimes, Sir," smiled the old Sergeant. "He'll snap out of it in a moment – he always does."

Bashford did not pursue the matter, though it was obvious he was not impressed – there was something different about the young Tan. He had not been in his regiment during the Great War and Bashford had not known him before this day.

Hayward was unaware of the Auxiliary Officer's scrutiny, as he lifted his head to sniff in the clear morning air, his bronze cheeks twitching with delight at the summer's heat. He wiped his forehead with the sleeve of his dark-green tunic, closing his eyes over pale, blue irises that contrasted sharply with his swarthy skin.

The noise of the company drifted away – his pondering pushed their gleeful chatter into the background.

"Hayward, are you with us?" A voice – distant then lost, in the sea of his serene introspection. He sighed at how improved life had become with this new occupation, unconsciously slipping his hand into his pocket and jingling some of his daily ten-shillings wage.

"Is he going to get the beers in at Cafgarven?" Another die-hard wag was swallowed in his musing wave. Shuddering slightly, he let his thoughts drift back to his native town in England. Unlike many of the men from home, he harboured no feelings of nostalgia towards his birthplace, being happy to leave the dismal rows of dirty houses. Dreary factory rooftops assembled under dull, overcast skies were all he could recollect, and Ireland, for all her troubles, was more appealing than standing among depressing ranks of unemployed men.

"Where is he now?"

Another irritating voice was discarded along the tunnel of his thoughts, as he smiled at his initial disappointment when first setting eyes upon Dublin city and Gormanstown – more dreary streets with people similar to those of his hometown.

He remembered his first reactions. "If this is the place all the fuss is about, the Fenians are blooming welcome to it."

Fortunately, his regret was short-lived – he found the west counties far more amiable, with meadows that washed up against the scarps of ancient hills – green waves captured in time, as if in a painting. He was beginning to enjoy life's finer pleasures – an experience long overdue.

Bashford had meanwhile become preoccupied with scrutinising the young man, sensing the calmness flowing through him, and for some reason felt ill at ease about the matter. Men with fire in their stomachs were more to his liking and Hayward, he decided, did not make the grade.

Unabashed by the Auxiliary's scrutiny and cushioned in his repose, Hayward allowed his recollections to drift back to the dark times of the Great War. Two years in the trenches – living on his nerves, only to come home to a land of depression and stagnation, had marked him.

The patronising Bashford began to impact upon his thoughts. He was not keen on the Captain. The Auxiliaries had not yet entered into police action and his visit was unofficial. It was to his ex-soldier Tans that he spoke.

"I suppose it was easy for you chaps to drift into a life of drinking and brawling in public houses. I can see those days slipping into a monotonous routine, which you all desperately wanted to escape from. You're soldiers at heart, and this new job must be a blessing in disguise for all."

Hayward half-listened; part of him still remained in the bloody quagmires of Flanders, where his dead friends were buried. The Auxiliary did have a point; something had moulded them all in that horrific war.

"So why are you here, Sir, and what's with all the plush uniform?" asked Turpin cheekily.

Bashford abandoned his observation of Hayward; he was searching for a response – hoping to strike a chord – and he did not appreciate being unnoticed.

"Yeah, and are we going to get them instead of this mixture of Army issue and police cast-offs?" Cuttings grinned at his ex-Captain.

More mocking cheers came from the Reserves, and Bashford responded with a smile. He noticed the unknown men were picking up on the fact that his old soldiers liked him – something pleasing to his nature.

"Well, you must have heard of us Auxies? We're coming as a new group of Police Reserves comprising ex-Army officers. We will be supporting you chaps that are already here – you 'orrible Black and Tans," he chuckled.

Hayward rested his gaze upon Sergeant Bradley, who sat a little apart from the rest. A Regular country policeman, he might throw in the odd catcall now and then but would not join in fully with the improbable Reserve Policemen. He guessed that Bradley was not too impressed with Auxiliary Officer Bashford.

His attention left Bradley and drifted along the line of happy men. All were bubbling with mischief because they had been drinking whiskey before going out on patrol. They stared at Bashford – their adulation of the man disturbed him, and Hayward wished he was in front with the driver Pulham.

He took another deep breath, happy none the less with the old comradeship without the constant fear of death. He had been in the same regiment as Barnes and Wright, and realised it was due to wartime experience that they had been recruited into the Royal Irish Constabulary – tough, hardened, war veterans who wanted employment. An amused smirk bloomed as he thought about the gossip concerning Black and Tans. Many of the locals believed they were being recruited from English prisons.

Hayward glanced at Bashford, resplendent in his dark-green uniform and self-assurance. A length of black ribbon, attached to the back of his beret, fluttered before his face as the truck rumbled along. The Auxiliary returned the scrutiny, and for the first time, Hayward realised that he had attracted unwanted interest – something he always did with authority figures. The Auxiliary's eyes glinted, flustering Hayward and making him feel as though his privacy had been invaded. Bashford, despite being popular with the others, unsettled him. Jones, Cuttings, Turpin and Baker he knew had served alongside the man in France and were completely at ease with their ex-Captain.

He quickly abandoned his attention of the Auxiliary and thought about how things were in Ireland. The Shinners were few in number, and seemed to spend much of their time in hiding. The odds against these small rebel bands brought a sense of relief to him. He wondered what motivated these desperate men. To get caught brought severe penalties – sometimes capital punishment – and the odds of getting caught were very high. Yet the Shinners, with their dreams of an independent Ireland, continued to crawl out of hiding places to attack, whenever an opportunity presented itself – often murdering policemen plus the odd soldier and being just troublesome enough to be a cause of concern for the British government.

"Why do you think the Regular Army are so reluctant to have a go at the Shinners, Sir?" asked Jones, looking for an educated opinion on this matter.

The question roused Hayward from his pondering – for the first time he showed interest. All eyes widened for the answer.

When Bashford noticed the sudden interest he met the distant Tan's sudden attention with a brief smile – glad that the unknown, young man was finally showing some enthusiasm.

Bashford cleared his throat and began. "Well, it's the Government really. They refuse to recognise the Shinners as a legitimate Army of an Irish Republic. After all, our military go to war against foreign nations that might invade us. Their function is not to hunt murderers. That's a police job and we, as policemen, are up against these organised criminals. This is our patch."

Hayward quickly lost interest in Bashford's patronising response. It was as though the party crashing Auxiliary was a schoolteacher addressing obedient pupils. Because he was from a higher rank and social class, the men would not question him further. He reflected on what would have happened if Inspector Callaghan had said the same thing. The unit would have shouted him down.

Hayward's attention returned to the lush, green meadows as the truck continued along the country lane. Above, the blue sky was crystal clear, apart from a kindly, bright sun that enfolded the world in a perfect radiance that spread across the placid pastures. Maybe he should have torn himself from the appealing view, as the brazen glory was a sanctuary for the Shinner flying columns.

He began to think about his exasperated father and tutors – all had the same criticism of him – their distant words echoed from childhood memories. 'The boy lives in a dream world.' Or 'He's always in a trance'.

They were, of course, right – though Hayward did not want to change his ways. Dreaming and wondering about things relaxed him – they provided a means of escape, feeding his temperate nature. However, his trances came at inopportune moments. When he was a young lad, such dream states occurred when his father tried to talk with him, or when his tutors were trying to teach him. Hence, the usual comments were passed whenever people in authority got together to discuss him. His entire growing life had been one long stream of ridicule.

"Come on, Hayward lad, stop trying to look majestic! It won't do! You're a Black and Tan laddie, and the natives hate you," shouted Bashford above the wind rush of the truck.

A roar of approval rang out from the rest of the Black and Tans sitting around him. Hayward gave the Auxiliary Officer a broad grin and pink wrinkles appeared around his eyes. He was suddenly with the mood of the rest, bursting from his solitude.

"Come on in, Hayward, the water's lovely," shouted Baker.

"Come on, all you boys of the bulldog breed," yelled Bashford, pulling out his pistol and firing a shot into the sky. It was against regulations but who cared?

Hayward tucked his upright rifle between his legs, put his index fingers into his mouth and whistled in response to the foolhardiness, knowing it was what the Auxiliary wanted. Another chorus of approval emitted from the inebriated policemen, followed by laughter. More shots were fired into the sky amid a fresh wave of exultation, which swept through the group as the rickety truck tottered merrily along.

Bashford pulled out a flask, from which he drank. After a couple of gulps he smacked his lips and let out a sigh of satisfaction. He gave the rest of the men a tormenting stare to which Turpin responded. "Come on, Sir, pass it round."

"Round?" mocked Bashford, good-humoured. "Or do you mean around, Turpin?"

The rest of the men laughed while Turpin adopted a silly, broad grin. The Auxiliary laughed and passed the flask along to Jones, teasing Turpin further, who looked back with mock disappointment.

The loud Tan knew his turn would come, as he was one of Bashford's favourites – one of the blue-eyed boys because, despite his lack of education, he had great aptitude and he thrived in chaos, making him a very valuable team-member for any leader of men.

Sergeant Bradley said nothing, but Hayward noticed the slightly raised eyebrow. The policeman was not amused by Bashford's antics, but he would not dare to say anything. He contented himself to watch, ignored as the flask was passed among the policemen one by one, until it arrived before Hayward. He hesitated for a moment, knowing the Police Sergeant was disapproving. He did not want to be the one to bring the issue into the open, so he complied and took a swig.

"Bottoms up, Hayward," shouted Joe Adams, greedy eyes sparkling. Impatience usually got the better of him where alcohol was concerned. He was the most compulsive drinker of the group, and had joined the Tans purely for beer money.

Hayward quickly got on with the drinking part of the request but then mischievously passed the flask to Higgins instead of to Joe Adams, playfully antagonising the tubby man who was shaking with excitement for a swig. Hayward loved to torment him, and it worked.

"Cheers, Hayward, I don't know if there will be enough for you, Adams." Higgins happily joined Hayward in the tormenting.

"Right, Hayward," muttered Adams with a facetious wink. "That one's on my little rainy-day list."

Hayward knew what Adams meant; in the not too distant future, the prank would be returned with interest. He stared at Adams sheepishly as the tubby Black and Tan's eyes flashed back with enthusiastic brilliance, knowing he had put Hayward on his guard.

A smile creased Adams big, fat, cherub face. "It's all in my little book, laddie. Don't worry, I won't forget," he added slyly, before accepting the flask from Higgins, who was crudely wiping his lips with the back of his grimy hand.

The flask eventually returned to Bashford, who leaned along the side of the driver's cabin and passed it through the window to the driver Pulham and passengers, Wilson and Stiles.

"That's that terrible trio happy," he joked as he accepted the laughter from the approving

Tans. "Well then, lads, what about a song – we've got a little more time before we get to Cafgarven so what about *Goodbye-ee?* That's one of my favourites."

An enthusiastic roar of approval rang out from the high-spirited men and the song began:

Goodbye-ee, goodbye-ee,
Wipe the tear, baby dear, from your eye-ee,
Tho' it's hard to part I know,
I'll be tickled to death to go.

They sang on, giving Hayward another precious moment to savour the green, rolling hills of Ireland and her glorious, unspoilt countryside. He sang along with the rest, but his inner self left them to follow its own thoughts. His vision settled on the long, uneven hills that ran parallel to the road. The superb sky seemed delicately folded against the luxuriant, green scarps. It was like being inside a bright, blue dome, whose internal borders were the distant hills. The expanse was almost as he visualised Heaven, and his thoughts began to drift to the Irish people. How rightly they idolised their land. Sometimes he felt unclean at the thought of policing them in such exquisiteness. He wanted to remain, but not in a uniform or carrying a rifle. For the few months he had been in the country, the change in the villager's attitude towards the Black and Tans had become very apparent. Because of their heavy-handed treatment of people and property, they were despised and resented – an affliction in a pleasant land.

The distant, sleepy village of Cafgarven, nestling in the distant greenery, drew nearer as the truck rumbled onwards. The singing ceased, and the men readied themselves for a surprise raid. Their banter died, leaving an eerie silence for the coming job. All knew there would be the usual protests as the doors were kicked in and the ransacking searches began.

Sergeant Bradley looked up at the Auxiliary, who had invited himself along on the raid, even though Auxiliaries were not officially operative yet. "Cafgarven has been rumoured to have a hidden store of weapons. We got the information from an informer that the R.I.C. had been using."

"Yes, Inspector Callaghan did mention this to me. Seems I picked an exciting morning to pay a visit," Bashford smiled.

"A flying column from a neighbouring county has been rounded up, so there will be no danger from them," added Sergeant Bradley.

"So little Cafgarven has been playing host to the Shinners, blast them. Will you be teaching them a lesson?"

"I hope not. Many of them would be too frightened to refuse such help because of reprisals. Also, there might not be any weapons anyway. I understand the informer has gone missing.

He may have become unreliable and run off, or he might have been caught."

Bashford frowned. "Caught by whom – I thought the flying column was rounded up and interned?"

"We have interned some men who we believe belong to the flying column operating in these parts. We could be wrong, but that is not likely."

"The villager's part in this cannot be tolerated – they can always hide behind the excuse of fear. They must stand up to these cowards," Bashford stated firmly.

Sergeant Bradley was quiet – if the new Auxiliary force had Bashford's ideals, things were not likely to improve.

Hayward had overheard their conversation and his loathing of the Auxiliary increased. Like Sergeant Bradley, he doubted things were going to get better.

TWO

Waiting for Special Guests

Sunrise, above the eastern hills, brought a fanfare of birdsong. The spectacle caused Sean to reflect on the marvel of the blessed land with its rich, rural beauty.

"Compelling beyond words," he muttered, his paisley scarf saturated with sweat from his big, bull neck. "Mornings are my favourite time of the day. Especially summer ones." He grinned and turned his gaze from the distant hills.

His companion, a tall, young man, was crouched by a boulder, shivering and unimpressed. "You can keep it."

Sean laughed at the sorrowful exhibit. "Good God, Cormac! There you are now – six foot of you aching away in the morning dew. Life in the Volunteers is not so romantic now, is it?" Then taking off his cap, he mopped his brow with the end of his dirty scarf. His black curly hair, flecked with grey, was gently ruffled in the soft, morning breeze.

Looking up from his melancholy self-indulgence, the young man sighed. "How can you, and the others, be so calm after what we've just done, Sean?" He was clearly nervous, and needed consoling.

"Oh, come now, Cormac! We're not so calm as you might think. I don't like killing, neither does Sammy or Daniel, but the man was an informer. He was working for the police. This is war, lad! It's a very dirty business. There is no glory in this, only necessity, and I said as much when you first came into the column."

He watched as Cormac sighed and looked down at the wet grass, shaking his head. "I can't get over the wretched way his eyes bulged as you and Sammy strangled him. Then Daniel muffling the gun and shooting him in the back of the head."

Sean nodded in agreement. "Daniel is a good lad. He held his nerve when it was needed. However, he has seen death before."

During the entire ghastly affair, Cormac had been useless. He had gone to pieces. "I've brought about distrust in Sammy and Daniel, haven't I?"

"God love us! What makes you say that?"

"They couldn't wait to get out of my sight after the deed was done."

"Don't be silly, Cormac. They're planting the corpse where it can be found by the Black and

Tans. The set-up has to look right." Sean was a little more forgiving than the others and knew his companion was not at fault. "You'll make good when the time comes."

"Christ! Daniel's just seventeen. Four years younger than me."

"He has been with us longer than you. With the rest of the column rounded up and interned, our operations have not been that daring of late. Before you joined, this sort of thing was commonplace. You're going to have to get used to it, Cormac. This is a big one and the informer's body is bait for the Black and Tans. You can't afford to be self-indulgent when you face these English Reserves. They're all ex-squaddies and most have killed before. They're good! Better opponents than our Regular policemen."

Cormac seemed oblivious to his advice. "Planting a murdered corpse in the pub's yard is just going to get the villagers into trouble." He looked down into the gully at the small village. "A nice little place like this – out in the middle of nowhere and we are going to lure the Tans in and frame its people. For what?"

Sean looked down upon Cafgarven. The sleepy little community nestled snugly in the gully. A small church, standing like a sentinel upon the scarp, looked out over the rooftops. The quaint Parochial House, close by, had a little vegetable garden to the rear, close to the grave-yard. It was a most tranquil setting.

He smiled. "It is a charming little village. The people keep well out of the troubles." He looked back at Cormac. "It's important that everyone gets a taste of the Tan's community policing. These people are our best weapon, combined with the brutality of these shell-shocked English soldiers. That's what they are, lad. Trigger-happy men who have endured years of trench warfare. They don't know how to react to their surroundings."

"What do you mean?" Cormac's blue eyes became focused and striking against his pale skin. He twisted his neck to get rid of the stiffness and blinked nervously. His black locks fell across his forehead, and it was obvious that he was not cut out for this type of thing.

Sean smiled soothingly. "These Reserves are not proper policemen." He lingered a while searching for the words. "They're unemployed soldiers who have been slung upon the scrapheap by their ungrateful rulers. They're desperate young men. A generation with no skills except fighting. These are, principally, what your Tans are made up of, my lad. In a way, I suppose one could sympathise with them."

"You have pity for them?" It was now Cormac's turn to show revulsion. "The stories that have been told about —"

"That's right," cut in Sean. "We need them to have such a press and we must encourage them to earn it. For it furthers our cause. Especially when we push them to the limit, keep them paranoid knowing that anyone of us has the potential to kill. Even mild-mannered people like those below." He looked back down at the village where the Parochial House's garden door opened and out walked the village priest, a tall, lean, spectacled man. "The Tans could be the best weapon we've got. Their brutality is winning worldwide condemnation."

"So killing the informer has been done simply to put the village under suspicion?" Cormac still disapproved.

"It will breed another pocket of resentment. We also need to see if we can kill a Tan. There's a fifty-pound bounty for the death of one. We need to let them know we are active and we can get them looking in the wrong places."

"Like the innocent village below."

"Yes, Cormac, especially the little place below. We need them to hate the Crown forces too. Likewise, we need the Crown forces to distrust them. Can't you see that these Tans are too heavy-handed for their intended job? They are a match for us all right, but the local, law-abiding sheep down there..." He pointed to the village, "... these people that would let us continue under British rule for another seven hundred years. We need them to hate too! And like it or not – these Tans are better at whipping their passions up than we ever are. Particularly if we can help our vicious, little, hunting hounds along the way with a nicely-planted snitch in the alehouse yard. Think of it. One of their pals viciously murdered. It'll make their English blood boil, and when they are nicely worked up we plug one and retreat.

"They're not logical men, you see, and the R.I.C. will not be able to contain them when they're inflamed. The Tans will run riot like they did in Balbriggan and Tubbercurry. They'll smack a few heads. Maybe kill a local." He scanned the village below. "Then little Cafgarven will become resentful and hating of British rule and another small village to suffer Tan hostility. We want to infect the countryside with hatred."

Cormac sighed and shook his head. "All this has become so sordid. I never thought it would be like this."

"I told you to get rid of the romantic notions and think about this seriously before you came in." Sean stopped and pondered a little, knowing recrimination would be useless. "This is what the reality of fighting is and, as you can see, the old fables become clouded. Poets and bards have a fancy of their own around warm fires with fine ale. Take the repugnant side of it on board and live for the Cause. We've got enough dead heroes for inebriated men to sing of. The British are still here and have always won. Your new outlook may be pessimistic, but it's a lot better than the idyllic one you've replaced, lad. Perhaps you'll learn to control it and put it to good use."

Cormac leaned back against the rock, holding his rifle upright with the butt resting upon the soil. "Do you see it all as loathsome then? I mean, you don't seem distressed by what happened to the man we murdered."

"I did not get pleasure from the killing, but I will not bask in self-indulgence about it. I'm distressed about confronting a police patrol with Black and Tan backup. In case you haven't noticed, there are only four of us, while the old flying column numbered thirty and more. We could do with that sort of firepower now." He allowed his gaze to scan the distant meadows. "No sign of their vehicles yet!"

"The village priest is up early." Cormac had calmed down. "Can he see the street from his garden?"

"No," answered Sean. "Besides, Sammy and Daniel have placed the body and are making their way back through the wood and along the other side of the scarp."

Almost immediately the two men appeared on the summit and stealthily made their way down, using the shrubs and bushes for cover.

Sean chuckled at their antics as they descended. "Will you look at those two now? Sammy's bald head shining like a second sun – he should keep his cap on. And little Daniel's ginger mop is screaming out in all directions from beneath his."

"They're on their way," gasped Daniel as they came into the clearing.

Sean held a placating hand out to Cormac as though gently bouncing a slow-moving bubble. The young man had stiffened and had almost clicked the bolt of his weapon in readiness. "The priest might hear." He then put his finger to his lips and looked at Daniel. "Not so loud, Daniel."

"Two vehicles," whispered Sammy. He, like Sean, was a brutish-looking man in his late thirties. "One car leading and a Crossley Tender behind. It's full of Tans."

"So they've taken the bait," replied Sean. "I was rather hoping they might give it a miss and all this become a waste of time."

Sammy smiled. "Then we could have pissed off home."

"We still could now. It's not too late," ventured Sean. "Do we really want to try and plug a Tan for fifty quid we might not live to spend?"

"And probably won't get because Dublin is hard up," added Daniel.

Sean winked at him. "Now you're thinking, boy." He looked to Sammy who would have the final say. "They'll find the corpse now and we can let nature take its merry course where a Black and Tan introduction, for the village, is concerned."

Sammy shook his head. "Sorry lads. We still need to shoot one before we make a run for it. One shot and out as quickly as we can."

"I had a funny feeling you were going to say that." Sean hid his anxiety and moved out of the clearing, leaving the others behind. He covertly moved downwards along the worn path, searching for a position that afforded a good view of the high street. As the marksman of the group it would be down to him to make the killing shot, and he needed to consider the probable things the Tans would do. He knew they would place lookouts on the high road in and out of the village, so there would be good targets among the guards. However, in the past, the Tans had displayed vigilance when doing such duties. They would, no doubt, be surveying the hillside, so he would need to keep himself well concealed.

Finding a small bush next to a rock, he lay upon his stomach and looked down into Cafgarven. He had a clear view of the high street and the main road where the police vehicles would enter the village. Content that he had a good line anywhere upon the approach road, he allowed his gaze to drift up the hill towards the church grounds.

The priest was still picking vegetables from a tomato patch. How oblivious the holy man was, and what would be his reaction when the Tans arrived? Sean could not help feeling a pang of remorse for the man, whose morning contentment would soon be shattered.

THREE

Father John.

The summer morning was most invigorating, which contributed to Father John Joseph Abbott's joy as he wandered in his small garden. First to the much-loved vegetable patch, to check his runner beans and pick some tomatoes. Then to his cherished flower garden, to delight in the bright colours and the chirping of distant birds. The contentment his garden brought him was immeasurable; perhaps he would raise it during one of his sermons. After all, it was something people should learn to appreciate, in making the hazardous journey through life. He reflected on the matter, taking off his spectacles and cleaning the lenses with his handkerchief. The thick glass enlarged his green eyes when he put them on again and allowed his gaze to stroll beyond the garden, into the church grounds and across the gravestones of late Cafgarven people.

He smiled contentedly, taking gentle pleasure in his thoughts, and walked to the fence to read some of the stones close to the garden perimeter.

Suddenly his zealous housekeeper, Maureen, smashed through his tranquil contemplation, startling the priest back into the real world.

"Father John, would you like some fried tomatoes with your bacon and eggs?" asked tubby Maureen, also full of the morning's gracious vigour.

"Oh, why yes, Maureen, I had meant to ask, and have picked some from the vegetable patch already." Father John proffered his hand, which held three tomatoes.

Bemusement flashed upon Maureen's big, crimson face, and her eyes widened in disbelief, as though she had witnessed a miracle.

"You have some in your hand, Father John," she whispered quizzically. "Yes Maureen. It is as I just said. A moment ago I was in the vegetable garden, and I picked these for the purpose of frying," insisted Father John blandly. Maureen was a gentle soul but apt, on occasion, to be a gossip. This, combined with her ability to spin a colourful yarn, made Father John keen to stress that he had already picked the tomatoes in anticipation of her wishing to cook them. The last thing he wanted was for her to put some lavish tale, with her wondrous, likeable wit, around the village. He could just imagine her telling people he performed miracles.

"Oh, of course, Father, you had me going there," she giggled, and taking the tomatoes from him made off back to the kitchen door. "I'll bring them into the dining room in about fifteen minutes."

"That will be splendid," he called delightedly, relieved that he had been able to convince her. She would still spin a comical yarn about the incident, but it would be for what it was – a little incident, nothing more, nothing less.

He watched as she entered the kitchen, shutting the door behind her. When the jovial housekeeper was out of the way, he walked quickly towards a small set of French doors that led into the dining room, noting that the wooden framework could do with painting. He would have to let it be known among the congregation's men, when he next visited Flannigan's Bar. During the course of a light-hearted conversation, he would subtly mention the dilapidated doors, over a pint of stout, and be sure to get a tipsy promise from one of them. That would be all he needed, as the promisor would be fully committed, in front of witnesses, to his pledge. Knowing the Lord could see into his thoughts, Father John crossed himself and whispered a prayer for forgiveness. He then allowed a cheeky, little smile to corrupt his solemn face, confident in the knowledge that God would overlook such a small misdeed. Secure in being alone, he uttered aloud: "Just one more little grievance for which I must humbly ask you to forgive me, Lord."

He stepped enthusiastically towards the book cabinet, delicately avoiding the worn, tapestried chairs. Opening the dark, wooden-framed door, he carefully removed a leather-bound book, which was only half the width of the other volumes in his collection. This was apparent only when the book was removed. In the space behind was a secret bottle of Irish whiskey, which he had bought from Flannigan's, purely for medicinal purposes – at least, that was what he had told Flannigan. However, as a result of Maureen's gossiping, it was the worst-kept secret in Cafgarven. Among the village children the hidden alcohol was known as Father John's lemonade. He was unaware his little tipples were an open secret.

He sighed with relief as he reached for his "little livener". He daintily referred to his vice in this way, when asking for the Lord's forgiveness. It was his morning kick, to which would be added an afternoon one, and an evening one before retiring to his bed. The vice was not too excessive, as his congregation knew. It was his efforts at discretion that provided amusement to the villagers, though they would never have let him know as he was apt to be a little sensitive. The next, practised move was to open the drawer below the cabinet doors and take out the small whiskey glass. Carefully pouring a generous measure, he observed that his bottle would need replacing in the near future. This would combine neatly with a visit to Flannigan's to claim a favour from one of the customers in the matter of the French windows. He first raised the glass to the sunlight that filtered through the curtains then put it to his appreciative lips.

Suddenly the dining room door burst open, as he was in mid gulp. In rushed Maureen, with a startled look on her face, catching him in the act.

"Father John, it's the Black and Tans. Here, here in Cafgarven," she blurted out in panic, seemingly unconcerned at the priest's tippling.

The whiskey went down his windpipe, and he choked and started to cough violently as the liquid burned. He hastily slammed the glass upon the polished-oak table, so that he could focus on this predicament. He continued to cough and splutter while Maureen, in panic, tried to assist him by vigorously slapping him on the back. As the determined housekeeper got to the third slap, the action qualified as a rather hard punch. Father John's coughing instantly stopped but was replaced by a new pain in his back.

"Are you all right, Father John?" she asked innocently, believing that she had been of some use.

"Bless you, Maureen," he spluttered ironically, knowing his tone would go over her head – the joke was between God and him. He looked upwards in despair, as though the Lord might be laughing at his expense. He attempted to compose himself, while Maureen began to brush him down like a fussy mother wanting her little boy to look tidy before walking out into the world.

"Yes, thank you, Maureen, now please stop fussing. You'll be getting yourself all vexed by the commotion going on outside." He was growing agitated with his housekeeper's persistence.

Calmly drawing breath, he slowly allowed himself to settle after her activity. The clock on the mantelpiece showed the time as six-sixteen. He glanced again at the excited Maureen, then ventured out of the room into the hallway. The watchful housekeeper was in hot pursuit, excited with curiosity to see how the Father John would deal with this matter.

FOUR

A Messy Job to Get Out of the Way.

The car and the lorry came to a sudden halt at the entrance to the village high street, with screeching of tyres and raucous shouts. Behind, a wake of dust lingered, as though reluctant to proceed further. The Black and Tans and the Regular Irish Police began to get out of their vehicles

"Come along now, lads. Let's rekindle that good old spirit," bellowed Bashford, in his full, dark-green regalia and matching beret decked with a comical bobble on top.

Shots were fired into the air, letting the forlorn villagers know the "Boys of the Bulldog Breed" had arrived. Curtains twitched. Hayward could not help noticing the look of agitation on the face of Inspector Callaghan.

Preferring the proximity of Sergeant Bradley, Hayward edged closer to the car from which the Special Branch Irish policemen emerged, knowing they would wish to speak with the R.I.C. Sergeant.

Hayward had a strong sense that Bradley had developed some tolerance and trust towards him. The rest of the Tans, with a few exceptions, were kept at bay – most of them were undisciplined in handling police work. Sergeant Bradley preferred to use them as low-profile guards, and to use R.I.C. personnel when possible. However, the Tans were not easy to command, and Irish policemen were getting hard to come by.

Inspector Callaghan cursed, despite Hayward's close presence. "These ex-soldiers have made a bad situation worse through their indifference towards the local people. Christ! What a bloody bag of ruffians."

"We have to make do with what we can recruit," responded Sergeant Bradley. His big, red face looked brutish, yet his voice showed moderation.

"So the Castle sends us this bunch of bastards?"

"Yes, Sir."

Callaghan shook his head and muttered: "Soldiers are good men to have when fighting wars against a defined enemy, but Ireland is different. Unemployed soldiers can't understand that Shinners are indistinguishable from the civilian population. Towns and streets are the battleground, and innocent people are in the crossfire when the lead starts flying." He watched Bashford laughing among them. "And now, Auxies. Tans with posh voices."

Sergeant Bradley agreed, adding. "I don't much like the idea of this new Auxiliary turning up either, Sir. He still seems to think they're his men and they're a little too fond of him for my liking. His lot are not even mobilised yet. But he's poking his nose in around here, where it's not wanted."

"Are these Tans any good? Reliable, I mean." The Inspector was reluctant to confront the Auxiliary, being after all nothing more than a rural Police Inspector.

Hayward could not help but sympathise with Sergeant Bradley, who was obviously trying to get his officer to take command of the situation. But then Callaghan, a simple countryman, liked to take things easy and had never, in his wildest dreams, foreseen himself in charge of such a police operation.

Resigned, Bradley answered. "They're all good when it comes to a fight, Sir. They just don't know when to stop, and they're not fussy over who they get stuck into. None of them like to dance the side-step, if you get my meaning. They like to confront things head on. However, if I had to choose, Hayward here is fine. His temperament is sound. Henderson and Cuttings are level-headed too, but I don't think our visiting Auxiliary likes them much."

Hayward frowned, surprised and amused at the effrontery. They spoke as though he was not there, but Bradley was also letting him know that he was aware of him listening.

"Why would that be?" asked Callaghan, perplexed.

"They were in different regiments during the War and these three don't seem too keen on him, especially young Hayward here."

Hayward was surprised by Bradley's astuteness. The old Sergeant had obviously read the reason he had left the truck's company.

"Right. If needs be, use them before the others."

Callaghan's reluctance was plain, and Hayward knew the man had a loathing for village raids.

They all fell silent, watching the brash Auxiliary. The man basked in the adulation of the Tans. It was as though he was trying to relive the days of trench warfare, and was totally oblivious to Inspector Callaghan's authority. Impudently taking things upon himself, he blew a whistle, which cut through the excited yelling like a hot knife through butter. His men came together.

Callaghan flinched and looked up to the heavens as the shrill sound sliced through him. "Why ever were the English created? God, what I wouldn't give for the good, old Regulars, instead of these heavy-handed ruffians."

Again Hayward was aghast, wondering if the Inspector knew or cared that he could hear him. Officially the man was in charge, but it was difficult to command the undisciplined Reserves. Bashford, with no authorisation, was better able to supervise them.

It seemed to Hayward that Callaghan had reluctantly decided to let the interloper get on with it. The Inspector turned from his scrutiny, combating a growing feeling of amused embarrassment and unable to contain a smile that spread across his face at the unholy disorder. "Of all things, someone from a goblin's horde has managed to bring a smile to my face. Lord, what's the world coming to?"

"Right! Adams, Higgins, Cuttings and Wright – go to the eastern approach," Bashford bellowed. "Stop anyone from leaving."

"Yes, Sir," they replied, and jumped to the task.

Hayward wished he were among them – it would have eliminated him from the house searches. Still, there was the western approach. Maybe he would be chosen for that duty. "Wilson, Stiles, Pulham and Henderson, go to the other end and do likewise," added Bashford.

Hayward cursed under his breath as the Auxiliary stared at him, reading him like a book. He shuddered as a small, vindictive smile creased the man's face. The Auxiliary clearly took a malicious pleasure in his discomfort. Fortunately, all attention was diverted to a small, bleak Parochial House next to the sombre, stone church.

All turned as the door opened, and a tall, thin, Roman Catholic priest emerged. Hayward thought him a rather dour-looking man, with a concerned expression. Yet he could not help studying him. It was strange – he had never met the fellow in his life, yet he found he liked him. The housekeeper, who followed him, was stopped at the door by the priest, who looked back and said sternly. "Now will you get back indoors, Maureen? There's nothing for you to see out here."

She reluctantly stopped and watched him leave. Then run through to the lounge where she could watch the commotion from the window.

Father John composed himself before proceeding with long, firm strides towards the policemen's truck. Hayward was struck by the air of confidence that he exuded. His deep respect for the clergy was stirred, and he briefly wondered if Bashford would offer such respect.

Father John halted before the Auxiliary, as though perceiving that Inspector Callaghan would be of little use. He was dealing with the Tans who, he obviously knew, were a law unto themselves. Prudently he indulged them.

Regretfully, Hayward watched the sad encounter, as Bashford smirked in triumph. Unlike the Tans, he was more impressive in his new uniform. Officially he was a guest on patrol, but his credibility among the rogue policemen was fully established. The ammunition belt over his shoulder made him an intimidating sight. Father John nodded his head in silent greeting.

The sombre priest's spectacles sparkled, drawing attention to the magnified eyelids that lazily closed over enlarged, bright-green irises. Hayward thought the priest showed a quiet, yet authoritative manner, and he noticed it irritated Bashford, who was scrutinising the solemn man before him.

Like a theatrical performance, the scene unfolded. Bashford and Father John appeared to be acting out a ritual. The arrogant Auxiliary looked deeply into the green eyes of the priest, only to be confronted by a look devoid of fear – just a calm challenge.

"Sir! What is wrong? Why are your men firing their guns?" Father John was unfamiliar with the details of rank, but he had fortunately massaged Bashford's ego with his mistake.

"We have to search the place, Father," answered Bashford, after a pause. "I'm sorry for the inconvenience, but we believe there are gunmen hiding in your village."

"Good God," replied Father John, laughing at the absurdity. "You can't be serious. Everyone in this place is a member of my congregation. If one person were involved with gunmen, I would know. This is a small village and everyone gossips. You must be mistaken."

"I hope you are right, Father," replied Bashford.

The priest's face creased into a broad smile. "I'm Father John, and may I know your good self, Sir?" His tone was gentle and refined, though self-assured. He waited for the Auxiliary to give his name.

"My name is Bashford, Auxiliary Officer Cadet to the R.I.C." He then turned away with rude disregard. "Sergeant Bradley."

"Yes," replied the Regular, in some doubt whether to cooperate; but like Callaghan, he thought the Auxiliary could handle the Tans better. He did not want an argument in front of the priest.

"Could you take Turpin and Barnes? Assemble the villagers in the street! Everyone – women and children too."

"Yes," he responded awkwardly, and went about the task.

Father John scratched his head and looked down at the road. "Is this really necessary?" His tone had become noticeably more mocking.

Knowing exactly what the priest was doing, Hayward continued to observe. Sometimes he had to turn his attention elsewhere, for the priest's gall was comical and he found himself unable to contain the amusement. He decided to watch Sergeant Bradley who, with Barnes and Turpin, went about rousing the villagers from their homes.

The first street door opened and the search party barged in past a woman of about forty years. She was shocked at first, then enraged as she turned to pursue them, shrieking oaths. After a moment, Turpin and Barnes re-emerged, and forced the woman from her home. She twisted her plump body, wrenching her arm from Turpin's grasp, and tried to go back inside.

"I want to dress properly," she spat angrily, as she stood in her tatty, old nightgown, covered by a man's grey jacket – grabbed hastily before being forced out.

Turpin shouted back. "Shut up and move. The quicker we're done, the sooner we're gone."

A younger woman then ran out of the house shouting: "Leave my mother alone! You have no right to be treating her like that." Her dressing gown fell apart, revealing a pink petticoat beneath.

"Do it up, you dirty cow," snarled Turpin vulgarly.

"You can't use that sort of language on my mother," she retorted as she retied the gown, ignoring the wolf-whistles coming from some of the Tans.

Barnes, standing at the street door, gritted his teeth; frustration was getting the better of him. "Move, don't make things awkward. The sooner we are done, the quicker we go." He grabbed the young woman by the scruff of the neck, then slung her forward. She stumbled, and was prevented from hitting the ground by her mother, who clutched her desperately.

"You thug!" shouted the mother. "What gives you the right to do that? Leave her be, she's never done you wrong."

Turpin stepped forward raising his rifle butt, threateningly. "Shut your mouth and get moving." The women flinched before his threat.

Hayward was surprised at the behaviour of Barnes and Turpin, but then they had been drinking from Bashford's flask on the truck.

Father John was shocked by the commotion. "Please control your men, Sir," he implored.

Inspector Callaghan tried to defuse the situation. "Come on now, ladies, don't be making the job more difficult." He turned to Barnes and Turpin. "Right boys, go into the house and help the Sergeant. I'll take it from here." He winked at them and nodded his head sideways with a discrete "run along now" gesture. "Here, Madam, let me be helping you."

"I can manage myself," spat the mother, wrinkling her nose in revulsion as she caught a whiff of his pungent body odour.

"Keep your stinking hands off her," added the daughter in disgust. The pair of them moved towards Father John, while the Inspector, who had developed a thick skin to criticism, thought their abhorrence of him was because he was with the hated Tans.

"I'm just doing my job, Madam, now will you come along? We'll soon be done," he replied.

Hayward was now nervous that things could quickly get out of control, but Callaghan, despite his shortcomings, managed the situation well. Suddenly, Bashford's harsh voice summoned him.

"You there," he pointed at Hayward, then turned to a couple of his old soldiers. "Jones and Baker, come with me."

Hayward reluctantly unslung his rifle and followed them. Bashford lingered to whisper to him: "Don't forget, young man, you're not on ten shillings a day for nothing."

As he moved off with the Auxiliary his gaze met that of Father John, just as the priest dipped his head to look over the rim of his spectacles. Clearly he had observed the mild rebuke.

Along the street the bitter and frightened villagers were herded – forced to stand in the middle of the road, while the Tans went about searching their homes. Mattresses were turned over, cupboard contents were brutally strewn across floors, tables and chairs were thrown aside. The wretched villagers looked on in desperation, not daring to further antagonise the Tans. Forlorn faces stared, while tormenting sounds issued from within their violated homes. Adults, and children, gulped back tears. The villagers were suffering; they felt debased by the incompetent policing, recognised the corruption and were sickened by it. Father John put a soothing arm around the distressed mother who, with her daughter, had suffered Turpin's scorn.

"My son fought for King and Country, Father John. Why are they doing this?"

He gently stroked her cheek, anxious to calm her, feeling that the mood of the Black and Tans should not be trifled with. "Come now, Mary, they're likely to take any antagonism out on the men. Try and be bold now, or one of our boys could get shot."

She sank her matted hair into his chest and continued to sob. As he consoled her, he watched Bashford return with the strange, detached Tan who had been rebuked earlier. There was something different about this young man. He could sense it, and he knew the Auxiliary recognised this odd Tan too. Bashford was clearly unsettled by peculiar young fellow, and Father John began, in his mind, to look for ways to exploit this.

"Do you not think this is fine countryside, Auxiliary Officer Cadet Bashford?" said Father John, pleasantly though his face was grim. His big, green eyes fixed him in a hypnotic stare. He continued. "The noise from the houses destroys it all. Brings home the sad reality of the troubled times we live in. Fenians or Tans, it doesn't matter really. You're all reckless imps that have somehow managed to sneak through Heaven's gate. All of you are an affliction in a pleasant land."

He momentarily turned his gaze on Hayward. To his astonishment, the young man never flinched. He looked back naively. There was no challenging defiance, but neither was there shame.

"I'm not about to argue with you, Father John," replied Bashford, after a brief pause. Evidently he would have liked to. He walked away and stood before the dismal villagers.

"Hayward," he called.

Hayward stood to attention. "Sergeant," he responded loudly, hoping Father John would now recognise the man's rank. Bashford said nothing, but he was not impressed. If he said he had not been mobilised yet and the rank was incorrect, he could invite criticism of being on duty without authority. He stared at the villagers as though unable to withdraw his gaze. Finally he sighed. "Go to the truck and fetch the register for me, Hayward, there's a good chap." His scrutiny was still fixed upon the crowd.

Hayward did as instructed, pleased to be away from the man, even for a moment. He returned, with a clipboard containing the names of Cafgarven's residents.

"Thank you. Stay here while I call the register," Bashford ordered.

"Yes, Sergeant," he replied, wanting him to say something that would invite a rebuke from the priest. The man was using his status as a gentleman and ex-officer to take liberties, and these rural policemen were letting the bastard get away with it. The Cafgarven folk were of the same mind too, and it was clear that this isolated, little village wanted no part in the troubles.

"Listen clearly, please," called Bashford. "As I call your names I want you to answer, then step forward. Anyone who does not have his or her name called must stay where they are. If I find anyone stepping forward without his or her name being called, I will accept it as a mark of contempt. That person will be immediately arrested and taken back to the police barracks to be questioned more intensely. Do I make myself clear?"

Murmurs followed.

"If any of you want to score points by playing the dumb, Irish yokel, then believe me – you'll bloody earn them. Perhaps you are unfortunate enough to be half-witted. In that case we will flatter you. We will credit you with more sense then you have, and we, being a mere bunch of thick heads, will assume that you have something to hide. It is our duty to apprehend the gunmen that have infested this country, and any fool getting in our way will not be tolerated."

Bashford then began to call out names from the register in family groups. One by one the inhabitants of the village stepped forward. When the roll call was finally done, a nervous man, of around thirty years, was left standing at the back.

Hayward pitied the wretched fellow who trembled with fear. His brown hair stuck to his sweating forehead, while his big, red, cherub face flushed. The man's eyes looked as though they were about to fall from their sockets, and he began to babble nervously about his presence in Cafgarven.

"I'm visiting my fiancée, Sir, and I have been staying with the said young lady's family," he stammered.

"Is the family here?" asked Bashford routinely.

"We're his hosts, Sir," a man cut in, standing with his family. "I can vouch for him. We own the bar, Flannigan's Bar."

"Right," accepted Bashford. He turned back to the nervous man, and became a little more polite. "What is your name, please?"

"Lynch, Sir. Michael Lynch."

"Where are you from, Mr Lynch?"

Before Michael Lynch could reply, Sergeant Bradley came out of Flannigan's bar and shouted for Inspector Callaghan's attention. Callaghan walked brusquely across the village road.

"What's the problem, Sergeant?" he asked.

"We have a corpse on our hands, Sir," he whispered. "Shot in the head, the usual way the dirty bastards like to play their games."

"Lead on, Sergeant," ordered Callaghan quietly. He motioned with his head, directing Bashford to accompany them.

Hayward glanced back at the crowd. Who, among them, was capable of such an act? He felt that something did not make sense. He shook his head, wishing to rid himself of such troubled thoughts. He was uncomfortable at being the recipient of the priest's continued attention, and wanted to ask the man if he thought of him as a part of the land's blight too. Silence had fallen upon the crowd, though Hayward was certain they could not have heard what the Sergeant said. For what seemed like an eternity, he was forced to look from face to face, and in each person's gaze he read questioning looks. What is it? What's wrong? There was no escape from the concern.

Finally Bashford emerged from the bar and his grim, red face was contorted with rage, while Sergeant Bradley jogged beside him, in what seemed like an imploring manner.

"Well, let's start with the so-called fiancé. He doesn't live here. I reckon the bar keeper must have been helping his Fenian pal with the body," he hissed, stopping by Hayward.

"We should just apprehend them and let the Regulars handle matters from here," Bradley remonstrated.

Bashford confronted him. "No Sergeant, we'll deal with this our way."

Hayward moved behind them, eyes wide with surprise, as the furious Auxiliary pulled out his revolver. Sergeant Bradley frowned despairingly – the situation was becoming increasingly serious.

"Jones and Baker," called Bashford. "The bastard calling himself the fiancé! Sling the murdering sod in the back of the lorry now!"

Bashford's face seemed about to explode as his skin fought to contain a storm raging beneath his crimson cheeks. He turned to Hayward and the Sergeant. "You two, arrest the landlord who vouched for him."

Frantic protests erupted from the Flannigan family, as they pleaded with Father John for help.

Jones and Baker arrested the bewildered Michael Lynch, while Hayward accompanied the Irish Sergeant and quietly instructed the inn-keeper to get into the truck.

Father John stepped forward. "Sir, please! I implore you. These men have done nothing wrong. You're making a mistake."

But Bashford ignored him, and in desperation Father John turned to Inspector Callaghan, who was then crossing the road. "Inspector, you're in charge! Please, do something. These people have done nothing wrong."

Bashford interjected coldly. "Don't interfere, Father John. We're arresting these men, come what may."

"There's been a murder, Father," added Inspector Callaghan meekly. "We must detain suspects for questioning."

Michael Lynch tried to reason. "But I haven't done anything wrong. I'm here with –!"

He screamed as Jones smashed a rifle butt into the small of his back. He fell to his knees, amid frightened screams from the women and children. Baker stepped forward and, for extra measure, slammed his rifle butt into Lynch's mouth, smashing the man's lips into his teeth.

Shocked screams arose from the crowd, and children backed into their parents, horrified at the sight of Michael Lynch on his side, clasping his bloodied mouth.

"Good God, Mr Bashford! In the name of Jesus, I implore you. There's no need for this," bellowed Father John. It was useless, and the priest's face twisted in repugnance as he realised the Auxiliary was immune to reason.

"Get the murdering bastards on the truck," shouted Bashford, while the innkeeper's family frantically insisted on the innocence of both men.

"Please, Father, you must help us," cried Mrs Flannigan. "We've done nothing, honestly. For the love of God, help us."

Sergeant Bradley struggled to find a compromise. "We should just take them back to the barracks. Let the R.I.C. take over from there."

Bashford stopped abruptly. Slowly he turned to face the impertinent Regular, who had dared to question his judgement in front of the villagers. A hush fell upon the crowd, hopeful anticipation gripping all. Even the innkeeper's family desisted from protesting. Michael Lynch was the only oblivious person – his fiancée and Father John briefly stopped attending his needs to watch what unfolded. For a moment, the villagers believed they had found an unwitting ally in the R.I.C. Sergeant. Their hopes were dashed when Bashford's face flushed trying to contain the mounting rage within.

Bradley wished he had kept silent. It was wrong to question the man so openly, despite him being a mere guest. God! If only the meek Inspector Callaghan would exert his authority.

The Auxiliary managed to refrain from rebuke, but his eyes blazed with a fierce passion. Hayward wished the Irish police would stand up to the pompous man. It was so plain to see what was happening. None would, and so all were at fault, including himself.

Bashford was a gentleman who had his own perception of what was going on, and he had been tempered by a brutal war where men had looked to him for leadership. The man thought he was in the same place under the same conditions, but he was clearly mistaken and no one would say anything. To him they were all working-class people, needing someone to take the helm. He carried his own authority from the trenches and his countrymen thankfully recognised it, but these bog-diggers were ignorant people and they clearly needed his help. Coupled with his low opinion of the rural police he ignored all.

"Comply with your original instructions, Sergeant," ordered Bashford quietly.

Sergeant Bradley feebly conformed, aware of having deeply offended the proud ex-Captain.

There would be a reckoning back at the barracks. He turned to go about his duty.

Suddenly a shot shattered the ominous silence that had just settled.

Some of the women screeched as the sound rang out along the high street. The villagers jolted, looking in all directions to see where it had come from. The Tans reacted instantly by going to ground. Quickly they gathered their wits. Rifle bolts clicked in response, amid shouts of where the enemy gunfire had come from.

More shots filled the air, thumping into the truck's engine panel and radiator, close to where Hayward had found cover. He looked to the panic-stricken villagers suddenly gripped by terror, running in all directions as they realised they were caught in crossfire. Children were scooped up and bodily shielded by parents, who frantically ran for the sanctuary of their homes. He watched as water trickled from the radiator onto the hot road while Barnes and Turpin, at the rear of the truck, started to shoot into the hillside.

As the confusion unfolded, he watched with his earlier, strange detachment – a condition further enhanced from his experience of warfare. His eyes narrowed as the events unfolded. He was transfixed and in awe, from his position of cover, as individuals reacted to the new terror in their own way. He calmly studied the way Inspector Callaghan responded – watching the grim-faced policeman kneel and take careful aim with his pistol. Two shots cracked from his gun towards the hillside, from where the enemy shooting was coming – a droplet of certainty in a sea of human bewilderment.

He was taken, too, by the pickets placed at either end of the village, and found their rapid response with return rifle fire fascinating. These men were already advancing, amid shouts of confident instruction, towards the overlooking hill where the enemy was located.

Then all around he observed the poor, wretched people of Cafgarven – they screamed and panicked amid the angry crossfire. Terrified parents grabbed their infants and tried to cover them protectively from the random bullets that zipped through the air indiscriminately. Others clutched love ones and ran for cover. Close to him, by the truck, he was aware of Flannigan and his daughter, kneeling by Michael Lynch, still badly hurt from his recent beating. Flannigan was shouting to someone beyond the cover of the truck. Hayward turned to investigate the bar keeper's concern: Mrs Flannigan and Father John were kneeling over the prostrate body of Auxiliary Bashford. The priest was administering the last rites, flinching yet steadfast amid the hail of bullets that hit the road or smacked into the truck. Bashford's lifeless body jerked when another shell thumped into him.

FIVE

Tit-for- tat.

Angry gunfire infested the hillside, forcing the Volunteers to keep their heads down, as the Tans rapidly got to grips with the situation. They had now switched to the offensive, and had begun to advance upon the attackers.

Sean flinched and swore as bullets cut through the nearby bracken. His eyes widened in astonishment when he saw four Tans moving in. Gritting his teeth to fight his dismay, he cursed. "God! One shot too many. Why did I go for a second shot?" He had not used his head. It was obvious his first round had killed the Auxiliary, even though the second had put things beyond doubt. He levelled his rifle upon a rock, wanting to get a shot at the advancing Tans. Before he could aim, a bullet hit the boulder, forcing him to bury his head in the dirt, while splinters of stone tore across his cheek. Fear nestled in his stomach, rippling across his skin. Sweat oozed from him. Wretched memories of the South African veld, and the Boer gunman, began to haunt him. These Tans were a bit too experienced for his liking. They covered one another admirably when advancing. More shots threw up the soil close by, forcing him to keep his head down. His fear intensified when he saw that as two policemen fired, two more advanced.

His situation was hopeless. If he broke cover to run, a Tan bullet would cut him down. Yet, staying flattened behind the rock would also mean his death. He prayed that Cormac, or one of the others, would see him from their higher position.

"Come on, boys," he muttered. "This old hand needs help, and bloody quick." He caught a fleeting glance of Sammy who, with Daniels aid, was fighting a fierce gun battle against yet more Tans advancing from the opposite end of the village.

"Sammy," he heard Cormac's voice. "Sean's pinned down. We've got to do something to help him."

"You'll to have to go it alone, Cormac. As you can see, Danny and I have our hands full. Try to do what you can! Get going, lad, we need you, Sean needs you." Sammy would not dare to leave his position or take his eyes away from the gun-sight.

Sean fired off a quick shot, then pulled back the bolt to let the empty shell case spring into the grass. He crawled to another shooting position as two more shells hit the soil, close to where he had just been. He hoped it would buy Cormac time to crawl into a position where he might be able to assist him. The air was thick with the sound of whining bullets – soft, thudding sounds mixed with the occasional ricochet when they bounced off boulders.

He prayed the young man might be using the rocks and foliage for cover, while manoeuvring to a vantage point. A shot rang out above. It was Cormac. The youngster had come to his aid.

Sean spied four Tans advancing up the hill towards him. They had become a little more cautious, discovering they were now up against two. He raised his rifle, knowing two of the policemen would move forward under cover of their colleagues' blanket fire. Two fired three rapid rounds at his precarious position, while the other two ran for the next cover. A shot hit the turf in front of one of them, who quickly jumped back to his previous cover. His companion continued, sheltering behind a small rise and aiming at the thicket from where Cormac had fired.

Two shots were discharged by the angry Tan – the bullets cut a path through the bush, one of them bouncing off the rock behind which Cormac had ducked.

"Careful, boy," hissed Sean, as the young man scrambled away on his stomach to a new position. He discharged a second round, which was wild and missed by some distance. His introduction to the contest, however, had brought about a more cautious approach from the Tans.

The two Tans covering now also aimed at Cormac's position, but were forced to duck when Sean returned fire. He then took the opportunity to dash from his precarious position towards Cormac's. More shots rang out, missing him by inches.

One of the Tans, in a moment of bravado, broke his position to get a better shot, but was forced back as a bullet hit the turf a few feet in front of him.

Diving down beside the youngster, Sean sighed with gratitude. The whole gun battle was becoming a wicked tit-for-tat affair.

"Thanks, Cormac, I owe you one for that. Let's get to Sammy and Daniel, then we'll withdraw further into the hills and the wood beyond. We'll use proper cover when retreating – the way the Tans do to advance. Do you understand me?"

"Of course I do. I'm not daft now," Cormac laughed nervously. Sean could see the lad was trying to hide the anxiety flowing through him. All were afraid, needing to put as much distance between themselves and the Tans as possible. They managed to get back up to Sammy and Daniel, the air still thick with whining bullets.

Hissing instructions to break off their engagement, Sean led as the four retreated over the thicket-covered summit, descending into a gully that meandered between hills blanketed with welcome foliage. Tree clusters scattered the way towards the next scarp, offering cover until they could reach the wilderness, where it would become more difficult for the Tans to pursue them.

As they went down through the foliage, Sean looked back and saw the first policeman to reach the summit. "Cormac, wait and cover while Sammy and Daniel get ahead."

He watched one of the Tans turn and beckon to others as more heads broke above the peak, then started to come over into the gully. One called in alarm and pointed towards toward Sammy and Daniel as they ran to a cluster of trees. Rapid fire broke out along the scarp, but both vanished.

Sean looked to Cormac. "Right. Two rounds rapid then run like hell. You got that boy?"

"Yes," replied Cormac, waiting for the word.

"Now!"

They fired, and the Tans went to ground.

"Run, boy," shouted Sean, and they fled through the bush towards the trees where Sammy and Daniel had found refuge.

He heard the thud smack into Cormac who was right beside him. Sean tried to stop him falling but lost his balance. They both toppled to the ground as the young man went down. The blue sky twisted into the hills as the grass came up to meet them. Quickly gathering his wits, he grabbed Cormac's collar and started to drag him along, cursing his burden. Around, bits of sod erupted with misleadingly delicate thuds. He heard Sammy screaming at him from the nearby trees to leave Cormac behind, but he would not abandon the young man to the tender mercies of the Black and Tans. Their clemency was never much good at the best of times, and with one of their brethren lying dead in the village, he doubted they would tender much to Cormac's needs when they got to him. He turned to Sammy.

"I'll not leave the lad. For the love of God, don't ask me to," he yelled, trapped by his conscience. "Help us or go, Sammy, but don't ask me to leave the lad. I can't do it. I won't, do you hear me!"

Sean sat down cradling Cormac's unconscious form, while small puffs of dirt continued to burst about them.

Sammy turned to Daniel. "Go and help them. I'm a better shot than you. I'll make sure the bastards keep their heads down."

"Right, tell me when to make the run," replied Daniel nervously.

"Now," called Sammy as he took aim at one of the policeman cautiously moving down into the gully. The distance was far, the target moving, plus the rifle's kick – all had to be taken into account. He opened his mouth, something he always did when concentrating. The target sat snugly in his sights as he gently squeezed the trigger.

Sean watched as the projectile smashed into the advancing Tan's thigh, knocking the man off his feet. The wounded foe's rifle went off as it clattered to the ground, the bullet soaring harmlessly across the gully.

"Come on now, move." Daniel had appeared beside him, and together they dragged Cormac into the wood.

"Fire into the trees." They heard one of the Tans yell. "Keep shooting and make the bastards keep their heads down." Everyone obeyed, and the woods were peppered with withering but blind firepower.

Bullets zipped through the foliage, some distance away, as they huddled beneath the leafy blanket. Cormac was groaning, unaware of what was happening.

"Where has he been hit?" asked Daniel.

"In the shoulder," replied Sean. "I want to take him to the apple orchard beyond the hills. I think I can hide him there while I get help."

"This will jeopardise all of us, Sean, we —"

"I'll not leave him, Sammy," interrupted Sean. "But I agree – all of us need not take the risk of helping when one of us will suffice. That'll be me."

Sammy knew it was useless to argue. He accepted Sean's stance. "All right then, Daniel and I will help you to the orchard, but from there we must leave you. When we get back to Limerick I'll see if I can get someone to help. In the meantime you must try to survive at large. They'll be combing everywhere after this. We'll probably be able to get some sympathisers to spread false information concerning your whereabouts. Get the police searching in the wrong places."

"Thanks, Sammy," replied Sean. "Now let's be moving, before the Tans get themselves down here. The sods can smell blood and they're not likely to let up now."

Gingerly, Sean and Daniel lifted Cormac as he groaned. They started to walk him along, while Sammy whispered words of consolation. The rebel band moved deeper into the wood, while each member encouraged Cormac with promises to be brave and hold on.

SIX

Back in the village.

Hayward had remained behind the truck during the gun battle, with Father John and the Flannigans, who were attending to Michael Lynch. Sergeant Bradley had joined them, but only to look on helplessly. Like Hayward, he had been numbed by the events. Although reluctant, both had participated in the search-and- arrest process and each felt guilty of contributing to the villagers' misery. Their guilt overshadowed Bashford's terrible death.

Father John regarded them, assessing them. His eyelids had descended compassionately over his green irises – humbling them, but also easing their feelings of wretchedness concerning the whole affair.

"I am most sorry about the Auxiliary Cadet, Sergeant, but there was nothing we could do for him." His regret was genuine. He watched as

Turpin and Barnes lifted Bashford's body onto the back of the truck. "We, in Cafgarven, have no connection with what has happened here today. You must believe us, Sergeant Bradley; we want no part with these gunmen."

"We believe you, Father, don't we Sergeant," offered Hayward, needing Father John to believe in their integrity.

Inspector Callaghan walked across from his car to talk with them.

"I believe that Cafgarven and we are both victims of this attack," he began. "But I will have to ask Mr Lynch and the Flannigans to accompany us back to the barracks, where they will be interviewed by the Regular Constabulary." The Inspector was at some pains to allay the fears of the Flannigans. He emphasised that the Tans would not take part in the questioning. "I'm sorry, Father, but this has to be done."

Father John's disdain for the Inspector was still simmering, due to his silence during the raid. "I feel that you should have stepped in during these antics. You're in charge, after all."

"With all due respect, Father John, I was in the pub's yard when the commotion was going on." The Inspector thought the priest's criticism unreasonable.

"Not when the searches began. You were still here then." Father John's anger was beginning to get the better of him.

"And you chose to converse with Mr Bashford, Father John – a man who is not officially on duty yet. You were happy with the way of things then. Now that the Auxiliary is dead, and I appear to have crawled out of the woodwork, you have the cheek to ridicule me. I can understand your frustration, but I must remind you, Father – you were as willing as I to recognise this ex-officer as being in charge. He commanded the respect of the men, because of the War."

Father John could not give in without having the last word. "It is very clear that the Black and Tans have no respect for police authority, yet still retain their old respect for Army ranking. The Auxiliary was allowed to exert leadership, and take liberties of his own accord, and you, Inspector, turned a blind eye. The only man who tried to help was Sergeant Bradley." He bit his lip, then looked to the frightened innkeeper's family. "I would like to accompany these people to the barracks, Inspector"

"Yes, Father John, I think it would be a good idea if you did," replied Callaghan, happy to offer some conciliation.

"Young man." Father John looked directly to Hayward. "Could you help the innkeeper to get Mr Lynch indoors until the relief truck gets here? The gunmen have caused considerable damage to your vehicle, and I am sure it's no longer road-worthy." He looked to Sergeant Bradley: "That is, do forgive my presumptuousness, if you can spare this young man for a while?"

"Yes, Father, we can do that for you. Hayward, help Mr Lynch."

"Yes, Sergeant," Hayward replied.

The daughter's eye's blazed fiercely. "Keep your filthy hands off him," she spat.

Henry ignored her scorn, while Father John stopped her, gently calling. "Come now, Joyce, this will not help Mr Lynch."

"Do as Father John says now, Joyce, we've had enough trouble," added Mr Flannigan.

Reluctantly, the distressed young woman agreed, allowing Hayward to take Michael Lynch firmly beneath one arm, while Mr Flannigan took the other. Together they hauled the wretched man to his feet and made their way slowly towards the inn.

Two Tans emerged from the public house with the informer's body, unceremoniously wrapped in an old blanket. As they passed Hayward and the Flannigans, one asked, "Where are they going?"

"It's the Sergeant's orders. They are to wait in the house until the relief column arrives," replied Hayward.

"Come on, we want to clear up this mess," interrupted Sergeant Bradley, becoming vexed with the Tan's questioning.

Jones, one of the taller members of the troop, looked down from the truck, grim-faced because of Bashford's death.

"They should be made to wait out here," he bellowed.

Father John felt a need to support the Sergeant. "Young man, I know you're angry at the death of your old comrade, but I assure you – Mr Flannigan is a good man and would never side with these gunmen."

"You're a priest. You would believe anyone," Jones replied contemptuously.

"It's true, Jones," added Inspector Callaghan. "This whole thing stinks of a set-up."

"Come on, Jones, this is not helping," Sergeant Bradley interjected sternly.

"We've got two corpses here, Sergeant," Jones protested, politely though he was still seething. "Two of our own boys —"

"That's enough from you, lad, shut it now," snapped Bradley with annoyance. "This might not be the Army. But you are still bound by my rank, do you understand?"

Jones remained silent. He bent down to help place the informer's corpse alongside the Captain's.

"DO YOU UNDERSTAND, JONES?" roared Bradley, finally losing patience and desperately wanting to get to grips with the situation. Jones's eyes narrowed and a fierce anger burnt within him as he quietly replied: "Yes, Sergeant."

The rest of the Tans, who had pursued the gunmen into the hills, came along the road carrying the Tan wounded in the pursuit.

At first Henry thought the man was dead and he wondered how long the volatile natures of the men could be contained. He tried to move the Flannigans along a little more quickly. They stopped to look back when they heard the wounded man cursing and swearing.

"Thank God the fellow's alive," muttered Mr Flannigan.

"What happened to the Shinners – where have they got to?" asked Sergeant Bradley with concern.

"They've gone, Sergeant," replied Henderson. "Wright got one of the fellows but his mates rescued him and got away. We were going after them but then one of the sods got Wilson."

"One for one," muttered someone, dismally.

"It's worse than that," added Jones from the truck. "They shot Captain Bashford dead and killed one of our undercover men before we arrived."

"What!" Stiles looked startled.

"Do you honestly think I'm joking?" Jones held his hands outward, and then he started to shout. "Do you think I would bloody well make a thing like that up, eh? It was the bastard inn-keeper and his future son-in-law that were in with them."

"That's not true, Jones," shouted Sergeant Bradley.

"The Captain thought so and overruled you, when you tried to give the bastards a smooth ride." He turned to the rest of the group. "You lot never saw it all, you were guarding the road. The Captain wanted the pair brought in for questioning —"

"Enough," shouted Bradley. "They're coming back to the barracks, where they'll be handed over to the R.I.C. for questioning. We can't convict them. It's probable they had no part in this."

Inspector Callaghan decided he should support the Sergeant. "They would have to be pretty stupid to murder someone and leave the body in their own back yard, for Christ sake!"

Sergeant Bradley stood firm. "Don't theorise, Jones. Don't assume anything. Let the proper people deal with it. People better qualified than you."

Henry edged the Flannigans towards the house. "For Christ's sake, get indoors will you," he grumbled, knowing the mood was getting ugly. He wondered if the Inspector and Sergeant Bradley could contain the angry Tans. Without proper restraint they could become vicious.

Once in the surroundings of the snug alehouse he thought they might be safe, but to his distress, the daughter began to berate him. "You're one of them, so don't be expecting any gratitude from us."

"Look, please!" he implored. "Now is not the time or place."

"Don't you dare be telling us when the time and place is —"

"For God's sake, keep your voice down. You'll antagonise them and that'll be all that's needed to really start them off. Please don't speak to them like this, will you."

Father John's entry was fortunate for him. The women seemed to sense his temperament was not like the rest of his over-zealous compatriots, and their anger had been aroused because of his association with such men. Mr Flannigan was less aggressive, more interested in trying to find out where they would be taken for questioning and when they would be released.

Hayward tried to assure him. "It's just routine stuff, mate, nothing more. They're only following standard procedures. You don't have anything to be worried about."

"There will be if those two great apes on the truck have anything to do with it," spat the daughter.

Mrs Flannigan fumed: "Good God! Look at the state of young Michael here. Is that part of your standard procedures, young man, eh?"

Father John coughed, and gained their attention. His enormous eyes seemed about to burst from his lenses as he stared at the daughter. She turned her head to look at the wall, unable to outface the priest. Mrs Flannigan looked at the floor when he turned his scrutiny to her. Mr Flannigan nervously rubbed the stubble on his jaw.

"Let anyone without sin cast the first stone." Father John knew them well. Finally his searching stare fell upon Hayward. He smiled benignly at the young man.

"What am I searching for? Is that what you're asking yourself, young Hayward?"

"Yes, Father, that had crossed my mind," replied Hayward mildly. The priest's gentle tone put him completely at ease.

"You called me Father, not Padre the way English soldiers do. That makes me wonder about you."

"Yes, Father, I did, though I can't see why you should be intrigued."

"You're Catholic, Mr Hayward?"

"Yes, but I fail to see how that surprises you. We do have English Catholics."

Father John smiled, then softly continued. "It causes concern, Mr Hayward, and yes, I do know that there are English Catholics. Most of you are of Irish descent, aren't you? Do some of your relatives come from this country?"

"What do you mean, Father?"

"I could not help noticing that you don't appear happy with the way things are concerning the suspects." He looked to the Flannigans.

Hayward turned to the innkeeper and said reassuringly. "You're not suspects. That's the wrong word."

"I'm sorry, Mr Hayward, I should not have said that," said Father John. "What I mean is, they are suspects to some of the other policemen. The man called Jones was most upset with

Sergeant Bradley wanting the Regular R.I.C. to handle matters. As I was coming in, the other man, Baker I believe, was becoming increasingly angry over the matter."

"Father John, these men are extremely upset because one of their ex-officers has had his brains blown out by the Shinners."

Father John raised his hand. "Mr Hayward, please! The men who did this foul and sickening act do not come from Cafgarven. You must believe this."

"In my heart, I do. They would have to be very foolish to kill someone and just leave the body here. Though it is also reasonable to expect any police force to question the proprietors."

"Yes, Mr Hayward, I agree with you and though you have not been trained, I think you would make a splendid policeman. Unfortunately, I can't say the same for the rest of your friends. They're undisciplined and angry, and I am concerned for the villagers' welfare."

"What can I do, Father? Why are you telling me this?"

"Because you should not be among these men. Many of you should not be here. Your fellows are being painted as a demonic horde, and history will not see the odd well-meaning person within the ranks of a corrupt organisation."

"We're a police force, Father, not an army," objected Hayward.

"You're trained soldiers, Mr Hayward, not policemen. You're part of an army that wants not to be recognised as such. Your opponents, on the other hand, are another army that is not acknowledged, but they want to be. Mr Hayward, leave the Black and Tans. Go back to England. You're better than these men. What's happening here is wrong. Both sides are wrong! People like us are being caught in the crossfire."

Henry looked into Father John's eyes and saw a cold, hard stare. He sighed and he turned away, making for the door. He paused to take a last look at Michael Lynch, now seated in a chair by the table. The injured man had remained silent throughout this discussion. Hayward felt pity for him – his face was a mass of congealed blood and bruises.

He went out into the street, which was alive with the joyful chirping of birds. Nature had reclaimed the glorious day, painting over the dreadful death of two men. He cursed God for what had happened, then quietly asked for forgiveness. How many times had he prayed, when the shells were falling around the earth during the War? What promises had had made to be spared from death and to pass through the hell of the Great War? Why had he tried to convince himself he was living a decent life? He was nothing more than a hired bullyboy. It was evident the civil population loathed his kind. Father John's words about leaving the Black and Tans echoed deep in his conscience and ate away at his will – a meek loyalty he was beginning to despise.

He stopped at the truck, where Sergeant Bradley was arguing with Baker and Jones. The quarrel had quietened to a more temperate disagreement. At the end of the heated exchanges, the men had realised that arguing with the Sergeant would not make him shift his ground. So they tried to reason with the old policeman, as though they were his friends offering sound advice. It was their firm belief that they were doing well by him.

"If it was you who had stopped the bullet, Sergeant, the Captain would not rest until we had the people responsible. These sneaky sods pretend they don't know what is going on, but they do and the bastards running the bar are in on it." Jones was assertive yet calm.

Sergeant Bradley became weary and was anxious to do the right thing – not wanting the resentment of the rest. "Listen, Jones, I've already told you that the Flannigans are being brought back to the barracks for questioning. Inspector Callaghan will take care of it."

Hayward surveyed the others, wondering if they would turn nasty. Turpin appeared angry yet able to contain his emotions. Barnes and Henderson were calm, and would not argue with the Inspector or the Sergeant. They thought it proper that any suspect should be apprehended for questioning, as was being done. Jones and Baker were the main problems – their emotions were getting the better of them.

Henderson raised his eyebrows and shook his head when catching Hayward's look. The man was obviously fed up with the bickering; it was alien to him but the times were very strange. No one argued with sergeants during the War; not if they had any sense. The whole world seemed to be going mad. Nothing functioned logically anymore.

Stiles, who had been sucked in by Jones and Baker, burst out passionately. "Torch the fucking pub and bring the bastards out into the open, make them wait out here."

Jones's volatile emotions were instantly inflamed. "Yeah, now you're talking my fucking language." He jumped from the truck, and fired shots at the wall of Flannigan's Bar, just above the ground-floor window. Puffs of dust and masonry exploded, as bullets smashed through the rendering.

"Wait, no!" Henderson shouted, trying to stop the indiscriminate violence.

Hayward was dumbfounded, as the wicked bullets zipped past him. A woman's shriek came from the building. Instantly, he ran back to see if the bar's occupants were all right. Behind came the angry shout of Stiles.

"Out of the fucking way, Hayward, you bloody idiot."

Ignoring them, he reached the door and glimpsed Baker filling a bottle with petrol from the truck's leaking engine. Quickly smashing through the door, Hayward was confronted by more screams, and the Flannigans had raised their arms in surrender.

Father John emerged from the huddled group, like a grain of order in a desert of confusion. "Mr Hayward, what on earth's happening?"

"Is anyone hurt, Father?" he interrupted.

"No, thankfully, but –"

"Sorry, Father John, no time now. Get everyone into the yard. They're going to torch the place and I don't think some of the men care if you are in here or not. Please get them moving now."

Suddenly the window shattered, and a petrol bomb smashed onto one of the bar-room tables. Mrs Flannigan screamed as flames erupted, wickedly yet gracefully. The cruel, orange tendrils glided across the smooth, varnished surface, shimmering and dancing like reckless scamps.

"Quick, get out the back!" shouted Henry, desperately pulling Mrs Flannigan with him as he led the way to the back door. Father John instructed the others to heed the urgent advice.

Outside, Henderson was shouting. "Get out, Hayward, for Christ's sake, get out."

All reached the back door, and stumbled out panicking. They stood in the yard, confused and sweating with fear, wondering what to do next.

The horrendous glow of fire was devouring the Flannigan's feeble sanctuary. It had to be stopped before everything they owned was destroyed.

Suddenly the outer yard's door was kicked open. Mrs Flannigan screamed, certain they were going to receive more blind retribution from the Tans. Hayward moved in front of the wretched people, shielding them. Father John stepped beside him.

Sergeant Bradley entered the yard, accompanied by Henderson, Barnes and Turpin. Henry was filled with relief at the absence of the Jones and Stiles. The four men present were not vindictive.

Turpin asked, "Where's the water tap?" It was the type of situation the man excelled in – the very thing that made him tick. His mind was racing ahead to bring order to the chaos.

Mr Flannigan pointed to a tap fixed to the wall. Turpin instructed him to get a hosepipe as he moved forward to gather two buckets that were nearby and began filling them.

"Come on, Hayward, give us a hand," he yelled urgently, as everyone joined to fight the fire.

Mr Flannigan, sweating and panting from his exertions, returned with his hosepipe and attached it to the tap, while Henry and Turpin each took a filled bucket. Charging through the back door into the bar area, they were daunted by the extent to which the flames had spread.

"Jesus Christ, we'll never stop this bloody lot from going up!" yelled Hayward, gulping back his fear at the scene before him.

"Don't give up yet," responded Turpin. "The best thing to do is get the hose in here now. Then ask Bradley to go to the front and get some of the others to work at this thing from the entrance."

Hayward promptly rushed back into the yard where, thankfully, the Police Sergeant was already attending to the matter. Relieved, he quickly snatched the hose that Mr Flannigan had set up and returned to aid Turpin.

Henderson followed with a second hose. "We can fix this one to the kitchen sink," he shouted.

"Good, get to it then," replied Hayward, above the crackle of the flames. He went into the bar where Turpin was anxiously waiting.

"There," he shouted, pointing where the spray should be concentrated. "Stop it from spreading."

Quickly Henry doused the flames that were climbing the walls and arching along the ceiling. A hissing protest spat back as smoke filled the room, causing greater concern. Henderson suddenly appeared with the second pipe spraying defiantly into the flames, amid the crashing sound of the front door opening.

Cuttings entered cautiously, observing the commotion before him, followed by another. Both stood dumbfounded, observing Hayward and Henderson as they grimly continued to spray the walls and furniture.

"Father John is rousing the villagers to help fight the fire," declared Cuttings. "He's got Callaghan and his Regulars to watch over the Flannigans out back."

"What about Jones, Baker and Stiles?" questioned Henderson.

"Bradley has sent them back to the barracks in Callaghan's car with Wilson," said Cuttings. "He needs to get to hospital. They'll bring another lorry for us."

Out on the street, the people of the village joined with the Tans by setting up a chain, to pass pails of water, which were slung through the shattered window. Shouts of encouragement became more distinct as the villagers' excitement gathered. The Cafgarven men were urging each other to keep the water coming at all costs. The inn, after all, was a focal point for them.

Turpin got a new rush of enthusiasm, once he saw that Henry and Henderson were coping well enough with the hoses. "Help get some of this furniture outside away from the flames," he called.

Cuttings and Wright responded quickly. They grabbed a table close to the flames and carried it outside.

Gradually, the fire died amid the spray, supported by the continuous drenching of water pails from the villagers. Wet, charred wood and a blackened wall, coupled with the smell of damp soot, was all that remained as a solemn testimony. All looked at the torrid aftermath. Maybe in another place, under different circumstances, they might have had a sense of achievement, but here the event should never have happened.

Turpin turned to Father John. "Tell your flock to keep their comments to themselves, Padre. After all we helped put it out."

Father John responded. "Young man, I'm under no illusions as to what you could do if they were not to keep their comments to themselves. I have the utmost faith in your abilities to respond to such chastisement and I judge you to be a person of your word. You showed great initiative in fighting the fire, and we would not want to be on the wrong side of such capabilities. I am most grateful for your assistance in stopping the fire that your compatriots started, though I do feel it might be a little optimistic to expect gratitude from the villagers. They have suffered much pain and humiliation, for nothing."

He bowed his head ingratiatingly, much to Turpin's annoyance, then left to advise the villagers that it would be prudent to go home until the Tans had left.

SEVEN

The Apple Orchard.

T he trek had been hectic and filled with anxiety for the hard-pressed Volunteers. They
cautiously made the final part of the arduous
journey beneath the red, twilit sky. Gingerly the
small band moved uphill, entering a wood amid
the gentle, rustling leaves and cheerful bird
chatter.

Sean resolutely struggled onwards, aiding
Cormac. He looked up through the leafy ceiling, relieved that the day would soon give way to
the welcome comfort of the summer night. His
injured friend could soon rest, while Sean set
about finding help.

"Just a short distance to go, Cormac. You've
done wonders to get this far, believe me," he
encouraged, aware of the effort his young companion was making. He was grateful that Cormac
had decided to try and walk unaided, though at

times the throbbing pain in the hapless man's shoulder was clearly severe. Sean was constantly helping him in his battle with demoralisation, bringing him comfort – letting him know that he would stick by him through thick and thin. His optimism was sustained by Cormac's continued determination. Such courage, he thought, had reduced the burden upon the rest. His intrepid assistance, when Sean was pinned down, had had an uplifting effect, sustaining everyone's hope of escape, and Sean made sure his wounded friend knew this. He kept encouraging the young man by praising him for so aiding the rest. True to form, Cormac responded grittily, pushing himself in stubborn bursts, like a staggering steam engine, fuelled by the constant urging, the fire of determination manfully stoked.

Ahead, Sammy and Daniel led the way, their rifles at the ready – alert to the last, expecting police to open up from the surrounding trees. After getting so far, it would be a wicked irony to be torn down by a blazing hail of Black and Tan gunfire. All the way they had harboured that expectation. Through streams and thicket clusters, over every mound and hill, they continually anticipated some confrontation. Thankfully nothing happened, but being suspicious men, the tranquillity of the fine, summer evening only made them more vigilant. When things appeared to be going well, fate could always deal a cruel hand. Constantly, the small band stopped to scan the area ahead.

On route, they had made as much use as possible of the scattered woodland and gullies. A tiny flower of hope began to bud within them. Perhaps they might just make it to the orchard. It was a thought they still found hard to believe – they were not being pursued. Slowly, and with grateful acceptance, they recognised that, despite Cormac's hindrance, they had actually managed to escape.

Making their way through the wood, the last part of the journey before reaching the apple orchard, Daniel was bewildered by their good fortune. "Why haven't they followed? They must have seen Cormac hit."

Sammy light-heartedly responded: "Your fear is beginning to subside, and you are left with a notion that divine intervention has aided our escape." He turned to Sean and Cormac with a big grin on his face. The sinking sun and the wooded cover engulfed him with a snug feeling of security that would surely last until morning.

"Don't be counting your chickens yet, Sammy," scolded Daniel. "The Tans will not want to disappoint you. They'll come, especially when they realise you're missing them."

Sean could not help but laugh. "Wonderful, Sammy! Now where did you get words like that? You should've been a poet."

Daniel, somewhat dismally, retorted. "Why are all you Jackeens so perky in such a predicament? You never stop joking, no matter how severe things get. Your outlook on life is always comical. Sometimes it's extremely annoying. I can't, for the life of me, understand how you can joke about it all. I've never known fear like this."

They reached the top of the hill, and the wood abruptly ended before a small crater-like basin, surrounded by green scarps. Within it, an apple orchard, bathed in the red twilight, displayed an inviting aura, welcoming them as to a new world – a small Garden of Eden, obscure and hidden. The place was an oasis of tranquillity, oozing comfort. Long lines of apple trees ran to the foot of the surrounding slopes.

For a moment, Daniel and Sammy were tempted to throw in their lot with Sean and Cormac, but then in the morning perhaps the allure would have gone.

"How long have you known about this place?" asked Daniel, taken by the spectacle. "Who owns this land?"

"I don't know who it belongs too, and right now that isn't important." Sean allowed the serenity of the orchard to flood him before continuing. "I know of a place down there where Cormac and I can stay. Once we are sheltered I can try to get help."

"We can get help sent back for you. When we get to Limerick," Sammy said, anxious to reassure Sean he would not be deserted.

"I know you will, Sammy, but there's a chance that you and Daniel could get caught, so I'll try to get help too."

"How do you propose to do that?" Sammy asked.

Sean grinned. "I don't know yet, but I'll think of a way."

Sammy smiled, well aware that Sean could be very resolute when he had decided to do something. He looked to Cormac. "Well, Daniel and I will get going now. Good luck to you, Cormac. If anyone can sort something out for you, it will be Sean."

"Get your asses out of here, you daft Jackeens," Cormac chaffed, stifling the pain.

They departed, reluctantly leaving their two friends to fend for themselves.

"God be with you," called Daniel, crossing himself before following Sammy along the summit, while Sean and Cormac negotiated the descent to the orchard.

The sun sank behind the hills, bringing an end to their trying day. Both knew there were more unpleasant times to come, keeping out of sight from the Empire's many eyes, which would be hunting every wood and thicket for miles. Capture would mean torture, then the final relief of the hangman's noose. The thought sent a shudder through Sean, though he would not talk about it to Cormac. He did not want the youngster to know that he too was fearful.

At the bottom of the hill they staggered into the engulfing coppice of trees, amid the eerie rustling of leaves and branches. The floor was littered with apples, and both cursed as they stepped on the fallen fruits.

"How far now Sean?" whispered Cormac, a little impatiently.

"Only a little, then you can rest up for the night."

"Just me? What about you?" There was a note of panic in Cormac's voice. He did not want to be alone in the darkness with the Tans still searching for him.

"Ease up there, boy," replied Sean soothingly. "Let's get to the shelter, then I can tell you what I am going to do."

Cormac was pleasantly surprised to see a small shed in the distance. "Is that it?" he asked.

"It is, Cormac."

"Christ, it looks like a coal bunker," laughed Cormac.

"Well, I agree that it is about the size of a coal bunker, but that can't be what it was used for. The roof lifts up and the inside is very clean," added Sean as he eased Cormac down onto the grass, amid the faint breeze and stirring branches.

At last, Cormac felt he could sit and look at the star-filled sky, happy they had made it this far. His shoulder still throbbed painfully, and he had to resist the temptation of putting his finger in the bullet hole to check the wound. It was worrying him, and he feared gangrene might set in if he did not receive proper medical attention. Remain calm, he reminded himself. Let Sean complete his efforts of help. He closed his eyes, allowing tiredness to engulf him while beyond, in the blackness, frogs and insects serenaded the warm night.

Sean lifted the lid of the bunker gingerly and, to his relief, saw it was still as clean as when he had last inspected it. Pushing the lid over, he climbed inside and laid Cormac's rifle down. He unslung an old satchel containing bread, cheese, tomatoes and a bottle of stout.

"I've been carefully preserving these, knowing you would need them. I've worked out a plan while travelling. I thought it best not to tell Sammy." After placing the satchel neatly in the bunker's corner, he climbed out to get Cormac. The lad had fallen asleep beneath the warm, night sky.

He smiled, grateful again that the young man had been there for him when he was in danger. No matter what obstacle stood in his way, he would save the lad.

This young man could not be wasted. Not like the other young men he had seen die on the grasslands of South Africa. The unsettling memory of the Boer farmers and the withering firepower from their entrenched positions haunted him.

His thoughts wandered back as he looked at Cormac's sleeping form. It had been on a very similar night when the Irish regiment had moved across the African grasslands at a place called Colenso. A river called the Tugela ran through it, and all he could recollect was that the British forces, for whom he was fighting, needed to get past in order to reach a besieged place called Ladysmith, which had been surrounded by the Boers.

Sean sighed at how naïve he had been. Then again, how fortunate to survive the ordeal, when so many of his friends had not. He remembered the dreadful event, when his regiment had advanced into the early morning, just before dawn was about to break on the horizon. The cap-badges on their khaki helmets were covered in cloth to hide the glint. Anything that might reflect was covered in drab material. Out they went, across the veld towards the position where they believed the Boer farmers were dug in. The regiment was strung out in a long line, moving stealthily forward with fixed bayonets. For about a mile, and what seemed like an eternity, they advanced, when suddenly a line of fire flashes lit up the blackness before them. Thousands of shells filled the air with hot hissing death.

Sean shook his head killing the terrible memory. "Enough, no more," he cursed under his breath, as he bent over Cormac and gently woke him.

The wounded man grimaced, gritting his teeth in one final effort before complying with his helper's bidding. He hauled himself up, supported by Sean.

"What are you going to do?" he asked, aware something was already planned.

"I'm going back to Cafgarven to get the priest to help us," answered Sean.

"Do you think he will help after what we've done?"

"Of course he will. He can't refuse. He's a priest, bound by oaths." "But I'm not Catholic!" Cormac was worried.

"You're a Prodie, then? God love us," laughed Sean. "We live and learn, don't we?"

"Well, he's not going to want to help me now, is he?"

"Of course he will. What kind of talk is that?"

Carefully, Sean helped Cormac into the bunker, gently easing him in to a lying position, and doing his best to make sure some meagre comfort could be arranged.

"Easy does it now, Cormac. Your gun is beside you, but most importantly, you have food plus a couple of bottles of stout."

"God love us, I might just move in permanently." Cormac tried to be light-hearted, though deep down concealing his fear at being left alone in the dark. The dreaded bogeymen who lurked in the darkness were real. They wore a mishmash of khaki and dark-green uniforms. Still, the darkness would be more helpful to him than it would be to the Tans.

"That's the spirit, boy. Now, I promise you! I'll be back by the morrow with help. You must try to bear up between now and then, do you understand?" stressed Sean, fearful that the young man was going to be spending some considerable time alone and in discomfort. It pained him to leave the youngster. He yearned to stay, fearing that Cormac might think he was deserting him.

"Do what you must, Sean, and God bless you for what you're doing." Cormac read his friend's anxiety.

"To you as well, boy. I'll not forget what you did, not as long as I live. I'll be back with help that's a promise." He gave Cormac a reassuring smile, deliberating as though not sure what to do next. After a pause, he hauled himself out of the bunker and closed the lid, then made off back through the orchard, his spirits low due to tiredness and hunger. Also, the thought of making the journey back to Cafgarven was daunting. Still, it would be worse watching Cormac wither in pain while he sat by helpless and unable to aid the wretched youngster. Resolutely, he willed himself on, believing his chosen course was constructive. The police, he hoped, would not expect any member of the unit to return to the scene of attack. The village priest would be angry at his request, but as a man of God he could not refuse to help.

EIGHT

Back at the Barracks.

Frogs serenaded through the glorious twilight. Their croaking created a serene ambience that drifted on the summer night's breeze into the compound, where Hayward sat with Henderson and Barnes. They had joined him, leaving the rest of the company squabbling in the barrack room about the day's events. All felt demoralised, each hiding his desolation from the others, as they sat on a small wall gossiping about the devastation that had taken place at Cafgarven. How miserably had things deteriorated in the last few months in this pleasant island. The lack of respect for innocent people, caught in an ugly war of sporadic murder, had caused Hayward, most of all, to reflect deeply. He had been on searches, before Cafgarven, had seen people manhandled unnecessarily, witnessed the vengeful wreckage of the property of resentful non-combatants who were suspected of being sympathetic to the Fenian Volunteers. It had been disturbing at times, but he thought he had adapted – learnt to drift with the tide. At least, until Cafgarven. Something shocking had happened there, culminating in a sequence of bloody events.

Hayward was more disturbed by his comrade's malicious reactions than by Bashford's murder. The sight of the ex-Army officer lying dead in the road was almost lost on him, for he had seen death before among men who had been much closer. He still saw their twisted and mutilated forms, coupled with flashbacks of them laughing before their cruel end. The anguish of these losses still cut deep. The Auxiliary's death was not in the same league.

"The day started so well," he muttered.

Henderson looked at him. "We lost control today. It was very unprofessional."

"You're a religious man, like Barnes – I thought you believed enlisting was a good thing. The Empire casting its benevolent light on under-privileged peoples with God's blessing and all that sort of thing."

"I don't number the Irish among such people," objected Henderson. "I believe them to be fellow Britons who have contributed to the Empire. They are an essential part of the Union and must remain. This is internal unrest, which needs careful handling. Attacking the Irish public, our own Britishness doesn't help matters. The confrontation should be focused solely upon the Fenian separatists."

Barnes added his support. "Of course, that's why this is a police action."

Hayward sneered, remembering Barnes' rough treatment of the young girl when he and Turpin had searched the house earlier. "The general public don't seem to think so, or haven't you noticed? In your world of clear right and wrong, can't you see how they regard us?"

Henderson grew enraged. "So Barnes and me are narrow-minded, stalwart men of justice, eager to embark upon some holy crusade? Are you any different from the silly bastards in the corridors of power that thought this one up? It's easy to be an armchair critic. Sit back, condemn everyone with your arse-numbing moralising about right and wrong. But how would you correct it, Hayward? Have you got a grand solution? If you were given control, you'd end up sticking your head up your arse and turning in ever-decreasing circles. Criticism comes cheap! Very cheap, and better men than you get paid to moan in newspapers. So get down off your soapbox, Hayward. We all know that we're becoming blackened because of some of the things that are being done. Only we can control ourselves.

God, you make me sick! You think you're the only person with a conscience.

Some of the men are thuggish in their approach. We know that. But you contribute to the problem as much as the bullyboys, who have no right to wear a policeman's uniform. You, like them, should not be here. If you don't want to try and do the job properly, then get lost. Don't analyse me, Hayward. You're not fit too."

Hayward thought before responding – Henderson was right, and he was well rebuked:

"Your heart is good, and perhaps you are right. Though I can't help wondering how you could have gone through the trenches and come out with such firm beliefs. You have the ability to think in such ways. If there were enough men who thought as you do, then maybe the R.I.C. would have a body that could operate as policemen. As you rightly said, I'm not like you, and I don't want to be. I can't help it. I'm not cut out for this. Not here! Things are different."

Henderson frowned; he was not to be pacified. "You're a defeatist, Hayward, content to wrap yourself in your humble benevolence. After all that has happened, we need resolute men who can think and focus on things. You, and the thugs among us, are a dead loss."

Barnes sighed despondently. "You never lost control, neither did Hayward. I, on the other hand, did. I slung that young woman after her mother when we were searching their home."

"We're all trying to do something that we are not suited to," cut in Hayward. "Christ, Barnes, you're so bloody weak minded. I've lost patience with your continuous acts of repentance. It's all irrelevant. You'll make the mistake again. If you were inside the barrack room with the bullyboys, you would find a way of agreeing with them in your usual, apologetic way. You get sucked in by anyone who does the talking." He softened, then looked to Henderson. "In any case, I'm losing all notion of the good-look-at-ourselves approach that you're in favour of. I can't help dwelling on the reasons why we're losing a grip on the local population."

Henderson stood up and took a pace forward. The distant hills were bathed in the dusk of the coming night. "Your bewilderment has become too deep rooted." He continued to stare into the dusk. "You yearn to distance yourself from this, don't you, Hayward? It's so compelling it aches in every fibre of you, but before you can turn and walk away, you're anxious for someone to understand you. Someone from this troop." Henderson shook his head. "Not me, Hayward, and after what you just said to Barnes here, I suspect his acceptance would be rejected anyway."

The dusk-laden wilderness beckoned Hayward, its celestial call couched in the language belonging to frogs and crickets, and he yearned to be swallowed in its hidden vastness. How grand to drop everything, and retire into that noisy oblivion. "Over the hills and far away," he muttered.

"What makes you say that?" asked Barnes, piercing through Hayward's trance.

Henderson wanted more of an insight too. "Come on, Mister Obscure. You have hidden ideas, and sometimes it would be better if you opened yourself up to others, instead of self-righteous scorn."

Hayward frowned. "It was something that the Cafgarven priest, Father John, said when I was in the bar, just before the fire. He knows why we're incapable of handling this situation." He liked Father John, and felt compelled by his words about leaving the Black and Tans.

"How do *you* think we are not suited to this then?" asked Henderson, deducing that Father John's reasons had become Hayward's.

"Yes, what is your opinion?" echoed Barnes in support. "We'd like to know."

For a moment he was at a loss as to how to begin. "We have to act as policemen against a hidden army who crop up anywhere and disappear into nowhere. Most of our time is spent waiting for them to hit one of us first. When we do make contact, it's very sudden and only if we are quick enough can we hit back. They jump out among the civilian population for a quick shot and then they're off. We need to be methodical, tolerant and show great restraint to fight them, and as policemen we need to consider the civilians among whom we are trying to function. Our hidden enemy use them and their towns for cover.

Farms and streets are the battleground, and it is difficult to do the right thing in such cramped conditions. Before we came out here, there was no training on the problems of dealing with ordinary folk – most of us don't care for them, and we are encouraged not too. Those we are up against don't wear uniforms – they look like the innocent people we should be showing tolerance too. So we find the easiest option is tarring all with the same brush. Everyone is a potential murderer."

Barnes nodded in agreement. "We never recognised them when they put on uniforms during the Easter uprising. The Volunteer leaders were executed. They were unpopular with many people until we started putting them before firing squads. That didn't do much for us in the long run, but it did a lot to further their cause and justify a new and more devious approach. They're not so sporting nowadays, and can you blame them?"

Hayward was impressed. Sometimes Barnes did have his own view of things. It was certainly a valid point.

"Since we have been deployed, the Shinners have had a taste of their own medicine," countered Henderson.

"Yes, but the cost has been paid by the innocent people. In some areas, the villagers are beginning to turn to the Volunteers as the protectors, while we are rapidly gaining status as barbarians. Nothing more than legalised thugs who do what they want, regardless of the consequences. Do you notice that the Regular Police keep their distance from us? We're not liked and are regarded as intruders by all, even among the Regular R.I.C," concluded Hayward bitterly.

Barnes was intrigued. "How long have you felt this way, Hayward? You haven't come across before as being against what we do."

Hayward remained silent for a moment, as though contemplating the words he would choose. Barnes and Henderson waited impatiently.

"I haven't always felt this way because, until today, my thoughts were more for myself and the countryside. I love it here, and would like to stay. Today, it really dawned on me. The people are afraid of us, when they should be pleased by our presence, relieved that we are here to hunt the Volunteers into oblivion. Yet it hasn't happened. All we see is the most beautiful scenery, and we get ten shillings a day for being here. The raids, searches and arrests are just minor, unsettling side shows really. I know that some units are engaged on a tougher level than we are, but until today we didn't have any serious meetings with the Shinners. Then, after one contact with them, we were ready to get nasty with the innocent villagers! We didn't care who we got, so long as it was a Paddy. Every one of them suddenly became a target, and the reality of it was that the villagers were terrified victims in the crossfire, wanting to get back to the cover of their homes. I was there among them. I saw mothers and fathers sheltering with their terrified children, desperate to get them out of the way, while the Flannigan woman was out in the middle of the road with Father John trying to help Bashford. After the Shinners had been chased off, we began to vent our frustration on the Flannigans.

As if they would leave a body in their own yard! The idea is ludicrous, but all we wanted were Fenian sympathisers at any cost. All we could see, in our blind rage, were a bunch of Paddy's who fit the picture we had painted. It was wrong, and now I feel that as an entity we are unable to check our prejudices. Most of the men in the unit can harden to it. Some like myself can't."

"Are you saying that you want to leave the R.I.C. then?" asked Barnes.

Hayward sighed despondently. "I'm lost, for I do love this country, but I would like to leave the Force. The thought of staying here is very appealing, but then what would become of an ex-Black and Tan after what we've done?"

Henderson mused: "So you wished you had come to Ireland before joining the Force. Putting the troubles aside, you just have a fascination with the land and would like to live here."

"Yes."

"Well, it's feasible, and some of what you said beforehand is too." Henderson began to pace back and forth. "We haven't been able to check ourselves, we've messed up and made bad mistakes, which means people like us should stay and try to bring the others into our line of thinking. Then we would be able to become something better."

"That's not going to happen," replied Hayward, abruptly. "The rest of the lads aren't going to be sucked in by you. They're game for the fight now." He tried not to laugh at Henderson, for the man was not wicked. Hayward did not want to offend him. He thought back to when Father John had likened the Black and Tans to a demonic horde. "We belong to a bad organisation, even though the individuals that comprise it are often well-meaning men, like yourself.

From history, we're told stories of heroes and villains. We imagine courageous champions up against evil foes. Take David and Goliath for instance, when the bad man Goliath was slain, the Philistine army turned and fled. We visualise them as wicked, cowardly men fleeing into the desert from David and his army of Israelites. You, Henderson, you could be one of those blackened Philistines. A decent man, a righteous tower of honest belief. But ultimately, a pillar made of sand, to be dissolved in sea of panicking, evil men. No one would ever know or spare a thought for you."

Henderson sighed and shook his head. "That's the prospect of defeat. I'm aware of such consequences, and I am prepared to face them.

You just want to flee straight away. Pretend you were never part of it. What use is that?"

"This will become an episode in history that will lurk in the back of the cupboard, like the other obscure defeats that we don't like to talk about. We're part of something that's wrong. We're not seen for what you would like us to be, and we never will be. Not with all the good intentions in the world."

"If we don't grit our teeth and try to be responsible, then I'm afraid that we'll be seen as men with no the real purpose. Men like you, who give up. What do you want, Hayward? Sympathy for your little self-indulgence?"

Hayward could not agree with Henderson, even though, deep down, he suspected the man could be right. He shook his head, wanting to dislodge the idea. "Already, it's too late, our metal has been stamped for the worse. We are the unwanted slag at the bottom of that forge. You won't be able to change things from within, even though you would be right to try."

"So why not try to help us change their thinking, instead of fighting us with your poetic little clichés. Sergeant Bradley can understand. Cuttings is different from the others too. They'll not be content with the vulgar approach of murder for murder."

Hayward looked at Barnes, wanting a way out. "Maybe you will adapt to *their* ways without knowing it. At the beginning of today's raid, you were pretty rough with the young girl that shouted at Turpin. She was trying to protect her mother from his verbal abuse."

"I agree it was over-zealous and wrong of me." Barnes dropped his head, as though eliminating himself from the discussion.

"Very clever, Hayward". Henderson was not going to let go. "Now you're diverting the argument, because you think you might be losing. Don't pick on Barnes for a way out, stick with it. He can change! That's the issue."

The talk came to an abrupt end as Sergeant Bradley walked across the yard with Cuttings at his side. He stopped before them, tired and pale. He had been in the interview room with Inspector Callaghan and other men of the plain-clothes division questioning the Flannigans about Michael Lynch.

"I want you three lads with Cuttings and myself to accompany Inspector Callaghan back to Cafgarven."

"Are we going to make any more arrests?" asked Barnes.

"No, we're to escort the Flannigans back to the village on the insistence of Father John. They're being released due to lack of evidence."

Hayward stood to attend the duty. "There's no way they had anything to do with the informer's killing. It was plain when we found the corpse dumped in the yard. We could have killed those people, burnt them in their home because of our own uncontrolled anger."

They gathered their rifles and walked to the truck, happy to leave the monotony of the barracks, even for a short while and with people that probably hated them. Hayward was first to climb into the back of the vehicle, with Cuttings and the Sergeant following. Henderson and Barnes got into the driving cabin.

The door of a nearby building opened, and a shallow light emitted from within, bathing the gravelled ground outside with its sombre glow. Dark silhouettes broke through the rays as people emerged, one in a long mackintosh striding purposely towards the vehicle. As he drew nearer, Hayward made out the features of Inspector Callaghan. Only he would wear a coat on a warm, summer night. Behind followed his two colleagues, attired in tweed suits. All looked at Sergeant Bradley.

"We'll lead in the car with Father John, you'll have the Flannigans and Lynch in the truck with you," instructed Callaghan.

"I would prefer to be in the truck with the Flannigans, if you please," called a voice from the doorway's light. Father John walked forward, beckoning to the others. The Flannigans reluctantly followed with Michael Lynch, who still looked wretched from his beating. Hayward studied their faces; they looked contemptuous and their eyes blazed with hatred. An aura of distaste was circulated to all who were to accompany them back to Cafgarven.

"No one will hurt them, Father John, they'll be all right with these men," whispered Inspector Callaghan, trying to ease the priest's concern.

"I am certain that my congregation members will be fine. I would, however, still like to travel in the truck with them. I find the company of these Black and Tans a little more bearable than yours, Sir."

The Inspector, stung by this rebuke, looked into Father John's eyes. Of all people, a priest was the last person from whom he would have expected such recrimination. His instinct was to respond with an insult of his own, but his ingrained respect for the Church forced him to contain his resentment.

"We all have our jobs to do, Father," he whispered, so that his men could not hear.

"My displeasure is not with the Constabulary which you represent, Sir. It's for your impertinent audacity at trying to convince Mr Lynch that his beating was due to his own foolishness when being questioned by your Reserves. I have never, in all my life, heard anything so outrageous, and you being a fellow countryman too. It is my belief that you should be ashamed of what you tried to get Mr Lynch to accept. I hope there is some decency in you, Sir! If there is, please remember the matter at your next confession."

Father John's final criticism was presented as earnest advice.

Callaghan turned and walked to his car without any further attempt at reasoning, perhaps feeling Father John was right.

The old priest looked to the Tans. "Mr Hayward, would you aid these good people aboard please, as you may be aware, like yourselves, they have had the most trying of experiences." He wanted the Reserves to know that he was not oblivious to the loss of Bashford.

"Yes, Father," replied Hayward, who moved to the rear of the truck to help the Flannigans. Cuttings responded too, knowing that Father John had developed some accord with Hayward. Silently, they assisted all aboard, including Father John. But no amount of help could make up for the wrong that had been done to the Flannigans and Lynch. They remained silent – not through hatred, but fear, which lingered wearily, like a volatile beast, in the nether regions of the mind. After all, to them, the Tans were men who could beat a person senseless and try to burn down a home, and then they could move Heaven and Earth to quench the fire they had caused.

The vehicles kicked into life, telling the night of their presence, before sluggishly moving out of the compound into the dark, country lane. Cones of light from the headlights of the car and following truck parted the blackness. It left Hayward with the feeling that the night was trying to envelop them in its arms. He became intensely aware of the sounds of bushes, rustling trees and croaking wildlife. Once again the unseen wilderness called to him with natural sounds that were more distinct, combating the noise of the engine. Through the darkness the uncanny deluge was soothing, and he could smell the delicately scented ferns. It was as before, and only the barriers dictated by hatred stopped him from walking into that enticing dark. He thought of the relentless killing of the Great War, and how he had wished for a return to the simple normality of everyday life in peacetime England. But when the War did come to a halt, those tranquil times had vanished, and he entered the unwanted ranks of the country's unemployed. He longed to escape the stagnation, even if it meant fighting again. Exasperated, he wondered what a person could do to find contentment. Maybe walk out into the blackness surrounding him and keep going until the darkness lifted. What would he find? Blue skies, green pastures and rolling hills, bringing thoughts of eternal peace? How long would it last, before a new desire drifted into his briefly settled being, forcing him to continue searching for something else?

"How long will it take to get back home?" asked Joyce, the innkeeper's daughter, in a quiet and reserved manner. She felt uncomfortable in the presence of the loathsome Tans, but was perceptive enough to know that those aboard the truck had fought the fire earlier during the day.

Father John looked at her with a comforting smile, then subtly diverted his gaze to Hayward who sat opposite them. He felt a desire to communicate with the disgruntled young man.

"Roughly how long will it take us to get to Cafgarven, Mr Hayward?" he asked.

"Not long, Father, it only took about twenty minutes this morning."

"People usually call me Father John," he smiled, showing a row of white dentures.

"Sorry, Father John, I shall remember that. We'll probably take a little longer to get back, because of the night."

"It is a fine night, too, do you not think so, Mr Hayward?" Unknowingly, he had struck a chord with Hayward.

Hayward assumed, beyond all doubt, that Father John knew what he was thinking and, taken aback by the words, he peered at the priest hoping to find those big, magnified eyeballs staring back and understanding his tormented desire. However, he could not make out Father John's attentive stare, for one side of him was bathed in a luminous radiance. The afterglow from the headlights shimmered upon his skin, as it did the rest of the passengers. It reflected upon his spectacles, behind, which hid the benevolent priest's knowing, eyes. Hayward was thinking during the day of those same eyes that bored deep inside him. They asked many questions, yet also offered salvation, making him wonder if this was what he sought. Did Father John offer a chance of contrition – a way out of the depressing dilemma which he was in?

"Yes, Father John, it's a fine night," he replied.

"Well, you took your time with the answer, Mr Hayward. Did it really need so much thought?"

"Our Hayward is a bit of a dreamer," interrupted Cuttings in a light-hearted manner and wearing a smile to let the silent villagers know that Black and Tans could laugh too.

Michael Lynch, with his bruised and battered face, stared at him, not finding the Reserve's remark humorous. The beam upon Cutting's face vanished instantly – he was reminded of the fact that these folk were not likely to enjoy light-hearted banter.

"I can well believe that," replied Father John in a jovial manner. He seemed immune to the silence between the Tans and villagers.

"Where will the innkeeper and his family stay, Father John?" asked Sergeant Bradley.

"Why doesn't the Tan's friend ask us, Father John?" spat Mary Flannigan, the innkeeper's wife, clearly annoyed that the Sergeant talked about them as though disregarding their presence.

Bradley sighed disconsolately and wondered what he could do to try and make these stupid people understand that he was just trying to do a job. He was about to explain, but then checked himself, knowing the villagers had a wealth of accusations with which they could come back. Like Cuttings, he was at a loss, and all because of rash actions earlier in the day.

"There is nothing wrong with having the odd dream now and then," commented Father John, wanting to keep the talking going in the hope of drawing Hayward out of his shell. He felt compelled to know the young Englishman, as there was something refreshingly different about him. Hayward was obviously unsettled with his lot and Father John presumed the young man needed to talk so that he might unburden himself in some way.

Hayward smiled back – tired wrinkles creasing his tanned face, giving him an older look. Like many of his generation, he had gone through much in his twenty-five years and, within the headlight's afterglow, the priest grasped that fact.

"I am given to believe that the employment situation in England is bad at the moment, is that true, Mr Hayward?" asked Father John.

"Yes, Father, it is very bad."

"I suppose that the lure of ten shillings a day in Ireland is a rather attractive proposition then? It's very easy to see how any dispirited young man would be enticed by such an offer, when the only alternative is the unemployment ranks."

"Blood money!" berated Mary Flannigan.

"Shut your bloody mouth," screamed Hayward, springing to his feet and moving towards the woman, his face flushed like an angry demon. Complete fury radiated from him, and everyone present thought he was about to lose control. But he had no intention of doing anything except intimidate the woman who was vexing him. He just wanted to rear up and growl at someone.

Sergeant Bradley and Cuttings jumped up to restrain him, as he expected; Father John was behind him too, trying to soothe his temper with kind words of consolation. Mr Flannigan and his daughter earnestly shielded the woman, nervously imploring her not to provoke the Tan. The bravado was quickly repressed, and Hayward felt a little better at getting the irritating woman out of his system. She seemed taken aback by his outburst. It was not something she had expected from him. Hayward was angered by the fact that she knew he was easier going than the rest of the Unit and had decided to take liberties by venting her frustration on him – something she would not have dared do with Jones or Baker. He sat down, staring intensely at her. When he answered Father John's question, it was in a low voice, and he kept his gaze on the woman.

"Yes, Father, it was an easy choice to make against the monotony of unemployment. Perhaps a little too easy, with the benefit of hindsight."

Father John smiled benignly. "Yes, it's one of our human failings to be wise after an event. I cannot help but believe our paths are already mapped out for us. What is was always meant to be. So possibly you were right to leave the misery of unemployment. You can't be wrong to search for a way out of an intolerable situation."

"Then do you think I was right to enlist with the Royal Irish Constabulary, and come to Ireland?" asked Hayward, with faint stirrings of interest bubbling inside.

"The decision was the right one to make at the time, Henry. But then you must ask if it was a decision that was of its time and now is of a different time. You had to choose a path which you thought was progressive. Our lives are spent choosing paths that we hope might better our circumstances. Sometimes the path is the right one for a short distance. Then you may have to consider changing course."

"I don't want to return to England just now, Father, though I do wish I could be in this country under more congenial conditions. It is, after all, a very magnificent land."

Hayward was beginning to feel comfortable with the priest.

"Well, Mr Hayward." Father John leant forward and paused to make sure he had complete attention. "If it is contemplation and contentment that you seek, I think it would be most unwise to go back to England. A place where you know there is nothing for you. Seek out solitude among the Brothers, where you could reflect upon what you want to do. Take a little time to choose your next road."

"Brothers?" exclaimed Hayward perplexed. "What do you mean, Father John?"

"I mean a brief stay in a monastery, Mr Hayward, here in Ireland. I know of such a place."

The priest held up the palm of his hand to stop the next question, knowing that the Tan wanted to talk on. Reluctantly Hayward stayed silent.

"Don't ask any more questions now, Henry! Don't answer what I have just put to you. Think about it for a while. You still have a little time before coming to a decision. Ponder it for a few days." Father John leant back and gazed along the vehicle's headlights that cocooned Inspector Callaghan's car in a bright orange glow, nestling the vehicle in a snug ball of light, while beyond the murmuring night was kept at bay. Hayward rested against his side of the truck and looked to Sergeant Bradley and Cuttings, hoping they had not heard what had been said. Both appeared uninterested in his chat. Inside he longed to continue the talk with Father John, but knew he had to dwell on what had been said to him. Everyone remained quiet for the rest of the journey – resistance to talk was easy for all, except him. A reversal of the situation from the journey's beginning. He held back with all his will, sensing that it was futile to try and push Father John on the matter.

He thought: "A monastery – me, of all people, in a monastery – the very idea is ludicrous." After all the killing during the War, how could the Brothers begin to consider a man like him? He shuddered, as images of the enemy soldiers appeared advancing towards him. He saw them scythed down in neat lines as metal projectiles harvested the ranks of human flesh. Somewhere, in another time and place, he believed that he would have to account for what he had done, even though he could not turn his back on the his duty. Refusal would have meant a firing squad, but then he knew fear of execution was not the real reason for his compliance – that was just an easy excuse, something he could shelter behind. He dwelt on this and admitted he had gone to War blindly, fearing more for his own survival than that of an unknown enemy soldier. He could accept living with the guilt of survival – obscure the mother's face that looked into his eyes, full of frustrated hate and sorrow. Did he dare do the same things again in a place where mothers and children could watch? Here he could kill a person then have to stare at the mother of the vanquished son afterwards. What if one of the village infants was hit in the crossfire between themselves and the Volunteers earlier that morning? How would they have dealt with the distraught mother and father? Tell them to shut up or be stricken?

The two vehicles finally rumbled into Cafgarven, amid the sounds of a commotion at Flannigan's bar, where some of the village men were at work, repairing the window that had been smashed by the firebomb. Others were whitewashing the scorched walls, while a homely glow radiated from the bar area. A big cheer issued from the repairmen when they saw Father John arrive with the innkeeper and his family.

Hayward watched and found himself uplifted by Mr Flannigan, who was clearly baffled by what he saw. The publican's face broadened into a relieved smile, as a younger man walked forward.

"We opened the bar ourselves and started the repair work with a whitewash. I think this was once done in Washington," beamed the man, cheekily watching the Tans. "Maureen is at the till, so don't be worrying yourself about the costs now, Mister Flannigan."

"My God, Patrick, this is most kind of you all. Don't you think so, Father John?" Mr Flannigan was clearly touched by such good will.

"It is, indeed, most kindly," replied Father John, sharing the joy. Mrs Flannigan, her daughter and Michael Lynch all jumped down with similar looks of mesmerised marvel. The older woman put her hands over her mouth in disbelief to cover the happiness that threatened to burst from her in an uncontrollable flood of tears. "Oh, how kind of you all," she wept in brimming gratitude. Her silent daughter put her arms around her, while the Mr Flannigan moved to comfort his wife from her other side. All three walked towards the bar, with Michael Lynch following. The repairmen parted to let them into the bar.

Hayward turned to Sergeant Bradley and Cuttings. He noticed they were touched by the good will of the villagers. Like him, they felt guilty for what had happened to the Flannigan family. The desire to depart was overwhelming. All three felt like trespassers.

Without saying anything to Inspector Callaghan, Sergeant Bradley stood up and moved to the front of the truck. He slapped the top of the driving compartment to let Henderson and Barnes know it was time to depart. The truck squealed in protest as it reversed, stopping with inches to spare from one of the houses. Then it rumbled off along the way it had come. As the light of Flannigan's bar retreated into the blackness, Hayward looked back and made out the distinguished form of the priest standing in the middle of the road, transfixed in a bold glow and looking back. Why did Father John show so much interest in him? What worth did he see in such a person? A mercenary, and unclean to many. The form was suddenly obscured by the bright lights of Inspector Callaghan's car, which rudely fell into Hayward's line of vision. Father

John was gone. He looked through the head-light's nimbus, out into the blackness where he knew the ever present and ancient hills still beck-oned, and wondered if he would ever see Father John again.

NINE

Back to Cafgarven.

The star-filled sky guided Sean and he was heartened by his progress. Fear that the Tans might be lurking in the night forced him to think of disadvantages *they* would face. He smiled. Thank God for the night! Reason told him that the persistent policemen would have a better chance of finding him during the day. All they could do in the blackness was to haunt his imagination – the night was his ally.

"Huh! Too late, Tans, the blackness is mine," he reassured himself, laughing to sustain his optimism and crush any furtive terrors that might take root in his mind.

Stealthily moving forward into a small wood, he held his rifle at the ready. He came to the very place from where he and the rest of the unit had run during the day, while retreating during the gun battle with the Tans. It was on the other side of the wood in which Cormac had been wounded.

He advanced carefully, peering into the blackness before each step. Maybe the Tans were still there? Suspecting that he might return, and waiting – it would not be unreasonable to assume such a thing. If the Tans saw that Cormac had been wounded, which he was certain they must have done, they might also realise that the priest was a possible source for help.

"No, the English are not that bright," he reasoned, not very convincingly. He checked himself, realising it would be a serious error to underestimate his enemy. Better to overestimate him. If only to preserve his own chances of survival and help Cormac. He paused, contemplated briefly, then made his apologies to God.

An owl hooted, causing him to worry that it might be a signal. Then he glimpsed the flapping wings through a gap in the trees as the creature launched off on its hunting flight, a silhouette against the stars. He crossed himself, thankful for the sight, a reminder to be alert at all times. Leaving the wood and entering the gully brought a new apprehension, as he imagined enemy eyes penetrating the open blackness. The craggy peaks were at first barely visible in the dark, but then he began to discern them more clearly. The welcome rise of the scarps was a comfort to him. Beyond was his goal – the village of Cafgarven, and the Parochial House.

A new dilemma now loomed in his mind. How should he approach the priest? Theoretically he could not be denied aid. Yet still the thought of facing the priest was daunting. All his wrongs would have to be confronted, one way or another.

"What type of person are you, Father?" he muttered, while recalling the man leaning over the dead Auxiliary and reading the last rites. He judged the priest to be a brave man; also resolved and strict in his commitments. Sean expected there would be some sort of harsh, verbal denunciation before finding out if the priest would help him. As he reached the summit of the hill, he saw the small village more clearly. Lights were shining from the inn, a sight that surprised him. He judged it to be about two o'clock in the morning, which was late, even by innkeepers' standards. Another light was shining from the Parochial House – a gleam of hope that the priest was still up. It would save him the job of breaking in and waking him from his slumber. Quickly but cautiously, he descended the hill. Moving with nimble grace into the graveyard, he crossed himself, to reassure the Almighty of his respect for the dead. He reached the cemetery's boundary, where the priest's garden began, and cursed as his attempt to clamber over the rickety fence met with disaster. Loud sounds of snapping wood ripped through the night, and he fell entangled in string and runner-bean vines. He was sure the commotion would wake the late people in the graveyard. Superstitiously, he turned to look back at the headstones, then stealthily moved to the French windows of the Parochial House, where the light glowed behind the curtains.

Suddenly the drapery was pulled aside to reveal a ghostly form at the window, and then a protesting squeak as the doors were pushed forward and the light-bathed spectre came out into the yard. Sean's heart thumped as his jumbled wits started to make sense of the illusion. He mastered his shattered nerves and refrained from squeezing the trigger, slowly relaxing his finger. The man at the door had to be the priest. Sean stood, his rifle at hip level, and pointed.

"Who's there?" The priest's voice was edgy.

The tone took Sean by surprise. He had expected an angry accusation, instead of this tentative enquiry. It then dawned on him that the priest must be as weary as he was at such an hour.

"Who's there, please?" he repeated.

"Is that you, Father?" asked Sean.

"Yes, it is. I'm Father John. And who are you?"

Sean did not respond, but advanced, still pointing his rifle at the priest, whose eyes momentarily widened in fear before regaining his composure.

"So, you bring the threat of death in the night? The way Unionists say you do. Of what possible use would my death be?"

"Killing priests is not on our agenda, Father John. You should know that."

"In that case, I would be obliged if you would refrain from pointing that thing at me." He calmed himself further, staring into Sean's eyes. It was a penetrating gaze, which burrowed deep inside, searching for some inkling of a moral being. The magnified eyes were now serene and enquiring. All traces of fear had evaporated in one slow blink.

Sean lowered his rifle. It was his turn to be apprehensive and he asked in frustration: "How can priests make people feel so unsettled?" He was angry. It was the only way he could confront this inspection.

Father John ignored the rebel's question, not allowing any respite. "Are you one of these Volunteers?"

"Yes, Father, I am."

"You seek something from me." He turned and walked back to the French doors. Before entering he called back. "I think you had best come on inside and talk. It is obviously something of importance to bring you here at this time of night."

Sean followed him into the study and was charmed by the appearance of the place. Despite looking like a priest's house, there was an unexpected brightness about the room, which surprised him. He expected something more sombre, not the delicate old chairs that were neatly covered with tapestries. He decided that the room must be in the constant care of a woman. Such was his experience on these matters. A man would not bother with such feminine and pretty things. Priests often surrounded themselves with good God-fearing people. Perhaps one female member of his congregation kept house for him. He went to the armchair that Father John gently gestured towards.

"Please sit down," he said going to the doors, and shutting out the world.

Slowly the priest moved to the vacant armchair and sat down. "Well, you make for the most peculiar of sights, dressed in working men's clothes, complete with ammunition belt and rifle. Rather comical, in fact! Though I suspect there is nothing comical about a man like you. I imagine you would prefer not to tell me your name. But I would like to ask – did you play any part in the horrific shooting incident this morning?"

"Yes, Father John, I did make a major contribution to the ambush," replied Sean, gaining in confidence, Father John not being the firebrand cleric that he had expected. He was not proud of the killing, but decided to grimly face up to the act.

"What makes you do such deeds? What compels you to take a man's life? I can give you no absolution for this! You know that, don't you?"

Sean lowered his head and looked at the hearth, allowing Father John's words to sink in. Only when he mentioned the word 'absolution' did he spare a thought for the dead Auxiliary. An image arose suddenly in his mind of the stricken form lying in road, with nauseating, red liquid wickedly garnishing the gravel around the corpse's head. Despite his distance upon the hill, the stark reality of the deed was not lost on him. What was it that enabled the priest to force him to revisit such actions? Could it be a hidden quality that the man of God possessed? Or was it his craven, ingrained respect for the priesthood? Sean realised that even he was not immune to the church and what he sometimes thought of as its accursed hypocrisy. On occasions he could shout in defiance at such doctrines. Not this time, however. He had to face the consequences head on. Hopefully his own beliefs and convictions could withstand it – convictions that would be hard to defend before the steadfast Father John. He would account for himself honestly, but he knew he would have to lower some barriers and make concessions.

"My reason for being here is not on behalf of myself, Father. I have come because someone else is in need of your help." He tried to move himself aside, wanting his conscience spared. The priest forced him to contemplate things he would have preferred to keep locked in the innermost recesses of his mind. In truth, he was uncomfortable with Father John's serene, yet focused, examination. There seemed to be no way of combating this unaggressive pressure. The priest was becoming his nemesis – exacting retribution and ready to pounce at any moment.

"What form of help does this person need?" asked Father John, resignedly looking to the floor. "Of course I will help, there can be no refusal. These things are not fundamental to the issue." He stared back at Sean. "Though such things will wait, they will not go away. You will be helped first, but when there are no more problems left to occupy us, there will be the matter of your ideology. That self-righteous doctrine, which leaves men dead in the roadside. Men no better than you, maybe worse – nevertheless still men, who have been secure in *their* beliefs, and have now gone naked and unprepared to the Almighty. Who made you that man's judge? One day you will be in such a position – standing before your Maker!"

Sean tried to evade the sermon. "My friend has been shot in the shoulder while trying to escape from the Tans this morning, Father. If he doesn't get some help, I fear his condition will become even more desperate than it already is."

"Such a courteous and diplomatic way of putting it," complimented Father John with another intense stare. "I'll get some things packed. Then you can take me to this person. Is he far from here?"

"Yes, Father, he is."

Father John sighed. "I had a strange feeling that he might be." He raised himself from the armchair and went to the study door, stopping at the entrance: "There's bread and cheese in the parlour. Some cold beef too, if you care for it."

Sean suddenly realised how hungry he was. "Thank you for your kindness, Father John, it's much appreciated."

All his inhibitions vanished at the thought of food. He followed the priest into the passageway and was shown to the parlour.

"You'll find all you need in there. Put the kettle on and make some tea if you want." Father John climbed the stairs.

Full of gratitude, he called, as an after-thought. "My name is Sean O'Sullivan, Father."

The old priest stopped half way up the stairs and smiled – a sign of trust.

The rebel went into the parlour, where a small candle burned upon the worktop and the light from the stove bathed the dour, little room with an exquisite glow, which Sean found invit-ing. A homely smell of peat filled the air, bring-ing soothing, childhood memories. The heat hit him, making his dirty shirt cling to his skin. He gasped while fondly looking down at the old smouldering stove. They were good things to have in winter, but during the summer they could be intolerable. He decided Father John must have had plans to stay up late. There was

a half-loaf on a wooden breadboard, some butter and cheese close by, and a green tea towel
was spread over a small lump, which he found to
be the meat, much to his euphoric glee. Then,
like a ravenous savage, he fell upon the food. He
was greedily worried that Father John might be
ready before he could eat his fill, but thankfully
the priest seemed particular about the things he
wanted.

Sean crammed his mouth full of bread and
beef as he re-boiled the kettle, still warm from
earlier use. He returned to the bread and beef
for a second helping, and contemplated the further liberty of making up more to take back to
the apple orchard. The kettle boiled and he was
filling the teapot just as the stairs began to creak
and Father John came down.

The priest entered wearing a light jacket. A
small duffle bag hung from his shoulder, and he
looked as though he was about to go on a week-
end ramble.

"You'll find cups in the wall unit in front of
you – could you please make tea for me too,
Sean? I think it will set us up nicely before we
push off."

"Yes, Father." Sean took two old, china cups
from the cupboard and poured from the pot.
As he offered Father John his tea, no hand was
forthcoming. Sean looked up, to see what the
matter was, and found himself confronted by
the mild, green irises centred with pupils that

appeared like gentle, black pools. Maybe a hidden trap had been laid within the murky depths. He shuddered, able to guess what was going through the priest's mind as he met the scrutiny.

Sean realised that he had been tricked, taken off guard by the wily priest. It had been a reckoned reflex action. He was snared, captured by his childhood in the authority of the Church and, somewhere in those dark pools, all those unwanted teachings that had been locked away for so many years, in the deep cellars of his reason, were clamouring to the surface. Screaming inside his skull and forcing him to face the rush of emotions that now engulfed him.

"Thank you, Sean." Father John raised his hand to take the cup. The difficult priest knew exactly what he was doing, and Sean could find no way of challenging him.

"You do realise, Sean...," began Father John, as if searching for the words. "... that it is not just your friend who I am trying to help. I also harbour a genuine concern for you."

"I know. I'm grateful for your concern, Father John, but I am aware there will be consequences to my actions. Somewhere along the line, I will have to face those consequences."

"Do you really believe that, Sean, or is it just insurance? In case we're not right and there is no afterlife – no retribution, no Purgatory?"

"When the time comes, I will answer, and pay for what I have done, Father."

"Do you think the time should come when you choose? Or is it in case there is just a black void? Then it would not matter. Is that it, Sean? Do you not have the guts to face it in the mortal world?"

"Good God, Father, why do you heckle me, when the country is full of these bastards from abroad. Ransacking and burning our homes because we don't want to be governed by them – all because we have the audacity to say no. They're the ones who have created me, with their stubborn refusal to listen – that has caused all of this, and now I'm branded a murderer for my actions. Twenty years ago the very same people were paying me to kill Boers in South Africa."

Father John put the cup to his mouth, gingerly so that he could test the liquid's temperature, and allowing Sean a brief respite. He took another sip.

"So they paid you to kill Boers, and you accepted their money. You fought for the British against men who, like yourself, did not want to be governed by these people you now reject. Forgive me, Sean, but who are the hypocrites here?" Father John drank the remainder of his tea, then put his cup aside. He let the matter go. "We had best get going, for the sooner we begin the better."

"Yes, Father."

Sean was glad for a way out, knowing the priest had mirrored his sanctimony – giving him time to reflect on the matter. He knew Father John would resume the conversation at another time though, if Cormac could be saved, it would be worthwhile. Gulping his tea, he grabbed the beef, cheese and bread before following Father John back to the study. He wondered why they did not use the parlour door to leave the premises. His question was answered when Father John went to the oak cabinet and pulled out a half book and produced a full bottle of Irish whiskey, that had only been replaced hours earlier while watching over the repair works of Flannigan's bar.

"Easy come, easy go," muttered the priest. Putting the bottle into his kitbag, he regarded the rebel and gestured towards the French windows.

Father John looked grim as he followed Sean through the doors. He would have to endure a rigorous journey, at the end of which there would be a person suffering and in need of his ungrudging help.

TEN

The Tinker Woman.

It was a fine morning, and Hayward found it hard to recall there ever being such a season as winter. "Could it ever be cold again?" he thought. Every day was hot and sunny – nothing but pure summer would exist, forever.

The birds twittered, like a choir praising the morning, as he walked from the barrack room onto the compound's gravelled yard. Life was teeming with joy and splendour. He wondered how God could create such fabulous things, and then bring on earthquakes and storms. A gypsy caravan stood framed by the compound gates. Strikingly green and yellow, with bold, red wheels, it burst suddenly into his vision. A splendid, brown shire horse stood to the front, chewing grass from Turpin's outstretched hand. Henderson and Cuttings were looking on admiringly at the splendid beast, while a tubby, little, old, tinker woman was chatting to Jones and Baker. Her hands gesticulating wildly, she prattled on, obviously undisturbed by the attentions of the Tans.

Inquisitively, Hayward strolled to the gates to hear about the wanderer's life. Altogether, it was an unusual occurrence. Encounters with the locals had been less amiable of late.

"Four and sixty years I have lived this way and I've never regretted any of it," said the tinker woman. "We're a dying breed, we are now." She charmed her listeners while telling of her life on the road and her splendid horse. "Of course, others like me don't use this breed of horse. I'm the only one. A bit of an odd ball among my own kind," she giggled.

Baker and Jones listened smiling, while Hayward wondered who was doing the patronising here. He noticed Barnes appear stealthily at the back of the caravan, scanning for anything that might look suspicious. To Hayward's amazement, Barnes beckoned him with a movement of his head, while his sly eyes motioned to the door at the back.

Hayward frowned. "What, me?" he mimed with his lips. He lip-read Barnes' scathing 'Yes'.

He shook his head negatively, wanting no part of any such antics, and turned back to the group around the shire.

"How long have you had the horse?" asked Jones of the old woman, as he stroked the beast.

"Well now, he's still a youngster, you know. Barely four years, he is. It clean broke me heart, when his grandfather died." The old lady was pleased with the interest. "He's an English shire and as I just said, I am an exception where using this breed is concerned."

Henderson whispered to Hayward: "She seems to be enjoying herself." Then he looked back at the tinker, while Jones bombarded her with pleasantries about the beast. It was obviously a ploy to keep her attention on him and not on Barnes.

"Barnes wants me to search the van," Hayward whispered to him.

"Rather you than me," replied Henderson, as he joined the rest of the group.

Barnes suddenly appeared beside him with a grin on his face: "Well, I think I'll go back to the barracks now". He added, obviously enjoying Hayward's predicament: "Bradley wants you to search the back of the van. His orders, not mine."

He briskly walked off towards the gates, chuckling. Hayward gritted his teeth in annoyance; after all it was this type of thing that alienated them from the civilian population. This old woman bore no malice and did not seem in the least perturbed by the fact she was surrounded by Black and Tans. This was how things should be, he thought. The only people they should be combating were the Volunteers, not the rest of Irish society. They needed cooperation from the locals! Something they were hardly going to get by sneaking around their properties. He sighed again, before catching Jones's intense stare. The man was clearly angry and frustrated by Hayward's reluctance to enter the caravan, and turned his back in exasperation.

Reluctantly Hayward went to the caravan door. Why? He could not say. Barnes had no rank over him and he had not heard Sergeant Bradley give such an order. The man was nowhere to be seen. He could have walked away, but instead he found himself gently lifting the latch, hoping the old lady's banter would not dry up. Thankfully, the door was well-oiled and made no sound as it glided open. Stealthily he went inside with a cat-like grace, something learnt when venturing into no-man's-land during the terrifying night patrols of the Great War. Silence was the key, and the reason he had succeeded in boarding the caravan unnoticed.

Inside the cramped living-quarters he was mesmerised. Everything was neat and perfectly placed. There were drawers built underneath a bed that was neatly covered with a patchwork blanket. A freshly polished table was fixed to the wall beneath one of the diamond-shaped, leaded windows on either side. Pleasing light-green and yellow square curtains decorated the windows. On closer inspection he noticed the table had hinges, so that it could be lowered flat. Along the upper part of the wall, running the entire perimeter was a shelf with all sorts of utensils hanging from it. Pots, pans, saucepans and various other implements, while in the centre of the ceiling hung an oil lamp. The front wall had a small, square door that was covered by a tiny, net curtain. Through it he could see the seating board where the driver sat. Everything was so neatly compact, with not an inch of space wasted. A twinge of excitement stirred at the sight of this little Aladdin's cave. He paused to drink in the fairy-tale atmosphere – imagining how he might himself live such a life, if he only had the courage. By the door through which he had come, he saw two darker, stained, wooden wall-units on either side, leading from the ground to finish at the upper shelf perimeter. He moved towards the units with an odd feeling of excitement in his stomach. He was unsure whether this response was from fear of being caught or from some other quality of the caravan. Carefully he slid a lower drawer open, revealing only an assortment of haberdashery items – various coloured cottons, neat compact balls of wool in various colours, knitting and sewing needles. The drawer beneath contained more bundles of wool and neatly boxed fragile-looking china thimbles, elegantly decorated with little paintings of birds and flowers.

He held one up in a ray of sunlight that filtered through the back door curtains, for closer inspection. The fine detail of a chaffinch on a dandelion was intense with colour, and despite having no interest in sewing, he could understand how a collector's mind might yearn for things of such refined facination. He opened a third drawer, revealing yet more thimbles, and realised that the old woman must trade such items – probably selling them at fairs while travelling about the countryside.

Outside, he could still hear the voices chatting. He became alarmed when the old tinker began to make her goodbyes.

"Where's Hayward gone?" he heard Jones asked.

"He went back into the barracks after Barnes," Henderson replied.

"Did he?" laughed Baker.

The rest of the unit obviously did not know he was inside the caravan just a few feet away from them. He smiled as the van rocked with the weight of the tinker climbing onto the steering seat. Her back came into view against the small window at the front. If he stayed put no one would be the wiser. His smile vanished and calmness swept over him as he looked at the latch. He could have crept off as easily as he got on. For some compelling reason, he did nothing.

A new commotion attracted his attention, and he looked through the window. One of the trucks was pulling out of the yard with Henderson at the wheel. Baker and Jones had clambered onto the back, while Turpin and Cuttings seemed to have gone back into the barracks. The vehicle pulled away, the noise of its engine gradually fading as it sped off into the distance.

Quiet returned, and with it the fluttering excitement in his stomach. What should he do now? The men inside the barracks would assume he was on the lorry, while the men on the lorry would think he was inside the barracks. It could be a long time before anyone noticed he was actually in neither place, missing, and if he stayed out of sight in the caravan as it left, no one would see his departure.

There was a sudden jolt as the caravan rocked into motion, and the old lady shouted "Gee up, Moogsly!"

"It's begun," thought Hayward. "Now is the time to make up your mind. What are you going to do, lad?" He crept to the bed and sat upon the patchwork quilt, certain the tinker would remain unaware of her passenger. For once in his life he felt sure of what he was going to do – with the wheels in motion he drifted effortlessly with the flow of things. The priest at Cafgarven would be his goal. Father John had said something about the Brothers and a monastery. It would not hurt to find out more on the subject. In the meantime, he would enjoy the ride and relax. He found it odd he could actually enjoy it – even while absconding. He would never have dared do such a thing during the War, as the penalty was death. But this was different. He was a Reserve policeman, free to leave whenever he decided. Though it was reasonable to assume the R.I.C. would be very unhappy that he had left with their property – the mishmash uniform and a rifle. In all likelihood, charges would be brought against him.

"There are probably others that can be brought as well," he muttered, deciding the powers that be could worry about such things. He was on his way out of the R.I.C., for better or worse, and this was the way he had chosen.

As the caravan rumbled on, he occupied himself in examining the drawers in the wall-units on the other side of the door. His curiosity was aroused and he wanted to explore the world of the tinker lady. He wanted to talk with her, be let in to her domain, if only for a short time. He stood and quietly moved to the unit, stopping momentarily to check the tinker had not been alerted by his activity. After establishing that she had not, he continued, compensating for the rocking motion as he went. His attention was drawn to some tatty looking books that were on the top of the drawers. An old book on herbs and medicines, another on recipes, plus a Holy Bible, which surprised him as he had assumed all tinkers were illiterate. But although she was obviously not illiterate, what need would she have for books? It occurred to him that the old woman kept these books because of their subject matter. All of the topics were appropriate for the type of life he imagined a tinker might need to understand. He picked up the old book on herbs and medicines, which filled him with fascination as he began to read pieces at random on how to cure particular ailments. Many of the remedies were finely detailed, to the extent of specifying the patting of pillows to ensure comfort when resting, and leaving potions to cool for specific amounts of time in order to avoid burning ones lips. These quaint little details enthralled him and he was full of admiration for the person who had taken the time to sit down and meticulously write such a thing. What a charming individual the author must be. The information was not lost on him as he began avidly to read the book, which contained cures for all sorts of complaints, setting out the administering of all assignments from start to finish. It would have made useful knowledge during the trench wars – though he had learnt to deal with many things while fighting in such hellish conditions. The book contained tips on all sorts of commodities that someone could use in a limited environment.

Outside, the old tinker lady continued to drive along, singing a gentle melody to the powerful Shire horse. Her soothing voice drifted through to him, and filled the space with song. He decided to put aside his reading for a while and to listen to the charming lyrics, some of which were jolly, while others were sad. They enchanted him, nestling snugly in the back of his mind to ease more painful thoughts, settling him into his strange environment; then he returned to the book, which held his interest. He found he was becoming avid to experience the art and craft that surrounded him in all its forms. Objects, sound and written word were now his to soak in. The book won the contest for word, while the surrounding furniture and song accompanied his contentment like subtle disciples that complemented his absorption.

Hours passed, yet there was no cessation to the tinker's singing or, for most of the time, his reading. He was perplexed by finding a treatment for bullet wounds, including fatal ones in which the doomed victim was made as comfortable as possible while being offered soothing words of hope. This was in case, by some form of divine intervention, the patient did not die. He shook his head in disbelief, smiling to himself, but charmed, nonetheless, by the optimism of the author whose meticulous endeavour appeared limitless. Finally closing the book with his forefinger inside, he looked for the author's name. *Domestic Use of Herbs and Medicine* he read off the title, then allowed his gaze to fall to a name. *Freda Mary Donavon,* inscribed in faded, gold italic. He opened it and found the publication date, which was eighteen eighty-two. He wondered what sort of woman Mary Donavon was, guessing that she would have been old when writing such a book for it must surely have taken a lifetime to acquire such knowledge. Now, forty years hence, the woman would surely be gone. The book was something of her that remained – a little piece of the lady's life captured in the pages. He judged her to be a woman of upper-middle class background, with servants who related such snippets of knowledge – one of those well-educated and elegant women living a life of carefree contemplation while her husband was serving as an officer in some far-flung corner of the Empire.

The caravan started to rock violently and the light inside, filtering through the window, became broken by the shadows of tree branches. They had now turned from the road into a wooded area. The tinker was preparing for another stop, which would necessarily bring about his discovery. He fought a bubbling anxiety that he might frighten the old lady. He was going to need her help. She was on the road to Cafgarven and Father John's Parochial House, where he wanted to go. How might she react if he explained himself to her? She might help, for the Bible showed the woman to be of religious sentiment. A person who might be relied upon to keep silent if she knew he was wandering the country. He faltered, allowing an image of an old woman, gossiping in villages, to cloud his reason. People with Fenian sympathies would be bound to hear the tale about a wandering Tan and the Volunteers would be searching the countryside for him. His execution would be a bonus in this war of ruthless murders – another notch in the ever-cascading turn of events that seemed to have no end.

The caravan lurched to a sudden halt, causing him to jolt forward. He managed to stop himself by grabbing the bedpost. Instantly he made the decision to acquaint the tinker with his honest intentions. If she became vexed and angry, then he would just have to walk back to the barracks and create some elaborate account of what had happened – clearly he would have a fair deal of explaining to do. He heard the old lady climb down from the front seat and listened to her progress along the side of the caravan as she panted and went to the back door. Why she did not come in the front way, he did not know as the latch slammed upwards and the door opened. He stood deciding to warn her before she put her foot on the step and was shocked by the unexpected sight of him.

"Don't be alarmed, lady, I mean no harm," he said clearly.

"OH BEJESUS!" she screamed in fright, throwing both hands up to her chest, as though trying to contain her thumping heart from leaping out. "My God! What in the devil do you want? Where in the bloody hell did you come from?" She started stamping up and down, muttering to herself.

Hayward thought at first she was trying to soothe her old body from the fright with Gaelic verses, but then realised, with some shock, that she was actually directing a stream of curses at him. When these came to an end, she stared at him with a look of bewilderment.

"Have you been in there since I left the barracks this morning?" She grumbled in disbelief, shaking her wrinkled face at the thought.

"Yes," he replied then stuttered. "I-I stumbled upon this b-by accident."

"Are you trying to tell me you tripped into my caravan now?" she gasped in miraculous awe at his audacity. "Of all the impudence, how could you expect me to believe such a thing?"

"Well no, that's not exactly what I meant," he answered nervously. "The opportunity cropped up in an accidental way – a temptation of sorts that I was unable to resist."

"Serendipity," added the old woman.

"What?" asked Hayward forgetting his dilemma when confronted with this strange word.

"It means happy accident. Now, can you please tell me how a Black and Tan happens to be in the back of my caravan?"

"I've just left the R.I.C. without announcing it. I was looking for a way out and you just happened along". He saw no reason to tell her about the intended search.

"My God, you'll be in great trouble, young man, if they find you. Why did you not tell them beforehand? It would have made things much easier. Now they'll be out searching the whole area for you. I'm aghast at this foolhardiness."

"If I did, they'd send me back to England, and that's the last place I want to go."

"When they start looking for you, believing that something bad has happened, they'll search the village houses – more vandalism upon innocent people's property. How could you be so foolish? Have you considered the implications of what you have done?"

She tutted and shook her head, not knowing what to make of the situation, while he tentatively stepped down from the caravan. The shade provided a welcome coolness amid the chirping from the green canopy. They were bubbled in a ball of foliage. The tinker looked up at the ceiling of leaves, as though aware of nature's isolating influence, respecting the fact she had to make a decision.

"That you're genuine, I'm not in doubt. But whether or not you're a fool remains to be seen."

"I need to go to Cafgarven," he said.

She stared for a moment, then turned away deep in thought and shuffled about amid the small clumps of grass and shrubs that were spread at intervals upon the dry, hardened earth. Taking a deep breath, then letting out a sigh, she finally faced him with a more subdued look, as though resigned to something she would rather not do. Her face was grim, but Hayward sensed the good beneath the old woman's features.

"What would you be doing in Cafgarven, when you get there?"

"I need to see Father John – he'll help from there."

Nodding her acceptance, she stared blankly above, meditating for a while, before reaching a decision. "We'll have to spend a little more time here than I had anticipated, then we can move onwards. It'll be better for you if we reach Cafgarven nearer nightfall. This is because I can leave you by some woods near the village. It'll make it easier to get to the Parochial House without people seeing you. It would not do for the likes of yourself to be seen out alone in present circumstances."

She scrutinised him, studying his features, looking for things that might be of significance. He returned the stare, hoping for signs of reliability, earnestly entreating God that she would prove trustworthy. Perhaps she was appeasing him through fear of being harmed – treating him condescendingly in case he turned violent.

"If you are afraid to help me I will understand, and if it is your wish, I will leave you and make my own way. I will not harm you, please believe that."

"I know that, and I'm not afraid of the likes of you, young man," she scolded flippantly, which relaxed him for her manner was kind. Resolved, though reluctant, she would help him. "First, I'll need some dead bracken to make a fire. Then I can cook dinner. The van cannot be seen from the lane, which is good, for I think there will be an almighty uproar over this matter and I feel your friends will be searching, fearful that you may have been abducted. I just hope the locals don't have to pay too high a price for your absconding."

"Shall I collect the bracken?"

"Yes please, it would be most helpful of you."

"What should I call you, lady?" He was unsure if she wanted to give her name, but felt impolite not to ask.

"My name is Freda Donavon."

"Mrs Donavon?" he asked assuming that the old lady would not have gone through her life a spinster.

"I was once, but my husband passed on long ago, God rest his soul."

"You wrote that book on medicine and herbs didn't you? The one that I was reading in the caravan," he stammered excitedly as he suddenly realised he had heard her name before. "How did you manage to get it published? I'm so sorry, I never thought it would be ..."

"What? A gypsy – a tinker, eh, is that what you are saying?" she smiled, gratified with his adulation for her little achievement. The young man was to her liking and he had the ability to flatter without pretence – having, what she would call, a young, innocuous charm.

ELEVEN

The Next Day.

Father John was severely fatigued by his adventure to the apple orchard and much troubled by his next course of action to help Cormac Doyle. The man, whom he had tried in vain to assist throughout the night, was very ill. The bullet, buried deep in his shoulder, would need to be extracted soon. He feared for the young man – if the wound did not receive proper medical attention it would fester and worsen. Gangrene could set in if something were not done swiftly.

He looked up into the cloudless, blue sky, using the palm of his hand to shield his eyes from the intense sun. Before him was the final hill, beyond which lay Cafgarven. At last he had made it back, though concerned at having to leave Cormac and Sean alone. His first desire was to eat something, then to ponder, knowing the journey to the apple orchard would have to be made again – a very daunting thought, and a heavy undertaking at his age. The long walk had been difficult.

"God, please help me to be clear on this matter," he muttered resolutely as he began to climb the scarp that rose gently at first, becoming steeper as he progressed. "I know that You work in strange ways, but I feel I need some help on this matter. I am at a loss for what to do and I need some sign from You – anything that might help. We are so desperate and in need."

He was almost pleading with God as he reached the summit. "I cannot get Cormac to a hospital, for he will fall into the hands of the authorities. This, in essence, would be betrayal. Lord, I know that this is asking a lot, but please send help or the wisdom to do what is right for this young man."

He paused and looked into the blue heaven, before gratefully descending to the village. His mind was a whirl of ideas by the time he crossed the graveyard, noting briefly that Sean O'Sullivan must have broken his runner-bean frame. Entering the garden by the small gate, he was confronted by Maureen who had come out to meet him. Her face was etched with concern.

"Father John," she scolded lightly. "Where in heaven have you been? I got your note but still a person can't help worrying over such things. It's most out of character for you do this. You look exhausted, are you feeling poorly?"

"I feel fine. Maureen, but I would love a cup of tea and something to eat."

"Of course, Father John, I will do it right away. My God, it's so late in the day. Have you not eaten anything while you've been out?"

"I'm afraid not, Maureen, for such was the nature of my visit. I could not make any provisions in advance."

She moved to his side and put her arm gently through his to bring comfort and aid. It warmed his heart, making him feel fortunate to have a person like Maureen to care for his needs. He allowed her to lead him into the kitchen, where the smell of the peat stove was a little too overbearing in the summer heat. Maureen swiftly led him through the hallway to the front room, where she gently ushered him to the comfortable, little armchair by the mantelpiece. He liked to sit here when he was in his contemplative moods – a disposition that Maureen had sensed.

He thanked her, grateful that she understood this part of him. She would not burden him with questions. She discreetly left to prepare something to eat. "Maureen," he called after her.

"Yes, Father John," She stopped at the door.

"It is very important that you don't mention my unusual actions to anyone."

"Father John," she began with a tone of gracious candour. "I know that sometimes I am apt to gossip, but it does seem to me that this matter is best left. I'll say nothing about this to anyone. This will go to my grave with me."

He smiled. What a phenomenally good woman she was at times, and how lucky for him to know such a person. Of her sincerity there were never doubts, and as he sat back, allowing the chair's soft comfort to ease his aching body, the door was gently closed.

The journey to the apple orchard had been demanding, more so than he had thought. When he and Sean had finally got there, the sight of poor Cormac Doyle filled him with pity. What a tragic place the world could be at times, and what made young men with promising futures put their lives in such jeopardy? How many men had died throughout Europe in the recent War – the War to end all wars? No sooner does one pass than new troubles begin with ceaseless vigour. Father John shook his head, remembering Cormac's screams when he had tried to extract the bullet. Sean had held the man down – drunken and whimpering from pain. The whiskey had been to no avail, for he was unable to reach the bullet, only succeeding in causing more withering agony with every futile attempt to remove it. Eventually he had to give up, and devote his efforts to cleaning and dressing the wound. He promised Sean that he would be back later in the day with better help for Cormac. He had spent more time persuading Sean not to come with him, knowing it was unwise to leave Cormac unattended – besides the countryside would still be full of police units searching for them.

An image of a nunnery sprang to his mind, the Convent of our Lady of Grace. If only he could get Cormac there. The young man would stand every chance of pulling through. There had to be a way. With the thought, he experienced a new vitality igniting within – a light spreading through his clouded mind. The nuns would surely help, but the problem was getting Cormac out of the apple orchard. It would be most ambitious to expect him and Sean to be able to aid the young man, but there seemed to be no other course of action to take. There was no person in the village with a motor vehicle. Only horses and carts – but he would never dream of risking another villager on such a venture.

"You knew about the Convent of our Lady of Grace," he whispered to God, with a thoughtful smile. "Now what, I wonder, have You got in mind for the journey to the Convent? A little sweat and toil on my part, or divine intervention on Yours." He closed his eyes and smiled, cheekily shaking his head at the thought that God might actually answer his humorous, yet liberty-taking, question. It was a bit much to ask, but then he reasoned, if you never ask you're never likely to get anything.

There was still the question of Sean O'Sullivan. What could he do for this man? He had managed to converse with him before leaving the orchard to begin the journey home. He relived the conversation, and Sean's distress. "Father John, in the name of God, please don't desert us."

With firm conviction he had let Sean know that he would adamantly stand by both of them. In gratitude, Sean made a promise, a bargain.

"If you do, Father John, I promise never to kill again. I'll turn my back on all this to save Cormac."

Father John had swiftly replied. "By hook or by crook, I will save your friend, Sean – though I will hold you to your word about renouncing violence."

Thus, with Sean's promise he had made his journey back to Cafgarven. He smiled, then fidgeted restlessly, as he dwelled on the matter. The Volunteer would be sure to keep to his word if help for Cormac was forthcoming and they reached the nunnery in time. All he needed were the remaining tools to do the job. A form of transport, and some trustworthy help. God, he decided, was working in strange and mysterious ways. He was sure, drifting into optimistic slumber, that something would happen before the coming evening's return to the apple orchard. Confidence swelled. One way or another, they would prevail.

Maureen allowed Father John his repose, knowing that her indulgence on this particular matter would be much appreciated. Of course she was curious to know what he had been up to all night. His bed had not been slept in. However, a sixth sense told her the affair was too important to be pried into, not to mention her own shortcoming for gossip; the ethical side of her nature came to the fore. Silently her imploring spirit asked God to keep her tongue firmly closed on the subject where other people were concerned. She would not confide in anyone. If not, the news would soon spread about the village, something Father John could do without.

When the clock had struck two in the afternoon, she decided to go into the lounge and wake him, supposing he might like to wash and change before lunch. Gently she opened the door and peered in where he was mildly snoring with an air of contentment. At first she was unsure whether to rouse him, he seemed so peaceful and she felt it would be a shame to disturb the man.

"Father John," she called softly. "It's time to get up now."

She stepped forward, when she got no response. Gently she reached out and prodded his shoulder repeating. "Father John, it's time to get up."

He bolted upright, looking around as though amazed, seeming for a moment not to recognise the place. Remembrance of his surroundings came suddenly. He frowned and looked to the clock before turning to face her.

"Good heavens, is that the time?"

"It is, Father John. I thought it best to wake you because I will be dishing lunch in thirty minutes. You may like to freshen before eating."

"Yes, indeed I will, Maureen, thank you." He got up from the chair to attend the matter. He stopped at the door.

"What's for dinner?"

"Pork chops, boiled potatoes, carrots and greens," she replied.

"I'll slaughter that for you, Maureen. I'm famished to say the least." Maureen smiled and added. "I made bread-and-butter pudding with custard for your sweet."

Father John smiled, knowing that his housekeeper was always pleased when her endeavours were given credit, and it gave him as much pleasure to compliment her table of gastronomic delights.

"Oh, too much, Maureen," he giggled. "You're certainly spoiling me today, aren't you now."

He went up the stairs singing, while she toddled back to the kitchen, invigorated with a new enthusiasm. Waking him had obviously been the right thing to do.

She went into the garden, where a table had been laid. During such warm weather the bright outdoors was alluring. The garden was splendid and therapeutic, and she believed it would help him to think.

Quickly she cleared the utensils, before laying a clean tablecloth and cutlery. The meal was being dished as Father John came down.

He wandered out and sat at the table, beaming with delight as Maureen laid his lunch before him. She stopped and bowed her head as he said a quick grace. This done, he looked up at her, sensing she wanted to say something.

"I'll be off now, Father John. I'll pop back in an hour to do the plates and dishes before I go home."

"Oh please don't worry about the dishes, Maureen, I'll attend to those. You take the rest of the day off."

"Thank you, Father John."

Maureen smiled, knowing the dishes and plates would still be there in the morning. She left, happy at being able to go home early on such a fine day. It would give her time to get her own spring cleaning done before preparing her husband's dinner.

TWELVE

The Surprise Return.

Hayward and the tinker lady started back upon the road. Awestruck, he listened intently to her life story, while standing just inside the vehicle, behind the curtain at the front door.

Freda, who sat holding the reins, prattled on happily. It was a long time since she had spoken so deeply of her past.

"How did you come to write the book on herbs and medical treatment?" he asked.

She chuckled. "Lord, is there no end to all your questions now? You're an inquisitive young man at that."

"I'm curious, that's all. It's a big achievement – you must be proud."

"Well, I must confess that I was most flattered and deeply touched at the time. It was originally a collection of little articles and notes, a minor pastime I enjoyed among many things.

The records were for an aristocratic lady, whose land I happened to stay upon sometimes when passing. She was a very graceful person, most articulate and a pleasure to talk too – like you in many ways. Always asking questions and finding much delight in my answers. Oh, but she was likeable and charmed by my wanderer's knowledge. I explained things in intricate detail you see, an ingredient in her affection and fondness to me. Surprised at my writing ability she was too, and positively thrilled when I bestowed my notes upon her. Of all people, I thought she should have them because of her kindness and interest.

Well now, can you not imagine my surprise when I next passed by her lands, to be presented with a book – a proper, edited version of my notes as a sign of appreciation. I was never so thrilled in all of my life and did not realise that I had written a book until she came walking up bold and graceful with a big, beaming smile. A small number of copies were actually sold, giving me a handsome earning from the publication."

"That's right bloody marvellous that is." Hayward was enthralled, and for a moment there was an awkward silence as both searched for another topic.

"How long do you think it'll take us to reach Cafgarven?" he asked, feeling a little more at ease.

"Oh, I should reckon about an hour, maybe less."

"Do you think we'll have to wait long before I can go to the Parochial House?" he added.

"I think it will be in our best interest to wait until it is dark, and then I should be the one to contact Father John while you wait in the woods. You can't take the chance of wandering the countryside in that uniform, not around these parts. Word will get out and soon you will have undesirable characters on both sides of the struggle looking for you."

"I don't want to burden you anymore than I have," he replied hoping to convey his appreciation.

"This is a particular burden that you do *have to* put upon me, young man."

"I am grateful for what you are doing, Freda – you do know that, don't you." He felt that he was taking excessive liberties with her good nature.

"I know that, lovely, and I don't expect you to keep thanking me. Try and get some rest now while we complete the journey. It will do you good."

Thinking Freda might want to be left alone, he quietly moved away from the window and sat upon the bed, reflecting on what he should do to pass the time. He thought of looking at the book again, but dismissed the idea, feeling that rest would be better. His stomach fluttered at the recollection of absconding, sending shivers through him. Maybe if he could sleep it would take his mind off of such thoughts, relieving the worry of his fragile freedom – a dangerous liberty brought about by his reckless abandonment of the Constabulary. He started to unlace his boots, making up his mind to lie down against the inviting pillow and see if he could sleep. After all, when would the next opportunity come? Neatly placing his footwear at the end of the bed, he lay back to look at the ceiling, watching the hanging oil lamp swing back and forth to the vehicle's motion, while Freda's light melody gently began to push his mind into what might have become a soothing slumber.

Outside Freda's singing stopped. The sound of a motor vehicle grew louder as Hayward, hit by a sudden panic, got up and peered out of the rear-door window. He saw a Crossley Tender truck in the distance, rapidly getting closer. His heart leapt in fear at the sight of the Black and Tan lorry. What if they were out looking for him? They might stop to search the caravan. He made a hissing sound to alert Freda, but she was already guiding the horse towards the rock wall, by the side of the lane, to allow the truck to pass.

"Keep your head down, Henry," she hissed. "The Tans are coming."

With hoarse cheers and waving from the boisterous policemen sitting in the rear, the truck passed. He watched her wave back as it sped harmlessly by.

"Things like this are a bit too close for comfort at my age," she muttered, once the danger had passed.

With a skilled flick of the reins she coaxed the shire to pull the vehicle away from the wall and back onto the road.

"I wonder where they were going – surely not Cafgarven? Lord, the state of the country today. So full of confusion, and me always trying to mind my way where these troublesome political issues are concerned. The entire business has become very dirty and messy. It's very difficult to travel in some parts, with Volunteers digging trenches to restrict police movements and all. It also stops everyone else from travelling. Are you not listening, Henry?"

"Yes, Freda, I am listening."

"How absurd, all of them."

"It always happens and it always will," he replied.

Freda shook her head. "Everywhere I travel, the stories are always the same. The midnight knock, not knowing which side it is, killings close by, followed with reprisals against all. That's regardless of whether you are innocent or not. It's strange that such ordinary people are capable of carrying out vile and dreadful deeds. They are often ordinary people whom you can meet and like – seemingly kind by nature, yet able to inflict cruelty upon others without a second thought."

He agreed. "Some revel in the brutality, and these people can be found on both sides, but, like you say – most are ordinary folk, caught up in the flow of mayhem."

"You have a nice way with words, Henry."

"Thank you."

"No, I mean it. You don't belong in that mishmash uniform. How did a fine, young man, like yourself, become part of such a horde?" She began to daydream and talk at the same time. "Then such mobs are made up of fine, young men, hidden by the collective thing they are part of. They don't exist individually anymore."

"They do, but you are only looking at the broad picture of what they represent, not the fraction that is part of their true identity, which, in the loathing minds of people, is an unimportant crumb on a rotten cake. The only way that such men can attempt to regain that identity is to walk away from the mob – the fake something that swallows souls and corrupts."

"As you have done, Henry? If that is what you believe, then you are right to leave. In a way, your absconding, rather than just leaving, makes sense, if you see things in such a light." She wondered how he had become so filled with an obvious dislike for the organisation he was in. He was aware of individuals. Good men corrupted by the collective thing they were in. "We live in a world where people are used as tools of murder for unseen idealists – artists with human life as their pigment. They are frustrated men, who cannot be heard and won't listen, because they think they don't need to. Sometimes their mantles are taken from them in attempts to restrict their words from being heard. This causes deep resentment. Then opposing artists want to hear their own voice and no one else's. They adopt force to gain or preserve dominance. Innocent people are the chequered board, and young men, filled with hatred, become the unwitting pawns."

The caravan rocked gently as he listened with interest, knowing she would continue.

"Individuals, like you, Henry, make a difference in the web of life. A tiny, yet complex, pattern made up of millions of other such threads, all connecting. Yours and mine have crossed! I believe everything has significance, and this was meant to be."

She was glad to help him, perceiving it was part of their destinies. More would come from their meeting, if they followed the course.

Time passed quickly – the meadows rolled by, lazily garnished by the distant peaks and wooded clusters that soothed and relaxed him. Freda sang to Moogsly as the brute pulled the caravan along in sluggish yet relentless steps. At times she would philosophise on life's strange journey, but eventually a mood of silence cast its warm blanket around her. In this state she remained for over half a -hour as the moments passed in splendid, summer weather.

She stirred to life when a small gathering of trees came into view. The lane twisted behind them. It was the little wood before Cafgarven's high road and she was filled with sense of urgency. The next stage of the quest was at hand. Impatiently, she flicked the reins to hasten the horse, who responded with a slight quickening of pace. The wood slowly came forward to meet them as Moogsly went into the cover of the foliage.

Inside, Hayward grabbed the door jamb to stop himself falling. A twinge of excitement replaced his earlier cautious mood, drowning the mild fear that hovered in the pit of his stomach. He reached for his boots and cursed as he tried to put them on. It was a difficult task when swaying about. They finally halted, enabling him to tie his laces as the rear door opened, revealing Freda.

"Have you been sleeping, now?" she asked.

"I tried but spent much of the time by your window?" he said pointing up.

"It would have done you some good. Now, we have arrived at a small wood just outside Cafgarven and it's my intention to go into the village alone to seek out Father John. I'll tell him about you, shall I? Then I think he is likely to venture out here."

Hayward was concerned for her. "I'll wait until dark. Then I can make my own way. That'll allow you to go on and dissociate yourself from me. I don't want to cause you any more inconvenience! You've done so much for me already."

She looked aghast and a little hurt, but then her face softened as she smiled, realising he was trying to oblige her. "Your concern is very flattering Hayward, but I do think it would be better if I were able to wander into the village. I'm a familiar sight; I would not arouse any undue attention, when going into the confessional to get Father John's ear on this matter. You wait here in the woods – hide yourself in some bush or tree, for I intend to take the caravan into the village. It all makes for a normal, summer scene, you know."

"Shall I make ready to hide now, or are you going to stay here for a while?" He smiled, knowing she had given the matter some thought.

"I think it will be better if I give it another hour. Things in the village will be winding down and it will only be a couple of hours before nightfall. I don't know why, but I think you'll be travelling further during the night. It would be a good time to move, after all."

"Shall I get some wood to get a fire going?"

She smiled and replied: "You're learning fast now, lovely," then collected the necessary utensils for brewing tea, while Hayward went into the woods for bracken. He returned in minutes, carrying firewood, and placed it by the various pots that had been set out.

"You seem to have done this sort of thing before, Henry. You work like a born tinker. Have you lived out of doors?

"Of course – eighteen months in the trenches. Often I would leave the front and go back into the sanctity of our own territory, just to the nearest woodlands. We gathered wood for stoves and things when in the dugouts. Some of the woodland was reduced to nothing but broken stumps, all flattened from shelling. Mind you, the wood was always well-shattered."

"I thought as much." She put out stakes with a spit from which she suspended a kettle.

"Mind you, we never made fires in the open. It would be asking for trouble from the Jerry snipers." He sighed reflectively over the bygone days. "It seems my occupation has become one of dodging sniper bullets. I've lost some great mates over the years. It leaves you with mixed feelings of fear and frustration."

Soon the fire was burning away and he went and filled the kettle from the small, water barrel attached beneath the caravan, then hung it over the flames. When the liquid began simmering, Freda poured a small drop to heat her teapot – stirring it as she looked at him, lingering with the chore, wondering about his past.

"How do you come to be in such a predicament? An ex-serviceman and all."

He looked up, snapping out of his trance – a sixth sense told him that she was taking too long as he answered. "Just going with the flow of things, that's all."

"Well, now you have a paddle to steer yourself by." She slung the hot water from the kettle into the mud and started adding tea leaves, her eyes firmly fixed on him.

"You're an enigma, young Henry."

He laughed. "In your world, Freda – as you are in mine."

"You know, this is the sort of scene that makes poems or nursery rhymes," she giggled girlishly. "I can imagine the scene when Father John gets here." She made a quick line of a poem. "Beneath the woods in the campfires light –"

Hayward cut in. "You come across an amazing sight."

"Ooh yes, you have it," she laughed and pointed at him. "Come on now, some more, you're on a roll, lad."

Quickly, he added. "There sat a tinker lady …"

"…A holy man and a renegade Tan," she added.

"The romantic Irish in you is bubbling to the surface, isn't it? Where is the holy man? He's not here yet." He laughed at her extravagant dreaming. It was an outrageous thought, but then Freda had written books and maybe, just maybe, she could compose some sort of nursery rhyme with him in. "Go on then," he said childishly. "Let me hear the rest of the lyrics."

She chuckled like an old grandmother who knows how to thrill infants, pleased with the joy she had brought from his frayed character.

"I can't recite lyrics, young man." She bubbled with glee. "I will begin to make up a verse in my head. It's sure to change, because we have not brought the priest here yet, and more interesting things might happen to us. All these things can shape the verses you know, so I think it is prudent to wait. It will make the little ditty all the more rummy."

Hayward's enchantment overflowed, and his smile developed into an open-mouthed grin. His pink-streaked wrinkles nestled by his eyes to contrast sharply against a sun-tanned face, while the smell of the burning bracken suddenly become stronger. He gladly surrendered his spirit to this bewitching feeling, allowing the mystery of the place to engulf him. Freda, he decided, was magic and oozing with charm that foreign people believed her race had in abundance. He viewed her in such a light – deciding that Irish was unique and non-British.

"Do you speak Gaelic?" he asked, leaving the subject of verse.

"When I'm in certain parts, where the Gaelic tongue is used as the vernacular, yes. Why do you ask?"

"I heard you singing during the day, before you knew I was in the back. The words seemed so colourful, even though I did not understand them." He looked into the fire. "You are very different us."

"In what way? As in I, being Irish, and you, English?"

"Yes, but the differences are what really make you interesting to me; being English and all."

"But maybe it is the similarities between us that enable you to appreciate those entertaining little differences."

He smiled. She was a complex creature. An existence so perplexing that she could not have been born into the world out of emptiness. Some almighty, all-seeing thing must have created her, and been greatly satisfied at the work of art.

"Do you believe in God?"

"Of course! My, but you are a strange young fellow, Henry Hayward. That mind of yours is ticking over all of the time, isn't it now?"

She poured the kettle. "Sit down, Henry."

While the tea brewed, he looked up into the green ceiling where javelins of light pierced through small gaps that were scattered about the foliage – united with the splendour of bird song that filled the arched canopy with wild melody. It reminded him of a choir in a cathedral.

She noticed his distraction and turned to see what had taken his interest. At once she was aware of the same splendid sight.

"Bird song and light – perfect nature," she said softly.

He smiled with a satisfied air then looked at her. "… in all resplendent glory."

THIRTEEN

The Meeting in the Church.

Maureen would be pleasantly surprised, when morning came and she visited the Parochial House. Father John had washed the plate and dish, something he never did, while dwelling on the matter of the two fugitives. He was concerned with how he would move Cormac to the nunnery. It would have to be done with his own sweat and toil, for he could think of no other way to perform the task without involving innocent people of his parish – good congregation members who he would never dare to risk in such dangerous affairs. His venture was by choice, and it would be most unfair to endanger others, who would feel compelled to help him from a sense of duty.

He wiped the plate and dish, then put them away, wanting everything in order before he went into the church. His intention was to pray before returning to the apple orchard. Perhaps God would provide some minor miracle for him before his journey. As he went to the kitchen door, he stopped and thought about the whiskey bottle in the cabinet. Should he take it? No, he shook his head – it would be of no use – even for Cormac's wound.

The cool evening refreshed him as he stepped into the garden, and brought him a small sense of relief. He walked by his flowerbed and vegetable patch, past the rickety fencing that was still in need of repair from Sean O'Sullivan's visit. That was another thing he would have to attend to. Still, it could wait a little longer. He entered the graveyard and walked briskly towards the church, entering the stone arch leading to the wooden doors. One of them was always open, in case the Cafgarven public felt the need for silent solace. He entered his church, where there was a quality of humble repose in the thin, gentle light beams slicing through the gloom – their piercing rays washed the stone aisle. Before him were two steps where a figure of the Virgin Mary looked up with hands uplifted. Behind was the altar, with a large, wooden cross and a statue of the suffering Christ.

He knelt upon the steps before the Divine Mother and crossed himself. Bowing his head, he clasped his hands. Before coming to the main reasons of his prayer, he asked God to watch over the people of the village, and then for the Lord's protection upon all people everywhere. This was something he always felt compelled to do when in silent prayer, for it seemed impolite to go straight to the foremost thing in his heart. Once upon this matter, his plea came in the form of asking God for a way – some form of strength - through which he and Sean O'Sullivan might somehow rise to the task of moving Cormac Doyle to safety.

Someone walked into the church, briefly disturbing him while in mid prayer – he raised his head slightly, but he kept his eyes firmly shut and continued. When he had finished, he whispered a quick amen and crossed himself before standing. He turned quietly, in case the person entering wanted solitude of their own, and discovered an old tinker woman. He had seen her passing through the village before, but had never spoken to her as she never came into his church. He knew her name as Freda Donavon, because on occasion, when visiting Flannigan's bar, he had heard the local men gossiping of her goodness, which had impressed him. He smiled and bowed his head respectfully, and was about to leave when to his surprise she returned his respects by nodding her head and entered the confession box. This surprised him, for he had always thought the tinker woman liked to keep to herself. Perplexed, though willing in his duty, he proceeded to the confessional to hear what the woman wished to unburden.

Going into his own compartment and sitting himself down, Father John slid back a panel to reveal a small grid through which he might hear Freda's confession. What came to his ears astonished him.

"I'm not here to say bless-me-Father-for-I-have- sinned," she said quickly and firmly. "Because, without meaning any disrespect, I go to other priests for that sort of thing. Ones that I know and trust, you see." Her manner seemed surprisingly abrupt.

Father John raised his eyebrows at the impudence of the old woman. He did not know whether to be amused or insulted. She continued before he could recover his astounded wits.

"I'm here on behalf of a young Black and Tan, who says he knows you and that you, likewise, are acquainted with him. His name is Henry Hayward. He has absconded from the barracks down the road, and reckons you can take him to a monastery. Can you help him, Father?"

Once again, the bewildered Father John's eyes widened as he drank in the news. Miracles! Divine intervention! No, surely this could not be.

But then, what else could it be? God had sent him a Black and Tan, along with a tinker, in response to his prayers. The priest's mouth gaped open as he stared into space, thinking of ways that this strange turn of events might assist him. The idea forming in his head was so outrageous that it might just have the cheek to work. Only God could have put such an ambitious idea into his head and it would be, he decided, wise to follow where his thoughts were leading him. Flukes of this nature just did not happen.

"Father John, will you not help him?" cut in the tinker woman, alarmed at the long period of silence that had followed.

"Yes, of course I will, without doubt," answered Father John to calm her. Then gently he continued: "My word, Madam, you have brought splendid news for me. Indeed, I'm sure that God must have fashioned things so. Please tell me, Madam —"

"You can call me Freda," she cut in.

"Please could you tell me, Freda, how it is that you come to be helping the young man. Where is he? Close by, I hope."

"The way he came into my company can wait for the moment, Father John. I can tell you that he is close by and I will be happy to take you to him now, if that is your wish."

"It is, Freda, and I will be happy to follow you, if you would lead the way."

He stood, opened the narrow door and left the enclosure, slowly crossing the stone floor to stop once again before the Divine Mother and the suffering Christ. He gazed intently at the large crucifix, transfixed by his absolute belief in the divine ways of his faith.

Behind him, the other door to the confessional opened and Freda walked out in respectful silence, knowing that in some way she had brought good news. The sight of Father John's placid bliss was infectious – making her feel that she was being happily led into some extraordinary adventure.

She quietly came up behind him, careful not to intrude upon his thoughts, and stopped a few feet away. She waited tolerantly, allowing him to finish his contemplation, aware that this was a small but necessary preliminary before they got on with the task at hand.

Father John turned and regarded her, a composed expression still on his face. He found that, unlike others, Freda could stare back into his eyes without the need to shy shamefully away from his tacit questioning. Her boldness brought him to the conclusion that perhaps she was a little more exceptional even than the patrons of Flannigan's bar had described.

"Will you be able to take me to him now, Freda?" he asked, a slightly anxious note in his voice.

"I will, Father John, but I would like to wait at least until dusk before you see him. I believe the people of your village might be a little too interested in your travels if you were to leave now, and seeing as the sunset is in process, it might be wise if for a short while we wait. Then I will take you, in my caravan, to meet him," she replied.

"It's not that far away is it, Freda? I must combine my help for this young man with that for some other people, whom I have promised to aid as well."

"He is not far from here, Father John. I will be glad to help you in any way I can, in both your efforts, if it means helping the young Englishman. This man has been through much and seems deserving of guidance, for I believe him to be a good person, despite the uniform he wears."

"I have great need of assistance from you, Freda. More than you could ever know. I also need Henry to help me. I am sure all of us, in this endeavour, will find it an irregular occurrence, even in these confused times we live in."

"What do you propose then, Father John?" Freda was growing suspicious.

"I am burdened with a dilemma, Freda. The other people I mentioned are two other men in distress, one of whom is wounded and whom I have to move somehow," he replied, knowing that he needed to invest a certain amount of blind trust in her. He hoped she would be able to assist him in what had to be done. He told her of the events that had occurred in Cafgarven during the previous day – the killing of the newly arrived Auxiliary Officer, the shoot-out between the Black and Tans and the Volunteers, the wounding of Cormac Doyle during the rebels' escape, and the burning of Flannigan's bar. He described Hayward's help in putting out the fire, and about his talk with the young man when the Constabulary were taking the Flannigan family, Michael Lynch and himself back to the village after their interrogation.

"I must have had more of an impact upon the young man than I realised," he concluded.

"Well, surely that was your intention when you spoke to him, Father, otherwise you would not have said such things in the first place," she retorted mildly.

"Oh, of course I hoped that I would, Freda, but in my wildest dreams I never thought I would hit home. I can't help worrying for him. It would have been better for him to have just left rather than abscond," he replied with genuine concern.

"He thinks like a soldier who has had enough of all this killing. Maybe he is frightened that his own superiors will persuade him to stay and it was easier to just turn his back rather than face his friends. Many of them might not be impressed by his decision to leave – we don't know what sort of pressures the other men might have put upon him if he tried to go about things the proper way. You, Father, have offered the young man a way out and he wants to take it," concluded Freda.

"Yes, and now I will need him to help me move the injured Volunteer to a nunnery. Do you think he will help me, Freda? It would be God's answer to my prayers if he did." He had let her know a little more about the plan he had formed in his head.

"You will need transportation to the nunnery. My caravan would be a good form of transport. I can't see why you need Henry to help you. Also, I could probably get the bullet out of the wounded man before moving him. Therefore I can't see why you will need to bring the Volunteers and Henry together. It could be like lighting the blue touch-paper." She was concerned, yet clearly becoming involved with Father John's intended venture.

"There is a little more to it than that, Freda." Father John was bubbling with enthusiasm as he shared his plan. "The two men are in a basin where your vehicle will not be able to get to them. I need two able-bodied men to carry the wounded man over the scarps. It was my intention to try and carry Cormac all the way, with me as the second able-bodied person."

"You will not be much help to the man. You're too old for such strenuous activity. Even to carry the man out of the basin. Did you think God would bless you with hidden strength now, Father?" She was showing signs of humour.

"I was rather hoping for something along those lines, or perhaps not feeling the strain till after the event. However, since Henry is here and you have some medical knowledge, we will still need him, even if you are to tend the wounded man in the basin. I assume you will want to deal with him before moving?"

"Well, it seems as though we have our work cut out for us. First, you will have to let Henry Hayward know of your plan. After all, the young man might harbour reservations about helping the Volunteers and they, in turn, most certainly will be disturbed by the arrival of a Black and Tan." Her eyebrows were raised.

"That's putting it mildly," replied Father John. "Can we not chance going to the young Black and Tan now? The time factor will be to our advantage, especially the wounded man's."

He watched as Freda, without saying another word, strolled to the chapel entrance. She peered up at the dark blue sky, determining whether the twilight was sufficient to shield them. She bit her lip as she pondered then, to the evident relief of the priest, beckoned him to follow.

He hurried after her, his blood rushing in excitement. The Lord had truly been looking down at them all, and maybe this extraordinary turn of events was His blessing.

Hayward was anxious as he waited in the woods. This was, after all, bandit country, where the rebels felt more at ease travelling during the night. The Volunteers were few in number and sparsely spread throughout this part of the land. This was the only place in which he had come up against them since he had arrived in

Ireland. What if they were to stumble across him now in the confines of the wood, far from the barracks and on his own? He shuddered at the thought, knowing that they would kill him without mercy. It had been rumoured that the death of a Black and Tan could bring the executioner fifty pounds in prize money – a tidy sum for desperate Fenians, who would also be grateful for the publicity of such an important kill.

The darkness had begun to affect him, as he waited amid the rustling trees and the distant insects. His ears strained for the sound of unfamiliar things, such as footsteps upon twigs, that would warn him of any approaching person. There were none! But it brought him no respite, because he knew Fenians would be experienced in the ways of stealth. Like all who fear a hidden enemy, his mind began to attribute the Volunteer rebels with more proficiency then they perhaps possessed.

His heart leapt as the sound of horse's hooves floated upon the night air. It filled him with relief, as he knew that it could be none other than Freda. He crawled from his place of concealment. The clop, clop, clop of horse's hooves drew closer as he advanced out of the wood looking for a glimpse of the caravan. He peered into the gloom and saw a dim light appear out of the blackness. From his daytime recollection of the lane bending into the wood he was able spot the light when it suddenly appeared. Logic began to return to his troubled mind, filling him with comfort as the recent paranoia began to subside.

The caravan drew nearer, and he could make out Freda's form in the dim light. If the priest was with her, he must be concealed in the back of the vehicle as *he* had been during his daytime travels. He held up his arm, the rifle still firmly gripped in his hand, and waved at the approaching vehicle, assuming that she was be able to see him. Suddenly the horse veered towards his position and he knew Freda had spotted him. He retreated into the trees, attentive to the fact that she would want to be well inside the welcome darkness of the woods before stopping the caravan. As the vehicle passed, Hayward fell in beside the wagon and looked up at the tinker earnestly. She gave him a quick glance. He held a thumb up, questioning if everything was all right. She smiled and nodded, to his relief. Things were beginning to happen. He felt that he was getting somewhere at last. Maybe the years of unrest were over. His trepidation during the trench war with its persistent slaughter, then the demoralisation of being unemployed, had made him feel he was living a wasted life. Now, by chance, he had reached out and grabbed at an opportunity that had come his way, in a land where people found it hard to come by a living. The country's biggest export was its migrating people, who seemed to live everywhere in the world.

"Did you manage to contact Father John?" asked Hayward, unable to see any light coming from within the caravan.

The door of the carriage opened, and Father John stepped on to the footrest, beaming at the sight of Hayward before him. The kindly, old priest jumped nimbly from the caravan, which was still in motion. The action caused Hayward to jump forward to assist the priest, fearing he might tumble.

Father John was equal to this small exertion, stopping Hayward with his uplifted hand and beaming with a delighted smile. "How are you, Henry? I can't tell you how overjoyed I am to see you here. Though I must say you went about it in a rather haphazard manner, from what Freda tells me. Why did you abscond, when there was no need too?" he asked coming forward to shake Hayward's hand.

"It was two reasons, Father John – one because I did not want to be transported back to England. The other was a little more cowardly, I admit. I was worried that some of the other lads would feel let down by my actions. Well, in truth, I did not want to have to look at their faces and answer to them. Bad I know, but you must realise how difficult it is," Hayward added solemnly.

"I understand the way you must feel, Henry." Father John showed sympathy. Freda came down from her seat at the front of the caravan and joined them. She regarded Father John with a raised eyebrow, as though there was some annoyance contained within her scrutiny. Then her gaze rested upon Hayward and her look softened into one of compassion. She had developed an obvious fondness for the young Englishman, which was fuelled by a determination that he should find the solace he wanted after his years of bitter fighting.

"I will light the lantern inside the caravan, then the pair of you will have light during the journey," she said, with another impatient glance at Father John.

Before leaving aboard the caravan on the ride back from Cafgarven, Father John had described to Freda the basin, where the two Volunteers were hiding, as being an apple orchard. It was a place she knew well, as she was familiar with all the wooded clusters in the area. She told Father John about the tree clusters around the external rim of the basin, and was also in agreement that help would be needed to move the sick man over the scarps. However, she had extreme reservations about using Hayward. What would be the reaction between him and this able-bodied Sean O'Sullivan? After all, both were capable of killing, and each had a weapon.

Father John had assured her that he would inform both men before they met, in order that no unpleasantness might occur. In Freda's opinion, Father John should inform Hayward of the circumstances as soon as possible!

"While I am seeing to the lantern," she said anxiously, "you must inform Henry of our intentions, Father John. He must be in agreement with you."

"All right, Freda, I will let Henry know of my plan, but I do need to talk to him uninterrupted please." Father John had to word his proposition in the best way possible, free from Freda's pessimism.

"That's why I will be putting on the lantern," she retorted mildly.

Father John looked to Hayward, setting his chin firmly down in his chest as if he about to belch the words. It was obvious to the Tan that the priest was attempting to put his thoughts across in the right way.

He frowned – maybe Father John was unable to help him now. He looked with concern to the priest and was caught by the return of the man's intense stare that drilled into him. The look, however, was not so much soul-searching as encouraging.

"Is there anything wrong, Father John? You're unsettled because I absconded, aren't you?" came Henry's response.

Father John grinned, amused by the Tan's assumption. He shook his head and put his arm around the young man's shoulder.

"Henry, I can and will help you. You are still considering contemplation in a monastery, aren't you now?" asked Father John.

"Yes, Father, I am, which is why I have come to you," he replied.

"Well, I also desperately need a favour from you. I need help to move a sick man, and you will also have the help of another man, very much like yourself, who I want to take to the monastery too."

"One of these men is to go to the monastery and the sick man to hospital?" enquired Hayward.

"Yes," Father John said.

"Is the sick man a wounded Volunteer?" A tone of foreboding was apparent in Hayward's voice.

"Yes, Henry, he is, and as a man of God I am bound by my oath to help all who come to me. I am now therefore pledged to help you, a Black and Tan, and these two men, who are Volunteers. The man who will go to the monastery with you is bound by his oath to me. You have left the Crown forces, and the sick man is in no fit state to do anything. I see no reason why you should need to fight each other. Let the killing come to an end for all three of you. I have to move the sick man to a nunnery, where he can get medical treatment and convalescence. I also need Freda, because she will be able to administer some treatment and move the man in her caravan." He stopped and looked at Henry, waiting for a response.

"How do I know whether to trust the two men? Won't they be likely to panic at the sight of me and get a bit trigger-happy?" Hayward asked nervously.

"I give you my word that none of them will harm you, and I will give them the same promise that you will not harm them. Can I do that?" Father John seemed most anxious.

Hayward gritted his teeth in despair and looked to the caravan, where a dim light was coming through the window. He was worried at the daunting prospect of coming face-to-face with the Volunteers. Most Tans that did so were executed, unless they were able to fire first. " H o w bad is the man? I presume he is the one that my troop got during the shoot-out yesterday."

"He is bad – the bullet is lodged in his shoulder," explained Father John. "And yes, he is the man who was hit in yesterday's engagement.

"Freda will know how to get the bullet out. I suppose that is why she is anxious to be moving." Henry was talking himself into the plan. Father John frowned – he was puzzled at the young man's belief in Freda's medical ability. She also seemed convinced, too, that she would be able to remove the bullet by her own hand.

"What makes you and Freda so sure that the bullet can be removed before getting to the nunnery?" he demanded.

"Freda has great knowledge of medicine. She has even written a book that contains methods for treating bullet wounds in various parts of the anatomy. Even in places where the injury is fatal. You know – how to relieve pain and bring comfort, all that sort of thing. She is a very remarkable person, Father John. I'll show you her book when we are on the move."

"How extraordinary," whispered Father John, thinking that the good Lord had really sent the right people for his quest – chance alone could not work in such inexplicable ways. It was nothing short of divine intervention, and his heart swelled with devotion for the task at hand – believing that the coming together of this odd assortment of individuals could solve all the problems. All were unique, and very special.

Freda emerged from the caravan, pausing for a few moments while her eyes adapted to the darkness. She squinted as Henry walked forward.

"Oh, so there you are. Has Father John told you of the circumstances, Henry?" she asked.

"He has, Freda."

"I can't help feeling a little dubious. Do you too?" she inquired.

"I do, but we have to take the odd chance now and then, so I've decided to go with Father John's plan."

Freda smiled, happy that the young man was still ready to go along with Father John. The whole day had been very bizarre indeed for her, with a further adventure still ahead. Deep down, she was pleased to go on this pursuit, feeling that it was a most Christian and good thing to do. She climbed down from the caravan and went to the front of the vehicle, seeing Father John standing alone in the gloom. His face was radiant. He was lost in his contemplation of God's wondrous ways.

"All aboard now, Father John, a sick man is relying upon our help," she interrupted him, with a sense of urgency.

Father John sprang from his Heavenly deliberation, and apologised embarrassedly.

"Are you sure that you don't want me to sit with you, Freda? You may need some help travelling in the night," he offered kindly.

"Father John, Moogsly and I are not unused to the demands of night-time travelling. We have done this hundreds of times, even in sleet and snow," she called back, with a firmness that let him know there was no cause to worry about her.

He smiled and held up a hand in recognition of her capability, before climbing aboard and shutting the door behind him.

Hayward was already sitting upon the bed, with Freda's book in his hand. "You really must look at this, Father John," he said excitedly.

FOURTEEN

Waiting in the Basin.

The day had been long and hot, which was difficult for Cormac – broken in body and shattered from his throbbing wound, with a pulsating ache of such intensity it would not allow him to settle. Sometimes he groaned, when the pain reached its peak, so that Sean would become concerned and frustrated by his own helplessness to do anything except talk.

"Father John will be here soon, Cormac. Try and hold on, there's a good lad."

Both had been full of apprehension during the daylight hours, fearing the Crown forces might suddenly appear upon the surrounding scarps, but misfortune did not come in such attire and the welcome night brought relief – a dark veil that soothed their anxiety

Cormac looked across to Sean, who was sitting against an apple tree. "You seem to place much faith in this priest. Are you sure he'll return?" he grumbled.

"I do, and I'm sure he'll have some food."

"Hunger is not the immediate problem. We've only just run out."

"I know." Sean looked up at the stars before continuing: "Our main anxiety is your condition, even though you've proved tougher than expected."

Cormac smiled and snorted with embarrassment in the dark, where the frogs and insects contributed their natural sounds. He whispered: "More hours for the dust of the shooting incident to settle – the Tans will start to assume that we have been able to disperse. Searches are likely to cease, giving us a chance to move to a place of more safety."

Sean nodded his agreement and thought of Father John. "I wonder how long it will be before the priest gets here. I hope he was able to remember the way back." He fell silent, considering that it would mean as Cormac's dilemma got worse. Again, he looked to the stars, twinkling magically in the black sky, and scolded himself for such a cynical outlook. Father John, after all, was a man of strong, moral convictions, who would dedicate himself to any task. When the priest made his promise, after having failed to remove the bullet, Sean was sure they would not be forsaken. In that moment a guarantee was made – a promise, and a belief within. It was also a resurrection of his faith – a deep belief that a priest would never pledge what he could not do. He, in return, would stick to his vow, forsaking the violent contribution of his struggle against the British, while Father John devoted himself to saving his friend.

Cormac coughed, blighting the natural sounds of the night, and Sean was filled with pity for him. "God bring us salvation." He cursed into the blackness as he stood to walk over to the compost box, which Cormac was sitting against, sweating with fever.

"You'll make it, Cormac?"

"Yes." He smiled. "Something will turn up. I know it."

"Has the pain lessened any?"

"It's the same, no worse. When Father John returns, like I think he is going to, it will be then that I will be howling – especially if he tries to dig the bullet out again."

Sean raised his eyebrows sympathetically. "All right then, let's hope he has a better plan this time."

"I do, with all my heart," Cormac humorously replied.

"You're a fine spirited man. I've always known that. 'Sean,' I says to myself: 'There goes the making of a very sharp fellow indeed.'"

"Good grief, thank God I'm not a woman. I think I'd have lost me bloody drawers by now. My word, you could charm the knickers off a nun."

Both laughed their mood light for the moment despite their circumstances. Sean bubbled with pleasure; his friend was chuckling. "Well, here we are, in dire straits, yet able to perk up one another's spirits by laughing at ourselves."

Then Cormac fell sideways and heavily against the dry ground and he yelped in pain. Sean was aghast as he watched Cormac roll about on the grass in the faint starlight, groaning as well as laughing.

"Are you all right?"

Finally Cormac lay still, panting. "I'm all right – just allowing the pain to subside." His eyes were shut as contentment began to fill his troubled face

"Well, you don't like doing things in half measures," mocked Sean humorously as Cormac gingerly raised himself into a sitting position, wincing as he did, yet able to bear the stabbing pains. Edging backwards, he rested against the box.

"I seem to take short cuts, though not through choice."

Sean sat down next to him and looked up into the night, where stars twinkled with a glory that made him feel inconsequential within the nature of all things. "Mental horizons broaden when you look at those," he muttered.

"Oh, I agree. Destroys that small lens we see life through, when we can drink in such immense expanses of universe."

Sean became indignant. "I'm trying to be serious. We've eternity in our vision."

"I know, and I'm very pleased for us."

Sean grinned. "You know Cormac, no one loves a smart-arse – I was just thinking, that's all."

"Well, I feel as though you're about to hit me with something big and metaphysical, and I'm in total suspense."

Sean smiled mischievously. "It certainly boggles the mind, and it's a rum little ditty, if an educated person like yourself, who has been to college and all, would care to hear it."

"Well you're looking up, mesmerised and all, so I think you should unburden yourself."

"You're beginning to sound like Father John."

"Heavens above, no! Or maybe yes. Well, seeing as we're now back on the subject, let's be hearing the ditty that's bursting to escape from your laughing gear."

Sean smiled before speaking. "Well, up there," he pointed to the heavens. "We're staring at eternity, all that there is, something endless that goes on forever, aren't we?"

"Yeah, I suppose you could say that," Cormac replied.

"And on the other side of the planet there is even more endless forever."

"Yeah, so what are you saying?"

"Well, if I am staring at everything, eternity and all, why can't I see the other everything, the eternity on the other side of the world?"

Cormac tried to contain his laughter. Sean's attempt to be philosophical he found comical, and he desperately wanted to laugh. An explosion of mucus splattered upon his hand as he began to giggle.

"Well," continued Sean, holding his outstretched hand to the stars, like a man who fancied himself as a classical actor. "If that's everything, what's the other shit behind us? That's what I want to know."

"That up there, what you are gesticulating at, is only a bit of everything." Cormac was convulsed between laughter and pain. "For the love of God, Sean, lay off, I can't handle this." He began to giggle hysterically.

"So I'm not looking at eternity and everything. Shit, and there's me, thinking I'm broadening me horizons and all. Then *you* tell me it's only a bit of things. I might as well satisfy myself with the world I live in, the circumstances we get embroiled in, because they are a bit of everything too, aren't they?"

Sean affected to be considering this deeply.

"The British Empire covers all parts of the globe, so theoretically they can see everything," added Cormac as an afterthought. "They always seem to get the best of things. Why do you think God allowed them to have an Empire where the sun never sets?"

"Because He doesn't trust the bastards in the dark."

Cormac started to giggle again. "You have an answer for everything."

Joy, fear, hope and defeat, all were emanating from Sean. Cormac reasoned such things were there in everyone, though not everyone had such a gift of appearing unwittingly to display such manifestation that decorated Sean's optimism with comedy. Perhaps only certain people would see how colourful this murderer was.

"You know, when I was at college I read a lot of books, and there were scientists who believed space has boundaries, that eternity is a myth," said Cormac, getting back to the original line of their talking and trying to gain Sean's interest.

"No, I can't believe scientists would write such a thing." Sean dismissed the notion.

"It's true – an eminent scientist wrote some sort of thesis on the subject, not in my line of study I grant but it did tickle my interest when another student gave me the paper. Just something to read, you see." Cormac licked his lips; enthusiasm began to grab him. He was about to continue when Sean, unable to resist interrupting, hit back with irony.

"The sort of light-hearted reading that most people occupy themselves with then"

"Aha, no, you've got to stop this." He went into another fit of laughter, and amid chuckles he attempted to continue his account of the theory he had read. "Honestly, this man reckoned space had boundaries." He then went to some effort to get a stick and sketch a big circle in a worn patch of soil, pointing with the stick inside the circle and saying triumphantly. "That in there is eternity, according to this scientist's theory on physics. Imagine it as a bubble and you are inside it. That is, what he believes is the universal boundaries —" "Tut, I never did hear such a load of shenanigans in all of my life. Is that the sort of thing eminent scientists waste their time upon? My word, it's no wonder we live in such a haphazard world. You don't believe such things do you?"

"I don't know, it's only a theory," Cormac light-heartedly replied.

"Well it stinks, even I could tell that scientist that things go on and on, there are no boundaries. What's outside the bloody bubble, eh? When they find the bubble wall, they'll want to look beyond it. There has to be a 'beyond the bubble wall'."

Again Cormac laughed, overjoyed at the simplistic ease of Sean's uneducated, yet logical, argument.

"I've just turned that poor scientist into a mouse with his foolish theories," added Sean.

Cormac smiled, saying "Then I think he'll be slinging himself on the mouse trap if you ever walk through his front door."

They prattled on, happy for the time with their lot, content with each other's company and hopeful of salvation in the welcome form of

Father John. Their joyful banter allowed a few hours of pleasure to slip easily past.

It was gone midnight when they finally fell silent and listened to the continuous sound of the nightlife laying claim to the dark. Amid the familiar sounds, a breaking twig snapped in the night – an alien and unexpected sound, which caused the commotion of night to briefly cease, and both men to sit bolt upright.

"Did you hear that?" Sean stood with his rifle at the ready and crept to the base of one of the apple trees, waving his hand behind him. "Hide on the other side of the container," he whispered, while trying to peer beyond the murky tree-clustered darkness. A movement. His heart leapt – someone was coming towards him, between the dim apple trees. Fear swelled in his chest, his teeth chattered and adrenaline pumped into his head. He gritted his teeth in desperation, fighting the fear, keeping it under control. Looking back, he could see Cormac, terror etched in his lined face, eyes wide with apprehension. The young man had retrieved his rifle from within the apple container, and was ready, if somewhat awkwardly, to fire at the approaching figure. The look of dread alerted Sean to the fact that his companion might be trigger-happy. He held up his hand with a severe look.

"Cormac," he hissed. "Hold your fire, lad. It's probably Father John."

Cormac composed himself enough to conquer his nerves, restraining from firing, allowing the distant spectre to come closer. Welcome relief stroked him with an invisible hand, soothing the mounting tension – destroying a yearning to pull the trigger.

Father John came into view, with a beaming smile causing his teeth to gleam in the night.

Sean stood, clearly relieved by Father John's appearance. "Thank God. I'm so pleased to see you."

"And I you – I have splendid news that will bring relief to young Cormac." Father John was distinctly bursting with excitement, as though he wished to fill his lungs with air before launching into a verbal flood of good tidings.

"Well, Father John, I'm grateful beyond words. What is it we're to do?" asked Sean.

"Back at the scarps I have a tinker woman, Freda, with a caravan for transportation. She is also knowledgeable on medicine and is most positive that she can extract the bullet inform Cormac's shoulder. I also have the help of another man, who like yourself has renounced violence. He is going to help us to carry Cormac over the slopes to the woods, where the Freda has her vehicle and horse concealed." He stopped and watched Sean intently, alerting him that there was perhaps more to the plan.

"How did you come by another man who has given you the same promise as me? Is this man a Volunteer? Where did you come across such a person, Father John?" Concern was marked on Sean's forehead.

"Yes, he's a Volunteer, in answer to one of your questions, and like yourself he's been involved in the Cafgarven incident. Disturbing things happened for many in the village that day, which caused this particular man to reflect upon his actions."

"Daniel Nelson has come to you too?" Sean was surprised and assumed it to be the other young man of their depleted group.

"I have never heard of the man to whom you refer."

Sean cursed his foolish and impetuous assumption – he had unwittingly given the name of one of his accomplices. Fortunately the priest was bound by oath, unable to disclose such information. Frowning, he looked into the priest's eyes and was snared by the consistent intensity of the man's scrutiny.

Father John continued. "He's one of the Volunteers of the supplementary police attached to the R.I.C. – a Black and Tan, as you like to refer to them. This particular man has absconded from his troop for reasons I cannot divulge. I'm taking him to a monastery, where the man will hopefully find his inner self. England has nothing to offer him, and he is sick of the fighting, more from the effects of France and its trenches than here. He can aid us when we move Cormac to the caravan, then he'll stay here with you, while the Freda and I continue to the nunnery."

"You can't mean that, Father John, in heavens name; tell me you're kidding, please..." His voice faded as he realised the priest was not moved by his protestation. "Good God, you're serious, aren't you. How do you know he is genuine? You can't trust him – it might be a ploy —"

"Sean, Sean. Please, I give you my word. The young man is all he claims to be, and you are bound by your promise to me. I have a vow from this person as well. Therefore both of you are removed from the contest, by your oaths to renounce violence. Now I would like you to meet him, or would you prefer me to bring him to you?"

Sean, open-mouthed and disbelieving, could not digest what had been said. "Your words are hammering upon my skull but I can't make sense of them."

"Your past convictions are making you reject them now, but you will come to them. This is no joke – what I am telling you is true."

Realisation dawned, and Sean was forced to accept – they were to be rescued from their plight with the help of a disaffected Black and Tan.

"Lead me to this man, Father John," he said, his face finally resolved.

"Promise me you will not shoot. He won't, and anyway Freda has put his gun inside the caravan. He'll be standing several feet in front of the vehicle, so that you can see he is unarmed." Father John was hoping to gain the same concession from Sean. He felt it to be inappropriate to ask directly, but his desire was conveyed in his expression.

Sean turned away with a sigh and a curse. Reluctantly, he laid his rifle upon the ground.

"Christ, I hope you know what you're doing. Show me the way." His nostrils had flared. Confusion and anger were contending on his face.

Father John led, going back the way he had come, increasingly anxious as they progressed towards the end of the orchard where the slope climbed upwards.

Sean had second thoughts about leaving his rifle back in the apple orchard, and he was fighting an inner battle to contain his rising doubts. His instinct was to run back and get Cormac. Maybe they should try to go it alone. Of course they would not get far, and if the Tan were not genuine, he would be able to pursue and catch them with ease. He tried to apply logic to the situation: a Black and Tan would have to be extremely brave to venture on such a mission of deception alone, in his uniform. Gradually reason began to overcome his trepidation, though only just.

They gained the summit and started their descent towards the wood, where the trees were much taller. Above them, silhouettes of branches and leaves partially masked the star-filled sky, while ahead a fire radiated. Its beckoning light flickered from within the wood.

Father John smiled. "We're here, Sean. There's nothing to fear, trust me."

As they entered the clearing, the fire was burning brightly, and Sean set eyes upon the Black and Tan, who was gathering twigs and branches for the fire around the edge of the area. Having looked once at Sean, he turned away to continue with his fuel collecting. Sean noticed the man seemed unnerved, as though Father John and this strange, tinker woman had subdued him.

Anxious for the two men to resolve their differences, Father John wasted no time in bringing them together. "Henry, would you come over here please?" he asked, wearing his diplomatic smile for the occasion.

Hayward obeyed, putting the wood down beside Freda, then walking to him. He hesitated momentarily and looked back to Freda for some form of guidance. She smiled reassuringly, and he seemed to trust her completely.

Sean scrutinised the young Englishman, with his dark-green cap pushed to the back of his head so that the peak pointed up casually. It made him look roguish. The man's aspect was that of a bohemian, an outcast – unable to conform, yet receptive to some of those who welcomed such non-conformity. He wore a worried frown when he returned Sean's scrutiny.

"Come on now, I know the both of you for the men you really are. You'll have to learn to get along with one another," said Father John, noting the hesitation. Henry stood beside him, eyes still fixed upon Sean. His anxiety seemed to subside – which made Sean feel more relaxed.

"Right Sean, this is Henry Hayward. Like yourself, an ex-British soldier, who is tired of fighting and is searching for something different. He is bound by a promise not to kill, as you are."

Father John then turned to Henry and began. "This man is Sean O'Sullivan. He is one of the opposing side, and was present at the Cafgarven ambush – a foul act, in my view, in which both sides showed their complete disregard for the innocent people of my village. With Sean is a young man called Cormac Doyle. He is injured, and is in the basin on the other side of the hill. I want Sean and you to go back into the apple orchard and bring him back here. Then Freda can extract the bullet. We will then put him aboard the caravan, and take him to sanctuary and then out of the country, hopefully Canada, where he has expressed a desire to emigrate. I'll return for the both of you and we'll decide what to do next at that point. Henry will be going to a monastery for a time, to convalesce. Maybe you would consider doing the same thing, Sean?" He looked to them, waiting for one to say something.

Accepting that one of them should make the first move, Sean finally ventured to speak. "Well Father John, do you want Henry and myself to get Cormac? I take it you'll come with us?"

"I trust the pair of you to work together on this quest, Sean. You'll be back in a very short time," replied Father John.

"Yes, Father, I'm sure that Henry and I can do this alone, but Cormac is back at the apple box with a gun. Suppose he panics at the sight of Henry, before he finds out he's with me. The lad's quite likely to start blazing away —"

"I'll take off the jacket and the cap," Henry cut in, trying to conceal the fact that the dialogue was not exactly building his confidence. "When we near his position, I'll stop a little way off and wait for your signal to come forward. That way you'll have time to let him know what has been arranged."

Sean turned, and for first time talked directly to him rather than through Father John: "All right then, Henry, we'll do it that way."

Quickly, Henry unbuckled his belt, pulled off his jacket and R.I.C. cap, then stood in his dirty vest. Only his khaki constabulary trousers remained of his uniform, so that there was nothing to identify him as a Tan.

"I bet those things aren't regulation issue?" Sean joked, nodding his head at the grubby, old braces.

"No, they're not," replied Henry with an amused smile. "These things are a bit more comfortable."

Together, they left the surroundings of the campfire, making off up the wooded scarp to descend back into the basin, while Father John and Freda set about preparing for the arrival of Cormac.

For a while, Freda sat in front of the fire mixing and crushing herbs in some wooden bowls. A big pot of water was in front of her, from which she took two strange-looking metal implements. These she placed in the flames, allowing them to heat until they began to glow.

"Do you think it's a wise thing to do, Father John? Throwing them in at the deep end an' all?" she asked quietly, still engrossed in her chore.

"Yes, Freda, I think it is." He sat on a tree stump beside her. "But you have your doubts, don't you?"

She shook her head. "No, no – not at all, Father John, I think it's quite ingenious. Only I wouldn't have thought so until I saw the pair of them amble away together. You had this planned from when I told you at the church, didn't you?"

"You came in when I was asking God to provide a way for me. Everything is being made up as I go along. Things seem to be falling into place, and ideas come up as obstacles arise. It's as though a path of destiny is laid out for us to follow. We will succeed, Freda. We have to, or there'll be no meaning to it all." Father John's optimism fuelled him.

"Everything has a meaning, Father. Sometimes, however, the meaning is not what we might expect. I believe you're doing the right thing, and there's purpose behind all your actions. Though I don't think the outcome will be as you expect. There will be achievements, but also tragedy – I can sense it."

"What makes you say that, Freda? Is it your belief that there might be another purpose to our enterprise? One we're unaware of?"

"Yes, Father, I have the strangest of feelings that Henry and Sean will walk different paths and achieve something beyond your aspirations, but there'll be a penalty to pay – there always is." she spoke like a true Romany, guided by her peoples' tradition.

"I never did hear such strange, gypsy superstitions," countered Father John, trying to play down such talk. "I'm surprised at you, Freda."

"Oh no, Father John." She would not be rebuffed by his light rebuke. "Don't be trying to patronise me now, like you might do with your congregation. I'm not about to be lulled. I've seen much in my time, and sometimes you get a gut feeling about things. You can't say why, you just do. Right now, I have such feelings. The wounded man will be our responsibility, and I think we'll be able to help him. After all, that was your pledge, was it not, Father John? The very promise you made to Sean."

"It was," he patiently replied.

"Well, somehow, leaving the two alone in the basin might be something else that is intended all along. Letting them find some sort of solution by themselves, without your aid. This seems fitting to me, and that is why I find the idea of sending them off alone a good idea. Leave them alone together in the basin until they decide what they have to do. Sometimes you can want too much, Father. Lots of things go right, and you can push just a little too far, take more than is offered."

"I'm sure that I don't know what you mean, Freda. In my heart I believe that the Lord has planted this vine of events – woven this destiny for us to follow. You came with this young Englishman, whom I had been trying to reach, the Volunteer coming to me and making his promise – it all falls into place. How can I doubt what has happened?" he protested earnestly.

Freda looked vexed. "I don't doubt this to be the Lord's work, though I mistrust your interpretation of events, and what your role may be in them. Has it not struck you that maybe, just maybe, you're as much a minor instrument in things as what you regard me, turning up at your hour of need, when you were praying in the church? The story seems to be revolving around you and some sort of moral quest. The wounded man is our project at the moment, and I just have this strange feeling that the other two have a path of their own to follow. The Lord might have a different plan for them, one that does not involve us. We should leave them in the basin to discover things about one another by themselves. You might spoil it by pushing the matter too much. Maybe bite off more than you could chew."

Father John looked into the fire, pondering her words. Could it be that he was being egotistical about his part in all this? With hindsight, perhaps he *was* thinking of the people around him being pawns, while he was the central character.

"You might be right. I will keep that in mind while we're on the road to the nunnery."

Freda smiled at him: "Leaving two little goblins, patiently waiting —"

"In a makeshift Purgatory," cut in Father John. "They will be living in anguish until I return."

"I think they might be able to get along and decide for themselves what to do," she countered.

"It would be delightful if they could, but I still think I should return to help them. However, I will give the matter much thought."

"It's dangerous to think you're more chosen for a divine purpose than the rest of us that are involved," chastised Freda mildly.

Cut by this rebuke, he was about to respond, but was then caught by her questioning stare – a scrutiny that was as searching as his own. She had a particular look that was every bit as challenging – something he found extremely awkward, not at all what he was used to. He baulked at coming to terms with the moral conflict she had stirred within him. Henry and Sean would be left alone while he was helping Cormac, thus leaving two former enemies together in the confines of the apple orchard. They would be there at least two days and nights before he could return to them and pursue the next course of action. In that time they might build a bond together and decide what to do without his help. He sighed, shaking his head and weary at the thought of 'beyond the nunnery'.

"Save it for the journey," said Freda, reading him well. "You will have a great deal of time to ponder the matter. Meanwhile, I will need your help with the wounded one – he'll be here shortly."

He nodded and looked into the brightness of the firelight flickering against the leafy ceiling. Beyond, in the tree-clustered darkness, the wildlife proclaimed its rightful presence as though protesting at the lit clearing.

FIFTEEN

Help for Cormac.

As Sean and Hayward descended the slope into the apple orchard, the Volunteer was struck by an urge to converse with the Englishman, remembering how he had felt a short time ago while following Father John to meet him.

"When we near the area, I will tell you to hold back. My friend has a gun, as I said. I'll need to take it. Then I'll tell him about you. The lad is bound to panic. After all, who wouldn't? If you can come as soon as I call, then we can settle his fears quickly." He was looking for some rapport with the Tan.

A little taken aback by the matter- of- fact way the situation was put to him, Hayward responded in his reserved English way when presented with something bizarre.

"Right ho, will do."

"Good," whispered Sean with a smile, impressed, by this apparent lack of concern. "God, you bastards are bloody tasty, I'll give you that," he added.

Henry, confused by this, frowned as he tried to discern the meaning of this odd remark. The two men moved forward cautiously amid the vibrant clamour of frogs and the rustling trees, negotiating the littered apples that could bring a man down with a thump if caution was not maintained. The star-filled sky twinkled with splendour. After a short distance, Sean held up his hand and they stopped. Satisfied the Tan had understood, he moved forward alone calling Cormac's name while advancing into the blackness. A faint reply floated back across the orchard. For what seemed a long time, there was silence. Then came the sound of a voice, full of panic, imploring and earnest.

"Henry, it's all right, you can come now."

Hayward's stomach muscles tightened and his nostrils flared as he gulped back dread. A murky tide in the blackness of night swept through him. What if the Volunteers were playing a trick? He could be walking out into a ready-made firing squad. There was a fifty-pound bounty for a dead Tan and these men had already claimed one. His reflex, something instilled from the trenches, forced him to advance, the way he had done against the German guns, where fear of not fronting the enemy was, in some bizarre way, greater than facing his fire. His highly strung imagination plaguing his mind, he propelled himself forward against a screaming assault of dead comrade's voices – warning him, cursing, imploring desperately as he moved through the trees. He willed himself on from a small alcove of conviction, somewhere within the innermost recesses of his rational mind. Once into the clearing, he could see Sean trying to calm the wounded man, who was sitting against a wooden compost box.

In panic Cormac pushed his sitting form back against the outer wall of the wooden box, pathetically, as though he could be swallowed by it.

"Cormac, please believe me." Sean appealed. "He's with Father John. It's strange, I know, but as far as being a Tan goes, he's not very good at it – ain't that right now, Henry?" He tried to calm the wounded man with a little humour.

"Yes, I'm out of a job on account of it all," replied Henry going with Sean's mode of things.

Cormac was dumbstruck! What in all of Heaven was happening? His friend had come out of the trees, cheerily telling him that he had acquired the help of a Black and Tan. Then, surprise of surprises, one such rascal had just walked out of the night, large as life, joking. He began to think that his logic had been influenced by some sort of delirium, that he was hallucinating and definitely in need of attention. But he also realised that Tans did not walk about in braces and vests.

"Where's your hat and jacket then, eh?" he giggled. "And your gun? My God, you're the sorriest looking Tan that I ever did see. I know that the British government was a bit light on police uniforms but that's taking things to extreme." He erupted with maniacal laughter, uncontrollable and increasing.

Henry turned to Sean, aware the man's mind was affected by his injury.

"Well, I don't know about you, Henry, but I didn't think it was that funny." Sean wore a serious look, wickedly contrasted by a naughty twinkle in his bright eyes.

"I think it's the sporting line in R.I.C. underwear that might have done the trick," suggested Henry cheekily.

"Why indeed, I didn't think of that. There's me now, gearing the poor sod up for the fright of his life, and all he gets is a man in his underwear."

Together they looked down at Cormac who was still laughing in short little bursts. Gradually he calmed down enough to observe them.

"Come on, Cormac, were going to take you to a kindly old tinker woman who is going to make you better." Sean bent down to gently lever him up. "Give us a hand here, Henry, will you please?"

The request got a positive response, as Henry bent down and carefully but firmly placed his arm around the small of Cormac's back, while Sean held him beneath the armpit. Gently they lifted. As they stood, Henry noted that Cormac's rifle was discarded upon the ground. The act enhanced the growing trust that was developing between himself and Sean as they struggled forward, through the woods, back towards the scarp that led out of the basin. Cormac flinched with pain as he was carefully carried over the apple-littered ground. Their progress was faster than expected, and although Cormac could walk with assistance, it was clear that he suffered less when carried.

At the scarp, Henry and Sean found the task more tiring, and by the time they reached the summit, their muscles were beginning to ache. However, they became revitalised when seeing the rest of the journey was all downhill, towards the distant glow of Freda's campfire, which shimmered through the wood – a pulsating brightness battling through the dark trees.

"There's your help, Cormac. Not long now me, boy," said Sean.

They watched, as Cormac peered at the distant crown of light and allowed a beaming smile to slice his face. He was obviously filled with joy at the beckoning sight. Relief began to reduce his anxiety. He looked up to the heavens and closed his eyes with a gaze of ecstasy, letting the exultation flow as hope became an ever-growing bubble in the pit of his stomach – engulfing his despondency. It undulated like an applauding crowd, joyous of salvation.

"I've always imagined my essence was in my head. But now I'm aware of myself from the pit of my abdomen to my chest," he laughed, reflecting on how precious his life was, and how remarkable the world he existed in.

Hayward was gladdened by Cormac's joy. He was privately pleased by the man's turn of fortune, for he was sure nothing would go wrong on the journey to the nunnery. He had great faith that Freda could aid the wounded man, firmly convinced of her exceptional abilities. Added to that was the ever-resourceful Father John's will, which, he was beginning to believe, could move mountains if put to the test.

Their descent was quick and easy, for the radiance of the campfire had a strong lure that fed the eagerness of all three. Once into the wood, the final stretch took no time at all. They burst into the clearing.

"We've got him," yelled Hayward.

Freda jumped to the task straight away. "Could you take him inside?" She pointed to the door of the vehicle, which was open. The men eased Cormac in, carefully so as not to knock him against the doorjambs.

"Right, I would like all of you to wait out here by the campfire," said Freda as she followed. She turned to Father John who had accompanied her. "You too, Father, if you please."

"Do you not want me to help hold the man down? The other two lads will be needed as well, surely." He seemed disappointed.

"I don't need any of you men in here, and this young man," she pointed at Cormac, who lay upon the bed. "He will feel little pain or discomfort. I have made a sleeping potion. He may feel groggy in the morning, but that will soon wear off."

"Oh." Father John's response was feeble.

"Well, Father," interrupted Sean, happy in the knowledge that he was not required to assist, and that Cormac would not scream the cabin down. "I'm sure the lady knows what she's doing, don't you, Henry?"

"Er... yes, I do," he spluttered, coaxed into supporting the impudent Shinner.

They walked out towards the campfire, Father John feeling most put out by the tinker's request. "Are you sure that I can't lend any assistance to you, Freda?"

"You can bring me those iron implements from the fire, and the bowl of water. Then you can close the door and sit with Henry and Mister O'Sullivan," she replied.

Hayward was about to do this but Father John persisted: "If you please, Henry, I would like to do this."

Sean looked back to Freda, who was standing at the caravan door. "You can call me Sean, lady," he invited mischievously.

"Can I, Mister O'Sullivan," she retorted sternly with a raised eyebrow.

Sean, pierced by her look, decided he would sooner endure Father John's soul-searching scrutiny. He sighed, looking at Hayward. "Best I keep out of the old biddy's way and not cross her."

"It appears she's not appreciative of your vibrant wit," agreed Father John, as he gathered the bowl containing the heated implements from the fire. He went back to the caravan and passed them up to the old woman, who turned and shut the door, leaving him standing like a disgruntled schoolboy missing out on a treat.

Sean grinned. "She's not going to have a change of heart, Father John."

"I honestly think the lady knows what she's doing." Hayward was trying to be consoling.

Reluctantly, Father John nodded his head and walked over to sit with them on a log, while Sean prepared tea in the large pot that Freda had left out for them. A big kettle had started to boil and Hayward grabbed a cloth to lift it from the hook and fill the pot.

Sean muttered. "Here we go, Father, there's nothing like a good old cup of tea now, is there?"

Father John sat reflecting on the bizarre situation. Here he was in a wood, during a gentle, summer night, sitting at a campfire with a Black and Tan and a Republican Volunteer for company.

"How strange," he thought while staring into the flames.

Henry caught the rapt look on the priest's face, and was pacified by it. It encouraged in him a sublime confidence and he wanted to converse with the priest, but refrained in case he appeared intrusive.

He ceased his scrutiny when Father John looked at him and smiled saying: "Who would have thought scenes like this would be possible?"

"Have some tea, Father John," offered Sean, feeling uncomfortable at the thought of the priest moving onto moral topics. The subject, combined with the priest's intense scrutiny, would be uncomfortable. When he presented the cup, there was the same lingering before taking the brew as at the Parochial House. Sean would not look up! If he did so, he knew a pair of pious, green eyes would ensnare him.

"Be careful, it's hot, Father John," he warned, keeping his eyes fixed on the cup.

Father John relented, knowing the rebel was playing an evasive game. He accepted the tea with an amused smile, then leaning sideways he lowered himself and stared up into Sean's face. Their eyes then met, and Father John couldn't resist saying: "Thank you."

Sean's head sprang up in surprise, while Father John straightened himself wearing a victorious beaming smile. "What's suddenly happened to your perky sense of humour? You seem to have come over all solemn and grim," chuckled the priest.

"Who me, oh no, I'm fine, Father," replied Sean, embarrassed. He turned to Henry. "Would you like some sugar in your tea?"

Henry was grinning back at him, amused by the evident torment of his situation. Sean's jaw locked and he stared back, as though warning the younger man not to enjoy himself too much.

Such bravado had no effect on the Englishman – he pushed back the peak of his R.I.C. cap, and stared in an audacious and challenging manner, standing boldly with hands on hips, with a broad grin that wrinkled his eyes with cheeky delight. In a short space of time he had discovered what liberties he could take with this killer. Then again, he had probably killed more and discounted the thought with greater ease. He continued to smile, knowing that despite Sean's capabilities as a soldier of the Republican Cause, he was also big enough to ride the effects of teasing. After all, the Volunteer had shown the first signs of humour between them, and surely took as good as he gave.

Sean's raised eyebrows gave him the appearance of a man who recognised the comical aspect of what was happening though he would not concede. This caused even greater amusement for Henry, who knew exactly what Father John had been trying to do. It was obvious to Hayward by Sean's evasiveness that he had been caught before. The Volunteer shook his head as though he was searching his mind for something to say. He was about to speak, when he looked from Henry to Father John, and was met by yet another beaming face. He uttered a feeble gurgle, which was quickly suppressed. But by then, it was too late.

Hayward hissed with the effort of trying to subdue his amusement, bending forward, covering his mouth with the back of his hand; he started to titter. Father John also laughed, but openly, while Sean looked on with raised eyebrows that pathetically announced he was not seeing the joke, though his open mouth told another story.

"Try not to enjoy yourselves too much now will you boys, huh?" he said in mock surrender.

With cheeky compliance, Hayward's tittering turned into outright laughter that brought tears to his eyes. Father John's deep laughter increased and his head was shaking in disbelief. Still Sean battled to keep his face serious, which only further fuelled the merriment.

Amid the continuous laughter, Father John took out a small, silver flask from inside his jacket and poured some of the contents into his tea, giggling during the process. He gestured with the container to Hayward, who brought forward his cup.

Father John regarded the rebel. "Come on now, Sean, you have a mind for the more acceptable qualities of comedy, and right now, you're the object of this little bit of good-natured banter.

Come on and offer your cup – Henry and I will toast you."

"Oh, that's fresh, Father, I must say." Sean could not help grinning as he held up his cup. He turned to Hayward and winked.

They sat upon the tree stump to drink their whiskey-fortified tea, carefully blowing to cool it. Henry was full of humour, all nervousness about the Volunteer having evaporated.

"Well, I bet that this is a spectacle that neither of you men would ever have foreseen, eh?" asked Father John happily.

"I wouldn't mind betting that you never imagined such a thing either, Father," responded Sean boldly.

Henry fidgeted, then said: "I must say, I never thought to see such a thing either, though I did hear about a similar incident in the trenches."

Father John smiled in wonder. "It's strange how people can be organised into colossal weapons of hate. The way we, the Germans, the French and many of the other races were. Tragic really, when many of the fellows you are shooting at could be friends if you were to meet them socially."

"When you say we, Father, do you mean as British?" asked Sean, reminding Father John that he was still a Republican and would not entertain the idea of being British.

The priest stood his ground. "We, as races of the Isles, have fought against the Germans, and whether you like it or not, Sean, many of your Irish brethren are dead upon foreign fields in distant desolate places. Like English, Scots and Welsh – like countless other races from the Empire – all went to fight against others who could not personally be hated, for their enemies were not known individually. We are conditioned to kill at other men's bidding. Wrapped in comradeship and blighted by the guilt of letting your friends down – would you not agree with me, Henry? After all, even when you could lawfully walk out of the Constabulary, it was the fear of facing our friends that made you leave more surreptitiously."

Before Hayward could say anything Sean jumped to his defence, unable to resist the opportunity that presented itself.

"Woo, woo, there, Father, you're being a little unfair with the Tan boy I think and, I'll be bold enough to say, hypocritical too – having the audacity to criticise the practice of keeping a flock of people together through guilt. Good God, who in the blazes are you to talk – you, a priest of our Roman Catholic Church – that glorious institution that has a most impressive flock? A flock that numbers more than the British Empire can raise armed soldiers. How do you keep them together, Father John? Are you going to tell me the Catholic Church never used the old guilt?"

"You can't compare them – they're not the same," spluttered Father John unconvincingly, needing time to formulate a response – and taken off guard by the bluntness of the rebel's argument.

Hayward was surprised, but also excited by Sean's argument. Hayward secretly agreed and desperately wanted to add his own thoughts, but he checked himself. His Englishness had taken over, inhibiting him from acting impulsively. After all, Father John had been there for both Sean and him when occasion demanded, and it seemed ungrateful to criticise the priest who had done so much.

But Sean was incensed and would not let the issue fade. "How can you say that, Father, when you don't believe it?" He aggressively stared into the priest's eyes and his adrenaline surged in a burst of triumph when the priest's gaze wavered.

"What is it? Have you taken your ball in?" said Sean, pleased with his achievement.

"No, I serve God as an individual through my church – *our* Church or do you deny belonging." He stared back at Sean with fearsome intensity.

"I didn't disown God," replied Sean.

"Well, I'm glad to know that, because you were quick enough to come to me when your friend was ill, and you were happy enough to hide behind the Church's doctrines when the government forces were hunting for you." Anger bubbled in his craned neck.

"We're getting a little overexcited," cut in Hayward, sensing this might be a good moment to intervene. "We've all got crosses to bear and axes to grind. But now isn't the time or the place. Let's try and be a little more understanding and appreciative. I know it sounds a bit rich coming from a Tan, but let's not get at each other's throats. Freda needs the silence, and so does the wounded bloke with her."

"Oh, nicely put, Henry," spat Sean, irritated. He knew he had let his feelings get the better of him, and was trying to calm down. After all, the man was right. Father John had brought help. "What strange days when forced to back down by a Black and Tan – and one doing me a service." He shook his head, pressing his lips together, restraining his exasperation. "Can I ask you a question?" he whispered.

"Go ahead," Hayward replied hesitantly.

"Why did you not just throw in the towel and go home? You could have done that, rather than abscond. Are you the ex-convicts that the rumour-mongers would have us believe?"

"No, they're old-wives'-tales. I don't think they would ever resort to that. There're just a lot of unemployed men who came here looking for a Regular wage – even the more well-to-do. Ex-officers are making up an Auxiliary unit – the man who was shot in Cafgarven was one. That's why he had a slightly different uniform. In truth, I absconded because I didn't want to go back to England. I couldn't look the rest of the lads in the face and say I wanted out."

The anger abated as Sean and Hayward indulged in conversation. Father John, still smarting from Sean's ungrateful impertinence, would have liked to join in. However, as they continued, he was struck by how much the men understood one another, clearly developing a rapport. Hayward was aghast at Sean's admission to being a soldier during the Boer War. He was shocked as the Volunteer described what it was like marching upon fortified positions. In return, Hayward shared his own experiences, relating his memories of the slaughter grounds of Flanders.

In this new light, Father John decided the two men should have an uninterrupted talk, while he observed. He thought of Freda's words about standing away and letting them discover their own direction. The thought had disturbed him with a feeling she might be right, and he had been reluctant to accept her advice completely, preparing only to half-heartedly consider it. Now things appeared to be taking a turn that suggested there was much in her wisdom and perhaps he *was* trying to take on too much. Was Sean's little outburst a sign from God? Could destiny be pointing the way? On one matter he had no doubt: he could and would leave the men together in the apple orchard while he and Freda took Cormac to the nunnery. It would be a good experience for them, perhaps even therapeutic.

Hayward and Sean continued to speak for a couple of hours while the fire gradually subsided to smouldering embers. Soon, only their glow, and the radiance from Freda's caravan, kept the night at bay. The darkness advanced – its dim fringes patrolled, waiting for the last vestiges of light to die before the main blackness engulfed them. Occasionally they turned to Father John, conscious of his silence. They were concerned by it, but accepted wartime experiences were likely to be topics priests would be unable to discuss – except in criticism.

The chatter came to an abrupt end when the caravan door opened and out came Freda smiling

"I'm rather pleased with myself."

Sean, heartened by her smile, asked: "Have you removed the bullet, lady?"

"Yes, he'll be fine now, but he needs to rest for a while." She stepped down and strolled to the campfire where Father John stoked up the dying embers and added a little more wood to rekindle the flame. The kettle was once again hung above the flames for the lady of the moment.

"I should think you could do with a cup of tea now, Freda," he suggested.

Once she was sitting among them, she put Sean's mind at rest by telling him about the removal of the bullet and dressing of the wound. The drugged potion had helped immensely. It had put Cormac to sleep while Freda dug for the bullet.

"His mind was so weakened, he did not know what was going on," she said. "He's a very fortunate young man, and you did well to stand by him – though you may have done better by not leading the man astray in the first place."

Sean would have normally jumped to defend himself, but decided to remain humble. "Thank you, Madam, I owe you a great deal – and thank you, Father John. I will not forget my promise to you."

SIXTEEN

Alone in the Orchard.

In a world alive with bird song – a chirping fanfare to the glory of a summer morning – Hayward awoke beneath a sumptuous, green cover, behind which stretched infinite, blue sky. He could see Father John and Freda making preparations to leave. The priest was putting equipment aboard the caravan while Freda was unloading other accessories. Peering up from her task, she noticed Hayward was awake.

"There are a few things here that might help you pass the time of day, until you decide what to do," she said.

"Will you be returning, or should I make my own way to the monastery?" asked Hayward, a little concerned.

Father John replied. "We can come back to help you, if that is what you want. Though Freda is of the opinion that Sean and you might fare better choosing your own path. I might be intruding upon your needs by not allowing you the freedom to choose. If it is your desire that I come back to escort you to the monastery, then I shall be happy to do so. Please understand, Henry, I am not deserting you. On the contrary, I am acting in the way you and Sean were, last night when talking with one another. You both seem as though you can reach a decision yourselves."

"We might do at that, Father John." Sean's voice caused them all to turn in his direction, where he lay under a blanket. He sat up and scratched his head. "I think that Henry and I might very well be able to get along in this place, but if we do decide to go to the monastery, how can we travel overland at night? During the day we'll surely be discovered."

"We don't intend to leave you permanently," countered Freda. "We shall return when we have completed our task with your friend. In the meantime, Henry and you can decide what you both really want to do. On our return, Father John and I will look in on you, and hopefully you will have reached a decision."

"I still want to spend some time in this monastery," said Hayward determinedly.

"Good." Father John smiled. "Then you shall, when we come back. In the meantime, Sean and your good self will live in the sanctuary of the apple orchard. I'm sure you'll be able to fend for yourselves. Freda seems to have it all worked out and is going to lend you some things that might be of help."

Hayward and Sean walked forward to look at the objects that Freda had left in a heap upon the ground.

"Will you take good care of them now? Because I'll be wanting them when I return," she said with a little worry upon her face. "The items are of sentimental value."

"Yes, we will," replied Hayward, as he and Sean rummaged through them.

There were two fishing-rods, one of them for fly-fishing, two reels and a box containing fly hooks in a variety of bright colours. There was also a container with fishing floats and various other things for an angler's use. Pen knives, lead weights, more unused fishing-line, pliers for the weights, and a wickerwork seat-box in which the items could be stored.

"My, oh my," Sean's face fizzled with pleasure. "I haven't indulged in this sort of thing since I was a nipper."

"Well, it mightn't be all it's cracked up to be," Freda advised. "For it's not going to be a picnic. You'll have to catch things to eat, if you want to stay in the basin. To the other side of the orchard is a small outlet, which is surrounded by a sharp rock-face where the river has cut through the scarp. It flows down from those hills west of the basin, twisting into the western end of the orchard, flowing between the rocks, and cutting a path through the wall of granite. You might try your hand at this part of the river."

"How would you know that, if you have never been able to get your caravan into the basin?" asked Father John.

"My late husband would go there with these very fishing-rods, and on a few occasions, in my younger days, we would leave the caravan and take the horse over the hills, down into that secluded area," she reminisced with tears in her sad eyes.

"Do you know who the land belongs to?" asked Sean.

"Yes, it belonged to an aristocrat, and as far as I know it still does, though not to the person I knew. The orchard and the surrounding lands are part of a stately manor that lay to the west of the basin, beyond the hills where the river flowed. A rather fine lady used to let me bring my caravan onto her land. The very woman that I spoke to you about Henry, do you remember?"

"Why, yes," he replied excited. "The lady who published your book."

"The very person, though she is long dead now, and I do not know which one of her uninterested offspring owns the land, for I never had a mind to come back when I heard she had died."

"What are these, Freda?" Father John picked up some metal wires fixed to stakes.

"Come on, Father, you're surely not that green, are you?" mocked Sean light-heartedly.

The priest smiled with the utmost innocence and sincerity. "I have no idea at all, Sean. Please explain?"

"They're rabbit snares," interrupted Freda. "They work well too. I still use them, and I'll be wanting them back."

"So we're to live off of the land are we," said Sean. "You left us a teapot and a kettle, plus a box of tea, all of which I presume, you will be wanting back."

Hayward started gathering the fishing equipment and made to leave, wanting to get on with things. Even though he felt reluctant to part company with Freda and Father John, a stronger sense of urgency to avoid police searches motivated him. It was feasible the R.I.C. might soon investigate the area.

Sean, appreciative to necessity, said. "I am just going to say my goodbyes to Cormac, I shan't be long, Henry."

"Right, I'll gather up what I can."

Father John stood before the Tan with a benign smile. He could not help liking the young Englishman, despite the hated uniform he wore. In the end, the man had come good, allowing his conscience to map his path, even though there remained a small misgiving about the Tan's absconding. It had made the young man an unnecessary fugitive because of unwittingly stealing a weapon along with a Government uniform. He put his hands upon Hayward's shoulders.

"God be with you," he murmured.

"And with you, Father John. I'll not forget what you have done for me."

"I'll return to see if you still want to go to the monastery. I hope you will, even if it's for a short while. It'll do you good, giving you the chance to get away from all of this. Who knows, perhaps all this trouble will be gone when you decide to leave."

"Maybe," whispered Hayward, quietly smiling. Aspiration sparkled in his eyes where visiting the priory was concerned.

For a moment dread seethed in Father John – perhaps the man would change his mind? Inside there was a faint inkling that when they next met, the disconsolate Tan might be unable to go to the community of Brothers.

When Sean emerged from the caravan, he too went before Father John and shook hands. "Thank you, Father. I'm forever in your debt and I'll stick to my promise. Not because I believe in it, but it has been made before God and you, his humble servant. What with Henry's appearance, it feels as though you and the big fella upstairs are keeping to the bargain." He looked to Hayward, who seemed ardent to get on with things. "Well, we're certainly an unusual pair – a Tan and a Volunteer. I think both our superiors would flay us alive if ever we were caught."

"Then we'll have to make sure we don't get caught. Let's go do some fishing," suggested Hayward. "In for a penny..."

"I'll have the pound bit," laughed Sean as Hayward, still smiling, made his way to the caravan where Freda had come expectantly to the door. She looked down at him smiling, knowing that he was grateful for her assistance. Grinning, he looked up, loaded with fishing equipment and his rifle, then permitted himself a glance at Cormac, asleep upon the bed.

"Tell your new companion his friend will be fine," she whispered.

"I will Freda, and I hope you'll be well — always."

"Oh, don't you be worrying about an old woman like me now. You have all your life to live. Live it well," she said teasingly.

If melancholy were a clear liquid he would be immersed, for she was a most extraordinary person, put upon Earth, and demanding to be liked.

"You sound as though you're not coming back," he said.

"Well, once I have left young Cormac in safe hands, I'll have to return, if only to collect my husband's fishing things. I dare say Father John will want to come back and look in on you."

"I'll always remember you, and forever grateful."

"Let's get going then," called Sean.

Father John waved them off as they left in the direction of the scarps, leading back to the basin's apple orchard. The priest turned to

Freda to discuss the forthcoming journey and noticed her gaze was firmly fixed on the retreating men and her face mirroring his own sadness. Deep down, both wondered if they would see the young Englishman and the Volunteer again.

"Sometimes I feel an insight into things," she muttered. "Something I like people to know about myself. At this time, beneath my emotions there is a swirling sea of optimism and doom. Achievements might be lost in ignorant oblivion, yet still an imprint will be left. Something small that can bring joy to those taking part, and all will share in it.

"When I spoke to Henry there was an aura about the young man. It was marred by the affliction of his tragic life. I think it's something he might never shake off."

Father John watched them leave and agreed with her. "He has been through much for a young man."

Nodding her head, she muttered. "In existence, there are always people who seem deserving of better fortune. Many are just cursed by a blight that lurks in their unfortunate shadow, ready to engulf them whenever courage fuels their desire. I've met many travelling, and Henry is such a person."

Father John looked to her. "Maybe he can enjoy some time in the apple orchard, fishing with his enemy. Both may learn something of value, and gain something rich from the experience."

"Henry is on borrowed time in my opinion. The government forces might catch up with him and he may have to face those friends he has walked away from."

"Well, if we get him to a monastery, he'll be fine." Father John was full of optimism.

"Do you honestly think so?"

"Oh, come now, Freda, please let us not be so pessimistic about things."

She sighed and clamped her lips, muttering. "I hope I'm wrong – for all the world, I hope I am wrong."

Father John was concerned by her misgivings, so compelling that they checked his usual rebuke. Tenderly, his words ventured forth. "Fear of provoking providence? I hope you're wrong too, Freda, and I pray that your wish comes true."

They returned to the caravan, ready to begin their journey, content that all things were packed.

"There'll be another day of travelling and one more returning Father. What will your people say when they realise you have not returned for a number of days?" she enquired.

"I'm depending on Maureen my housekeeper to spin a little yarn for me. It should hold for a few days. I did not have the time to inform anyone of my leaving, so my post will not be covered. I think I shall be able to ride the effects of a few days absence. There'll be a little explaining to do, but then that's feasible. Should I sit with you or stay in the carriage?"

She smiled. "You have the agony of choice, Father. You can ride in the wagon or you can sit up front with me. Cormac will be sleeping most of the time."

A big smile traversed his happy face. "The child that is still present within me is swimming to the surface. I've always wanted to sit at the front of a tinker's caravan. Now this little ambition can be put to rest."

"Come on," She said, and like an old mother who had read a child's mind she scurried off to the front of the vehicle, shaking her head with amusement, while he was close upon her heels, fearing she might have a change of heart.

Hauling herself up on to the seat, she looked down, wondering if he could do the same. He was beside her in a fleeting moment of agility, complete with boyish smile. She called Moogsly and flicked the reins gently. This was all the encouragement the gentle brute needed before responding with resignation. Slowly, as though tottering under the strain, then developing a rhythm, the beast began to trudge forward, pulling its burden with apparent ease. Father John looked behind the seat, through the small curtained window and observed Cormac sleeping.

They cleared the woods and moved onto the country lane, the first steps towards the Divine

Sisters of Mercy. A surge of gratification flowed through Father John, despite Freda's reservation on matters. The next part of the mending task was well on the way and so far all things had been effective. He looked to Freda as she sat lightly holding the horse's reins. She was a most remarkable person indeed, possessing an infinite resolve for doing things – even when unenthusiastic about a job.

"Your composure is awe inspiring." His heart was full of esteem. "Your help and understanding during the whole affair has been marvellous, to say the least. Your knowledge of medicine seems purpose-made for the situation. I can't help thinking that God sculpted you just for this deed."

Her face remained calm as she solemnly answered. "If an old woman was fashioned for such, surely her thoughts would be so too."

Father John checked his thoughts about her. "Is it because of your pessimistic view concerning, what you think might be Henry's demise?"

"Endow me with all the frailties and faults of a normal being," she countered. "Tell yourself that my one fatalistic view of you trying to help them, beyond this encounter, is nothing more than superstition."

"I stare at you and am struck by the fact you are too advanced intellectually to go for such superstitions. Why do you think some foreboding event will befall the Tan?"

"What happens is meant to be. It always was and will. Everything is mapped out, though something good will come of what they do. It is the right course of action to take. I just feel that the good things will come in a short space of time." She looked at the rock walls and the hedgerows, finding answers in visual things, using lumps, bumps and crevices as stimulants when shaping her philosophy on life and the way of things. She smiled, noticing a solitary rose growing in a hedgerow, standing alone in a wilderness, radiating its rich blood red joy to the world, bringing inspiration to continue and try once more to explain what she meant.

"The good that comes from their solitude, in that little Purgatory of yours, will be cleansing. Such goodness and understanding will be short-lived and like a flower it will bloom then end after a brief splendour."

He was amused by her romantic conception. "At least you see good in the idea of a renegade Tan and a Volunteer on the run being made to live together." He sat back surveying the countryside with its green grandeur and ancient hills. The gullies were playing host to wooded clusters, which were handsome in the summer brilliance. Nothing remained incomplete in what he saw – so many pleasing sights created by an all-knowing all-seeing essence. He took a deep breath and sighed with pleasure.

"You're obviously feeling very pleased with yourself," ventured Freda in some bewilderment, for she expected her forebodings to have disturbed him.

"Yes, I am pleased, Freda. Very happy with the way things are going, and full of hope for young Cormac."

"Now, for that young man I am much more optimistic. He is full of good fortune, I tell you. If ever fortune followed a man, it certainly does him."

"WHAT!" he spluttered merrily astonished? "The poor soul has been shot in the shoulder, dragged to death's door and back, yet you think he's lucky."

"Well, he is," she giggled, understanding the dumbfounded priest. "I know that it may sound a little foolish at the moment, but believe me, the luck is with that young man. He may have been at death's door, but he sure as hell came back. Don't be forgetting that now, Father."

His searching eyes contained a hidden amusement that shimmered behind the pupils. "Well, I suppose his luck has a sublime charm of its own – one which has a most strange and tantalising uniqueness about it. An advantage that is a little difficult to perceive on first encounter."

"Sarcasm doesn't suit you, Father John," she retorted with an air of joviality – she was game for some verbal banter.

Unable to contain his amusement, he surrendered to delight. His face metamorphosed into uncontrollable rapture. His mouth opened and his teeth shone through joyous wrinkles that swept away the recent strains and stresses.

"Well, Father, I think it will do you some good to laugh. Laughing can be a great healer, you know."

His chest heaved up and down, which, for a short moment, caused Freda concern. His laughing made him look like a person having a convulsion. It was still a long way to their destination, but Father John felt sure the journey would pass pleasantly enough.

SEVENTEEN

The Gully and the Winding Stream.

The clear water ran down from the lush, green scarps and meandered through the wood, cascading over rocks and toppling as pretty waterfalls into delicate pools. Elegant ferns and flowers scattered the river bank, adventurously hanging over the sweeping rivulet where the shallow stream's width provided enough space between the trees to allow in patches of brilliant daylight. Into such a clearing came the committed Volunteer and the renegade Tan. They had been walking for some time, and were relieved by the sudden change in the basin's physical geography. As they came to the western end of the basin leaving the apple orchard, the scarps had become more wooded with deciduous trees, which lent a feeling of security. The region appeared relatively unexplored, like a small, lost world. It brought comfort to the men as they made for the sound of the flowing water gushing over the scattered and worn rocks. Where the slope curved abruptly and followed the hill around, they found themselves within a tranquil clearing, where the shallow river ran a path through a ravine beyond the surrounding basin.

Sean jumped unsteadily upon a stone, keeping his balance by holding out his arms, with a Lee–Enfield rifle in one hand and an old sack of utensils in the other. He looked down at the crystal-clear freshness sweeping by him and sighed in wonder. The stream was only about knee-deep and turning to Hayward the rebel smiled contentedly. He raised his voice in order that his recent foe might hear him above the sound of the flowing river.

"Isn't this grand now, Henry. I feel as young as you." He jumped to the next stone.

Hayward followed with a rush of excitement, feeling free, more so than he could ever remember. Here he was with a hated Shinner, feeling released and free of past trauma. The visual aspect was utterly superb, with trees imposing their presence upon the wonder before him. The gushing purity was throwing up a cleansing, damp spray while the Fenian, complete with weapon and ominous ammunition belt, leapt from stone to stone like a child running out from drab school-lessons. The air was alive with the sound of the gushing current, while birds chirped their summer merriment from the high, rustling foliage of the wood's green canopy. Like the rebel, Hayward found himself wobbling on the stones.

He thought: "To hell with staying out of the water," then balanced on one leg to unlace his boot and discard it before proceeding with the other, teetering on his bare foot.

Sean got midway across the stream, and saw the young Tan's antics. "It's about waist-deep out here, Henry. What are you going to do, take your bloody strides off?"

The Englishman looked back with a grin, threw his boots into the wicker fishing-creel, then waded forward deeper into the cool water.

"I'll tell you something for nothing, Sean," he said as though he was about to give away a big secret.

"Fine, because I don't think I would have been able to pay you for telling me somethings." Sean was feeling rather witty.

Hayward raised his eyebrows in a mock look of indignation. "Oh, we are on form, aren't we?"

"Yes I am, aren't I?" The Fenian was clearly enjoying the moment.

Hayward opened his mouth as though he was about to come back at Sean with a smart reply, but then thought better of it and waded forward another few steps, white foam breaking around his shins.

Sean started to snigger because he noted the caution in Hayward. It was becoming obvious that the restrained young Englishman was a little self-conscious, which surprised him, as he had previously considered Tans brash, hardened men – all brawn and no brains. The Englishman had forced him to think more upon an individual basis – for a short moment, Tans were not a collective entity. He visualised them with mothers, fathers, brothers and sisters. People with strength combined with weakness. Sean was beginning to see Hayward's vulnerability as also a strength, which he found himself respecting.

"What I was going to say was that when we find somewhere to make camp, I'm going to wallow in all this water. I'm full of grime and sweat, it would be great to clean it off," declared Hayward.

Sean scanned the surface. "I can understand you, Henry. That water looks most inviting." He saw the splash of a trout as its tail broke the water. The moment brought a rush of excitement to him and he looked back at the Tan.

"Did you see that, Henry?"

"No." Hayward screwed his eyes as though trying to drain more vision from the water, peering intently at shoals of fish that had suddenly become clear. "Christ," he muttered. "The whole bloody river is alive with fish, look! Just below the surface, there must be hundreds of them."

Sean looked too, but could not see because of the sun's reflection glittering upon the surface where the Tan was pointing like an excited schoolboy.

"Right, I say we get to the opposite bank, find a place to put all of this gear, then we get the rods out and do some fishing." Sean had become even more enthusiastic.

"I'll have to let the bath wait until later." Hayward waded further into the river after the rebel.

"Where is your spirit of adventure, eh English? For Christ sakes, you're half way there now. Sling the rest of you in, then we can get on with the fishing bit."

As expected, Hayward stopped to consider the matter, while Sean began to chuckle. He knew that the Englishman would do it – his race was always the same when someone got them into the comical spirit of things, which had to be one of their more endearing attributes.

With a look of devilment in his eyes, Hayward grinned, while his mind ticked over. "I can't afford to get the rifle wet," he said feebly, knowing that Sean would have the perfect answer to his problem.

The Irishman did, shouting above the noise of the current. "Wait there for a moment." He turned and completed the journey to the bank – jumped upon the shingle and discarded the things he carried, before returning along the stones to where Hayward was standing knee-deep in the water. "Give me the gun." The rebel held out his hand to receive the weapon.

Hayward held up the rifle followed by the creel and thanked him in the politest of English manners for relieving him of his burden. "You know, when I first arrived in Gormanstown a wise old R.I.C. man told me that if I ever saw a Shinner with a gun, I should always address him as Sir," said Hayward humorously.

"Well, I would say that the old man certainly had a good sense of humour, but then Englishmen always call you sir. Even your coppers do, when they are politely arresting you for premeditated murder."

Hayward took off his peaked cap, which had become dusty and puckered since he had left the barracks, and unbuttoned his dark-green jacket, while Sean opened the creel and stuffed the discarded gear into it before asking: "Is that it, or are you going to go the whole hog and take your strides off too."

"That's it," replied Hayward as he turned to head further upstream to where a patch of deep water looked as smooth as a plate of molten glass. The depth was confirmed when Hayward started to feel the water level rise to his waist. His saturated trousers began to weigh him down and he winced at the cold potency of the fresh clear liquid as it splashed around his stomach.

Sean called from the rock. "Go on now, Henry, go for it lad. One clear plunge and you're there."

With gritted teeth and a look of complete determination, Hayward lurched forward into the river. The vigorous chill hit his torso causing him to smart momentarily with the water's briskness. However, it was soon over and he found himself immersed in the joy of the flowing stream, impaired only by the weight of his clothing pulling him down, while he paddled about clumsily. After a while he stopped, put his feet upon the river's bed and stood up. He looked back at Sean who was still crouched uncomfortably on the rock with the rifle and fishing-creel, lost in his thoughts, while peering into the water. Hayward surmised that he could see the trout swimming about in their carefree shoals, and was beginning to work up his own boyish enthusiasm for some fly-fishing.

"Can you catch trout with an ordinary coarse rod – you know, with a float?" asked Hayward.

"I reckon that you can always catch something. Have you not tried fly-fishing then, Henry?"

"No, though it's something I've always had a mind to do, but just never found the time."

"As you do when you're off globe-trotting fighting the British Empire's wars."

"You've been further afield than me on that score, if you consider South Africa and the Boer War.

"Yeah, well," muttered Sean dreamily into the water again, and then said aloud, but to himself; "Another person then – other ideals."

He looked back at Hayward, and changed the subject back to fly-fishing. "I'll teach you how to flick the rod. You can learn how to fly-fish today. We'll catch ourselves a few and have them for our eats."

"Sounds good to me," replied Hayward, pleased with the idea. He struggled towards the shoreline, making for the spot where Sean had put the rucksack and rods. As he came ashore dripping water upon the shingle, Sean arrived, gracefully jumping from stone to stone.

"I wonder how long these stones have been there."

Hayward took off his sodden trousers to hang them over a small tree by the edge of the shingle. There was a slight breeze, though the July day was scorching hot and he reasoned that it would not be long before the garments were dry. He went back to the water's edge in a pair of dirty, white long johns.

"I'm going back in for a spell," he said.

"Fine," replied Sean. "I'll get the rods ready and see exactly what we have got in the bags here." He rummaged through the contents of the rucksack, finding flour, matches, tea and a tin whistle. He stopped and picked the small instrument up, and was filled with delight. This was one little device he could play, and he wondered what made the old tinker woman put the object among the contents in the first place. He smiled as he put the thing aside, relishing the thought of the coming evening when he would play it around the campfire. He judged Hayward to be refined, and probably appreciative of the haunting sounds that could be made on a tin whistle, capturing the mood of a summer night. He laughed to himself at this newfound belief, for who would have thought he, Sean O'Sullivan, would ever have looked upon a Tan in such light. He was about to tell Hayward of this, but thought better of it, observing the Englishman splashing about in the sparkling water.

"Leave the Anglo-Saxon to his pleasure," he thought, as he turned his attention back to the things before him. He allowed his gaze to wonder over the items while the sound of the flowing stream and the surrounding woods enhanced his happy spirit. His mind clicked into motion, telling him the fishing-rods could be set up – a task he jumped to with great enthusiasm, once his mind was made up.

Going to the creel and pulling out the puckered R.I.C. cap and dark-green tunic, he began to choose his wants from the assortment of fishing-tackle neatly packed in various boxes. He set up the match-rod first, telling himself that he would look for some worms further along the bank where the shingle met the mud. Then turning his attention to the fly-rod, he selected a colourful hook with fine red, green and yellow hair delicately fashioned around the curved barb, looking like a tantalising fly. Hopefully, the fish would see the hook in such a fashion too. Quickly setting up the fly-rod, Sean returned to the stones to practise his fly-fishing, flicking the line out across the river, as though he was whipping the far off patch of water. He did a few quick flicks, unsatisfied with where the hook had landed. Then, after a while, he allowed the fly to rest upon the surface and travel with the flow for a little way, before repeating the process.

Hayward, happy and refreshed from his bathing, stood in the stream and watched the rebel's antics, fascinated by the flicking motion that he was performing. As a child, back in England, he remembered watching a man go through the same routine. It was on a day when his grandmother had taken him out into the country as a treat; leaving the squalor of the town's housing-estate behind, with its endless rows of alleys and dull brickwork. He shook his head at the memory of the town – God, how he hated that place. The mere thought of the exploited urban dross, in his mind's eye, was enough to depress him – the vision of wretched men lining up in the hope of getting work, while all the underhand dealings of employment selectors went on. He calmed himself looking at the foe on the rock, allowing the river, the birds and the trees to impose upon the dreaded memory of the abode that was his home.

"Will you not come up and give this a try now, Henry? You'll love it to death, I promise you," called Sean, realising that he had kindled the Englishman's interest.

"All right then, I'll give it a go," replied Hayward, moving forward into the shallow region of the stream. He jumped up onto the stone beside the rebel and shivered slightly as the light breeze began to chill the damp garment against his skin.

"Right," said Sean, "it doesn't take much to get the hang of it. You hold the rod like so and pull out this piece of line just above the reel. It gives you a bit of play and helps you to control the line when you go back and forth. Here, watch me."

Sean gave a few demonstrations and explained how this gave it the appearance of a fly skipping on the water. Then leaving the hook to go with the flow for a short while was when any would be predator would be tempted to take a bite. Hayward watched, enthralled by the act, wondering who originally came up with the idea of fly-fishing. What devious and cunning mind sat down and thought out the idea of making a hook look like a fly?

Sean offered the light rod to Hayward, who gratefully accepted, holding it with one hand and pulling the line out with the other, the way Sean had instructed him. He made a few unsuccessful flicks but was soon corrected by Sean's patient tutoring. After a while he developed a healthy swing, and for some time went through the motions, while Sean offered words of encouragement. Gradually he became more adept with the rod, and reached the stage where he was allowing the line to travel for a good way. Suddenly there was a splash and Hayward caught a glimpse of fish tail as the colourful fly disappeared from sight. He struck instinctively, while Sean jumped up and down upon the rock, full of mirth and shouting into the air with unashamed glee.

"Go on now, Henry boy, you've hooked one – careful now, that's our dinner. God love us, if you can bring one more in, we can go off to the fields just over the hill and swipe a few potatoes. No one will miss a couple of spuds in a dirty great big field," he babbled excitedly.

Hayward reeled the fighting fish in, watching the creature apprehensively, and hoping it would not escape as it twisted and thrashed about, splashing the water's surface in its desperate attempt to get away. He was filled with excitement, which was suddenly abated by the thought of the doomed fish. If he landed it, the creature's fate would be sealed and no one would care about it, not a thought for the woeful creature's unimportant life; only he and Sean would remember and they intended to kill the wretched thing for dinner. If he was alone he would be tempted to let it go. However, Sean's excited yelling, combined with the real need to be able to get their sustenance, caused Hayward to push the mild feeling of guilt to the back of his mind. Life and nature always took its course and one day he knew that death would take him. His contemplation of what lay beyond might briefly weigh heavy upon him, but no one would worry about his fearful demise when he was gone.

"Reel him in, Henry, you're doing good – that's it now," he yelled, while plunging forward into the water to pull out the thrashing trout. "I should have brought the blasted landing net over. I left it back on the bank." Sean pressed the fish against his chest and waded back to the stone while the trout's tail flapped to and fro.

Hayward jumped down beside him, aware that the hook and line were still in the creature's mouth. Both observed the fish briefly before making for the shore with their catch, pleased with the quick result of their first foray.

Once upon the bank Sean went to the creel and took out a small hammer with which he whacked the creature's head, killing it instantly. He took small metal pliers from the tackle box and unfastened the hook from its mouth.

"First blood to you, Henry – if we could get a few more of them, then go off to the fields for spuds – we could have ourselves a good dinner. What do you say to that?" Sean's excitement was growing with every passing moment.

"Sounds good to me, Sean, and on the way we can lay some of the rabbit snares," replied the young Tan jubilantly.

"The snares, yes, I forgot about them. I also think we may be able to find enough things to keep us going for a while. We'll have to be careful the farmer won't detect the odd little thing going missing here and there in the meadow. I know about mushrooms and fungi too. My grandmother taught me how to recognise the more edible of them, which is most you know. When she was a youngster she lived through the famine and would go into the woodlands with her aunt to collect all manner of edible things. She never lost her taste for mushrooms and other fungi."

It was as though the small step in the right direction of living off the land had begun to develop into a colossal enthusiasm, like a trickle of shingle rolling down a hill, becoming a huge rock fall.

Hayward was totally enthused by the Irishman's joy. "Well, why not have a go with the rod, while I go back through the woods and place the snares around the burrows that I saw at the edge of the orchard? I shan't be long, probably about twenty minutes. It'll be another string to our bow before the spud-hunting jaunt." He oozed with the fine spirit of optimism that had engulfed them since their little stroke of good fortune.

"Right then," grinned Sean. "I'll bet I can net one before you're back." He sat down and took off his damp boots and socks, then rolled up his wringing wet trouser legs over his knobbly knees before picking up the fishing rod and landing net that lay close by.

"Back to the heavenly pursuit," He beamed utterly rejuvenated, realising that he had not enjoyed himself in such a way for a long time and knowing the Englishman was of the same mind too.

Here they were – enemies finding more joy in life's simple pleasures than either could have imagined. It was as though the wilderness and the enchantment of the river had evicted the tension that lived in each of them.

Sean went back through the motions of casting, while Hayward waded across the river to make his way back towards the woodland. The Irishman watched as the departing Englishman ran off in his long johns intent upon his new venture.

"Make sure you're not seen by a wandering farmer! He'll think you're from some lost tribe of cannibals. You'll scare the poor devil to death."

Hayward, unable to hear the joke, only knew he had made some sort of humorous quip by the look upon the rebel's face. In response the young Tan shouted back. "I'm going to get them laid before the evening when the rabbits are more likely to come out and graze. Early morning and late evening is the best time to try and get the buggers."

Sean was a little perplexed at first, then realised that Hayward was talking about the snares and rabbits. He raised his eyes to the blue sky and smirked to the unobservable Almighty. "Well, that one was wasted on him wasn't it," he laughed and considered Hayward's funny little shortcomings.

He realised the Tan was, on occasion, a little distant by nature. Because of this, the young Englishman probably did not always grasp things straight away. Not for reasons of being slow, but because sometimes he was deep inside himself and when rudely awakened from his daydreaming it was on the tail-end of an abrupt word to get through to him. Sean thought that Hayward might have been a little distant among his own kind. Not needing the constant companionship of friends, yet not able to do without them all of the time. He seemed able to ride the effects of teasing, grasping the funny side when he knew he was the butt of a joke. It was probably something that he had got used to in life, yet still the Englishman was sensitive, which caused Sean to ponder two facts that did not add up. How could a self-conscious man be able to ride the effects of teasing? It was something that Sean decided to investigate for he was intrigued by Hayward's strange mannerisms. He seemed too polite to be a Black and Tan and Sean was at a loss as to how this seemingly docile man had ever come to enlist in the R.I.C., albeit he had the look of

a veteran soldier who had endured trench warfare. The man's qualities had helped him survive
the Great War – a campaign that Sean knew had
claimed the lives of many men throughout the
Isles.

A splash near the fly distracted him from his
thinking. His heart leapt in excitement – he had
hooked a splendid specimen, which was kicking
and thrashing vigorously.

EIGHTEEN

The Way to the Nunnery.

Pleasantly, the morning rolled by. The sun rose into the clear, blue sky to reach its zenith over a world seemingly at ease when viewed from the caravan. Father John continually checked Cormac through the small window and had to be scolded on one occasion for his persistence. He wanted to get down and go to the back for a closer inspection. For some reason, known only to Freda, she kept the front door behind the seat permanently locked. His final attempt succeeded in vexing Freda to such an extent that he was now trying to soothe her grumpy mood.

"Come on, Freda," he raised an eyebrow in comic fashion. "I know that you've done much off your own back, and you know what a fuss pot I am. Let us be at peace with one another. I'm truly sorry if I upset you. Your knowledge on these matters is superior to mine."

"Well, Father, I'm certain that at times you can be a most trying person, despite your good intentions." She was clearly vexed, but prepared to respond to his words.

His smile broadened. What good qualities she had. Even when tried by continuous pestering, her temperament always adapted.

"Freda, you're an absolute joy to behold."

Her eyelids narrowed suspiciously – always wary of compliments and prone to think that charm was a prelude to dire things following.

"What is the reason behind such kind words, Father? Are you after going back to take a look at young Cormac?"

He leant back against the leather backrest, eyes wide with astonishment and began to laugh. "My word, Freda, you're suspicious of me."

"Whether it's by your intention or by coincidence, something always follows one of your compliments that gives you your way, and the receiver then has a task to perform."

"Not more tinker superstition, Freda." If any of his congregation were to say such things he would have been quick to reproach them. With Freda it had to be different! His habit could not humble her; she could come back at him with equal strength of character and bare honesty. Also, her blue irises could penetrate in a way that matched his – even better it on some occasions.

Freda pulled on the reins – a look of concern was etched into the lines of her forehead. She grimaced as the beast stopped, and Father John wondered what he could have possibly done to offend her.

"Quick, climb down and get Cormac out of the back," she said urgently. "You will have your wish, but not for reasons that either of us would like."

"What on earth's wrong, Freda? What has come over you?" Perhaps his teasing had finally inflamed her. "If I have upset you then I do apologise, I assure you —"

"Father John, please, I'm not angry with you, LOOK!" She pointed through the bushes where the lane bent around the foliage.

He peered through the trees. The part of the lane they were yet to traverse was now visible. Just beyond the bend behind the trees a group of people stood around a truck – a Crossley, the very vehicle used by the R.I.C. The reason for Freda's abruptness was clear.

"Oh, my word," he exclaimed in dismay. "Have they seen us?"

"No, luckily I've spotted them before breaking cover at the bend ahead." Her mind was racing ahead with a plan. "You'll have to take Cormac into the woods, while I get the caravan past them. The lane bends around in an arc, so if you head north-west using the gullies and woodland for cover you'll break out upon the road further up and beyond them. I'll camp up along there in some wood lands. You'll find me eventually."

"But Cormac's not in a fit condition to walk," he replied.

"He'll be a little better than he was yesterday, though he'll be in some discomfort and his condition will be considerably worse if the Tans get their hands on him."

"Right, I'd better get to it then," he said, fully committed to the improvised plan. He jumped down, ran to the back door and went into the living quarters where Cormac was stirring, aware that the vehicle had stopped.

His bleary eyes opened and he sat up, scratching his ruffled hair. "Are we there?" he asked.

"No, we have a slight problem on our hands which demands immediate attention," babbled the priest, hastily helping him out of the bed. He was a little encouraged by the ease with which the young man managed to stand. There appeared to be a most remarkable improvement in his condition. "Right, we'll make for the woods and then go cross-country coming out, upon the road a few miles up."

Freda stood at the doorway, concerned. She knew the young man would be a little better, but he still needed to regain energy. He could go into a relapse from the exertion, and the effect of the herbs would be to make him dizzy.

"You'll have to stop and rest him at regular intervals. Say five minutes for every fifteen minutes of walking. Please stick to this meticulously or you will find the young man's condition will worsen," she stressed.   Her emphasis was not lost on Father John, his mind already making preparations for the short journey. Carefully he helped Cormac from the wagon as Freda stepped aside. Together the two men struggled into the cover of the woods.

"Good luck to you, I'll be as quick as possible," she called after them, before going back to her seat and taking the reins. A little flick and whistle got the docile horse moving again – dragging her world towards the ominous roadblock as she rounded the bend, where she came full into view of the ill-clad Tans. A small throng of people were being held in a line at gunpoint by two policemen.

Turpin looked up at the approaching tinker and called: "Sergeant, it's that bloody Jonesy again."

"What did you say?" asked Jones, thinking Turpin was referring to him.

"Not you – you numskull. I mean the bloody gypo, a Romany Jones," he retorted, brazenly insulting the unit bully, which he was able to do with impunity and receive no chastisement in return. The rest of the group always stood back from his defiant brashness, for he could make things difficult for any person who challenged him.

Sergeant Bradley came over and watched the approaching woman. He had seen her many times before, though he had never spoken with her. She was a familiar face and he knew her name. He guessed that she was the person the Tans had been talking about the previous morning, before Hayward vanished.

He looked back at Jones, standing before three local people, an old man and two young women in their early twenties. The bully was enjoying intimidating them, delighting in scaring the women by pointing the gun at their Father. "Jones, is that the biddy you were talking about outside the barracks yesterday?"

He let the gun barrel drop, and walked over to Bradley and Turpin for a closer inspection. He peered, recognising the old woman: "That's the biddy all right, Sergeant."

The caravan came to a halt, while Cuttings and Henderson took Jones' place before the three locals in a less menacing posture. Cuttings actually took time to calm the two women, telling them they would shortly be allowed to go.

Jones moved along the horse's right flank while Bradley and Turpin came to its left side. Freda found the appearance of the two Tans more intimidating than Bradley's old-Irish-policeman look. She decided the mishmash of police and army uniform was most unethical – from the moment she first set eyes upon them.

"All right, Granny, where are you going?" asked Turpin brashly with a beaming smile. He seemed to mean no immediate harm.

"I'm a wanderer, you cheeky little whipper-snapper, and I've been so since before your mammy was rubbing powder into your nice, shiny little bum," she answered, knowing the nature of the man before her.

Turpin grinned, deciding she was fine by his way of thinking. Bradley and Jones started laughing too, approving of any person who had the measure of him.

"It's not so shiny now, he's got a few splinters," laughed Jones.

"Yeah, he's a right hairy-arsed sod now, Mrs Donavon." added Bradley.

Freda smiled, gratified that the Regular policeman knew her name. "How would you two know? Does it get that lonely in the barracks then?"

All three laughed. "Not that bloody lonely," said Jones, who was a person easily amused by lavatorial humour.

"What's all the commotion about then? Or ain't I allowed to be asking such questions?" she queried craftily.

"What's it to you, nosy." Turpin grabbed his chance to make a retort.

It was delivered in a manner that she knew was good-natured, though she realised he was a cut above the rest. At a glance she knew this particular Tan possessed an aptitude for grasping things quickly. He would need to be handled carefully - something in his demeanour demanded respect.

"Oh, we are a sharp one now, aren't we," she smiled down at him.

Sergeant Bradley sighed. "There's been a bit of a shoot-out. We've bagged two Shinners."

"I never heard the shots," she said quizzically, and a little disappointed that he should refer to his countrymen the way British Tans did.

"It happened over two hours ago now. We're just bringing the bodies down from the farm house," he answered.

"The bodies – you mean there're dead? You've killed them?" She was appalled.

"I'm afraid so. We believe they were involved in an ambush that took place at Cafgarven a couple of days ago. Have you seen anyone else on your travels lady, anything suspicious?" He suspected she would say no even if she had.

"I've seen nothing upon the road, except you lads at the barracks yesterday," she replied, looking at Jones who she remembered.

"You seem tired, Gran," Turpin said in a perky manner. "You can't have had much sleep."

"I'm fine, young man, and when you reach my age you'll look a little worse for wear." She laughed nervously at the impudent Tan's grinning sunburnt face. She looked beyond and recognised some of the other faces, while a plainclothes Police Inspector walked among the chattering group, giving out orders to the Tans.

Upon the floor, beneath two shabby look-ing blankets, she saw the boots of the dead men protruding from the coverings. Her attention returned to the Inspector who appeared to be in charge of the proceedings, even though it was apparent the Tans were not taking too much notice of him. Their response was not that of disciplined men, though she reasoned they must be, because of their War experience. They did as instructed in a relaxed and casual fashion, as though they were deliberately trying to vex the Irish Police Inspector.

"So, did they try to shoot back at you then? Where were they?" she asked nonchalantly, while climbing down from the caravan. "Are the young girls all right?"

She walked over to the old man and his daugh-ters, where Cuttings stood with the butt of his gun on the ground, legs astride and both hands clasped around the barrel. He did not seem to have the greatest of enthusiasm for the job, but the other man – Henderson had a manner that suggested he took his duty more serious, though he was not menacing towards the locals. His manner was cordial and polite with rifle slung over his shoulder – not threatening in any way. As she approached she heard the words; "*just routine questions*" and gathered that Henderson was trying to allay their fears. Sometimes Tans burnt down houses and she knew the men she was among were capable of such deeds, if what

Hayward told her was true. So far, however, the only person she had seen who looked capable of such a foul deed was Jones. She watched two others lift one of the corpses and put it on board the truck. She stopped before the locals. "Are you good people all right?"

A slow nod came from one of the girls, not daring to speak.

"They're a little shaken by what has happened, but then that's to be expected," said Cuttings. His manner was dry, and perhaps a little snooty, but there seemed no malice. It was just the Englishman's way. He certainly had the air of a man who could not get another job, and had been forced to consider the rather distasteful position of a supplementary policeman.

"Oh well, perhaps if you all came and stood by the caravan I could make you a cup of tea," she said with a kindly smile.

Turpin and Sergeant Bradley stood beside her and, the brazen younger Tan cheekily blurted. "You could do us all one, Gran – charge a farthing a cup, you'll make a killing."

Freda laughed at Turpin's idea, for she was quite happy to do it without charge. However, the bold scallywag looked at the rest of the group and shouted. "Hey, you lot, tea at a farthing a cup," then pointed at Freda.

Caught unawares by such impudence, she was confounded as the Tans moved towards her with hands in pockets enthusiastically, jingling change, before she had a chance to protest. The bedraggled and motley ruffians descended upon her with big, red, cherubic faces, enquiring if she had enough crockery for such a venture and had she got any cheese rolls.

Behind them, the incensed Inspector Callaghan took off his hat and slung it on the road, muttering and cursing because the entire Tan contingent had assembled around the popular tinker. They had only done half the job instructed. One corpse was still on the roadside.

"Bloody useless English bastards," he muttered. "Sergeant Bradley, O'Hara! Would you come here please?"

Both police officers obeyed, knowing that Callaghan would not compel the Tans to complete the task. They seemed to be a group to be handled with kid gloves, while the Regular Irish policemen still got the brunt of things. O'Hara stood next to him and whispered. "Do you think those bloody Jackeens in Dublin put up with their Tans the way we do?"

"I can't imagine them being much different," replied the Sergeant. "After all, they haven't got much to threaten them with, apart from slinging them out of the force."

"That's not going to cut much ice."

"No, but if we were to start their antics, our livelihoods and pensions would be on the bloody line." Callaghan walked off in a huff.

"He's going to leave a lively deposit in his underpants if he keeps straining himself like this," added Bradley, watching the Inspector walk to his motorcar where he began to complain to two plainclothes policemen, who were sitting in his vehicle eating ham-salad sandwiches. They stopped as he ranted about the useless English Tans he was forced to work with. Their mouths were now motionless but bulging with the contents of their enjoyable packed lunches. They shook their heads, looking sympathetic and appalled. One of them gulped down his food and muttered. "You just can't get the staff nowadays."

Baker looked back at the flustered Inspector and called. "Inspector Callaghan, do you want a cup of Rosy?"

The Inspector forced his hands into his pockets, pushing his grubby raincoat back. The heat was sweltering, but for some reason known only to him; he loved his mack and wore it in all weathers. Silently, he strolled over to the Tans, who were congregated adoringly around the tinker.

He left the men in the car to their repast and reluctantly joined the Tans. Both Irish policemen breathed sighs of relief. One fanned the air, dispersing the strong smell of body odour.

"Look out, lads, here he comes, make sure he's down wind," whispered one of the Tans.

Callaghan bit his lip in annoyance, feeling these English ruffians were toying with him. After another brief sigh, he gritted his teeth. The group had dispersed giving him plenty of room, which eased his frustration. Mistakenly, he read this as a sign of respect for his rank and not the perspiration.

Freda tried to explain: "I have a small peat stove but I very rarely use it, so it will take a little time to get going. Better would be a small fire by the road side."

"No problem, Gran," said Turpin, as he jumped to the task, recruiting Henderson and Barnes in his little rush of enthusiasm.

In no time at all, Freda found herself by the stone wall with her kettle over the fire, silently cursing to herself at the unfortunate turn of events, which was certain to cause delay for Cormac and Father John. She spared Turpin a glance of irritation. The little loud-mouthed English rascal had caused all manner of problems.

Again the impudent man gave her a cheeky grin, knowing he had caused her a bit of work. He winked at her as though doing the biggest of favours. "Am I in for a cut of the profits, Gran?"

"You most certainly are not, you forward scamp," she laughed in reply, imagining she was cheerfully throttling him. The mite didn't miss a trick, and was likely to get suspicious if she appeared upset at making a bit of money on the side. He would realise she was in a hurry and wonder why. "At ten shillings a day you don't need a cut of my little earnings, do you?" she added in a fake jovial manner.

"Who the bleeding 'ell told you we're on ten bob a day, Gran?" he countered quickly with a sparkle in his eye.

She was momentarily stunned. "My word, you don't let much go! That's common knowledge." She shook her head with pretended disbelief.

He smiled broadly: "Your charms are wasted on me, Gran. I'm not sucked in by that old Irish approach." His smile suddenly vanished.

"Your mother?" she enquired, realising he had mixed blood. "Dad's English, me mother's from Belfast," he answered. "Both patriotic, British citizens and right proud of me they are."

"I'm sure they are," she replied, careful not to offend him. He was in the Tans for personal reasons, and it was obvious that he, despite his nonchalant manner, took some pride in the job, perhaps harbouring aggression where the rebels were concerned. She turned her attention to the preparation of tea, not wishing to look on or antagonise the Tan.

Tea was finally brewed and the farthings began to be exchanged. The old farmer with his daughters came forward, dipping his hand into his pocket. "Three cups please."

"Keep your money where it is," she said and gave it to them free of charge.

Turpin was about to make a joke about favouritism, but checked himself as Freda pointed her spoon at him. He indulged her stern look and grinned once again deciding, for once, to hold his silence. He strolled across and took a cup, still smirking and staring at her. She met his manner with a smile, but was agitated by his downright impudence, responding with a nod of her head, to let him know that his tea was also free.

He chuckled, then put his farthing on the table. "Don't take me too seriously, Gran," then left, allowing her to deal with the rest of the Tans, who were lining up with their money ready.

Sergeant Bradley, after finishing his chore, was the last and purchased two cups, for Inspector Callaghan and himself. The former gratefully accepted and walked towards his car, where the subordinates still ate their sandwiches.

"I don't know how he can walk about in suit and coat in this weather," said the Sergeant, noticing Freda's nose wrinkling.

"It is a bit close for such clothing, though your lads don't smell the way he does, and they have to wear thick jackets too," she stated introducing a little compliment. Though she neglected to mention that most Tans reeked of alcohol and tobacco, something she found equally intolerable.

"Well, there are good wash facilities in the barracks. In this heat it's a godsend," he admitted.

"So what happened with the two men that were shot then?" she ventured.

Bradley looked behind to check none were in earshot. "They're more like bloody mercenaries," he laughed, then began two enlighten her on the dead men. "Well, we found out that these men, who are not from around these parts, were holed up in a cottage, belonging to the old boy over there." He nodded to the farmer and his daughters. "We reckon they were part of a flying column that attacked us in Cafgarven two days ago – killed an Auxiliary Officer, who was part of a new cadet force of Reserves to be dispersed throughout the country. You might have seen some of them..."

"Oh, ones with posher voices then, these boys – upper crusts eh?" She had heard of such men.

"That's right, all ex-officers – stiff-upper-lip jobs. Well, one of them comes over to see us for a day while we go on a jaunt to Cafgarven. This Auxie was with a couple of the lads in the War, so it was more like a 'Halloo chaps how are you?' visit. Do you know what I mean?"

She nodded, while Sergeant Bradley talked on, telling her about the shoot-out and the wounding of two men in addition to the killings – one was a Tan, the other a Volunteer, who she assumed to be Cormac Doyle. She shook her head, adding the odd tut here and there, encouraging him with her willing set of ears.

"So they are not local lads then, Sergeant?" she asked, trying to get more information concerning the two dead men.

"No," he replied. "Though we don't know how they got separated from the others of their so-called column. We only caught a glimpse of three men running away during the shoot-out. The one that got shot, plus two that helped the wounded man into the trees. We couldn't pursue because the lads were being shot at by other snipers hidden in the woods, who were giving a lot of covering fire."

"So you never saw most of the men shooting at you?" she sounded appalled as though it was a statement rather than a question.

"You never do with these flying columns. So we've been told anyway. They're usually comprised of about twenty to thirty men, who hit you when you least expect it to happen," he admitted.

She started to clear her things, anxious to go as she pottered about in a kindly manner, politely declining assistance from the Tans. When this was done, she returned to Sergeant Bradley and asked if his men would see to the smouldering embers of the fire.

"No problem," he replied and walked to the kindling mass, seeing to it personally. She pondered whether or not to take a chance and ask one question, which might cause suspicion. Not the identities of the dead rebels, for that would be too obvious. The Sergeant would not give that type of information. It would have to be more for the farmer and his nervous daughters, who were being held, for some reason, in connection with the incident.

"Sergeant, please don't think me intrusive but I'm rather concerned for the wellbeing of these people. Have they done anything wrong?" she asked humbly as he dispersed the clicking and popping embers with his boot.

He stopped, looked at the farmer and his daughters, who were again standing with the more tolerable Cuttings and Henderson, then answered. "They were being forced to shelter the bastards at gun point. It's not their fault that they became targets for the Shinner needs. Luckily we were able to get them out before the shooting started. Right relieved they were when we turned up, as well."

"So, they'll not suffer any reprisals on suspicion of helping rebels then? They would, most definitely, have had no choice in the matter – not when these men knock on your door."

"We know that, lady," winked the Sergeant in a sincere manner, thinking her an unassuming woman.

She smiled, believing his sincerity! He was a Regular Irish policeman from around these parts and the troubled times must have been especially hard for him. He doubted some of the Tans he was forced to work with, of that she was sure, but he equally resented the Volunteers too. She wondered whether he and Inspector Callaghan would be able to keep the Tans in order. Before returning to her caravan, she decided to wander over to the farmer and make sure they were enduring well under the circumstances. The

Tans might stop her, but she had attained some favour with them, due to making tea.

Cuttings and Henderson made no attempt to move her when she stood before the farmer and asked "Are you going to be all right?"

A nervous yet grateful smile greeted her as he glanced wearily at his two Tan guards. Perceiving they were not interested, he spoke in an over obvious complimentary tone towards them, not wishing to incur their displeasure. "Well it could have been a lot worse if it were not for these boys turning up when they did."

Henderson, flattered, came over and stood with them, lending his voice. "The two Volunteers were holding this man and his daughters hostage. Forcing them to give shelter at gunpoint." He was ready to tell the whole story, which was a bonus for Freda.

"Ooh! Well I never," she added outraged and hoping to fire Henderson up so that he would tell more.

"We saw the whole charade through their windows," he continued obligingly. "We had already surrounded the place."

"Oh aye, they saw it all through the window. Did well too, did these boys. Got me daughters out before they give the two of them what for, didn't you mate," agreed the farmer looking to Henderson, who nodded blindly to the patronising man.

"Oh," replied Freda in mock admiration. 'How on earth did you manage that?"

"Well," he added, adrenaline fuelling his ego. "We were a bit fortunate because they sent one of the lasses out to do a chore. When she came out that man over there…" he pointed to Turpin. "…confronts the lass and tells her to call for her sister, which she does.

"We get a result, 'cause she comes out straight away, without the Shinners suspecting a thing. So, we takes the liberty a step further and gets the second daughter to shout out for her Dad's assistance.

Well, this time the lad over there knows that the father will come out with one of the Shinners standing watch over him. Blow me if our bloke ain't got it right. Out comes the farmer here with the older Shinner right behind him.

Our bloke is on one knee with his rifle aiming straight upward. The sodding Shinner walks into his own ready-made firing squad – didn't have a chance. BANG! The end!"

Freda looked at Turpin. Not cruel or vindictive yet probably the most dangerous of all. His happy-go-lucky manner was charming, which won people over, despite being a Tan. However, he had the ability to channel his energy towards the heart of matters, probing and searching a problem – always focused. She was nervous of him, despite liking him for his devil-may-care, roguish manner.

"So, how did the other one die?" Her manner was casual.

Henderson nodded his head towards Jones. "He burst open the back door and blasted the younger one before the kid knew what was happening. Shame really, he's only young. Caught up with the wrong sort, but then that's the sort of thing these Shinners do."

"His name was Daniel," said one of the daughters nervously.

Her father frowned, and for a moment he feared she might have known the young man. "I heard the other man call him that name," she said.

"His name was Daniel Nelson, the other, Samuel Fergusson," confessed Henderson, offering information that no Regular policeman would.

Generally, the Tans seemed unconcerned by the deaths. So too were the Regular R.I.C for that matter. Their lack of concern disturbed Freda! She could not understand how they could be so unmoved. They were not filled with morbid joy or a sense of victory, just an indifference that made it more sinister, as though they had long ago adapted to such gruesome things. She felt that the rebel bands, in their unholy quest of attacking the Constabulary, had given birth to this vulgar horde of ruffians from England. They were fast becoming a match for the Volunteer flying columns.

Henderson walked away with Cuttings, leaving her alone with the farmer. "These phoney policemen have the ability to be so brutal, yet at close quarters they seem amiable."

"I think I know what you mean, lady," answered the farmer.

"It strikes me that any human can be corrupted to believe in killing as a sign of strength. Learning to take reprisals upon the innocent, in the hope of catching a stray rogue, becomes the accepted norm. Callous revenge is distorted into justice with warped ethics backing it up. If you tried to tell these men of the wrong they were doing, most would look you in the face and laugh unashamed."

"It's a shame that such fine men can be corrupted so," said one of the daughters.

Freda thought: "Except for Henry, of course." He had been among these rough, sturdy men. How out of place he must have been. Still, his falling among them was heartening, in the opinion of Father John and herself – a small grain of sanity in a desert of derangement.

She looked at the farmer and his daughters. "What fires men up to such degrees of passion, and when the killing is done, what quenches such feelings into calmness, like now?"

"For the life of me, I don't know lady," replied the farmer, watching them drag the bodies to the front of the truck under vigorous instruction from Inspector Callaghan, who seemed to assume the Tans could not perform any task without constant supervision.

In return, he was tolerated but usually ignored. The only weapon he had over them was dismissal if they become too unruly. It was easier said than done, and held no threat – they were more inclined to smirk when he administered such ultimatums.

When the task was done, he was once again vexed by their lethargic attitude. He gritted his teeth, but managed to contain himself. Instead, he turned to his car where the reposing subordinates were wiping and dusting themselves with handkerchiefs like a comedy duo. Obviously they had enjoyed their lunch.

"Have you two quite finished?" he asked sarcastically.

The only response was silence, apart from two pairs of blank eyes staring back, which further fuelled his anger. The strained resolve on his red face brought open laughter from the Tans.

Henderson turned to the farmer. "Well it's up to the Castle men now."

"No one likes Castle men," said Cuttings. "They're a law unto themselves."

"I thought they were the law?" The Farmer looked confused.

"They are," said Freda, and cheekily added. "The irony is they are a law unto themselves. There's a lot of scope on that issue." She smiled at Cuttings who politely returned the compliment.

Sometimes other men of the unit would tell him he wasn't the sharpest knife in the drawer.

"So now things are normal again?" asked the farmer.

"Two people have been shot dead, but all is fine now."

Freda smiled and added, "Yes, but life goes on after ironing out a bump in time's path and continuing as though nothing has happened."

Cuttings enchanted, shook his head. He was from a different world – looking at life from a completely different perspective. "You Irish have a right way with words. You all think you're blooming poets."

Freda closed the caravan door and walked to the front, where Turpin stood with a broad smile as though knowing something that he would not let on about. She smiled back with a raised eyebrow, thinking: "Let the cheeky scoundrel make up his own mind."

She hauled herself up onto the seat, ignoring him.

NINETEEN

The Potato Field.

Vigour, like sap nourishing a healthy plant stalk, coursed its way through Hayward's veins, finally tingling at his fingertips as his arms were splayed, imitating the trees about him.

"God, I love my life. Thank you for making me – for my victories and defeats." There was no one, but himself and God.

After a huge breath of summer afternoon air, he ventured back through the wooded scarp leaving the apple orchard where he had carefully laid the snares. He was feeling particularly pleased with himself and whistled as he made his way towards the river. The summer heat was beginning to redden his back and arms to the same colour as his face, adding to the excited itch of his skin. He was a world – a realm with colossal oceans about his flesh. Yet still, he felt above such minuscule things as he made his way through scattered sunbeams that pierced the green ceiling in an array of grandeur. Bird song enhanced the allure. Their high notes entwined the shafts of light, and the trees seemed like apparitions of a grove that had once been.

As though ejected, he came out upon the riverbank where Sean still sat upon his rock in the middle of the stream. He had adapted his fishing to suit his stance, still able to flick and whip the surface of the water with the fly.

"You look as though you should be a gnome decorating some gentry flower beds or fishpond," laughed Hayward.

Exuberant, he waded into the cold, refreshing stream once again.

"God, Henry, you are a glutton for punishment now, aren't you?" called Sean. "All Englishmen must be slightly eccentric, even working-class ones, if you're anything to go by." He watched with awe as Hayward swam towards the rock. "You could have just waded over, but then, you seem to have a feel for the water."

Clambering upon the rock, like some boisterous otter, Hayward sat beside Sean, dripping wet but content to let the sun dry him.

"Well now." Sean's eyes glistened with mischief. "Don't we make a sight – a Volunteer and a Tan, sitting on a rock, fishing in the most sanguine manner? It has a certain irony about it, do you not think? Children could sing nursery rhymes about such a bizarre event."

"You Paddies are a nation of blooming poets and romancers," laughed Hayward, thinking of Freda's ideas about nursery rhymes.

"That's what fascinates you about us Irish though, ain't it? You're not into the reality of things because you're a dreamer – that's your thing – it makes you tick – don't try and pretend otherwise."

Hayward's mouth opened then faltered. He made no reply. Instead, he looked across the stream, and asked. "Did you catch anything while I was gone?"

Sean sniggered. "Your ways could be a tremendous source of light-hearted entertainment. The way you falter in mid conversation, when you realise you've no quick reply to someone's banter." He decided to be lenient and with a certain amount of pride held up two fish.

"One more will be excellent, as with the one you caught first we'll have two each for supper." He offered the fly-rod to Hayward who gratefully accepted and began flicking across the stream, the way he had been shown.

"You know, Henry, I think you have a real feel for this, and would be most competent if you were to take it up as a hobby."

"Well, as hobbies go, this could be one that I would enjoy."

"Then let the hobby begin here, while we fritter away time on these stones chatting about trivia. A thing of significance when building a bond or breaking down strong walls, crushing the memory that each of us was once a killer —"

"All right, don't start off on one of your poetic jaunts." Hayward gibed.

"Well, it's hard to believe that a few days ago we would certainly have slain one another. Now, amid the sound of the fresh running water my hatred's washed away, diluted until the cloud of abhorrence is so thinly scattered, it becomes lost to the clear purity about us."

"My God," Hayward laughed. "You have a great way with words, but it helps to see things in such a poetic way." He struck the rod, hooking another trout, while Sean clasped his hands with a firm clap, rubbing his palms briskly. Ebullience oozed at the thought of the coming campfire supper. They landed the fish, then went back to the shore and killed it, putting it beside the other three in the creel before hiding their meagre belongings, careful not to leave signs of their presence.

Sean picked up his rifle and ammunition belt. "I think it will be wise to take these with us," he said.

"Yes," replied Hayward, picking up his own weapon along with a sack. "I must admit, it does make a person feel more secure."

"You, fearing my fellow Shinners, while I tremble at the thought of your Tans. It's a strange circumstance that we must tolerate the other's fear."

"Would we have the courage to help each other, becoming in the process a traitor to our own country?" asked Hayward.

"It's a thought best tucked in the back of our minds."

"Agreed."

"I thought it would be a good idea to follow the stream through the ravine, rather than travel over the hill. What do you think?" asked Sean.

"I think a jaunt along the river will go down a treat," replied Hayward cheerfully.

They set off, wading into the stream for, as the shoreline ended, sharp cutting rocks jutted out from both sides of the gorge.

Hayward looked somewhat irregular, clad in long johns, an ammunition belt and holding his rifle above his head to keep the dampness from the barrel. Sean had discarded his shirt and was wearing a shabby vest with his baggy trousers rolled above his knees. Like Hayward, he wore an ammunition belt and carried his rifle above his head.

The woodland ended abruptly as they entered the cascading waters of the small gorge, but they could see a continuation of trees at the other end of the ravine. The foliage arched over the gushing stream, giving the appearance of the interior of some strange Abbey, fashioned from the undergrowth, allowing the torrent's gentle flow to pass through. It was a though fashioned at God's pleasure and both felt they were venturing into a different world – one of natural gothic splendour. To reach the new enticing woodland they followed the stream through the corridor of rock, wading up to their chests in the brisk flow.

Sean, deep in the water and with teeth gritted against the cold clash upon skin suddenly felt a strong urge to submerge himself completely. He called to Hayward: "Take my stuff."

The Tan took it, while Sean gave way to his desire, slinging himself below. For some time he held his breath, causing Hayward some concern, before breaking the surface, like a banshee escaping from hell. Wiping his eyes and pushing back his wet, matted hair, he felt greatly invigorated from days of accumulated perspiration, the grime and sweat finally removed.

"Do you think it's just dirt we've washed off?" asked Hayward, offering back the gun and belt.

"Oh Henry, how I wish it could be more. Though, like sweat, guilt accumulates gradually and before you know it, the stuff has caked your body and soul."

"In that monastery, I aim to wash for a long time," replied Hayward. Soon the depth was such that they were forced to swim, each lying on his side, paddling with one hand, and using the other in an attempt to hold their guns. This form of travel lasted for a short time, through the middle of the ravine, until both were able to stand again. They waded the last bit.

The rushing water suddenly quietened after they had passed through the cramped gorge and its echoing stonewalls, settling as it entered the arched canopy of foliage. Their expedition was becoming a joyful adventure, each feeling more at peace than they would dare to admit as they stood in the smooth flow with the inviting woodland about them.

Sean still wanted to talk. "Once upon a time there were vast, untamed areas like this. Before we cut down the trees and put meadows in place. Townspeople come out of their dens of iniquity to look at tame fields and meadows, contrived by man's hand, and think themselves in the untamed wild."

"Yes, it makes a person think doesn't it?" Hayward felt the same disdain, and also good fortune that the light of nature was shining for him.

They waded further along the stream under a canopy of green with sparkling gaps flaring here and there in quick flashes of brilliance. Fish still broke the surface occasionally which, combined with bird song, caused both to feel as though God was bombarding them with an abundance of life's glory.

"We'll have to come back a different way," called Hayward. "I don't fancy the idea of swimming against the flow when we return."

Sean grinned and nodded his head in agreement. He was feeling the effects of the swim a little more than Hayward. But he was enjoying the benefits of such exercise: "Perhaps I'm not quite as old as I to think."

Above, the twittering of birds enhanced the spiritual feel of the woods, filtering through the trees with a haunting and compelling hollow melody. A cuckoo's call broke through the common chirping with a decorative introduction to the new world.

"My word, Henry – isn't this fine-looking?"

"Yes," he replied, entranced by the splendour. He stared in wonder at the criss-crossing light shafts, breaking the ceiling, while specks of pollen danced along the transparent stems. "This is, without doubt, the most agreeable place I have ever visited. Who could believe in such wonder without first seeing it? Words do not exist to describe this."

"It *is* very noticeable," agreed Sean wading towards the shore.

Following his example, Hayward clambered up the mud bank and came across a dirt track. "This is good! But bare feet and stinging nettles don't go."

Sean stood beside him. "Yes! With hindsight, perhaps we should have brought our boots."

Finding a track, they followed the course, dripping wet and feeling as though a bubble of silence was about them as they moved. The birds seemed far off to the sides, to the front and rear. Their sounds stopped when they passed a particular area and restarted once they moved on.

Sean peered behind and whispered. "I feel as though we're some form of intruding blight, polluting the tranquillity of this place."

Hayward agreed. "It gives me a guilty and unsettled feeling, as though we're trespassers."

"Oh aye, but thankfully there's tolerance in the bird song. Can you not hear it, Henry?"

He nodded. "Yeah, it's as if hidden eyes are beginning to accept us – brings a settling effect."

The sanctuary of the wood was rudely interrupted by a barbed-wire fence, beyond which lay a potato field. In the distance, a line of small, grey mountains shimmered in the heat haze. Crickets had now supplemented the birdsong, and the expanse left the two silently adapting to a new feeling of vulnerability.

Sean's gaze combed the woodland border, where the timberland arched outwards to either side. "We must stick to the wood's boundary. It'll be better if we conceal ourselves."

"I agree," replied Hayward, not keen to set foot in the open field. "We can get what we need by putting our arms through the fencing." He got down and crawled halfway under the wire, reaching for the nearest plant.

"I suggest we take one from this spot, then move along the boundary towards the river," said Sean. "We'll stop at intervals, taking others here and there, as we go. The riverbank offers some protection too. It probably goes past fields with different crops. We might find ourselves a cabbage field, or one with carrots."

"Sounds good to me," admitted Hayward, crawling back and putting a fine potato into his sack. They retreated just inside the wood and slowly made their way along the perimeter, venturing out at intervals to steal another potato. Before long they were content with their gathering, and decided to press on towards the sound of the flowing stream with an excited urgency in their stride. The ambition of following the river's course into open meadow thrilled them as they waded in.

"We're sheltered from view by the stream's cutting," called Hayward.

"Oh aye, it all helps," agreed Sean as they continued, stopping now and then to peer over the bank and see what produce was growing in the field they were passing. A rush of delight swelled in the pit of his stomach. He descended the bank with a look of joy.

Hayward picked up on it at once. "Well, what is it, something different from spuds, no doubt?"

"Big, juicy cauliflowers, neatly standing in rows," answered Sean with a grin. "Just like British soldiers, nice and pretty they are."

They scrambled up the bank and lay upon their stomachs, surveying the bounty before them, a most welcoming sight after the continuous fields of potatoes. Sean stretched his head, peering beyond into a neighbouring field where the river bent along its further perimeter. Peering, he tried to identify the plant leaves. "Can't see what's in that field," he conceded.

Hayward moved forward upon his stomach through the clumped patches of long grass that bordered the cauliflower rows. A cricket jumped out of his way. He edged forward, ignoring the irritating itch the grass caused against his bare skin.

"I don't think it matters about that next field, Sean. What we have here is plenty." He selected a fine looking vegetable then retreated back to the bank and holding aloft his prize trophy, he waited for approval.

Sean smiled his agreement, then added: "I'll wager that it would turn heads at those dainty little country fetes you have back home. I can just see it now, white and blue checked tablecloths, wicker baskets and old ladies and men in light jackets and straw hats passing judgement on lines of cauliflower. I reckon that one would have a big, blue rosette with first prize written upon it."

"You forgot the scones and cricket," added Hayward.

"Oh such sacrilege, do forgive me," replied Sean with horror.

"We must never forget the scones and cricket."

Sliding down into the stream, they continued to follow the flow, happy with their gains, though Hayward was intrigued as to why they travelled on when they had acquired their two vegetables plus fish.

"You seem to be looking for something. What is it?"

"I'm sure the next field has carrots." Sean could not contain his childish excitement. Another vegetable to complement their supper was too good to resist.

A dog barked a short way off and both froze and looked at one another. Fear grew in the pits of their stomachs, making their hearts thump in dread.

"It was in the direction of your carrots," Hayward whispered, concern etched in his face.

Reluctantly Sean agreed. "If a dog is close by, then its owner must be too."

"In this weather the stream would be a most inviting place for a dog to walk."

Sean looked at him. "That's what I like about you, Henry. You certainly know how to put more excrement onto the dunghill."

Hayward's mind raced ahead. "We can't afford to be seen."

"I can easily kill the mutt if it's alone, but if the owner is with it …" Sean stopped then added: "These fields cover a wide area. I would not be surprised if the land belongs to that large manor Freda was talking about. That means a person or people loyal to the Crown forces."

"Well, at this moment both sides are an unattractive prospect to me." Hayward began to back away the way he had come, as more excited yelps were heard. "The animal seems excited. Maybe its master is throwing a stick or something."

Sean held his rifle ready and began retreat with him. Their world was suddenly a threatening place. They turned and quickened their steps, wishing to put as much distance as possible between themselves and the dog-handler. Slashing their way forward, the two men hugged the shoreline but stayed in the water at ankle depth thinking the dog could not pick up their scent. Soon they reached welcome cover of the woods, and fears began to subside, though a sense of urgency persisted.

"We may take a bit of time moving back through the ravine," suggested Hayward. "It's a lot harder moving against it, but we would not leave a scent."

"Agreed," yelled Sean above the sound of the stream as it broke from the fissure. "But we could go up and over the scarp along the cliff edge. It will probably be quicker and I don't think the dog walker will bring his mutt around here, especially if we use the opposite bank."

"Which side is the opposite bank?"

"This way, follow me." Sean moved to the further bank.

"Are you sure? We never even saw them."

"Trust me Henry. I know which side of the stream they are on."

"All right then, but when we reach the summit I would like to try and see if we can get a view of the stream as it runs out of the woods. We may get to see who the dog belongs too." He needed to determine if there was a threat, and where it was likely to come from.

Sean agreed, and together they ascended the wooded scarp, the rock-face to the ravine growing ever deeper at their side. The tree cover was dependable and the pitch of the water's path, through the gorge, enhanced the echoes from the narrow wall. They finally reached the summit and crawled to a ledge that hung over the chasm, where a good view of the surrounding fields lay before them. The stream, along which they had just been, wound its way through the meadows out towards the far-off, grey hills. At a distance of about half a mile, they spied two figures of a man and his dog ambling along the river.

"Not of working-class background." Hayward sounded positive.

"Oh, and how do we figure that one out then, Henry boy?"

"The man's wearing a neat-looking, brown jacket, and he has a walking stick."

Sean was amused and secretly impressed. "So you can deduce all that at sight?"

"Well, from what I can make out at this distance, the man seems as though he's from a well-to-do background and all, ambling along with that sort of ..." Hayward was searching for the right word, conjuring his fingers.

"Gait," suggested Sean.

"Yes – gait is the word."

"He does seem neat in appearance – might be Lord of the Manor."

"I can't make out the dog's breed from here, but I don't think it's a sheepdog."

"Why? Is that important?"

"Well, a common farmer would have a Border collie, or the like."

"He has the manner of someone who is used to living in grander refinement than a farmer. The dog is a good, old Irish wolfhound" said Sean.

"I reckon he's some sort of Paddy aristocrat then," added Hayward.

Sean agreed, "I would think so – a Brit at heart, loyal to King and Country. Probably talks like a posh Englishman too."

Hayward peered intently out across the meadows. "Why is it that all Celts think Englishman have posh voices, when posh toffs come from all four countries of the Isles?"

Sean smiled – relaxed – no longer concerned about the distant man and his dog. He thought of Hayward's northern-English accent. "I don't know," he admitted. "I think of an Englishman and get this view of some arrogant, posh-voiced dandy. Yet I do know that you have your various accents."

Laughing at Sean's humorous insight into his countrymen, Hayward shook his head fascinated, trying to see the world through his eyes. Sometimes it was hard to believe this happy-go-lucky man could ever get angry about anything, let alone kill for his beliefs. Then he wondered how Sean viewed him, since being forced to spend time together in the basin. Surely the man realised he was not quite one of the devil's horde that Black and Tans were supposed to be. Everyone could do unforgivable things – Tans and Volunteers alike.

"What do you think would happen if you put two foes like us together in normal times?" he asked, with the sound of the river flowing up from the gorge.

"Most likely the way we are now, I hope." Sean frowned and looked out above the meadow to the grey hills beyond. "Most would find a way to get along."

"It would be nice to believe that," agreed Hayward.

Sean thought for a while, then turned and looked directly at Hayward. "Do you believe what you're doing is right?"

"What, absconding or becoming a Tan?"

"Becoming a Tan."

"At first I did – that's why I was one. Now, no! That's why I absconded."

"What made you become a Tan at the time?"

Hayward sighed and lay on his back looking up at the clear, blue sky.

"No job at the time – no trade, on account of fighting a war when I should have been learning one. England doesn't much care for its surplus of unskilled labour at the moment, and I believe things will get worse. Ireland, on the other hand, offers ten shillings a day to police a country that has armed bandits running about shooting people."

"Is that honestly how you see it, Henry?"

"When I was back in England I did. I was approached and sent to a recruiting house in Glasgow, across the border in Scotland."

Sean laughed whimsically. "So that's how you found your good self a most unlikely policeman – a militia, geared up for reprisals, where and whenever the Volunteers strike."

"That's the way it seems to be going. I have to admit, it's not what I expected. In a short space of time we have upset the local population and contributed more towards an Irish Republic than you Volunteers could have dreamed of."

"Is that what made you quit then? The way local people have been caught up in the crossfire?"

"Of course it is. It's certainly not because of the rebel Volunteers."

"So you hate us still the same?" Sean did not appear upset. It was an answer he could accept.

"Hate – it's unimportant – we get by through being bloody scared of them, if it makes Volunteers feel better."

"I think a healthy fear is apparent in both camps. In some ways, Tan aggression is giving the flying columns a hard time, now that Reserve Policemen are being dispersed far and wide. Trying to adapt to the Tans has been difficult. The Castle men round up suspects in large numbers from all major towns, but many are innocent. They don't make many friends like that."

He looked up into the serene blue sky, pondering why they attacked Cafgarven with just four men. It was something their Brigade Commander would never have allowed. No one attacked Crown force units in such small numbers. It was foolish, but necessary to get credit for the attack. The Castle men would assume the rebel flying column had more gunmen than it actually had. They might then think the men they were holding were not flying-column members.

"Let's go back to the stream, where the gear is. We'll make do with what we have for our eats," he suggested.

"Right, I'll go for that. We've done well." Hayward stood and stretched.

TWENTY

Resuming the Journey

Father John had been waiting in the small wood, by a bend in the lane, keeping watch at the roadside for Freda's caravan. The quiet appeal of the wood was lost on him as he grew more anxious, thinking the Tans may have arrested her. His mind began playing all sorts of tricks as he imagined her being treated harshly by the intolerant policemen.

Behind, Cormac sat against a tree exhausted from the vigour of his cross-country walk. He had performed this undertaking exceptionally well. However, he had no desire to continue, fearing a relapse.

"Still no sign of her, Father John?" he asked, concerned.

"No, young man. It's been a very long time now, and I hope she has not passed this spot before us. I'm dreading the thought that she might be further along the lane, seeking us out." The priest could see a good way down the road, and felt hell would freeze over before the comforting sight of the caravan would appear. "It has been three hours."

His trepidation was on the verge of taking a further slide when the big, brown horse, Moogsly, appeared with his familiar blaze running from forehead to snout. The beast's head went up and down as it heaved. Behind came the caravan in all splendour, with Freda looking content and sitting at the front of the vehicle.

All Father John's misgivings melted as the sound of birds singing, in what seemed like a fanfare of achievement, suddenly became alive to his senses. All the sounds of nature had been there, continuously beating for recognition against the wall of his recent anxiety. Now they had broken through his defences, he turned to Cormac with a big smile. "She's here."

The young man struggled to his feet, and Father John moved out into the open lane so that Freda might see him. The caravan drew nearer, moving towards the side of the lane next to the wood with the priest falling in step, where Moogsly was brought to a halt.

From the trees emerged Cormac, his arm in a sling, yet standing and walking with less difficulty than before. This pleased Freda and she smiled, encouraged by the sight.

"We've been very worried about you," said Cormac, relieved that she was finally here.

"I've been rather concerned for you too, young man – though I see that you are managing well enough. Better than I expected. You'd better get in the back. Try to get some rest. There is still a little more of that settling liquid I made for you during the night. It would be wise if you drank some. It will numb any potential aches that may be lurking."

"Thanks." He smiled and went to the back of the wagon and climbed aboard, while Father John pulled himself up to sit beside her.

"I take it you were slightly delayed," he ventured.

"I was indeed, Father John, and have learnt some tragic things too. I will not tell young Cormac about it until we reach the nunnery," she replied.

Curiosity aroused, he began to bombard her with questions regarding what she knew. Freda related the story of her meeting with the Tans and of the two dead men – confiding her suspicions that the men were companions of Sean and Cormac.

Horrified by the news, Father John agreed with her. It brought home the dangers of the escapade they were embarked upon. The terrible acts that these Reserve Policemen and Volunteers were capable of made him shudder.

"My God, these are desperate and dangerous times, Freda. I wonder if there will ever be an end to these vile murders."

"I can't see an end to any of this, can you, Father? It seems that many of the young men who get recruited into the flying columns are captured, but there are always more to take their places, and the Tans, likewise, have a surplus of young soldiers out of work throughout Britain."

Father John raised an eyebrow and sighed, leaning back against the black, leather rest, which was hot because of the day's intense heat. He felt mentally tired with all the wicked commotion that inflamed the countryside. It seemed as though his little area was now in the thick of it all.

"You know, Freda, I have heard that in some counties none of these terrible crimes are happening. Is that correct? You of all people would know, because you are constantly travelling."

"Yes, Father, there are a number of counties where the trouble doesn't appear to have made its wicked presence felt. It's like nothing is happening."

"Dear little Cafgarven was like that, until the Volunteers and the Tans picked out our village for their special attentions. Slinging lead about, they were, and the innocent people of our village caught in the crossfire, and paying the price for other people's wrong doing. This is a foul and very dirty war."

"You'll never find a clean one Father. Conflicts are a filthy and disordered business," she added.

He nodded his head absently in acceptance while staring at Moogsly's sweating back. The animal's hide glistened – steam was rising due to its labour as the beast pulled ever onwards towards their goal.

"I know that Dublin is very bad," she added. "There are soldiers, policemen, the special kind in their multi-coloured uniforms. Everywhere you look there are roadblocks and searches. You can sometimes be stopped on up to two or three occasions, even more when travelling in Dublin. Things are so much more intense there."

"Do you travel into the city then?" Father John was surprised that the tinker might venture to such a place.

"Never in a million years, Father. I hear such things from others. Even the Black and Tans will tell you what it's like in Dublin."

Father John shook his head. "It's a terrible state of affairs. Most of us Irish have become criminals in the eyes of the Constabulary, and it does offend and hurt people when we are all tarnished with the same brush as these rebels. It's just so unfair, and I don't know what can be done to make amends to the way people's feelings have been hurt. These Reserves have inflamed the situation to such an extent; that some of the villagers are beginning to look upon the Volunteer flying columns as heroes, when a few months ago they were a nuisance, and looked down upon. It's so strange how delicate people's feelings can be. I don't think Ireland will ever feel the same again towards being British. Not after the events of the past few months."

Freda agreed. "If the Volunteers get their way, I reckon they will thank the Tans for it. They seem to be winning the war for them with their brutality."

They settled to the journey, trying to relax but anxious about the patrolling Reserves. What if they came across these men again? It began to dawn on Father John how precarious their situation was, and the enormous risks they were taking. Capture held forbidding consequences.

Freda stared at the road ahead, with a concerned frown. She was every bit as humane as Father John. Neither wanted any part in the troubles, but both found themselves helping people from opposing sides of the conflict. If the Crown forces were to catch them harbouring the wounded Volunteer, it would be treated as subversion. Both would be interned, at the very least. She consoled herself with the belief that Father John and she had clear consciences and, whatever happened before God's eyes, they had done what each believed to be right.

She watched as Father John looked through the small window into the vehicle's living quarters. He peered through the dim light.

"I'll bet he's sleeping now, Father." Her gaze went back to the road. "He must be exhausted from all this unwanted exercise and trauma."

Father John nodded his agreement. "He has borne the emergency with great fortitude. Perhaps the real thought of escaping from the Tans had given him the will that has spurred him on."

"Plus some good medical attention." She smiled broadly, content the young man was settled.

"What we've done over the past few days is really quite remarkable. Three men removed from this nasty conflict. What would happen if all well-meaning people could get such results by focusing on odd individuals here and there?" He became excited, imagining such an event.

"Are you beginning to feel as though you are on some sort of crusade, Father John?"

He stopped dwelling on the subject, knowing Freda was firing a warning shot across his bows. Instead, he smiled and adjusted his spectacles, realising that dreaming was a weakness that could get the better of him.

"You're quick to notice my limitations, Freda – over enthusiasm for the work at hand. You bring me down to earth."

"It's all mapped out! What will be, will be, and win or lose there is a purpose."

"Yes! Always," he agreed, feeling he was in need of her healthy council.

As expected, she responded positively.

"Father John, with the upmost respect, I want to make it quite plain that your enterprise and commitment has already achieved much. A little step in the right direction is worth more than miles of travelling in the wrong one. You should consolidate and be proud of the good work you've done, for it is already an achievement. Sometimes it's better to point people in the right direction and then let them find their own way. The more you take a person's hand and lead, with the aim of helping, the more you can become corrupted. It can seduce a person, and the very help offered can bring about downfall." Once again, she had ventured upon the notion of leaving the Tan and the Volunteer to their own concern. "I know that this causes you great concern, Father John, but I do feel that you should leave the two at the basin. Let them sort out their problems themselves. You have pointed them in the right direction, and they are fit men who can travel better on their own. Henry likes the idea of the monastery, and I think that Sean will guide him there. Who knows, the rebel may just take up the option himself. I'm certain that you have put together all the right ingredients and now you need to let things simmer."

"I would feel as though I was deserting my duty before God," he replied, fearing that she might be right. If he could only be certain. Freda had an enigmatic power he could not ignore.

"I can't help feeling we may push our luck too far and overcook the broth. The situation begun in the apple orchard must be allowed to continue under its own steam. You had the vision to bring about this situation, but I feel you should leave your creation to run its course. God brings things about and then lets the pattern of events run their course. Why can't you see the merit in this?"

He gritted his teeth! Part of him wanted to heed her advice, for he could see the excellence of her wisdom, but his own doubt threw a shadow of fear and guilt.

"How can you make things look so plain and logical?"

"Your own emotions get the better of you, don't they, Father John? You fear my advice may be perilous for Henry and Sean."

Beseeching eyes gazed back at her and for once there was no scrutiny contained within them. They were open doors that beckoned Freda to look deep into him and understand the anguish that her sound words were causing.

"Please Freda, your wise council is so disturbing, for if I were to heed your advice, Henry and Sean might come to some terrible pass. I would never forgive myself. I would always wonder and it would plague me till my dying day. It would be marvellous if you were right, but I dare not leave things to chance. Please believe me. I respect your counsel beyond words, but I fear betraying these men. I have promised to help and I will. Can you understand my side of things, Freda?"

"I accept your position and your perspective on things, Father John, but let this turn over in your mind between here the basin. Maybe logic, as you accept it, will triumph over your fears." Her softly spoken words were consoling – submerging the guilt beneath a blanket of tolerance. She sighed and then pursed her wrinkled lips. "It's a trouble with people who become too attached to the way of things. You know what I mean, Father John?"

"No, Freda." He smiled. "But I would like to hear anyway."

"Well, it's the same old way of things – the general nature of how days go by. They can't change and adapt to a situation. People become methodical, never changing, constantly nursing, and never allowing something to develop on its own. A tinker has to find ways of improvising for the unexpected and must learn to leave things to go their way."

Freda turned and looked at him. He was lost in his thoughts, realising that she was caught up in his way of things too. She was unable to desert him, even though she felt he was trying to do too much. She accepted he could not follow her advice about leaving Hayward and Sean to fend for themselves. His fear of betrayal was too real, and the thought of some kind of mishap falling upon the two men was ever present in his mind. In her heart she was convinced that they would eventually come to terms with their situation. Then, together, they would formulate a plan of their own, taking control of their predicament, working together in the way Father John had always intended. She found it frustrating when he could hit upon such good ideas, bringing about reconciliation between enemies, and then be unable to let his creation bear its own fruit. His one failing was that he looked upon the Tan and the Volunteer as children. Both men had the capability to get up and tackle problems off their own back. When they needed something they could take the risk by themselves to venture forth without guidance from anyone. Hayward took a big risk by hiding in her caravan, right under the noses of his own men, while Sean elected to help his friend and came back to the village he had attacked the last place anyone would expect to see him after such a disturbance.

"I do believe you want to do your best for them, Father John, but then I have the feeling you believe you're on some sort of holy crusade. Humble yourself before the situation that has arisen. We are all just pawns in the game of destiny. Be aware of your own mortality, and try not to get too carried away with the contribution that you think you should make. Even a pawn can mess things up if it is not properly placed." Her words were kind, but firm.

He smiled and nodded his head, though he still had reservations.

"I feel that I have gained much from you, Freda, but the extra you have delivered as well as your solid reason is an unwelcome bonus." He looked down at Moogsly's back, losing himself within the steaming perspiration rising from the beast's glistening hair, and dwelling on the plight of Hayward and Sean.

"How long will they get along with one another? Sean seems to have adopted a light-hearted manner to the idea of staying in the basin and I trust him to his promise of no killing.

"Henry, for his part, will not violate the faith that is placed in him. He wants the sanctuary of the monastery. Maybe if they were left to their own devices, both would eventually go to the Brothers of Christ. Sean would know the way without my guidance. Then again, what if they don't? Two men left out in the wilderness without the help I promised them." He turned to Freda. "You lent them things for their stay in the basin – the fishing-rods and the old kettle. You said that you wanted them back."

"I have two more kettles. What I lent them has no use anymore. I shan't miss those little things. So, you are at least thinking on what I have said."

"God, Freda, you've set bells ringing in my head. This is tearing me in half, honestly."

"Father John," she whispered softly, putting a consoling hand on him. "It is not my intention to vex you. I would be overjoyed to see these young men removed from this ugly, little conflict that we have about us, and like your good self, my thoughts are on the best way to achieve that purpose. We are all mortal, we can all make mistakes. Now if you find the guilt of leaving these men to come to a decision too much, then you should carry on and do what *you* feel to be right."

He smiled. "Your wise words cannot be ignored. Therefore, I must live the torment before reaching a decision. At least I have your blessing on the matter being my choice, and I thank you."

"I'll mention the subject no more," replied Freda contentedly.

"Oh, don't give up on that score," he retorted mildly. "I rely on your honesty, dear Freda. You have a great gift – an aura of logic in which I have a steadfast trust. Sometimes I need this and seek it from you."

Freda felt greatly flattered by the words. One moment he was vexed, then he could manage to suppress his anxiety, taking time for his fellows as a priest should do.

"Thank you, Father John, that's most kind of you. I would like to say that you are a remarkable man, containing and dwelling on the matter I have put upon you. Yet still you can find time to be concerned and reassure a person. This is a good quality, and I commend you for it."

"Thank you, Freda." He sat back in, holding his face up to the hot, summer day's splendid sunshine.

The little caravan pressed on towards the ever-nearing goal. Above, the sweltering sun burned the side of Father John's face, causing him to shift uncomfortably. He took off his jacket and pushed his fingers inside his habit, wiping the sweaty grime from his neck. He longed to bathe in cold water, and wondered if he would be allowed to when they reached the nunnery. He breathed more deeply while taking his glasses off to wipe the rims and the bridge of his nose.

Here and there they passed through a small village, where the presence of a priest and tin-ker caused some excitement among the children who ran beside the wagon, asking questions. In reply, Father John blessed them, remarking on how sunny the day was. Women stood at the doorsteps, nodding their respects though not daring to ask questions. They encouraged their children to do this, or at least Father John sus-pected they did. Wherever possible, Freda would make deviations to avoid villages that she consid-ered too big.

"Ideally, I'd like to do this for all the commu-nities we come across," she groaned.

Father John had suggested that he should go into the caravan at the first village, but she had objected, on the basis that many people stopped and showed her hospitality, which she would need to refuse. If she had a priest at her side it would give her good reason for politely declining without having to answer questions. Fortunately the ploy worked, even though there was an element of risk from the Crown forces finding out from gossip of their strange companionship. Father John even came face-to-face with another priest, standing at the front of his Parochial House. He knew the man and he gave him a short wave, raising an eyebrow, allowing him to read the look that asked not to be detained. The stout, bald-headed priest nodded, smiling with congenial complicity, allowing the caravan to pass without question.

"The one fortunate thing is the lack of Regular R.I.C. men," said Freda.

"They have taken to remaining in their barracks unless reinforced with Tans," replied Father John. "There is noticeable lack of local, inquisitive village bobbies. In better times, they would have been on the beat, or pedalling bicycles."

"Lone policemen make easy targets for a gunman," Freda sighed, feeling uncomfortable with the situation.

"Many have been murdered during the last year," he added. "You can't blame them. When they do come, it is usually mob-handed, with drunken Englishmen as back up."

Onwards they went, through the summer day, until they finally reached their destination. Surrounded by the green, rock-strewn hills stood the nunnery. It was a grand, stately place with a large wall in front, in the middle of which was an arched entrance and a track of mud and shingle leading down to the roadside.

Freda turned – a satisfied smile on her face. "Oh joy. I was beginning to think we would never get here."

"Well Freda, we have and it's all down to you." He turned to peer through the small window grating into the caravan.

"Cormac, are you awake, lad?" There was a note of excitement in his voice.

"Are we there, Father John?" Cormac answered. He had been asleep.

"We are, Cormac, the nunnery is here."

He watched the young man stand and reach for the steady bedpost as the wobbling vehicle rolled on.

"Our objective has been reached, and all that remains is the agreement of the Sisterhood to permit your stay – then, perhaps, safe passage to Canada. Something can be worked out through the Church on this matter, though it will have to be done secretly, as in some areas the Volunteers have been able to impede young men from emigrating. They would be sure to find out about you if we try the usual channels. Then again, young man, you might want to stay, and see the conflict out."

"I'm not sure what I want to do, Father John."

"Cormac, when Freda passed through the roadblock, she came upon the aftermath of a sad commotion. Two men, believed to be Volunteers, had been surrounded in a small cottage and shot dead in a gun battle with policemen and Tans. Freda saw both these men lying dead in the roadside and was able to find out their names."

Cormac's jaw muscles clenched as he gritted his teeth, bracing himself for the answer, which he knew would be forthcoming.

"Go on, Father."

He resigned himself, looking down at the floor.

"Their names were Samuel Fergusson and Daniel Nelson."

"Oh Christ, no!"

Father John said no more, preferring to observe as Cormac, muttering curses, walked back to the bed and sat down.

He left Cormac to his thoughts. Outside the sun was a big, orange ball that lingered in the sky above the western scarps. The wild petition of the craggy hills and the day's twilight had a compelling splendour. He thought of the dead men who would never see such glory again.

He and Freda both looked behind as Cormac had come to the window.

"God I hope they are in Heaven, where both can be at peace," he muttered.

Father John was about to console him, but Freda subtly held up her palm to restrain him.

Cormac continued. "A place where all killing is meaningless."

He shuddered as another thought came. "A void, a black void is a place where this strife is meaningless."

Distraught he looked at the varnished plank floor with an elaborately decorated handmade rug tacked over it. "The rug in here is so colourful. Perhaps Freda, you make such things on nights beside a campfire. Content and free from the vexation of killing – living for the joy of pure being and taking each day as it comes. Making your comforts and beholden to no one. Yet still you have the heart to help people from all backgrounds." He stared at the rug's pattern. "All the joyous things that can be created and yet I use my energy for killing – or, at least trying too."

His mind drifted back to Cafgarven as he pondered the intricate planning to lure the Crown forces into an ambush with the taking of an informer's life. Then hiding the corpse in the backyard of an Inn to incriminate innocent people and win over more hatred against Volunteer enemies. The attack, to make the Reserves think they were under fire by an entire flying column, when most of the brigade were being held in custody on suspicion of other charges. The foolhardy attack, to make the police believe they were detaining innocent men – the killing of the new Auxiliary Officer as a bonus – all that effort, all the elaborate intrigue and clever planning, to leave men dead and innocent people traumatised.

He then reflected upon the quick response of the Crown forces, using their own brand of devious and unrelenting enterprise. It had left him wounded and desperate to remain at liberty. Now Sammy and Daniel were dead, after retribution of devastating consequences – again more unrelenting violence to leave more men dead.

"The real, notable, praiseworthy deed has been done by both of you," he finally muttered, in abject defeat as the caravan halted outside the Convent.

"We're here, Cormac. Now you shall have sanctuary, plus a chance to mend physically and mentally from the trauma of the last few days."

Father John climbed down and went towards the big gates of the nunnery grounds.

TWENTY ONE

Evening in the Woods

The campfire had a spiritual glow, and both the men had finished eating their gains of the day. The fish, potatoes and cauliflower had been very gratifying and, like fellows who feel they are at one with the world, they sat back to enjoy the fine night. The wood sounds were different from those of the orchard, with many strange noises harmonising with the rustling of trees. A creature shuffled through the nearby bushes, uninterested in the firelight, wanting only to go about its business in peace. The two fugitives spared it a brief glance, before turning back to the fire's gentle radiance.

"Oh, if only," remarked Sean with an air of contentment.

Hayward raised an eyebrow and asked the expected: "If only what?"

"It would be fantastic if every day could be as good as this, no hassle, just foraging and eating," he replied. "We have a little Garden of Eden around us – fields bearing bounty in the form of potatoes, cauliflower and carrots."

"A river for fish and rabbits on the scarps," added Hayward with a smile. "I will not mention the apples in the orchard, on account of you saying it is the Garden of Eden. You're not meant to eat the apples there, are you?"

Sean laughed at the Englishman's superstition. "You don't have to fear a bloody serpent, Henry. There are no snakes in Ireland. Saint Patrick told them all to get lost and they went."

"Well you might get a substitute snake or something that can take the role. I reckon we should leave the apples alone," he replied.

Sean chuckled, realising that Hayward was in earnest. Gradually his amusement faded and he frowned. "You're serious aren't you now. Oh, come, you don't believe in such shenanigans, surely not."

"Well no, but it wouldn't hurt to indulge the superstition, would it."

"If it makes you feel better, we will." Sean rummaged in the creel and came upon the tin whistle. He pulled it out and held it up, his eyebrows raised in expectation of his friend's approval.

"Do you know how to play it?" asked Hayward, suspecting that he might be in for an ordeal as

Sean blundered about with various uncoordinated musical notes.

"Of course I do! I can play a mean jig on a fiddle too." Putting the tin whistle to his lips, he began to play a lamenting sound that was both haunting and compelling with shrill notes that rippled out into the dark wood. The tune was slow, allowing the listener to linger on each note and explore thoughts. Hayward felt as though the trees and bushes were alive, and he leaned back enthralled against a trunk savouring Sean's ability with the instrument.

Soon both were lost in their deliberations, Sean intent on his tune, while Hayward allowed the music to feed his imagination. The powerful attraction of the slow, lingering melody led him to think of his life, its catastrophic path and where it was heading. He imagined a future in the fields and scarps of Ireland. He was detached, staring out of his hollow shell. His eyelids were like two cave mouths, allowing in the sight of vast grasslands with the craggy hills at the end of the expanse. Beyond the hills a mauve, angry-looking sky raised and arched the capsule of his being. He felt himself twisting to watch the torrid sky going over and beyond to descend upon yet more rocky scarps that skimmed the encircling horizon. His only link with the campfire was the sweet, haunting sound of the tin whistle that he had taken with him into the dream world. He walked around for a while feeling a tingling aura along his calves and arms. His chest inflated with pleasure as the music followed where he trod. He was a ghost in this world, and dwelt on the matter a little, deciding he could accept an afterlife like this. Then the subject of death came, keeping unwanted company with gentler thoughts – an unwelcome guest that irritatingly followed, allowing no privacy. He was sucked into the morbid topic, and saw a rumbling, black void rising over the craggy summits. It hovered, reminding him that the black beyond would always be waiting, no matter how many conflicts he survived. It would draw ever nearer, until he was consumed into the blackness.

He jerked forward, back to the firelight of the campfire. Sean was staring at him, having taken the tin whistle from his mouth. The fire crackled amid the rustling trees, but the sudden pause of the melody left an eerie silence, as though both felt they had been left bobbing in the wake of some prophetic enigma.

"Are you all right there, Henry? You've gone an awful strange colour," ventured Sean.

"Just morbid thoughts," he replied nervously. "Sometimes it's not always a good thing to think too much."

"What type of thoughts?" asked Sean.

Hayward grinned. "I'm terrified of dying. The mere thought of going beyond, fills me with dread. I get scared that there is nothing but void – black void."

"If it depresses you, why do you think about it?"

For a while Hayward was silent, staring into the flickering flames, as though searching for the right words. There were many reasons, but all of them boiled down to the dread of death. There were smiling faces of good friends that had departed forever, their empty shells remaining in the fields of Flanders. Some of them had died hideous and tragic deaths, while others bore mutilating wounds and were locked away, waiting for the black unknown to take them.

"I've seen hordes of people mown down – thousands in the space of a few hours. Some of them screamed and squealed in their death throes like wretched pigs in an abattoir. The indignity of death, when it comes, is always terrifying to me – is it not so for you?" He looked up, his voice filled with loathing for the distasteful topic.

"It is terrifying to me as well, Henry." Sean looked into the fire. "My dread is standing before a court and justifying my actions. Do you fear that as well? Maybe there is a God, maybe they have it right and all of the Christianity that is preached will come true. Sometimes I feel a void will let me out of becoming some focal point of attention."

"So you do feel guilt for killing? You have killed in your time, haven't you?" Hayward supposed the rebel might not have taken a life, even if he had the countenance of a man who had.

"I have on a number of occasions, during the Boer War. I could not really say if I actually took a life there. I fired at positions where the enemy were, and saw my own countrymen, and yours, falling about me. But since this trouble began I have seen death on a much more personal basis. I've looked into the eyes of men before they died and heard their mothers scream in my imagination. They give you a wretched stare of disbelief sometimes, when their lives are ebbing out of them. It was me who shot your officer in Cafgarven. His death filled me with a mixture of feelings. First, when all the rest of your lads went to cover and started to return fire, I felt like a little boy who had dropped the milk bottle that I was stealing from the pantry. Then, when you all began to ascend to our position from two directions, I was terrified that I was about to be killed. It wasn't until I reached the apple orchard with Cormac and started back for Father John's help, that I began to think about the life I took. The guilt was not so obvious until confronting him. I had to look into his eyes you see. When I killed that Auxiliary, he was quite some distance away and the effect was different during the heat of the moment. The informer was worse. My associate took his life with a muffled shot while he was being throttled. It was a very messy affair. We were trying to kill him without wasting bullets. If we can, it's advisable and worth it. *The Big Man in Dublin*, our leader, advises that. It was the informer's face, just before we took his life, that haunts me. His is not the only one – just the most recent. He stared, silent and resigned to his fate – looking me straight in the eye, burning himself into my memory with fateful resignation. It's horrible face-to-face.

Did you ever come across that in Flanders? The terror must have been overwhelming during the heat of battle. You look like a man that has come through it. I don't mean it offensively, Henry, but the War has taken something from you. That's why you dwell on such things."

"I should imagine that it is so. I can remember the lights and the roar of the guns during the night. Crouching in our dugouts, we were, under ceaseless bombardment." Hayward was developing a desire to talk, to clear out his system. "Sometimes you could not stand it anymore but there was nowhere to run. We were paralysed with fear, and then when it suddenly stopped – you knew that it would be either ourselves or the enemy that would swarm across no-man's-land. It was better for us if it was them doing the attacking. You would scream out in rage and let the turkey-shoot begin. Lines of men mown down, murder on an unimaginable scale, and you would go along with it because you were glad that this day was not one when you were among the poor sods that were screaming and hollering. Men become snivelling little children as they wither and thrash, or sometimes just huddle up and die in the mud. I never wanted that. I prayed to God not to let it happen to me. It's not death so much that scares me; but knowing when it will come, being forced to dwell on such a thing. When I go it will be ideal if I don't know anything about it. Just turn the lights out, and let it happen."

Sean nodded his head understandingly. "My fear is different from yours. I do believe in an afterlife —"

"I don't disbelieve, Sean, I hope and pray above all things that there is," cut in Hayward.

"I'm sorry, Henry. I did not mean to imply that you are a non-believer. My point is that my fear is of retribution. Yours is standing upon the abyss of life and death, having time to dwell before you make that fateful plunge into that unpredictable cloud."

"Yes," agreed Hayward. "You're right, though I have never really had time to look into the faces of the men I have killed. This is a dirty war really, isn't it? No constant fear of attack, much of it is quite pleasant from a Tan's point of view, just a corpse turning up now and then, followed by the anger and a desire to go into the nearest town and take revenge for it. That's when I have seen the faces, the women and the children. Here they are part of the battlefield. The innocence is much more apparent. It's difficult to find words to explain, but for all the fear and terror, this place is more difficult to function in for me. I can't take it here. I'm broken and unashamed of it. We don't look at them before they die, but we do see into their faces when we are searching their homes, ransacking and slinging their property about. They stare at you, filled with anger, but unable to do anything, because if they do – they know what to expect. I've seen the bemused looks of the children who can't understand what's going on, as we bring degradation on their parents."

Sean sighed in sympathy and leant back. Who could believe that he was sitting in a wood on a glorious summer night with one of the hated enemy and finding he had much in common, gaining truth and understanding from a Black and Tan – more than he had ever expected?

"Let's talk hypothetically," he suggested, after a little thought. "What would you do, as the leader of your country, if I came to you with my complaints about British rule in Ireland? Would you back off and allow Irish people to rule themselves?"

Hayward pondered the question before answering. "First I would like to know just how many would like to break away from Union. Since I have been here, it has been said that Ireland was always a colony, not part of Great Britain. This is something that I never knew. I was also unaware of the fact that many Irish want self-rule. We don't get a clear picture at home. It was not until I arrived here that I began to get some idea of how diverse the situation was. During the War, I saw many

Irishmen in the trenches, and quite frankly the Easter uprising was a shock for the Irish boys, as much as it was for the rest of us. There are also the blokes in the R.I.C. These are the Irishmen that I have spent most of my time with. They appear mainly pro-British. In the North, where I confess I have not been, we hear of Orange Orders that are extremely loyal to the Crown."

"There are a sizeable number in the North. But these people are in a minority of their own Irish people," added Sean, patiently trying to introduce a broader picture of things.

Hayward looked into the flickering campfire, allowing Sean's words to sink in. He became lost in the flames, trying to think of all the conflicting things that he knew of. There were probably more than he could bring to mind. Whatever Irishman he chose to listen to – Loyalist or Nationalist – he knew a great deal of bigotry would come from whoever argued their cause.

"It doesn't matter which one of you fellows starts preaching – at the end of the day, you're all divided. You can't live without killing one another. If I agreed with your views and gave in to them, there would be other Irishmen that would feel let down. You people have got yourselves a nice, little war without us British. God! Why am I talking like this? One moment you have me talking on the woeful things I feel about being here, in this little tit-for-tat conflict – then you inflame me against your people when you ask me what I would do if I had the power of judgement. Suddenly I feel hypocritical. The truth is – I don't know what to do. I can't make that type of decision. What I will admit is that I don't believe the police action, in which I was involved, will be able to fix things. Plus I do not sympathise with your approach to what is going on."

Sean nodded his head, glad of the Tan's honesty, knowing the Englishman was no traitor to his own country even though he disagreed with the methods employed. "I'll agree that we have a bloody good conflict here, without you boys. Though if the English never came here, in the first place, it would never have happened. Your Norman Barons came over seven hundred years ago."

"Sean, seven hundred years ago these Norman Barons were kicking the shit out of us Anglo-Saxons, who didn't care much for their rule either. It's no good going back in history. What's now, is real, and arguing with pointless recriminations, and lots of ifs, will not improve the mess we have out here. Our mess, for even though I may be English my people are involved in this. We are entwined, and there must be a way of disentangling the plight we are all in. At the moment, all we can do is kill one another, and not give a toss about the innocent people, who get caught up in the crossfire.

"Look at what we both did in Cafgarven. It was a despicable act by both sides – your people and mine. None of this will ever be right, dress it up with any philosophy you want. At the end of the day people, who don't deserve to, get killed. Something has got to be done about it all and I do realise that if people are not listened too, then frustration can spill out in other forms of protest."

"Like mindless violence," suggested Sean, putting things in the perspective of how he felt Englishmen looked upon the Volunteer gunman.

Hayward looked, knowing that his tone contained a little patronising tint. "No, not mindless. Your *Big Man*, as you call him, seems to be causing all sorts of problems. There is some coordination among you, but it seems to be less intense nowadays. When I first come out here, we were told stories of police stations being deserted, because of the Shinners ability to strike at the R.I.C. men barracked within. Now you're being forced to ground, though you still manage to catch us with our trousers down, every now and then. It's all tit-for-tat killing, and the body-count is mounting up in a place that pretends to be normal."

Sean nodded. "I don't think our demands are wrong though, and I feel you haven't any great desire to condemn our ideals – even though you should not be allowed to judge on the matter, being foreign. I'm not accusing you of anything by the way, Henry, it's just a statement. I believe the English don't have the right to preside over the way we would like to rule ourselves. Freedom is a right, and no other person should assume some sort of entitlement to grant or refuse it. The British should stand back and let us get on with it. Then if their loyalists did win, they could have the country as part of their own."

"You mean, step back and let you all kill one another, while international opinion blames us for doing nothing? Let's be real, Sean. Personally I couldn't care less if Ireland wants to go her own way, but the British Government is not going to let go. They will arm any loyalist faction to the teeth. Even now they are containing you with police action – you're fighting policemen, not the Army."

"Oh, come on, Henry, you're all Reserve policeman made up of ex-soldiers. Are you sure none of the Tans are recruited from prisons?"

"No, we are not," laughed Hayward. "Though a blind eye has been turned on some previous convictions. We are soldiers really, I admit that, but on paper we are Police Reserves, part of the Royal Irish Constabulary, making it seem that Ireland's police are dealing with matters themselves. The Castle in Dublin employs us. The British Government is trying to give the appearance of sitting back and letting you get on with it. If you do come out on top in this little affair, which I honestly think you will not, the government will probably say that Irish policeman put it down. We will never have existed."

"I don't think Irish people will ever forget what you boys have done Henry," stated Sean grimly.

Hayward sat back, bit his lip, and stared at the flames again, finding solace within the pulsating, orange embers. He wondered whether Sean was right. Without taking his eyes from the flames he asked: "What do you think they will make of the Volunteers, Sean. Do you think they'll see you as the heroes you think you are?"

"I don't believe any of us think we're heroes, Henry, including your blokes. Both sides think it's a messy business that has to be thrashed out. Our countries could get along so much better if we respected the differences of one another." Sean wanted to take the sting out of the conversation. Both were becoming impassioned and, despite each man's shame at what was being done, there remained a reluctance to disparage his own particular faction.

Hayward nodded in reluctant agreement, feeling the need to stop talking about politics – accepting he was blundering blindly into a dark realm of which he knew nothing.

"Do you know any lively little tunes? Like those jolly, Irish-type jigs that are usually played on a fiddle?"

Sean smiled, catching the new spirit of things, and also wanting to be away from issues that neither of them could solve.

"Sure I do," he grinned. "So you like jigs, eh? Well, let me see now."

He put the tin whistle to his mouth and started to play a merry, little tune that lent a new mood to the wood and the firelight. It was as though the trees and bushes were made to be serenaded by the melody. It was the night's anthem – perhaps since time began. They spent the night under the leafy foliage while Sean played to his heart's content – even getting Hayward to sing to some of the tunes, which he was surprised to find were folk songs of Irish origin when he thought them English. Sean conceded that he was unsure himself on some of the songs origins, confessing that the odd one here and there might have been English or Scottish.

"Never mind, they're rum little ditties anyway," he laughed as the two of them found they had a common love for folk music. Hayward spoke of the public houses in and around the north-east of England, where folk singing entertainment was common, saying they would be most impressed with such fine tin-whistle playing.

Sean, having his appetite whetted by such a tempting prospect made a pact. "When all of this madness is over," he ventured. "I'll show you some of the best pubs in Ireland if it's the jigs you want to be hearing, and you can show me England's north-east. I would love to see some of the things you talk off."

"We'll do that for sure. I reckon they'll pay to listen to you."

"I can also play the fiddle, as I told you. That's my main thing. I used to earn a few bob in Inns doing that sort of thing when I was younger," added Sean.

"Well, if you can knock out jigs on a fiddle the way you do on a tin whistle, I'd say we English would love you in the rural parts."

Sean, flattered by the compliments, was fired with enthusiasm. He scratched his head with a dream-like stare on his face. "Do you really think they would like to hear my playing then?"

"Your talents would be greatly appreciated." He asked for a few more tunes, and Sean readily obliged. Soon the haunting sounds were floating into the night.

TWENTY TWO

The Way Home.

Leaving Cormac at the nunnery had caused a commotion, requiring a great deal of heated explanation. Sister Superior was most put out by the young man's unexpected arrival, and Father John had become very vexed at her reluctance to help. It caused him to ask the Sister some blunt questions on her Christian commitment, drilling her with his eyes, most valuable weapons. She had buckled under the intense scrutiny, not used to people firmly standing their ground with her. Father John was also adept at turning the lady's own words against her, cleverly twisting them and throwing them back.

After gaining her consent for Cormac to stay, the question of passage out of the country was then discussed, with a satisfactory commitment from Sister Superior. By then she felt it was safer to cooperate with the forceful priest.

Fortunately, the darkness had long settled upon these tense issues when Freda steered the caravan along the lane with the aid of a lamplight. She peered into the dimness, trusting in Moogsly's senses more than her own.

Father John sat beside her deep in contemplation, worrying about his congregation back at Cafgarven. If he could get back to the village before the morning, then his one-day absence would not arouse too much suspicion, and he could easily dismiss questions on the matter if raised by any of the more inquisitive people of the village. It would mean going back to Cafgarven without stopping off at the basin, which would no doubt make Freda happy and also allow him that little time extra to consider the question of leaving Hayward and Sean to fend for themselves. He reflected on the fact that he was even considering Freda's proposal at all. It was utterly out of character for him to do so. In his own mind, he saw the Tan and the Volunteer as lost children, whereas in reality they were anything but. Here lay the wisdom of Freda's advice, desperately campaigning against his resolve. His mind was once again a raging battlefield of logic, conscience and clemency – and his need to get back to Cafgarven represented a welcome postponement of the final decision.

Freda knew the problem weighed heavily on his mind, and remained silent, not wanting to cause him any more anxiety. She looked up at the stars, which flickered in their resplendent glory and told of the tiny insignificance that contributed to the way things were. Minute to gigantic, everything was meant to be, and played its part in the overall way of things – from an ant in some distant meadow crawling into a spider's web, to men flying. All these tiny events were vital parts of the matrix of destiny. A raindrop, falling from the sky, might explode into a massive ocean, making its little effort of good. So, Freda told herself, every raindrop had value. When combined in their millions upon millions, they were equal to an ocean. That tiny speck was part of everything and carried importance in its own right. She smiled as she looked up at the black star-speckled ocean – she was a part of eternity and always would be. Nothing could change or deny the essence that was Freda, for she occupied that time and place and always would. Nothing vanished without trace whatever the outcome of its venture – there would always be a reason behind it. Even if things did not turn out as expected – the will was there. With this thought in her mind she looked to the priest to console him, for she felt much of his perplexity was of her making.

"I will still help you, even if your final decision is to go back to the apple orchard," she said.

He responded with a relaxed smile. She was most assuredly a true and honest friend, something for which he was most grateful.

"Thank you, Freda, I realise that all that has been achieved so far is due to your contribution. I will need your help again, once I have got back to Cafgarven. As much as I keep going over things in my mind, the conviction is still there. I will have to return to the orchard and complete the final part of what I need to do, to bring salvation to these two men. I must witness it, just to put my conscience at rest. Perhaps it is selfish, but I have to see it through, even though you may be right in thinking they can find salvation for themselves."

Freda's face wrinkled – deep furrows formed into a smile of happy acceptance. It was a show, for deep inside her doubts remained. Still, he had to reach his own conclusion. He had, after all, done very well by Cormac, and brought two foes together. It was a remarkable feat, and who could blame him for wanting to see things through to the end? She would stand by him throughout his venture, to the bitter end.

"So where am I to take you, Father John – straight back to the apple orchard or to Cafgarven?"

"I think it would be wise for me to return to the village first, Freda. If we could get back before daybreak, it would be most advantageous. In the villagers' eyes I will only have been missing for one day. They will not take much notice of the two nights in journeying, for they will have been lost in their own dreams. What are our chances of getting back before daybreak?"

"I will try my best, though I do think we'll be pushing it a bit to reach Cafgarven before daybreak. Travelling at night is hazardous at the best of times, and slower than in daylight. We will have to put a lot of trust in Moogsly for guidance. The beast is good though, and we will give it our best attempt. If we don't get to the village by daybreak, it certainly will be in the early morning," she answered.

"Splendid, Freda, and I do hope we can get back without any mishaps. Most people will be tucked up inside their beds while we are travelling."

Together, they talked on matters at hand, giving one another a degree of praise for the achievement concerning Cormac. Both agreed, it was work well done and were most pleased with it. The task remaining, with the Tan and the Volunteer, had to be performed towards the following evening, when the darkness was ready, once again, to descend.

Time passed quickly, and the ground covered was considerable. They travelled for about three hours with the dim lamplight from the wagon throwing its glow to guide them against the silhouetted foliage. As they turned a bend they saw, before them at a distance, a light. Freda halted the caravan, but immediately cursed herself for doing so.

"A roadblock at this time of night?" enquired Father John, nervously.

"Not Crown forces,' hissed Freda concerned. "They must have seen our lamp light. They know we're here."

Suddenly there was the click of a rifle bolt from the wood at the bend the caravan had just passed. They turned, terrified at the sight of armed men – much closer than expected. Ominous, dark shadows emerged from the dim tree trunks and moved towards them. Father John lifted his hands – a reflex action, letting those approaching know that he was unarmed. Four men came into the caravan's lamplight, immediately recognisable as Volunteers from one of the rural flying columns. They carried ammunition belts, like their counterparts in the Tans, but wore civilian clothes.

One, a tall man in a shabby, old cap and a rough-looking jacket, walked closer, his rifle menacingly pointing at them. His wrinkled and brutish face, with flat nose, was severe.

He had obviously done a fair amount of box-ing in his time, decided Father John. "Could you point the gun away from me please?" He was ner-vous but annoyed.

"SHUT UP!" the brutish man replied. "Get down and come here." "Don't you be talking to a man of the cloth like that," scolded Freda in response. She nimbly clambered down from the caravan and walked towards the man.

"No, Freda," berated Father John, fearing she might provoke him.

"Stop!" shouted another voice from among the three men standing behind.

The brutish man, who appeared poised to hit Freda, froze. Abruptly, Freda stopped, reading concern in the voice. She wondered whether the command was for her or the big fellow pointing the rifle at Father John. It was then she realised her act of shaming the thug would not have worked. The ruffian would not have hesitated to strike her down. She lingered uncertainly before the brute, who stared back at her with complete contempt. A younger man came forward and she realised he had called the command.

"Come down, Father," he said in a surprisingly well-spoken and educated English accent. His dress was refined compared to the rest of the men, and it was evident that he was in charge.

Father John obeyed the command and climbed down from the caravan to stand before their scrutiny. The other two men, standing in the background, moved forward with their rifles levelled at them.

"What are you doing, abroad on such a night," asked the young man.

Freda distrusted him – he seemed to be a dandy and adventurer such was the flamboyant air he portrayed.

Father John composed himself. "I have been attending to some important business in a nearby village. A fellow man of the cloth has been helping me with matters of the Church," he answered, hitting upon an idea that could aid him. In a flash of inspiration, he decided to pretend that he thought these men were from the Castle in Dublin – Crown forces doing undercover work. He would use the Volunteer's English accent to aid him.

"I'll tell you government bullies no more on that score, and I will not disclose the name of my fellow man of God. You can tell that to your employers back at the Castle too. I want no part in your fighting – do you understand me, young Sir?"

There was a brief silence among the Volunteers, who looked at one another, frowning.

Freda unwittingly aided him. "They're Volunteers, not the Government."

Father John feigned open-mouthed astonishment – followed closely by an intense stare at the leader. His scrutiny appeared full of suspicion.

The leader held up a placating hand. "Please, Father, don't be fooled by what you perceive to be an English accent. I assure you I'm a good and loyal Irishman, and my heart is with the Cause."

Father John frowned, then regarded the rest of the men with startled expression. Deciding to not overdo things, he added. "If you are Volunteers, you'll get no blessing from me, young Sir. I'm a man of the cloth and cannot offer you any support for your cause. You're an adventurer, nothing more than a man whose head is full of romance."

The young man nodded in acceptance, satisfied with the vexed priest's manner. Father John, for his part, found the ideal way of appearing to accidentally inform them of his position – letting them know he was in disagreement with the Crown forces and willing to say so.

"How do you come to be with a tinker? Accepting that you have been to visit one of your fellow brethren – what reason do you have to be riding with this woman?" asked the rebel leader, sounding like an affluent Englishman.

"This lady is my friend, and she is doing me a great kindness," was all he would say.

One of the others spoke in defence of Father John. "He would have to travel when the old tinker wants to move, Sir. She's a little eccentric and is a common enough sight around these parts?"

The young leader looked around at the man who offered the information and gave a nod. "You're lucky, Father, or we would have recruited you to help dig up the road."

"Oh," muttered Freda. "So you're making another blasted roadblock. Have you no consideration for folk like myself, who need to use the lanes?"

One of the men replied: "It's an inconvenience that you'll have to live with."

Both noted the harsh Belfast accent – another man who was not from the area. The flying columns wandered far and wide across the county and could often be based in an area where they did not live.

"You have men working up by the light," said Father John getting a little bold. "Are they Volunteers like you, or are they poor, local men press-ganged into making a roadblock for you."

"They are local men called upon to help the Cause," replied the young leader.

"They will be the ones to pay the price of retribution when the Tans visit their village. It will be their homes that are smashed up and searched. Their persons injured when the beatings start, and maybe one of them will take a bullet for retaliating against harsh treatment, which these new policemen are apt to administer," scolded Father John.

"Policemen! You call those bastards policemen?" spat the Belfast man, trying to offer some form of criticism, and clearly missing the point.

"It doesn't matter what they are called, you ignorant oaf," retorted Freda, angered by the northern man's pathetic impudence. "These Black and Tans take their frustrations out on innocent people because of what you are doing here."

The man gritted his teeth and stared back, simmering with anger. The young leader next to him held up his hand for quiet and, like an agitated dog, the thug backed down reluctantly, snarling and wanting to be let off the leash. "We know what these Tans are capable of, Father. Could you at least tell me where you are going?"

The tone of his voice was still polite, but he wanted an answer.

"Cafgarven. I'm the village priest there," answered Father John, knowing that, by now the news of the incident would have spread about the countryside.

There was a gasp of amazement from the group, who were visibly impressed by what he said. They all seemed suddenly more amenable.

"Were you at the village —?"

"Yes, I was," cut in Father John. "It was a ghastly deed that I witnessed, and the retribution was thankfully small, compared to some stories that I've heard. The inn was set alight, but luckily the fire was put out before too much damage was caused. I realise that I cannot divert you from the Cause that you follow, but I must ask you to let me pass. Will you allow us to do that?"

The young leader looked at him, considering. He glanced along, through the darkness of the lane, to where the light of the saboteurs was glowing.

"Most of the trench has been dug. I'm not sure if the wagon will be able to pass," he was deep in thought. "Come over with us, and I'll see what we can do for you." It was funny how people normalised in peculiar situations – suddenly the young rebel had become a tradesman keen to help a customer in any way he could.

Father John, for his part, was willing to be indulged by the young leader's attentions, while

Freda followed in disbelief. He walked among them – men who were part of a vicious, killing campaign. Everyone was laughing and exchanging in small talk! Even the press-ganged village men, who were being forced to dig the trench across the road, had adopted a spirit of light-hearted indifference toward the gun-swaggering henchmen watching over them. They seemed resigned to the fact – not having much choice in their work, as there would be consequences for refusal, and at that moment no Black and Tans were present. When they arrived in their Crossley Tenders the next day, the rural men would no doubt be just as cheerful filling the trench in if need be.

Freda observed these easy-going local men, appearing to be so full of cooperation, while the Volunteers gave them the necessary gratitude for their efforts. "Laugh today and worry tomorrow," she thought, for though people were fond of saying tomorrow never comes, it always did. They would have to watch the English Reserves, because they would be immune to their light-hearted charms. The rogue law-enforcers would gladly drink the frightened villager's ale for them with a smile and a bit of light-hearted banter, but then they could just as easily burn and loot if they decided too.

All combined in an effort to get the caravan across the trench, finding a small area of ground at the verge and the meadow's rock wall border.

The trench, which was still being worked upon, had a short fall from the rough stone wall of about six feet. Steering the caravan close to the wall still left an overhang, which would cause one side of the wagon's wheels to fall into the trench. A solution was proposed by one of the villagers. He knew where there was a big, sturdy, old barn door, which could take the weight of the caravan.

"If we fetch it, I'm sure it would make a fine bridge," he said.

The Belfast man instructed the local, and a few others, to lead him to the place. Instantly, they clambered out of the pit, sweating in the hot night – steam rising from their bodies because of their exertions. The break was welcome to the tired men, who dearly wanted to return to their beds. Many of them would have to be out in the fields by morning, getting on with their farming.

"I'm sure they will not be long, Father," said the young Volunteer leader. "We'll have you on your way in no time at all." He turned to the others who lazed around nonchalantly in the darkness. One asked to smoke, a request which was bluntly refused.

"No, you know the rules." He was furious that his fellow conspirator had even asked – tutting and shaking his head in disbelief. "Where on earth is your blasted head at, man?" he added in his elegant accent.

Father John decided to probe, knowing it was unwise. "Are you ex-British Army?"

The young man turned and smiled, pleased by his attention, then replied. "Yes, how an earth did you know that."

"You have the air of an officer."

"Oh, my accent gives you that impression does it?" replied the rebel leader. "With the rest of the chaps it goes down like flatulence at a Royal banquet."

Father John laughed. "Yes, I can well imagine it would. Does it not cause an inconvenience for you?"

"Not now," confessed the young man, matter-of-factly. "Though in the early days – my word – the chaps were suspicious and they were certain I was an English spy."

"Well, I don't think the English would send a spy with a nice, plum, Oxford University accent," admitted Father John, waiting to see if the young man corrected him by saying something like 'Cambridge actually'.

Instead, he received an amused, yet suspicious, smile.

"Naughty, naughty, Father – my word, you are a slippery fellow, aren't you?"

Freda decided to butt in. "My word? Is this the real you, or is it just an act." She still found him irritating.

"I beg your pardon, Madam, but what you see is the real, unpretentious me."

Father John smiled. The man had a sense of humour that was able to withstand Freda's scolding. She calmed down, not wanting to be the object of the man's wit, hearing chuckles in the darkness and men settling themselves down for the entertainment that might follow.

"I, like many of my fellow Irishmen, have been born and bred in England's pleasant land. I do emphasise, however, that I am Irish and a loyal patriot," he stated.

"Do you not think of the young, Irish boys who lie out on the fields of the Somme and Flanders as loyal patriots then, Sir?" asked Father John.

"I most certainly do, Father, and the young English, Scots and Welsh men too. We agreed to settle these disputes after the conflict. We stuck to our word, many of us anyway. Instead we are penalised by a Parliament that does nothing but drag its feet then sends out Reserves from England because they can't get enough Irishmen to do their dirty work for them."

Father John added. "The Easter uprising happened in the middle of the conflict —"

"That was an unpopular event, even among Irish people. The people of Dublin openly booed the men involved in that, and many of the Volunteers were in France at the time. What did we get for our consideration – nothing? Nothing, except a new police force and a new type of freedom, which allowed English rogues to go around the countryside doing exactly what they want."

"Not that you people don't provoke them," countered Father John in the most settled of voices, allowing his magnified eyes to stare down.

The young rebel was absorbed by the priest's scrutiny. His humorous mood disappeared as serious issues inflamed his passion. He seemed to be about to babble out his beliefs, needing to justify his reasons for taking the gun.

Father John wondered why the young man did this. Why indulge him? He would never be allowed an audience by the British thugs who terrorised the villages.

The young rebel leaned forward, obviously wounded by the priest's words. He put his face close to Father John then, through clenched teeth, whispered:

"Tell it to your Black and Tans, drunk on hate and the Greenwoods they have been told. See if they listen to you. The Church, Father, must get down off the fence and decide whose side it is on."

Father John stared back. "Don't use a man's name in vain, young Sir. I know people are apt to say 'Greenwoods' instead of lies, but surely an educated young gentleman does not use such common slang."

The rebel leader slowly pulled himself away from Father John, still staring into his luminous eyes, not allowing a flicker of the eyelid to show weakness. The rage within him subsided, and his face creased with a vindictive yet victorious smile.

"Confront the bastards all the way. Every time they hit you, hit back. Face everyone with aggression. Even blasted priests like you. Save your sermons for those congregation members you call your flock. The sheep that will do anything you tell them, including accept British rule."

Father John stared with his gentle, accusing eyes for he sensed the frustration would burn out, and when it did – the young man would still have to meet his stare before leaving. He assumed the rebel would walk away, though to give him credit, the young man was able to make him waver a little with such bravado. It was quite an intimidating response, which caught him off guard.

Pleased and fuelled by anger, the rebel swaggered and strutted along the trench, believing he had gained some advantage over Father John.

He did not realise Father John had the measure of him. The priest continued to stare back with the calm, tranquil radiance of his church – an invisible haven that Father John always fell back to.

Before long the rebel leader's zeal lessened, but Father John's scrutiny remained – big, green, soul-searching eyes.

Finally, the young rebel, his face burning with frustration, turned away. Almost sulking, he went and stood among his men who were quiet. Their leader's usual quick wit and bold talking was a match for radical minded people bold enough to confront him. This time he was at a loss. His aggression, blind and unfocused, had faded under Father John's scrutiny.

An uncomfortable silence settled over the group, and the surrounding blackness of the night began to mark its presence with the chorus of clicking and croaking wildlife. The sounds swelled in the darkness settling upon the silent group, who ambled about, waiting for the return of the villagers with the old barn door.

Father John wondered if the vexed leader would change his mind now that he had been rubbed up the wrong way. He turned to Freda and whispered: "I do hope that I haven't upset him too much, Freda. He might not be so willing to help us now."

"Don't worry yourself on that score, Father John. I think he will be only too pleased to get rid of you, even if he has to carry the blooming caravan across the ditch by himself," she sniggered.

Welcome voices drew close, above the other noises of night. Freda turned to Father John with a hopeful look. The fear of the Volunteers had gone. They posed no threat now, but a type of disdain was apparent, making the return of the villagers welcome for both parties.

They suddenly appeared out of the darkness by the rock wall, with the Volunteer barking out encouragement in a harsh, northern drawl. All clambered over the meadow wall, dragging a heavy barn door with them. More men came forward to assist, surprising both Freda and Father John. Neither had realised that there were so many of them outside the glow of the fire. How many more could be hiding in the darkness?

The young leader moved forward and lent his strength to the task. Carefully, the door was placed over the trench, providing more width to accommodate for the caravan's axle. Once laid, it became obvious that the crude bridge was more than adequate for the caravan to pass over. The rebel leader, pleased with the efforts and the promising strength of the old door, turned with a renewed vigour.

"Right, Father, it might be a good idea to come forward. We shall take it slowly though."

Freda clambered up onto her seat, asking Father John to lead Moogsly by the reins. He smiled, gently guiding the anxious beast forward. One half of the wagon was steered on to the small area of the grass verge, while the other side rolled on to the bridging barn door. The villagers pushed when the wheel hit the thick edge of the door, while others held it steady, standing in the trench to grip beneath. As the first wheel lumbered onto the crude bridge, the rest of the vehicle followed easily. Within seconds the caravan was safely on the other side.

"Right then, get the chaps to take it back to the place where they found it," ordered the young leader to the brutish man.

The villagers left with the heavy barn door in tow. Once again the company fell silent and the previous strain swelled within Father John and Freda. They looked to the young leader ominously, expecting him to become vexed again.

He smiled instead, pleased that he had been able to assist. It did, after all, pay to keep in with the Church, even if it was to appease the every-day folk.

"Well, you're free to be on your way, Father," he said with an air that showed he would like to see the back of them. "We'll not detain you any longer."

Father John smiled, and then became solemn. "Thank you for helping us across the ditch." He climbed to sit beside Freda, then looked back at the group standing beside the Volunteer leader. He sighed then after a pause his eyes widened with conclusion to his thoughts. He blessed them with the sign of the cross.

There were murmurs of thanks from the men, who knew he did not approve of what was being done. They edged forward in a tighter pack as the caravan resumed its journey. Within a few minutes the wagon turned the bend and the incessant sounds of nocturnal life imposed their presence, mingling in the blackness.

"Well, that was a little close for comfort," ventured Freda in the glow of the lamplight.

"Oh, I am not so sure really. I think that the police would have been much more inquisitive, and I'm certain we would not be on our way so lightly," he replied.

"I think it may have been respect for the cloth," she added.

"Again, on that note, I am positive you're right, though now I'm anxious to put as much distance as possible between us and these Volunteers."

"I'm afraid that in this darkness it'll be unwise to try and push Moogsly for a little more speed. Believe me, Father John, we'll be well clear of the rogues before long."

"Yes, Freda," he smiled submissively. "You are, of course, right."

He looked behind and made out the silhouetted shapes of hedgerows. He sensed, rather than saw, the blackened scarps rolling away in the distance – still waves in the night.

"At least the local villagers were creative in finding some form of help for us." He looked ahead, through the yellow glow of the lamplight and out into more lingering blackness.

"When the Tans come in the morning, they'll be equally as creative in helping them fill the trench in," added Freda with a glint of humour in her voice. Father John laughed, nodding his head in agreement.

"They will, and who could blame the poor fellows?"

TWENTY THREE

Morning in the Woods

The heavenly twitter of a nightingale was the first of many gorgeous manifestations to enter Hayward's waking consciousness. More birds chirped far off and a ceiling of luscious, green leaves gently rippled against the blue sky, giving promise of another fine day. The sound of the river called gently in the background, as though lingering politely, allowing the other noises of nature to enter his being first. The kind smell of crackling embers filled his nostrils, bringing all his receptive senses to life from slumber, already forgotten as he sat up to see Sean sitting by the small fire.

The rebel was poking at something in the ashes and, sensing Hayward was awake, he turned and smiled. "I'm cooking a few spuds and the kettle is about to boil."

"It smells good," replied Hayward standing up, arching his back and stretching his arms. "How long have you been up, then?"

"About half an hour," he replied. "Thought I'd knock up some spuds, before setting about anything else."

Hayward moved to the fire. There was coolness in the air that he knew would give way to warmth as the sun began its journey across the vivid, blue sky. Still, the shade would be more than adequate as the day progressed. Unbuttoning his police jacket and laying it by a tree, he returned and squatted next to Sean.

"How long until they are done?" he asked.

"Not long, about ten minutes. The tea is ready now, though," he said and reached for the kettle, holding it with a cloth to stop the burning his hand.

Hayward reached for the teapot and placed it before Sean, who carefully poured the boiling water into it. With a long spoon, Hayward stirred to help the brew along.

"So, what's for today?" he asked.

"When we've done this, I thought it might be a good idea to walk over to the scarps where you laid your rabbit snares," suggested Sean.

Hayward's face blossomed – he had forgotten the rabbit snares. He wanted to go immediately. Sean was most amused. "Whoa there! Henry boy, have your tea and potatoes first," he laughed. "They'll not be running off, you know."

Smiling, Hayward crouched again and continued to stir the tea, though the excitement had made him seem more agitated.

"Maybe a fox has taken the rabbit," he began.

"Woo boy!" laughed Sean, as though to control an unruly horse. "They'll be there. I know because I have a feeling, that's all. Come on now, Henry, drink your tea and then the potatoes will be ready. We can eat them walking along, if you like. That way you can get your breakfast and investigate the fruits of your work at the same time."

"That sounds good to me. Where are the cups?"

Sean pointed behind him with a raised eyebrow.

"Oh!" Hayward looked up in mock exasperation because of his inattention. He picked them up and placed them before Sean, who was poised with the kettle.

"It's a pity we have no milk but then, with a dab of sugar, I find the taste quite acceptable," he replied rather tartly as he poured.

"Indeed," mocked Hayward, with an old lady's aristocratic demeanour. "One learnt to become acquainted with the taste during the trenches where such luxuries, as milk, were often absent."

They sat back in the grass that grew in odd clumps where there were gaps in the foliage, and allowed the sounds of nature to occupy them as they sipped their black tea. The birds, the rustling leaves, and the distant sound of the flowing stream engulfed the small area with a spiritual quality that both were keenly attuned to.

"Today makes a person glad to be alive, don't it, eh Henry?" Sean had an air of satisfaction.

"It certainly does. I've not seen such splendour for a long time. I'd almost forgotten how ideal life can be. No killing, no accusations. It's like Heaven, or someplace en route. A pleasant waiting zone,' replied Hayward.

"Like a happy Purgatory – one that eases you before a journey."

"Yes, that's an apt description of it; a happy Purgatory – a pleasant, waiting zone, before my journey to this monastery."

"Do you seriously want to go to a monastery, Henry? Is it really what you want to do? Or is it Father John's influence."

The fact of Hayward wanting to go to such a place confounded him. It did not seem like the sort of thing a Tan would do – especially after his wartime experience.

"Why do you think it so strange?" asked Hayward.

"Well, it just doesn't seem like you."

"Because of the blood on my hands from France, or the blood money I have accepted for being a Reserve policeman in this country? Are these the things that make you sceptical?"

Hayward sipped his tea and waited for Sean's reply.

"Yes, in a way I do think of these particular things. It seems so strange that a fighting man like yourself would want to live among monks."

"I've seen too much death." Hayward looked up through the foliage, into the clear sky. "Now I have become obsessed with it. I lie at night wondering how long I've got. We spoke of that last night, remember? Well now, most of all, I need time to contemplate and think among good men who believe in an afterlife. Maybe you would too?"

"I could never see myself as a monk," laughed Sean. "God knows, I could do with taking time to contemplate for a while and a monastery, in that particular respect, offers some form of attraction. But actually going into the Brotherhood? I don't think so. Not on a long-term basis. Maybe you should think along those lines."

Hayward stared into the fire and nodded his head, pondering. Maybe Sean had a valid point – one that certainly could provide a more careful and non-committing approach where going to the monastery was concerned.

He sighed. "I suppose I want the time to think and reflect in a place of peace. I need to make a decision on what I really want to do with my life. I'm sure I don't want to go back to England – not now – too many things have changed." Then he looked directly at Sean. "How long do you think we should stay here, waiting for Father John to come back?"

"If he is able to come back," replied Sean. "I think you might be pondering on the same things that I am. We should consider what we must do for ourselves. What if Father John and Freda have been caught while helping Cormac? It's a real possibility."

"Do you know where this monastery is? Me being what I am, there is no other place that I can go to. We should be making plans ourselves."

Sean rolled the blackened potatoes from the embers then stood, wanting to pick them up but knowing they were too hot. He looked to Hayward, his face intent on the issue, allowing the potatoes to cool. "If you want, we can decide what to do between us. I'll go to the monastery for a while and I do know of one, which is probably the very place that Father John was thinking of. We'll spend today here, and then begin the journey at nightfall. It's always best to travel at night, away from the roads."

Hayward nodded in agreement: "That sounds good to me. We'll try and do it for ourselves if there is no sign of Father John by nightfall then."

Sean turned his attention back to the potatoes and picked one up, which he started to juggle about from one hand to the other. Hayward copied him and together they walked from the campfire towards the stream, still juggling their potatoes as they went. In the distance, a nightingale trilled as though calling after them.

"Ouch," spat Hayward dropping his potato to the ground. "How bloody long do these things take to cool down?"

"A little while yet," Sean laughed, trying to peel the burnt, black skin from his. He was partially successful, revealing the soft, snow-white inside – a hot and inviting steamy substance easily pulped in the mouth once properly cool.

Hayward picked his up and tried to peel it too – being moderately successful as he exposed the inside.

When they reached the river, the forest seemed to open up, like a grand set of doors, revealing the shingle of the ford and the stepping-stones that crossed the fresh flowing water.

Hayward was tempted to dip his potato in the water to cool, but then refrained, considering it would destroy the taste. Instead he placed it upon a clump of grass just at the edge of the shingle. Deciding he could at least wash his face and arms in the cold water, he pulled off his braces, allowing them to hang loosely by his side as he knelt upon the first stone, cupping his hands and lowering them into the river.

Sean followed suit, removing his dirty shirt and neckerchief to reveal an equally grimy vest, containing a veteran beer-consumer's belly, which hung over his thick, leather belt.

When both had completed, Sean squatted upon his stone, looking to his companion who lifted his wet face to the sun.

"Do you think that all this trouble will come to an end?" he asked.

"It doesn't seem like it," replied Hayward. "We've been at one another's throats for hundreds of years and it seems whenever this sort of thing comes about, it always ends in tragedy. I don't want to be part of it."

"You're a part of it already, Henry. You can't change that. All this …," he gestured towards the woods and the river. "You're here because of your involvement in the affairs of Ireland."

The Tan jumped back on to the shingle and walked back to his potato, calling back to Sean. "Then on this account," he waved at the woods in imitation. "I'm glad to be here. This is a very important thing that's happening to me. It has deep meaning."

Sean hopped on to Hayward's vacated stone, then returned to the shore. "You're not going to start getting all poetic on me, are you, Henry? There's that slight touch of the romantic in you. I've noticed it crop up on a few occasions now. Definitely not Tan material. You must have slipped through the net when they were doing the interviews," he joked, but with an undertone of well-meant honesty.

"If I could have a penny every time a person has said that to me, I would be a rich man now,"

Hayward smiled, as he picked up his potato, which was now cool enough for him to peel away the burnt skin, while Sean returned to his. Each took a bite and smiled, pleased by the taste.

"Well, my compliments to the cook," said Hayward.

"And the farmer," added Sean. "Bloody good crop he's grown."

They started to laugh, and discussed another excursion to the potato field later in the day, while hopping back across the stepping-stones, chatting as if they had known one another for years, each enjoying the other's company. They had drifted beyond the boundaries of enmity, into the realm of friendship, without realising it – Sean, no longer a Volunteer, and Hayward certainly not a Black and Tan.

Reaching the other side, Sean found that his enthusiasm for fly-fishing had returned, as tempting trout broke the surface of the fast-flowing stream, twisting and flapping in a tantalising display of freedom, oblivious to predatory scrutiny.

They entered the wood and came out upon the scarp to face the basin's orchard, deliberating over a timetable of events that they planned for themselves during the day. Fly-fishing had become their focus, although each would have preferred something different, preferably rabbit.

"Rabbit would be great for lunch," said Sean, firmly believing the snares would yield one victim.

"We can then squeeze in an afternoon dinner before starting our journey to the monastery."

"That would be another trout for dinner then?" asked Hayward.

"It would leave us a pleasing memory of the stream cutting its glorious path through the hills."

"Now the poet in you is coming out," Hayward laughed.

Sean smiled. "First, however, we'll have to get preparations in place for our rabbit lunch."

As they entered the gentle slope and followed the wood around, they agreed upon getting all the necessary items. If a rabbit was snared, the potato and cauliflower gathering must be done next. Also, the campfire could be moved closer to the riverbank, so that they could cook while fishing for trout. Excitement about the forthcoming day began to stir and they quickened their pace around the scarp. In a short time they were back in the basin and standing upon the open slope, with the wood behind and the apple orchard to front and below.

"Where does the water come from?" asked Hayward.

"On the other side of the basin's opening, I think. It trickles down in a sequence of falls through the woods. I don't reckon we'll have time to see it now, but I do believe it is a sight to behold," answered Sean.

They moved along the knolls of the rocky slope and then went down into the grass floor of the basin. Sean moved off in the direction that Hayward pointed, while the Tan went to another trap. His heart leapt with excitement when he spied one of the creatures lying by the burrow entrance. Moving closer he saw the animal was dead – strangled by the snare. He was about to call but Sean beat him to it.

"Got one," Sean shouted excitedly.

"One here too," replied Hayward, pleased with the results, and went on to check the rest of his traps. He found one more rabbit. Again he called out, and Sean responded with a shout back, also finding a second among the traps he was checking. The final result, four rabbits, would be ideal if Father John and Freda should make an appearance.

They returned to the scarp and sat on a rock overlooking the orchard, happy with their gains.

"What if we have to leave by ourselves tonight? We'll have to leave two of these," said Hayward.

"We'll cook them anyway. If Father John and Freda come, we'll give them the rabbits cooked. On the other hand, we may be glad of them if we have to travel by night, even after a fish supper," added Sean happily.

"Do you think they will return? Or do you think that they've been apprehended by the police with your friend. If they have, the Castle men will be called in, you know that don't you?"

"Yes," answered Sean. "We'll need to go tonight. That's an absolute must, Henry. If they don't come back tonight, we'll assume the worst, because the Castle men will break young Cormac." He crossed himself, praying silently, asking God not to allow Cormac's capture. His forehead creased into a frown as he grew concerned about the absence of Father John. They should have got Cormac to the nunnery by now if everything had gone to plan. Still, he reasoned, it would be unusual if the two helpers were to come to the orchard in daylight – previously, the priest had always arrived by night.

"Come on then, let's get the rest done, before the trout swim off," said Hayward standing up. He sensed the anxiety in his companion.

Sean smiled in readiness, knowing that worrying would do no good. Reason returned and with the thought of doing some more fly-fishing he became calm.

"First, we may as well go over to the fields. We can go by the edge of the ravine, the route we took back yesterday. That way we'll be able to see if that fellow with his dog is wandering about, before we go into the fields."

"Agreed," replied Hayward.

They made their way up the scarp towards the trees that carpeted the basin's summit line.

Neither thought of their rifles, back by the smouldering campfire, as they basked in the secure bosom of the basin's wood, amid the peaceful twittering of birdsong and gentle rustling of leaves. The calm morning's temperature gradually increased to summer heat, even though there was still much of the morning left – a warning of what the afternoon might bring. Both developed a sense of urgency to gather potatoes and a cauliflower quickly enough to enjoy the rest of the hot day by the river, in their little sanctuary, secluded from prying eyes that might threaten their liberty.

"Why don't I collect potatoes, while you get a cauliflower?" suggested Hayward.

"That sounds good to me," agreed Sean.

At the bottom of the basin's outside scarp, under cover of the wood, the stream broke from the ravine. They separated to carry out their respective tasks.

Hayward jumped knee-deep into the stream and crossed to the opposite bank, remembering the wood ended at a fence before the potato field.

Sean stayed on his side of the bank to follow the river's course, knowing it would lead out into the open fields, one of which contained cauliflowers. As he reached the end of the wood, his first instinct was to survey the area before leaving the protection of the concealing trees. Satisfied that he was unobserved, he splashed down into the stream and followed its course into the open countryside. His presence was concealed by the height of the steep banks. Moving stealthily along, knowing exactly where the cauliflowers were, he came to the bank they had climbed the previous day, and was alarmed to see paw prints around their old foot marks.

The dog must have been sniffing around, though this was not apparent when he had been observing the previous day.

A frown of stress crossed his forehead. He was gripped at the pit of his stomach by a prophetic fear that slowly climbed into his chest. Quickly clambering up the bank, he discovered prints belonging to the dog's owner. Someone had stood there, looking down at the dog while it sniffed around his and Hayward's clearly visible footprints.

"Christ Almighty," he cursed and wondered what the walker and his dog had concluded from the footprints. His desire for another cauliflower had now vanished, and he became apprehensive. The walker could pass by again and notice there had been another theft from the field. In his mind, he was convinced that anything he took would be missed. Cautiously, he withdrew and went back down the stream, the way he had come. One thing only was on his mind! He must find Hayward and warn him. The prints put a whole new complexion on matters. They were no longer safe and needed to lie low and be vigilant until nightfall. Then, at all costs, Hayward and he would leave for the sanctuary of the monastery.

Wading up stream, pushing his shins against the flow of the stream, he staggered in panic, falling forwards as the chill water immersed him.

Curses and splutters issued forth as he struggled to get up, drenched from head to foot. Quickly he moved, on reaching the cover of the woods then climbing the bank on Hayward's side. Dripping wet and leaving a sodden trail upon the dry mud path, he hurried along to reach the perimeter fence. As he came into the clearing he encountered Hayward, looking equally concerned.

"There's a man and dog's footprints by the very spot where we took the potatoes yesterday," Hayward reported worriedly.

"There are prints by the bank too, where we took the cauliflower," replied Sean equally affected.

"Christ, we've made more now. The fact that the prints appear to be standing about in the spots that we had previously been, suggests someone reading our presence. If the walker comes back this way again, he is sure to find our return prints." Hayward began to grow more vexed.

"Maybe it was just the mutt that smelt us, and then the dog's master stood around while the animal was sniffing. It's possible that only the animal got our scent. Everything else is just speculation," remarked Sean, though he was not convinced.

"Let's hope so. Either way, we best not steal any vegetables today." Hayward looked about at the ground to see what fresh marks they had made. "Let's get back over the hills." Sean turned to leave.

"What happened to you?" He noticed Sean's soaked appearance for the first time.

They hurried off back to the stream, crossed and ascended the woods towards the ravine's edge. Upon reaching the top, they turned to survey the area, looking out for the lone man walking his dog. No such person came to sight, just meadows bathed in glorious sunlight. The stream widened as it twisted and turned into the tender countryside while, in the distance, ancient hills ran along the horizon.

"It all looks very inviting, don't it, Henry?"

"It does, but now we can only venture out into it at night, when we can't see its splendour."

They turned and walked over the summit, feeling safer and becoming attuned to the noises of the wooded scarp. A little way down, the slope began to twist back towards the stream, where it flowed into the ravine.

"I don't think we should stay by this part of the river, in view of the recent turn of events. Do you?" asked Hayward.

"No, I think we should go deeper into the wood and cook these. When nightfall comes, we can be on our way. We'll have to go back through the apple orchard; then leave by the other side of the basin, the way we came in."

"No fishing then?" added Hayward. "How quickly things can change. One moment we are full of the joys of summer. The next, we are down. I'm wishing for the bloody day to end so we can be on our way."

Sean nodded in agreement. "I know the feeling."

They reached the stepping-stones and hopped across to the opposite bank, quickly going back to their campfire that was still smoking away. They began to gather and pack, grabbing their ammunition belts and rifles.

"There's not much we can do to hide the evidence of the campfire. We'll just have to hope that the dog-walking man doesn't come over this side of the hills," said Sean, optimistically.

They moved off, fearful for their liberty, against the flow of the river, and up into the wooded hills. The stream narrowed, becoming a sequence of waterfalls that cascaded down through the woods and rocks in a sumptuous awakening to the magnificence of Mother Nature.

"It'll be a shame to leave this place. I could quite happily pass the time here." Hayward's mood was forlorn.

"No time for regrets. We must be on our way by nightfall." Sean had adopted a firm resolve. After all, he had evaded capture since the uprising, some four years ago.

Hayward sighed, accepting the mild rebuke. Still, they were amid the grandeur and both could enjoy the beauty for what it was – an idyllic portion of life – a brief moment only, yet one to savour nonetheless. The falls reminded him of the truck journey before the Cafgarven raid. Like the enticing hills, he wanted to be swallowed by the kind memories of the miniature waterfalls. His ultimate desire, to lose himself within the wilderness, still burned within. He would not squander such precious moments.

TWENTY FOUR

After the Morning Slumber.

Father John went to the book cabinet for his afternoon tipple, making sure that Maureen could be seen through the French windows. She had come out through the kitchen door into the garden, pulling out a worktop on which to complete her cooking chores. The heat of the peat stove was proving too much in such fine weather. Cooking, however, had to be done and he knew it was her absolute conviction that he must have a cooked meal. She had been concerned with his gallivanting off about the countryside without taking proper care. He turned his gaze upon the Freda's caravan, which was at the back of the yard, and at the big horse grazing in a field on the other side of the graveyard. Freda, he presumed, must still be asleep and he had given strict instructions not to disturb her.

He finished his drink and put all the things back before going to the doors. As he was obscured from outside by the net curtains, Maureen was unaware of his presence as she got down to her cooking preparations. By her side was a chopping-board with a few carrots for the meat-and-potato pie that she was prudently preparing for him.

A fly caused her to tut with annoyance and she flicked the air in an effort to be rid of the pest – sneering in disgust as the repulsive insect evaded the lazy swing of her palm.

"Oh, I absolutely abhor the things," she muttered to herself, frustrated to the point of anger.

"As vile and nasty as they may be, they're all God's creatures, and therefore have a purpose," Father John said.

Startled, she turned with a hand on her chest. He had a gracious smile that let her know he was jesting.

"My word, Father John, you clear frightened the living daylights out of me." She laughed, and then became grim. "A lovely spring-cleaned living room, with the sun coming through the windows is violated by the cutting buzz of such vulgar germ-carrying mites. They spoil summer." She angrily swished the old cloth at the insect again.

Still smiling, Father John held out his hand and said: "Will you let me have the cloth please, Maureen?"

She passed it to him, and Father John set about flapping the air to drive the fly away. "There, now the little pest is on its way, though just in case it should return, I'll stand guard while you go about your work."

She smiled in appreciation, and set about her chore with renewed vigour. Quickly, she peeled the last potatoes, put them in a large saucepan of water, added a little salt, then hurried off into the kitchen to place them upon the stove to boil. Returning with relief to the garden, she intently scrutinised him as he stood over the table like a sentinel.

"Well, you certainly seem to be devising a rather special lunch today, Maureen. It is most kind of you to do so." He was in good spirits and considered his housekeeper was deserving of his praise. Day in and out, she was ever reliable. Often, there were times when he took her for granted – after the trials and tribulations of the previous days he had realised that perhaps he did not show her enough respect.

"You need a proper meal inside you, Father John. You've been missing a whole day." She paused before continuing, looking around as though to make sure no one was listening. Then, in a hushed voice, she added: "People have been gossiping all day, and I'm sure to get a grilling from them once I leave here."

"Well, there's no big secret really, Maureen. I have been on very important Church work with

Freda the tinker woman. She came to me on a matter and I had to help her. It was very vexing issue and I've had to see some Church colleagues to help with this problem. That's the best I can tell you at present. Don't give the villagers all of it at once. Make them work for it." He smiled and winked, knowing she would be glad of such liberty where interesting news was concerned.

She grinned girlishly. "String them along a bit, shall I?"

"Now, that's you at your very best, Maureen. You can colour it up the way you like to do – just don't say things that aren't true," he added.

She started to roll some pastry, and then neatly laid it in the pie tray, while he flapped off the fly again. Turning her attention to the carrots and peas, which she had taken from the vegetable patch earlier in the morning, she put them in a smaller saucepan then placing them next to the simmering potatoes in the peat oven. As she returned, she caught him leaning over the table with his finger pointing down towards a small jug of stock.

"Don't you dare," she let out a high-pitched squeak, slapping his hand.

He jumped back like a naughty schoolboy with a look of mischief on his face, subservient in her domain.

"Sorry, but I do love the gravy," he confessed sheepishly.

"Well, you'll have to wait until lunch is ready, Father. Now, I was going to pour out some tea but I dare not leave if I think you're going to be after the stock."

"Maureen," he replied emphatically, though still with his bright smile. "I promise faithfully that no more attempts will be made upon your delicious stock until lunch is served."

"Well," she thought, "He is a man of the cloth and I was a perhaps little quick-tempered in my scolding."

He sensed this and offered an idea: "Why don't I quickly pour the tea, thus leaving you with a feeling of security with respect to your splendid preparation. Though you will have to watch out for the fly by yourself – just for a moment or two?"

She smiled, radiating pleasurable acceptance of the idea, and returned to her pastry-making. He meanwhile went into the kitchen to make tea. Her efforts were barely renewed, when the caravan door opened and out stepped the tinker woman, bleary-eyed and wearing a tatty, old nightgown and bearing a chamber pot.

Maureen opened her mouth, but then stopped without uttering a word, thinking that it would be more polite to let the tinker attend to her business before engaging her in talk. She continued to observe as the old woman made her way towards a cluster of bushes by the fence where the giant shire horse stood. As she returned, lost in her thoughts and seemingly oblivious to anyone's presence, Maureen felt compelled to call.

"I'm sorry if I woke you."

Freda stopped abruptly, as though noticing Maureen for the first time. For a short moment, the old tinker just stared, as though drinking in the sight of the woman and bearing, in Maureen's view, a rather haughty look.

After some deliberation Freda replied, in a gentle, comforting voice. "Oh no, you did not wake me, dear."

The severe look fell away – revealing a warm and kindly person. Maureen was pleasantly taken aback, and responded with a smile.

"Would you like some tea?"

"That's kind of you, I would dearly love a cup," answered Freda. Maureen quickly went to the kitchen doorway to tell Father John, who was craftily taking a rock cake from under the fly net.

"Could you please make Freda a cup of tea too, Father John?" asked Maureen, waiting for him to pop the cake into his mouth first, thus catching him completely in his sly act.

He turned, wide-eyed with amazement, his cheeks stuffed with the cake, and looking shocked to see her at the door. Leaving her cooking preparations to the mercy of the flies was most unexpected. He thought he was home and dry on the cake-pilfering front but, alas, he had not bargained on Freda waking up, and Maureen dropping protocol to order additional refreshment. With a mouth full of the evidence of his second misdemeanour, there was quite literally nothing he could do except nod to Maureen, regarding him with one eyebrow raised and her arms folded. He turned away sheepishly and attended to the task of tea-making, while Maureen returned to her garden table.

Freda had put the chamber pot away and now had with her a bucket, with a towel and flannel. She asked politely for some water to wash with.

"Good Lord, dear, Father John has a washroom. I'm sure he would let you use it," replied Maureen kindly.

"Oh no, please, I don't want to be any trouble."

"Oh, but it's no trouble. It's no trouble at all," stressed Maureen, as Father John came out carrying a tray with three cups and saucers, a teapot, milk and sugar.

"Please do, Freda," he added in support of Maureen. "It's really no trouble at all."

Freda smiled coyly – the truth was, she would much rather heat a pail of water upon a campfire and take it back into her caravan, but then it would not do to light a fire in the garden. She allowed Maureen to show her into the hallway and give her directions for the bathroom by the bottom of the stairs. Before proceeding, Freda's attention was drawn to the loud, ticking grandfather clock in the hallway – its continual, throbbing tick-tock, tick-tock tapping through the silence. Her own clock, in the caravan, never ticked so intrusively. She was surprised that the housekeeper appeared unaware of its noise, oblivious to the constant ticking because it was part of the stationary world she lived in.

Freda looked up the stairs she needed to ascend to get to the bathroom. The Parochial House seemed so uncomfortably grand, and her wish was to be gone from such a place, which became more imposing by the second. Her eyes scanned the surroundings as she climbed, absorbing the fixed, entrapping abode, with all its beckoning finery. But then, the grand, old clock ticked away to remind a person that one travelled through time with one's life ebbing away in a stagnant place racing towards the unknown dark wall, beyond life. Rooted to the same spot and never moving. Just waiting!

Maureen hurried back to the garden, and found Father John pouring two cups of tea, leaving the third empty.

"I'll wait until Freda comes down before I pour her tea," he said.

Maureen nodded in agreement and returned to her cooking preparations. "How long have you known the tinker woman, Father? I never knew you were that well acquainted with her. I'm surprised we've not seen her stop at the church before." She wondered whether Father John and

Freda had been friends even before she took the position of housekeeper.

"Not long, Maureen. Like you, I have only seen the lady passing through. I knew of her, but didn't actually know her to speak to." He had an air that suggested he was not going to go any further on the matter, and to confirm this he strolled off towards the caravan.

As much as he liked Maureen, and valued the work she did for him, his caution, where imparting too much information was concerned, had to be maintained. He was sure that, in her heart, Maureen would try to keep things secret if she knew that there was a need, but when she did not need to know it would be wrong to burden her with such trust in troubled times.

Maureen watched as he strolled over to the wagon, guessing he was troubled in his mind concerning Freda. She did not, however, connect this with the recent trouble in the village, and would not have connected Freda with such events.

"Terrible things have happened in Cafgarven of late," she called after him. "Yet you, Father John, are still here for our humble needs."

Once again the annoying fly came back, causing her to tut and swipe her hand as he walked back exchanging his cup for the teacloth.

"Oh thank you, Father," added Maureen before he swiped the air, driving the pest off. He remained vigilant, while she continued to prepare her pastry.

"Well the meat must be added next, but I'll leave it a while. Need to let the potato-filling boil a little longer." She seemed pleased with her endeavours.

"Your cooking is a pure delight to observe, Maureen. I feel hungry just watching you," he said appreciatively.

Then a deep frown crossed his face and his words drifted out upon his sombre thoughts: "Maureen, you are a person of great flair and skill. Doing the things you know best, but receiving little appreciation. The world seems so unfair, when men who use guns for killing and maiming are considered heroic, yet what of the Maureens of the world, hmm? Those who contribute to making people's lives comfortable, cleaning their homes, cooking meals, and lovingly bringing up children – preserving life and serving the ones they care for, yet receiving no credit – until it is too late. Do men realise the extent of such duty? Selfish men, in general, rarely recognise the value of the small things that are good. They are too busy revering lesser men who drive people to mass destruction. Why do they turn such people into icons while somewhere a lady like you might grieve for one of the tiny individuals who pay the cost of such adulation? How robbed some people are by inconsiderate statues standing in fake benevolence, caked with pigeon droppings."

Maureen had put a handkerchief to her watering eyes. "Oh Father John, you say such moving things sometimes, but there are men who are sucked into the ambitions of others, like the two murdered gentlemen of our village. How silly and brave they would have been to walk away and not get involved in the first place. Somewhere inside – there must be a spark of salvation."

"Indeed, Maureen," asserted Father John. She had reminded him of Hayward and Sean. "Indeed there must."

Freda reappeared, feeling most awkward. "I'm sorry to trouble you like this, but because of the unusual amount of travelling, I've been a little neglectful where collecting water is concerned. Something I never usually fail to do."

"Here, Freda, we have some tea for you," offered Father John, leaning over the table and pouring a cup.

"Oh thank you," she answered, holding up her towel and nodding to the caravan. "I'll just pop back with these." She sauntered off.

"I think she's a little ill at ease, Father. She seems unsure of herself, like a fish out of water."

"Well, I have a small suggestion that might help," he responded.

"What's that, Father?"

"Seeing as the weather is so fine, why not have lunch out here? I will put a table close to the caravan, and then Freda might not feel so uncomfortable."

"On the other hand, it could lead her to believe that you are snooty and don't want her in the house," she ventured.

He frowned. "Why do you always put that little element of doubt in my head? I'm sure that Freda would never think like that, but just in case, I'll ask her what she prefers."

"She'll be too embarrassed to make a choice, and would feel most uncomfortable at being asked."

"My God, Maureen, you always seem to look on the downside of things. Let me handle this one. I'll make the decision myself. I can tell you – when Freda is not happy with things, she lets me know. I'm going to suggest eating lunch in the garden. Then I'll say: 'But if you prefer the dining room?' – just to be on the safe side."

Maureen smiled. Father John was dithering, and when the problem of diplomacy had to be faced he would probably shy away. "Are you sure you don't want me to put it to her, Father?" she asked quietly.

"Oh no, no, Maureen," he replied, pretending to have things under control, but then after a pause conceded: "Well, all right then, perhaps it would be better if you suggested the choices."

He watched, relieved, as Freda came out from the caravan and made her way towards them for her tea. Maureen noticed his big, beaming smile and seemed to be at ease, so she decided to get the problem out of the way immediately.

"Freda, I'm making lunch, and was wondering where you would like to eat. Being as it is such a glorious day and all, we thought it might be nice to dine in the open, unless you would prefer the dining room of course."

She smiled and looked at Father John. "I love the outdoors, especially in summer. Would the garden be to your liking?"

Serenity descended as Maureen left for the kitchen. Freda offered to help, but was told to relax and talk with Father John who was most anxious that she would, lingering until sure of her compliance.

"Let me get some chairs for us, Freda, then we can sit and chat." He went to the French windows, disappearing behind the curtains and reappearing with two chairs.

He placed them and held out a hand for her to take a seat. She did, and he followed her example, while clasping his knees, as though reluctant to begin.

She chuckled. "You are dithering, Father John, which means you want to go to the apple orchard. We've already discussed it and agreed that we will do so this evening. Why are you still uncomfortable?"

"Because, Freda, I know that you are unhappy with this," he replied.

She laughed and put her cup down, shaking her head at the same time. Recovering her composure, she looked at him directly: "Why linger on things, when we have already decided to go back. I can't understand you when you're like this," she added.

"Because I do not want to disregard what you said yesterday, as we were approaching the nunnery." He looked down at the grass.

"Well, Father, I have resolved to do what you want. I did before we reached the nunnery, because it was my desire not to leave you unsettled. Do you pursue the subject because you want me to believe that you are totally right? Do you want me to say that I am now persuaded that you are now right? I can't wrap up a kindly lie, even for yourself, Father John – I don't believe that you would want me too."

Her voice was slow, but her words clear and focused.

He now understood that she did not want to go through the issue again, and thought intently on what she said. "Every time I get my way, I seem to need little something more. This is not right, I know. I have your consent and help, but there is something inside of me that wants you wholly on my side, heart and soul."

It was more of a confession and a mild apology.

"Well, I can only do that if I'm with you heart and soul." Her voice was soothing. "I have said that you are not always content just to do enough. You want more – you can overdo things if events aren't allowed to run their course and your continuous desire to help can sometimes interfere. I, for example, don't agree with returning to the orchard, as I have said. But despite wanting to remain quiet on the matter respecting your wishes, you are plaguing me in order to get more commitment spiritually, I suspect. It's only enhancing my sense that you try to do too much in pursuit of your good intentions. I believe you're overdoing things, and in continuing with your persistence where my help to you is concerned. Please, Father John, accept that I will come back to the orchard with you, but don't ask me to believe you're right and I am wrong.

"As far as humble priests go, you are a good man, but power can corrupt. You can't intimidate people into giving over their hearts and souls if they don't want too. Be content for someone to reluctantly go along with you. Don't deny people their feelings, even if it means they have to bite their tongues while they hesitantly help you. If you were privileged with a position of power, you might well become obsessive with your will. With no one able to resist, you could become a tyrant without realising it."

Father John looked down, wounded by her words, but not having any defence.

"On reflection, you are again right. It's ironic, I suppose – earlier I was thinking of Maureen's humble ways, and ruthless men seeking glory, leading millions to destruction and war. Could I ever be such a man?"

She leant forward and touched his hand. "No, Father John, you could never be like such men."

Slowly he raised his head, staring into her steadfast eyes. He blinked as a small tear appeared in the corner of his eye. "Freda, how could I ever apologise. I am truly sorry for my persistence, please forgive me," he stuttered.

"We will go back to the orchard for the two men because it is what *you* want to do, Father John. I shall be there with you, because I feel I will be needed."

The topic of the two fugitives was discreetly put aside in the splendid sunshine, and a new mood of relaxation descended. They sat back and flitted away the time with small talk, concerning Maureen's celebrated meat-and-potato pie.

TWENTY FIVE

The Decision to Leave the Orchard.

The joy of the woodland was lost to Hayward and Sean for long periods of time. Anxiety, due to pessimistic imaginings, constantly beat back the serenity of their surroundings. The cascading waterfalls and the overhanging plants were quite captivating for short periods of time – interspersing their agitation with small patches of relief – a remission short-lived! The thought of the mysterious Dogman always came back to vex their thoughts.

The cool, damp air, produced by the spray from the small waterfalls, was the one constant thing that eased both. Their fervent desire was to see the daylight end. Then they could make their way, travelling through the night in search of the monastery, which had become a burning goal. The isolated basin had lost its appeal because of the Dogman – the malignant spoiler of their little sanctuary.

After a small debate, they decided to risk a fire in order to cook the rabbits. For a short time during the afternoon they had contemplated going down to the river to fish for some more trout. However, the thought of the Dogman wandering past caused them to reflect on the matter. They elected to stay in the upper confines of the wood where, from their vantage point, they could see anyone who might approach.

Searching among the wicker creel's contents, Sean pulled out a sharp gutting knife and picked up one of the rabbits.

"I'm beginning to wonder whether we'll ever get rid of this smell," he muttered.

Hayward agreed. "Everything reeks of rabbit, even the tea cups. Now my appetite has gone. I wish we'd tried for more trout instead."

Sean raised his eyebrows. "Well, we must make do for now. It's late afternoon and I think it's important for us to eat. We are likely to be walking most of the night."

"Will we get there by dawn, or will we have to hole up for the day?" Hayward had no idea of the monastery's whereabouts.

"I think we'll have to hide for a day," answered Sean. "But we'll get there tomorrow night." He started to work on the limp rabbit, going about the skinning in a vigorous manner. More stench of putrid entrails filled their nostrils as he quickly gutted the meat. "Will you wash it in the falls, please?" He held the carcass up. Hayward stifled his reluctance and took the thing.

He walked through the trees, towards the cascading waters, and where he held the raw meat inside the tumbling freshness. Washing the flesh thoroughly in the cold spray, his face was refreshed at the same time, bringing forth an invigorating smell of vegetation. Staring contentedly into the splash, he drifted into oblivion, daydreaming about the course of events that might arise if they were successful in reaching the monastery. His vision of a Spartan life style inside dark, stone walls, similar to the mediaeval churches of England, had an appeal. Perhaps it was a naïve and romantic view as he envisaged wandering the dark confines of gothic corridors. He imagined a contemplative lifestyle, praying to God, building a stronger sense of purpose, dispelling the dreaded, black void that he feared might linger beyond death.

Sean's harsh voice called out, bringing him into the real world again. "Come along, there. Are you daydreaming again?"

Hayward hurried back and saw Sean beaming with his wide grin and mischievously sparkling eyes. It was as though the man had been inside his head and knew his every whimsical thought. It felt most intrusive, yet he could not take offence.

"I thought that you might be trying to bring it back to life," joked Sean.

Feeling a little more at ease, Hayward laughed as Sean gave him the second rabbit carcass to clean. "I should have waited for you to do all of them before going the first time."

"Wait for me and I'll come to the fall with you," added Sean. "I want to wash some of this stench from me."

"I'll second that." Hayward felt a fresh enthusiasm. "I think I'll take the cups and plates too. Give them another wash. I never realised how much the smell gets into everything."

Sean gutted and skinned the last rabbit, and then stood to go to the falls. "You know, I've been dwelling a bit on this idea of going to the monastery. I think that I *might* just stay for a while. See if I can sort myself out. Try and find where I am going – you know what I mean don't you?"

Hayward smiled. He had been hoping Sean might come to this decision and nodded his approval. There was no need for him to comment. It also allowed the rebel to talk on. Hayward sensed the man wanted to speak, and his only requirement was to listen to his new friend. Friend! A momentary reflection! A few days ago each would have killed the other.

Sean continued. "I've had a bit of time to reflect on things, you see. There are all sorts of mind-confusing notions going through my head. I believe it's a just thing to want to rule ourselves, and I could never go against the Volunteers, who are frustrated men. I want to see the British

Government out of Ireland, but all this back-stabbing – this cycle of murder for murder. It's getting out of control. There has to be another way of trying to resolve this horrible situation. The things I've done in the name of Ireland have left me feeling unclean, and I must ask myself if many ordinary people of my country would be grateful – if they could stand next to me and watch some of the things I've done. I'm sure they would be disgusted. I know they would." His manner had become forlorn.

Hayward understood and had a similar view: "Well, I happen to know that we Tans are not basking in popularity back home. Even the Army stationed here dislike us, which makes me a little angry. Most of these soldiers have had it cushy in Ireland, while we, the men in the Reserves, have been out in the muddy fields of France, living with the constant fear of death, day in and day out. People often look upon others with disdain from their safe vantage points. Are they really any better?"

Sean responded: "Yes, but you are drifting off of the issue, with your resentment against those who might be judging you. My point is – it's not what others think of us, but what we think of ourselves. Do *you* think what you are doing here is right?"

Hayward quietly accepted Sean's point. "Well, I am obviously disillusioned about things, otherwise I would not have absconded. Maybe I should

have just left and gone home. But going back ..."
He lingered for a while as though searching for
the words. "Well, the very idea of going back to
Newcastle depresses me even more than staying in
the Reserves." He looked to Sean. "I think our reasons may differ slightly. Perhaps I have more selfish
desires for going to the monastery than you do."

"Why do you say that?" Sean was intrigued.

"Well, I think I'm doing this because I don't
want to go home."

"You also left because you did not like the
way the Reserve police force go about things as
well, Henry. This is to be commended. By saying it's just because you don't want to return to
England, I think you're discrediting yourself.
Though I must admit – you must have been the
first lot to come to Ireland because unemployment in England was so bad. It's usually the other
way around."

They came upon the little rock fall, and each
took a rabbit to the cascading water while reflecting on their talk.

"You know Henry, I can just visualise the head
of the monastery looking at us two knocking on
his door. My God, he's going to have a shock
now, isn't he?" Sean's wicked grin had returned.

Hayward laughed. "I'm conjuring up an
image of a little, thin priest with a bulbous nose
and an oversized tonsure, staring at us in total
disbelief – a Tan and a Volunteer. Let's hope that

God has a sense of humour, and the holy men are also blessed with it."

"I hope the good Lord has got a sense of humour too, or we'll be in a lot of trouble when we get to the other side," laughed Sean.

"I keep seeing the shell-shocked old priest answering the door and dithering about letting us in," sniggered Hayward.

"What's his name? Brother Peter?" mocked Sean.

Again they burst into fits of uncontrollable laughter. The new mood of joy was invigorating.

Hayward added: "We'll be saying things like, 'Come on, Pete, let us through your gates?' And he will be one of those meticulous, little, skinny men with a clipboard and pen saying; 'No, your names are not on this here list'. "

"Oh, for the love of Jesus, stop it," chuckled Sean. "My bloody stomach is going to split."

Hayward was encouraged and continued to laugh at the sight of his happy companion. Who would believe such a thing? What would those from the conflict think, seeing foes joking and laughing, enjoying reckless banter together in a sanctuary free from hate and oppression?

Satisfied that the rabbit carcasses were clean, they began to wash themselves as best they could, rejecting the idea of washing their clothes because the garments might not be dry when they started on their journey. They made their way back to the campfire with the ambition of cooking their morning gains.

"Two to eat right away, while we keep the others for the journey. We'll need skewers," said Sean, wandering off to a bush to make some from twigs.

Hayward stoked and added bracken to the fire while waiting. "How much can we read into the Dogman's footprints, loitering around the areas where we were doing our pilfering?" he called.

"I don't know really," answered Sean, snapping a long twig. He began to sharpen the end. "It could be that we're getting a little paranoid about things. If we had followed the tracks, I reckon that we might have seen other patches where the mutt stopped to sniff."

"So you're beginning to calm down about it now?"

"Well, let's say that I may have read too much into it but just to be on the safe side and leave nothing to chance, I think we should leave tonight regardless. The sanctuary of a monastery will be more assured than here. Staying and dwelling on the Dogman would be too much like Purgatory. For me, that's something that can wait until the proper time." He snapped another twig, judging whether it would hold the weight of a rabbit.

Hayward sighed and nodded his head, staring into the flickering flames. "I think I'll feel a lot more settled when we start the journey. This whole place has lost its appeal since those footprints. I keep thinking this Dogman is hiding in the bloody trees, watching us."

"Let's just get these things cooked." Sean walked over and skewered the meat. "Good God, Henry, I don't think he's going to come charging out of the trees."

"It doesn't hurt to be alert. I've seen such things in the trenches."

"Come on, Henry, the Dogman is becoming a big, green-eyed monster. We must be cautious, I know, but let's also be sensible about things. When night comes, we'll discreetly leave for the monastery."

Sighing again, Hayward hung his head, knowing his friend was right. The Dogman was an imp of his own making. He watched fat drop from the burning rabbit meat, falling into the flames and crackling. An inviting smell floated up and suddenly the anxiety was gone.

"The smell ain't so bad now, is it?" said Sean.

"No, it's not that bad after all. Our efforts have been worthwhile."

"I think it's time we brewed ourselves another pot of tea." Sean reached for the kettle, which was still half full of warm water from the last boil.

Hayward daydreamed: "Since joining the Army, I've always been told what to do, by one person or another. Now, for the first time, I'm stepping out and taking a chance alone. It feels extraordinary. I wonder if Freda would be able to read my destiny, the way Gypsies are supposed to."

"She would probably scoff at such a thought. She seems far too level-headed for such things." Sean looked about the trees and smiled in satisfaction. "Could you live in a world that was like this everywhere you went? No cities or towns, just woods and hills —"

"Don't forget rivers and the sea," cut in Hayward.

"Oh yes, those things too, how absent-minded of me to forget. It makes you think of things the way God intended them to be, where enemies like you and me can get along without trying to get at one another's throats."

"I've heard stories about America, Canada and Australia being like this. Only the mountains are bigger, the forests stretching for hundreds of miles. It would take months to walk from one end of the woodlands to the other. Can you imagine what it was like for the men that went out to places like that, when it was untamed and unspoilt?" Hayward's imagination began to stir.

"Yes," agreed Sean, staring up into the foliage, daydreaming about the Rocky Mountains and an endless wilderness. "Then along comes the human race with its big ideas about towns and industry. All over the globe men would be doing this, overrunning the place to make factories and cities. Although it's never really happened here in Ireland, thank God. It's still very much an agricultural country. Maybe that's what you like about Ireland, Henry. You don't care for the dirty factories and smoking chimneys of Newcastle, and find yourself drawn to the wilderness about you."

"Yeah, but you can keep Dublin," Hayward laughed. "It reminds me too much of home. We were born about a hundred years too late. It would have been glorious to wander those mountains and forests in the new world countries before the farms and cities were planted."

"Much of it is still there, Henry. We could go and see it."

Hayward was taken aback and fascinated by the suggestion. The idea had never crossed his mind, but now that it was mentioned, the notion caused a twinge of excitement.

"How could we get to such a place without being stopped by the authorities? What about the monastery?"

"We can still go to this place, and think on what to do. If we decide to move on, I'm sure the Brothers will help us," replied Sean.

Hayward thought while sipping his tea. "Canada! I've always liked the idea of Canada."

"That's where Cormac wanted to go. I wonder if he made it to the nunnery. If he did, he stood a good chance of fulfilling his wish. The nuns might try and persuade him to go, rather than get mixed up in any more of the violence."

Maybe it was just talk. Perhaps they would not go after all, but it was pleasant to fantasise. Both lost themselves in thought, blocking out the dread of the Dogman. Sean pulled out his tin whistle and began to play a haunting little tune to aid their drift into dream worlds.

Hayward stared into the trees and once more the ambient sounds of the woodland filled his senses. The tin whistle combined with twittering birds in gentle, rustling trees, plus the delicate, flowing water engulfed him.

Neither was aware of the distant Border collie bitch sitting obediently beside a silent observer among the trees. The animal's tongue hung out from the side of her mouth. She was panting from her prior exertions. Since her master had put his finger to his lip, however, she had come to heel – obedience without hesitation.

"Come, girl," whispered the voice, and they moved away from the distant campfire.

TWENTY SIX

The Coming Night.

Freda looked beyond the scarps. Upon a distant summit were two tiny silhouettes, a man and dog running against the red sky. They seemed in a dire hurry about something, but then it was of no concern to her. She had far more important things to worry about.

The carthorse moved onwards laboriously – pulling the caravan, while the impending twilight prepared to bathe the surrounding hills. She turned and looked into the living quarters, where Father John was reading her book.

"We're almost there now, Father."

"Oh, splendid," he replied, putting the book aside and making towards the open doorway to where she sat with the reins. For once she had broken with tradition and unlocked the door so that he could wander back and forth at his own leisure.

He climbed out and sat beside her, allowing his body to ride the rocking motion, just as she veered off into the woods. The ground suddenly became uneven, and the wagon started to lumber about and the ride became bumpier. He was hard-pressed to keep his seat, grasping the door jamb for support.

The relief was uplifting when he recognised the same old tree trunks from before. This was indeed where he and Freda had first brought Henry to meet with Sean. Small details about bushes and trees had remained in his mind. Strange, how such trivial things could burn into one's memory.

Once into the wood and out of sight, Freda brought the caravan to a halt, and he climbed down. His one thought was to get up to the scarps and into the basin before the dawn set in. He wanted to take advantage of the remaining light.

"Wait, Father John, if you go any faster, you'll meet yourself coming back," said Freda.

He checked his impatience and waited, only to be vexed further as she climbed down to wave him on.

"I'll get a campfire going," she said, deeming it would be better to prepare something in advance of the fugitives' arrival.

Father John allowed himself a frustrated sigh, careful not to let Freda see his annoyance. It would never do to offend this kindly lady. He set off briskly through the trees and up the scarp, hardly able to contain his excitement, and fearing the pair might have taken it upon themselves to wander off on their own initiative. Upon reaching the summit, he peered down at the neat rows of little apple trees stretching across the basin. Slowly and with caution, he negotiated his way into the orchard. His first inclination was to go to the old, empty compost box where Sean and Cormac had been hiding. As he expected there was no one there, so he resumed his brisk pace with a stronger and more urgent sense of purpose. Reaching the western end of the orchard, he felt a flutter in his stomach, an anxious desire to see both men again. They had become enigmas from his viewpoint – a rebel and a renegade policeman. His hopes lifted at the sound of rushing water. It was invigorating and full of expectation. Entering the wood brought further joy in the form of birdsong sweeping down from the foliage in sweet splendour. The fresh odour of the ferns wafting on the damp air of the close running water was heaven. He broke into a clearing before the fresh vibrant stream cascading into the ravine and saw the stepping-stones.

A voice called from the woods on the opposite bank and he looked up, alert, scanning the trees.

"Father John, we're over here?" It was a distinctive, northern-English accent.

He smiled, even though he could not see Henry until he burst forth from the foliage. His trepidation dissolved as he gasped joyfully and Sean followed from the trees. Both were jogging along the shingle, waving and equally pleased to see him. They looked comical, burdened with a creel, haversacks and fishing-rods, plus their rifles.

"Boy, Father, you're a sight for sore eyes," called Sean.

"I am most gratified to hear that," he answered, beaming at the spectacle of such happy runaways.

"Is Freda with you, Father?" shouted Henry, above the flow as he came across the stepping-stones. There was a note of anxiety in his voice.

"Yes," replied Father John, with a smile that quickly dissolved the Englishman's apprehension.

Sean made the final leap on to the shingle next to him, wearing a cheeky grin, which was, as usual, a prelude to an impending piece of wit. "I thought we would have to carry this lot all the way to the monastery by ourselves."

Father John looked surprised. "I take it, then, that you are also going to accompany us to the monastery. What made you decide to come along, then?"

"Well, it's this here Englishman of yours, Father. He has a persuasive manner about him —strange coming from a person wearing such a uniform."

"I think Sean would make a splendid Brother, don't you, Father John?" Henry grinned.

"I do indeed, Henry. Well now, it'll soon be dark. It's quite late. We'll make our way back to the woods and see if we can get a bite to eat before we set off. Freda is cooking something."

He took the rods and a rucksack, lightening their burden, then turned and led the way back.

Henry and Sean followed, confident as they progressed through the woods and into the apple orchard. They walked briskly, occasionally breaking into a jog to keep up with the sprightly, old priest.

Father John stopped once, to pick up some apples, then quickly moved on, his nervous zeal burning passionately, like a furnace of hopeful heat. Finally he came to the end of the orchard.

"My word, Father," laughed Sean. "Where in God's name do you get your energy?"

"I get it in God's name," he replied humorously.

Sean was about to reply, but stopped, realising that he was at a loss for words.

"You walked right into that one, mate." Henry grinned, delighting in the rebel's flummoxed look.

"Enjoying ourselves, are we?" replied Sean tartly.

They climbed the final scarp, knowing Freda would be in the wood on the other side, brewing tea and preparing something to eat.

"We have two rabbits left from our supper," called Henry after Father John, who was once again pressing onwards up the hill.

"Splendid, perhaps Freda will want to cook them," he replied.

"They're already cooked," said Sean, deciding to indulge in a little liberty. "Henry and I would prefer something different, if possible. We saved these for you and Freda."

"So, the rabbit didn't exactly go down a treat, eh?" smiled Father John. He stopped and faced him.

"Oh, everyone is enjoying themselves, aren't they, and all at my poor expense," Sean grumbled, playing the victim.

"Well, I'm sure you'll adapt," added Hayward, wanting to get in on the act.

"God, everyone is jumping on the bandwagon, aren't they. You know, Henry, I'm playing for you as well on this rabbit issue."

Father John sniggered too. "We're just enjoying you, Sean. And I'm sure Freda will make good use of the rabbits." He turned and went up the hill.

The delight of the burning campfire wafted on the twilight breeze, filling their nostrils. The lower woodland was aglow with the inviting light. Daylight was still brushing the leafy tops of the woodlands, but it was unable to penetrate and illuminate the gentle interior. Carefully, they descended towards the exquisite radiance, carefully negotiating the scarp for better footholds.

Already crickets were starting their rhythmic ticking and splendour began to enhance the clearing. Hayward, who cherished such feelings, spoke. "Don't you notice all of this? Do you grow so used to it, and take it all for granted?"

"Oh, of course we do, Henry," replied Father John, patronising him. "We allow ourselves to become part of it, don't we now, Sean?"

"That's right, Father, we bathe in this sort of thing," added the rebel in support.

Realising that he was now the butt of humour, Hayward shut one eye and stared back, concentrating with the remaining receptive organ. His chin developed a comical pointed look as he grinned. "Well, it's nice to see you're being so condescending."

Father John looked pious, while Sean, still in support, faked a look of complete innocence.

"Irish charm is so … how can I put it?" muttered Hayward, looking up for inspiration.

"Beyond words?" offered Sean.

"Yes, that's it. Beyond words," he concluded.

"Your words, Henry," added Sean, achieving another jovial dig.

"I'd better shut up. It's obvious I'm no match for your agile wit," he stated sportingly.

Father John burst into laughter. "It is clear that you two have developed a rapport while together. Learning to take liberties with each other, and to ride the effects of banter, is a good sign."

They walked on, with the smell of bracken growing stronger. Everything was engulfed in the summer twilight, and as they entered the clearing they were greeted by the sight of Freda sitting by her simmering pot.

Beyond stood her caravan, with Moogsly close by, nosing around for snippets of anything that might be edible.

She looked up. "I heard you all, way off. I must say, you seem very pleased with yourselves."

"We're enjoying life," answered Sean happily putting everything down. He ambled over to Moogsly, hands in his pockets and whispering to the beast: "Hello boy, how have you been on your little journeys, eh?"

Seeing an opportunity, Freda called. "I have oats for him. Do you know how to attach the bag?"

"Yes," he replied, glad to be of service.

She quickly went to the caravan and got an old, blue bag, which she offered to Sean. Then, with him nicely out of the way, she returned to the fire, where Father John was emptying his pockets of apples and smiling in expectation of approval.

She frowned. "Did you take them from the floor or pick them from the branches?"

"They were littered about the floor, Freda. Why?"

"Always pick them from the trees, never from the floor, because you don't know how long they've been there. Look!" She held one up for scrutiny. There was a black hole where a grub had been.

He looked disappointed. "Perhaps Moogsly would —"

"Certainly not! I never give Moogsly bad apples," she retorted indignantly.

"I'm sorry, Freda. Perhaps if we went back to the orchard and got some better ones before the night draws in."

A resigned, broad smile came to her face and she nodded. They walked out of the clearing and called. "Pour yourself some tea Sean. It should be nicely brewed by now – you too, Henry."

Outside the woods, Freda and Father John went up the scarps towards the basin, unaware that they had been observed.

TWENTY SEVEN

Silent Observers.

Once the tinker and the priest had been allowed to pass, the group stood in unison. They emerged from rocks and thickets and, as one, moved towards the woods, like ghouls intent on devious mischief. The hullabaloo of crickets and birds camouflaged them, destroying all evidence of their presence. Theirs was a well-practised and subtle art. All had survived the trench war – ex-officers from the carnage of French battlefields, veterans of night-time raids, men much more ruthlessly focused than their Tan counterparts. They were the new Auxiliary cadets, and they were angered by the death of their own man in Cafgarven a few days earlier.

The harp of Ireland, on each man's lapel, had been dulled so as to prevent any glimmer it might reflect into the dusk. Nothing was to spoil their chance of revenge upon the hated Shinners, who had killed one of their own on a remote village street.

The hills and meadows were carpeted with sublime tranquillity as the men approached the fire light that glowed between the trees. They entered the wood, armed with rifles and pistols, carefully confirming that the Dogman's report had been reliable. Their faces set in determination, they were keenly anticipating their first blooding in Ireland, and letting the Shinners know the Auxies had come and they meant business. Peering ahead before moving on, the men came to a halt at the edge of the firelit clearing, lingering just inside the gloom, using the foliage for cover. They grew hungry at the sight of their lush, unsuspecting bounty awaiting their most solemn attentions – watching with wicked fascination the two men before them, one bending over by the campfire stirring a cup of tea, the other walking away from the Shire horse and making for the campfire.

How unaware they were, as rifle barrels carefully penetrated the ferns or rested upon logs to prepare for a deadly engagement. The officer cadets waited patiently – one of them held his clenched fist up.

Not yet.

Wait.

Settle a target snugly in sight.

A crackle of laughter came to their ears, as one of the targets teased his companion. He had the appearance of a typical armed scallywag – the type who would happily terrorise the countryside. In a moment, death would visit him – fire would spit through darkness from a multitude of gun barrels. Retribution was etched in each avenging face as the hunters indulged their prey, allowing them their nonchalant banter in the radiance that enfolded them. It was as though the condemned were inside a bright, orange-tinged hall, while outside, in the blackness, their nemesis awaited – ever tolerant, amused by what was to come, and waiting for the opportune moment. Maybe an unwitting signal from one of the luckless men would precipitate their execution.

Father John and Freda descended into the apple orchard, unaware their travels had been observed. They had walked a short distance into the apple trees when the Black and Tans appeared, with rifles raised. Freda recognised them at once, from the barracks and from the roadside when travelling to the nunnery.

Sergeant Bradley came forward with Inspector Callaghan at his side. Behind was a country gentleman with his dog.

"What's up, Nanny," asked a brazen English voice from behind. Freda turned and saw Turpin – a big, cheeky grin upon his face as he pointed his rifle at her middle.

"Don't you go pointing that there thing at me, young man," she scoffed angrily.

Turpin's grin twisted and his face suddenly contorted into a malevolent sneer. His teeth gritted as he moved forward and poked her in the stomach with the barrel. Leaning down and holding his face inches from her he spat: "Shut it, Gran." He poked harder, just to drive the message home.

Henderson physically pulled him back, worried that Turpin could lose his temper and do something stupid.

"Ease up there, son," Sergeant Bradley said calmly. "Let it go now."

Callaghan remained silent, staring at Father John. The disgruntled Police Inspector knew he was unable to exert any kind of discipline upon his English Reserves, who held him in contempt.

"What are you two doing here?" He eventually asked. "Why are you so far from home, Father John?"

The priest pursed his lips and replied: "I'm about God's work, Inspector. Please understand me when I say I can't disclose it to you."

Callaghan moved forward – his body odour was intense in the stifling humidity of the summer night.

"You can't expect us to leave things at that, Father John. These are bad times, and for reasons of security we must be more thorough."

"I can't divulge my reasons to you, Inspector."

Sean took his tea from Hayward and noticed the discarded apples that Father John had left scattered.

"Has the old boy gone to get more apples?" he asked.

"Yes, Freda's gone to make sure he picks them from the trees," replied Hayward.

"Do you still feel the same way about eating them? You know what you were saying earlier in the day, about the Garden of Eden and all – your notions about the serpent getting Adam and Eve to eat the forbidden fruit," Sean mocked.

"Well," grinned Hayward, picking one up. "I've realised I need not fear. After all, there are no snakes in Ireland."

Sean chuckled and sipped his tea. "Not unless we count you English."

"Wow, easy there," laughed Hayward. He put the apple to his mouth, and with a wide-eyed grin bit into the fruit.

A roar of gunfire smashed through the night, obliterating the sound of the crickets. The explosion caused Sean to drop his cup, momentarily losing his wits. He recovered, only to be thrown into further confusion. Hayward was no longer standing before him. Instead he lay lifeless, a few feet away, amid the apples. Briefly, he registered the fact there had been a loud bang and he looked towards the foliage. Realisation came to him through clicking gun bolt actions.

Before he could act further, another fusillade felled him alongside Hayward. The sound faded into the silence of the shocked night, and as the smoke drifted from the scene the Auxiliaries emerged. Three moved ahead of the rest, administering an unnecessary *coup de grâce* with their revolvers.

The sound carried over the hills upon the night air, bringing a stop to the heated discussion the Tans were having with Father John and Freda.

"What was that?" she exclaimed, as everyone jumped.

"Bloody gunfire," said Sergeant Bradley.

"The bleeding Auxies have got a result," retorted Turpin disgruntled.

Suddenly, everyone moved towards the scarps and in the direction of the gunfire. Father John and Freda struggled up the slope, while around the Black and Tans cursed and bickered at the very idea of the new Auxiliaries encroaching upon their patch. The usual comments were passed about officers having everything their own way.

Inspector Callaghan reached to help Father John up. Flashlights were turned on, allowing the Auxiliaries to know of their approach. As they entered the woods, Father John was surprised see the new Reserve troop, dressed in the manner of the late Cadet Officer Bashford. He noticed these men looked a little more disciplined, and perhaps more refined, than the unruly Black and Tans. And each spoke with an air of affluence.

They entered the campfire clearing and were aghast to see Henry and Sean lying dead side by side. The Auxiliaries wandered about, searching the area.

The sight was disturbing. Freda turned to comfort Father John, who hung his head remorsefully. He was devastated, and the grief was eating away at him, infecting his spirit.

"Jesus Christ, that's Hayward," shouted Turpin, standing over the corpse.

Suddenly, there was a commotion as Tans gathered around the dead men pushing and shoving to get a view.

Sergeant Bradley disengaged from the throng and called to one of the Auxiliaries.

"You've shot one of our lads!"

All the heads turned to him as they moved forward.

"Which one?" asked one of the Auxiliaries.

"Him," Sergeant Bradley pointed at Hayward's lifeless body. "He's one of ours – absconded a few days ago."

"He came to me for help," added Father John. "So did the Volunteer. It was a strange turn of events, but both had to stay in the orchard while I went about preparations to take them to a monastery. We were about to set off in an hour or two. Both had renounced violence and hoped to be admitted to the sanctuary. They found a friendship in each other over the past few days and were well at ease with one another's company."

"We were surprised to find a police jacket and supposed it to be a trophy of sorts. We had no indication that this man was a Reserve, though now, I must confess, his trousers are obviously R.I.C. issue. But at a distance they both looked like Shinners."

They chattered among themselves excitedly, while Father John, bewildered, allowed Freda to lead him apart. His grief was profound. The achievement he had been so proud of had been blown away in one swift fusillade of gunfire, and with it the good that he believed was in all men. He shook his head and groaned, while Freda gently patted his back.

"Oh sweet Jesus, I should have listened to you, Freda," he whispered. "When I found them, they were about to set off for the monastery by themselves. They would have left in time to avoid the search parties and —"

"No, Father John, you mustn't be talking like this now. Everything has meaning, even this happening. Such a meaning may not be for us to know, but you have played your proper part. I am sure that Henry and Sean will be looking down at you, proud of what you did for them." She gulped back the lump in her throat, and fought tears that swelled in her puffed eyes.

"I think things will get worse before anything changes for the better. God! When *will* this nonsense end?"

He looked about the campfire clearing, and heard the Tans bickering among each other while Hayward and Sean lay prostrate – empty shells that moments ago were laughing and joking.

Printed in Great Britain
by Amazon

34022997R00245